ARTIFACT OF THE DAWN

The Cycles of Revelation
Book One

GRAYSON BELL

DEDICATION

Without the enthusiastic encouragement of my late husband, Dave Balhiser, this story would not exist.

Thank you and miss you, always.

JEVAN

Jevan blinked awake as the sun glared through the open window. Squinting, he moved his face away from the stream of sunlight and groaned as he slowly sat up and oriented himself. The spot next to him in the pile of furs he slept on was empty, meaning his bed partner from the night before must have already gone to do her daily chores.

Rolling over as he yawned and stretched, Jevan was startled when he saw Taela watching him from across the room. The pretty elf brought over a bowl of fresh fruit, laughing at his awkward attempt to right himself.

"I thought you might be hungry. Do all your people sleep as much as you do?"

He grabbed a piece of fruit and grumbled. "No, most of the people in my village wake long before I do." Then Jevan gave her a fond smile. "Thanks."

She settled down next to him, grabbing a piece for herself. "Where are you going next?"

"Home. Your settlement is the last one I trade with along my route," Jevan explained, taking a bite of the fruit and savoring the tangy sweetness.

"What about Maala'naa?" she asked.

"I don't dare go near that settlement," Jevan replied. "The one time I got too close, their rangers warned me to stay away. They made it clear that *my kind* was not welcome there. I wish I could see it, though. I hear it's the largest of the elven settlements, right?"

Nodding as she chewed on a piece of fruit, a red rivulet of juice ran down her pale chin. "Elder Syvan says Maala'naa has a population of over five thousand *Athla'naa*," she confirmed, using the word her people called themselves.

Jevan reached out and wiped the juice away from her chin with his thumb before licking it off and making her laugh again. He admired the way she laughed so freely around him when most of her people were far more guarded. Jevan took one of her pale four-fingered hands into his, loving the contrast between their skin tones. Bringing her hand to his lips, he pressed a kiss against her fingers.

She rolled her eyes at him, before she ducked her head, her pointed ears flattening and tilting downward, in what Jevan had learned was her people's version of a blush. She smiled and squeezed his hand before getting up. "I have to go. There is a rope bridge they have asked me to help repair. Please, finish the fruit. It is better for you than those rations you carry."

"You're not wrong," Jevan agreed. "Thank you for last night. I enjoyed your company."

"I enjoyed yours, as well," she admitted, looking at him for a long moment with her dark, fathomless eyes. When she exited the dwelling, she looked back one last time. The sun shone brightly on the short, dark purple hair framing her ethereal face. A moment later, Jevan sat alone with his thoughts.

After enjoying the rest of the fruit, he grabbed his waterskin to slake his morning thirst. His mind wandered to when he'd arrived at this settlement for trade. This was one of the few elven settlements that openly traded with his people, and Jevan was among the few traders who had even attempted to trade with them. Because of the tentative truce between their people, only two settlements had welcomed him within their confines.

Elder Syvan was unusually warm and welcoming compared to most elven leaders, so Jevan had added her settlement to his regular route. One thing he loved about visiting these settlements was how the elves were so open to having multiple partners. Once they had warmed up to the tall Medellan, they occasionally would welcome him into their beds. It was quite the contrast from the monogamous pair-bonding his people practiced.

Jevan frowned as he recalled the argument he'd had before leaving on this latest trading run. The ard, his village leader, had once again impressed upon him the necessity of planning his pair-bond. That was something Jevan was not eager to contemplate, despite being almost *too old* at twenty-five.

Sighing, he slowly clambered to his feet. Jevan ducked to avoid hitting his head against the low ceiling of the small treetop hut. The elves were not a tall people, so Jevan always had to stoop when inside their dwellings. Searching for his scattered clothing, Jevan unhurriedly dressed himself. After pulling on his boots and donning his cloak, he looked around one last time to make sure he didn't forget anything. Jevan let his mind linger for another moment on the pleasant night he'd spent here, before picking up his pack and making his way toward the nearest rope ladder.

As he reached the ground, the elven elder stopped to speak with him. "You're getting a late start, even for you, Jevan."

"Greetings, Elder Syvan," Jevan greeted as he looked up to check the position of the sun in the pale sky. "Yes, I guess I am. Thank you again for your continued hospitality."

"I'm not the one you should thank," Elder Syvan said with a sly smirk as the breeze ruffled her short silver and purple hair. "Please don't forget to bring more of that lovely cloth. It's much softer than our roughspun."

Adjusting his pack, Jevan smiled down at the elder. "Now that I know you approve of it, I'll include a few bolts every time I make a trip out to these parts," Jevan promised.

"Thank you. I won't keep you any longer," Elder Syvan said in parting. "Take care on your journey home."

"Have a pleasant afternoon," Jevan said as he began heading northeast into the surrounding woods.

Jevan walked cheerfully as his pack of wares clanked in rhythm to his steps, making a pleasant cacophony to accompany the tune he hummed. The morning had dawned clear and warm when Jevan had left the elven settlement, putting him in good spirits. It wasn't until the mid-afternoon when clouds rolled in, and Jevan realized a storm was about to break.

Spotting a large, old, hollowed out tree that had fallen many seasons before, Jevan made his way toward it, intent on taking shelter within. He took off his pack and attempted to crawl inside. It was a small space, and he wasn't a small man, but he managed to curl himself up enough to fit, dragging his pack in after him.

Moments later, the storm broke, and Jevan was grateful for the modicum of protection the old tree brought. Storms like these could last until well past sundown, so Jevan made himself as comfortable as possible and let his mind wander. Unfortunately, his mind wanted to ruin his previously pleasant mood, as that last argument with Ard Mathias bubbled into his consciousness again.

"Jevan, be reasonable. It's mid-summer and you are twenty-five winters old. You know you're expected to pair-bond before you turn thirty! If you do not choose someone soon, you will force me to choose for you."

What was so special about turning thirty? Mathias refused to explain, simply citing the law.

Everyone Jevan knew had pair-bonded in their early twenties, many caving to the pressure from their parents or village leader. Jevan wasn't sure how much longer he could delay making a choice before Mathias would make good on his threat to arrange a pairing for him. The problem was, Jevan didn't want to choose and become bonded for life with only one person.

Jevan had become a trader, so he could leave his village for a cycle of the moons or longer. He enjoyed traveling and learning about other people and places. The elves had especially fascinated him because their culture was a stark contrast to his own. Elves took many lovers, living in large, polyamorous families. While they rarely took Medellans as lovers, with his good looks and charm, Jevan found he could easily persuade any sex into a tryst or two.

Sighing to himself, Jevan wrapped his cloak about him and let his eyes drift closed. The steady rhythm of the rain, interspersed with the crack of lightning and rumble of thunder, lulled him into a restless sleep.

◆◆◆

The next morning, Jevan pushed his pack out of the trunk with his feet before slowly unfurling his long limbs. He stood, stretching to get all the kinks and aches out of his tall frame. Hearing the gurgle of flowing water nearby, he grabbed his pack and followed the sound. He found a small creek, where he freshened up and refilled his waterskin. After eating some rations, he oriented himself based on the position of the sun and shouldered his pack as he began his trek homeward once more.

Again, his mind wandered toward the inevitable confrontation with Ard Mathias when he returned home. Jevan debated the limited options he had, including the potential unpaired adults in his settlement they might force him to bond with. All of them were quite young, most barely past the age of twenty, and he had little interest in any of them.

Still completely lost in thought, a slight stumble over the root of a tree brought Jevan out of his reverie. Looking around, Jevan stopped when he realized his surroundings didn't look familiar. He shielded his eyes and looked at the angle of the sun.

Damn, I've wandered too far northwest. I must be deep into elven territory. Now I'll have to back track if I want to avoid running into any of the rangers protecting Maala'naa. I'm damned lucky I haven't run into one already.

As Jevan was about to turn around, a flash of silver caught his attention. Turning to watch as it disappeared into the undergrowth, he recognized the beast. A lone triwolf was a rare sight, especially one so large. Jevan stashed his pack and grabbed only his bow and quiver before following in the direction the creature had been heading. It may be foolish to go against a beast like this alone, but the pelt would be quite the prize.

He slowed his approach when he caught up with the beast faster than he'd expected. It had stopped, crouched low, having cornered its prey. Keeping his distance, Jevan crept silently behind the beast to get a closer look at its quarry. The same instant that Jevan had spotted the elven ranger, the triwolf lunged forward, knocking the elf to the ground, poised to rip out his throat.

On instinct, Jevan nocked an arrow into his bow. He gave a yell to distract the beast as he aimed. His arrow flew true and hit the creature in the neck, dropping it like a dead weight upon the lithe form of the elf beneath it.

After the elf scrambled from under the beast, Jevan walked toward him and greeted him in his own language. *"Yawen uthera'ior. Kerros'nor Jevan."*

At first, the elf studied him, cocking his head to one side, with his ears lowered and wary. Then he looked down at the beast, noting the arrow protruding from its neck, and looked back at Jevan and his bow. His ears rose as he looked up at the taller Medellan, and much to his surprise, the elf replied in Jevan's own tongue. "Greetings, Jevan. My name is Ardyn. I owe you my thanks."

"You're welcome," Jevan said, putting on his most charming smile as he reached out his hand in greeting. "It's always nice to meet such an attractive elf."

When Ardyn backed away from him, Jevan's heart stuttered a little. *Oh, no. Is he afraid of me? Falx, that's adorable!*

ARDYN

Several cycles of the sun earlier.
The settlement of Maala'naa was still in the quiet of the dawn. Ardyn always rose early, preferring to prepare for the morning undisturbed. He exited the small treetop dwelling as quietly as possible, to not wake his still sleeping parents, and made his way across several bridges, interconnecting the many dwellings in his settlement. When he arrived at the outermost edge, he untied a rope ladder, lowering it before climbing it to the ground.

Once on the ground, Ardyn made his way to a nearby creek to take a bracing bath in the chill waters before anyone in Maala'naa stirred. As he approached the burbling creek, he undid his long braid of light purple hair so he could wash it. At the creekside, he stripped off his clothes and submerged himself in a deep pool naturally created by a rock formation.

Ardyn was still re-braiding his hair as he walked back toward the settlement when he encountered an Elder of the Triumvirate. "Good morning, Elder Aelrynd," Ardyn greeted, lowering his ears in deference to the somber-looking female. "You're up early today."

"I have a task for you, Ardyn," Aelrynd said gravely. "A *sar'ora* took another child last night. All the other rangers are too far afield. As you are the only one here, the task must fall to you. I know you only returned yesterday, but it is urgent this beast is dealt with."

"Which child?" Ardyn asked with concern.

"Not yours," Aelrynd assured him. "It was Corae's youngest, Athandrael. It seems he left the safety of his hut in the night, alone. His mother thinks he needed to relieve himself and did not want to disturb her."

"He turned four winters only a few cycles of the moons ago," Ardyn recalled, shaking his head. "Such senseless tragedy. That's the third child the *sar'ora* has taken now, isn't it?"

Aelrynd nodded. "Yes. We believe this one hunts alone."

"That makes sense. Their packs usually never stray so close to our settlements," Ardyn mused aloud. "Where was the child attacked? Did anyone see where the beast headed afterward?"

"On the northern edge of Maala'naa," Aelrynd replied, pointing a finger. "Those who found the remains of the child said they saw tracks headed north into the woods."

Nodding his head with determination, Ardyn placed a reassuring hand on Aelrynd's shoulder. "I will prepare myself and hunt it down," he promised.

"Be safe and well, but make haste," Aelrynd said before turning to Ardyn, placing both of her hands upon his shoulders. "We think the beast may take refuge in the Aria'una. That is where the other rangers have lost it before. Hurry, before it crosses the border and eludes you."

Ardyn nodded. Every Athla'naa knew to avoid stepping beyond the line of *bhat'laa'arh*—tall trees with bright red leaves—that marked the border into the Aria'una. *The forbidden place*.

Leaving Aelrynd, Ardyn hurried back to his family hut and packed his gear, causing his mother to stir. Wiping the sleep from her eyes, she frowned at him. "Leaving so soon?"

"I'm sorry, Mama Saelyn," Ardyn apologized. "Aelrynd needs me to hunt down a beast. That lone *sar'ora* has taken another of our children in the night. Aelrynd can tell you more."

"Oh no, how awful. Taesys, say goodbye to your son," Saelyn said, shaking Ardyn's father.

"What? So soon?" he grumbled.

After making his goodbyes with his parents, Ardyn grabbed his bow and quiver on his way out. He'd descended to the ground near the site of the most recent attack when he turned to see his eldest daughter, Myria, and her mother, Cylaen, approach him.

"Going off again so soon?" Cylaen asked with a disapproving scowl. "You never remain long anymore. Not even to spend time with your child. How long will you be gone this time? One cycle of the moons? A whole season?"

Rolling his eyes, Ardyn adjusted his pack before addressing her. "Aelrynd has tasked me with hunting the lone *sar'ora* that has been attacking our children," Ardyn explained. "The beast took Corae's youngest last night.

Please, tell the others. Keep the children in the treetops until I have brought back its pelt."

Cylaen's eyes widened, and she gave a curt nod. Myria waved as her mother herded her toward the ladder. "Bye-bye, Papa Ardyn!" Myria called as she climbed up into the safety of the treetops.

Ardyn waved back, even as Cylaen gave him another scowl. He sighed before turning to make his way toward the site of the attack. Ardyn's mating with Cylaen hadn't been a pleasant one, and she still resented him for his reluctance to mate with her.

When an Athla'naa came of age, the elders matched them for their first mating. It was a tradition everyone followed when they came of age, but Ardyn fought against it. The elders insisted and forced Ardyn to mate with Cylaen against his will. Because of this, he had little involvement in his daughter's upbringing.

Myria was now nine summers old and looked more like her mother with each passing season. A part of him cared for her, but the circumstances of her conception still deeply troubled him. Seeing the child or her mother always brought back painful memories.

Sighing again, he shook his head and hurried toward the scene of the attack. Once there, he studied the blood pattern and tracks that were still fresh on the ground. This *sar'ora* had been needlessly vicious with its kill. From how much blood there was, this was not a kill made from necessity. The tracks were deep in the soft ground. This beast was large and well-fed.

Shouldering his gear, Ardyn strode northward into the forest where the tracks led.

●●●

Ardyn crept silently through the brush, his eyes focused, his ears scanning for any signs of the beast. He had been stalking the *sar'ora* for the past five cycles of the sun, waiting for the right moment to catch it unaware and get a clean shot. When Ardyn came upon the beast again, he found it sleeping next to the remains of its latest kill. A *paal'dak*, a small creature that would jump into low-hanging branches of trees when startled. The *sar'ora* had gorged itself and felt secure enough to take a nap within the small clearing.

Ardyn, his ears lowered back, fixated on his prey, disregarding the sun vanishing behind clouds that were swiftly blanketing the sky. He crouched low and noiselessly pulled out his bow and an arrow from his quiver. He had scarcely nocked his arrow when the beast stirred, blinking its three luminous, silver eyes. The wind picked up and howled around them, causing the *sar'ora* to rise and shake out its silver-gray fur before darting into the undergrowth.

Barely having time to curse the wind, the clouds burst open, and rain pelted down in heavy sheets. The dense cover of trees did little to prevent Ardyn from becoming soaked to the skin in a matter of moments. Putting away the arrow and his bow, Ardyn rose to his feet and ran to seek shelter. The rain and wind whipped tree branches into his face as he ran toward the cliffside he'd seen that morning.

Bright flashes lit the sky, followed by the crack and boom of thunder. Ardyn ran faster, hating to be caught out in the middle of such a fierce storm. He'd seen one too many trees obliterated by lightning in the past.

Ardyn didn't know how long he ran until he found the entrance to a small cave along the cliffside, nearly hidden behind thick brush. He was lucky to find it at all, with the rain obscuring everything within a few feet in front of him. Stumbling inside, breathless, he sank to his knees onto the dry cave floor.

Once he'd caught his breath, Ardyn sat at the mouth of the cave and watched the storm while he wrung water from his long braid. This storm would not relent soon, so he made camp for the night. Unpacking his gear, he pulled out his bedroll, his waterskin, and some rations.

Being a ranger, Ardyn always had enough supplies to survive in the forest for as long as a season. Most of the time, he'd hunt and gather the food he needed, but he always carried some rations for times when that wasn't possible.

Athla'naa rations were made from a mix of dried meat, fruit, and herbs. Rangers favored them, as they spent several cycles of the moons away from their home settlement, and these took a long time to spoil.

Ardyn ate his rations and washed them down with some water. Still soaked to the skin, Ardyn stripped out of his wet clothes and laid them out on the cave floor, hoping they'd dry without the aid of a fire. It would be impossible to find dry wood in a deluge like this. While he huddled nude inside his damp bedroll, Ardyn tried to rub himself warm.

He was on the verge of drifting to sleep when a flash of lightning startled Ardyn awake. Another flash drew his attention to the far side of the cave as the light glinted off something. He may never have noticed it if he hadn't been looking in that direction. Ever curious, Ardyn rose and made his way toward where he saw the twinkle.

In the dim light of the cave, he could barely make it out. There seemed to be something metallic, partially buried in the dirt that covered the cave floor.

If it's made of metal, that means it was made by one of those Medellan beasts. Could I have strayed into their lands while stalking the sar'ora?

Ardyn's curiosity got the better of him as he reached out to pick up the half-hidden object. When he brushed the dirt from its surface, he startled and dropped it.

It... *glowed.*

Occasionally, Ardyn had seen some metal tools the Medellans used when he traded with them, but he'd never seen one that glowed. Without touching the object again, he bent closer to study it. As soon as he'd dropped it, the glow had faded. Now it just glinted dully in the dim light. His heart pounded in his chest as he reached out again. As soon as he touched it, the glow came back, making him flinch away.

While his own people shunned technology, he had never feared it. However, he had never seen technology behave like this. What could cause this object to glow from a mere touch? Ardyn steeled his nerves before he reached for the object again, picking it up with a firmer grip. The light it produced was a faint, eerie blue, emanating from a pattern etched on the surface of the silver metal.

Looking more closely at the pattern, Ardyn's eyes widened in surprise. It wasn't some random pattern; they were words written in an ancient Athla'naa script. The script was too archaic for him to read, but he recognized it from some ancient scrolls and books the elders kept.

This made little sense. His people didn't forge metal, and they didn't have technology for anything like this. This object was more advanced than anything Ardyn had ever seen.

I've also never seen Medellans carry tools or weapons with metal this smoothly polished and certainly never ones that glowed like this.

Wanting to understand what this object was, he turned it over, studying it from various angles. It was small, just large enough to grasp comfortably with one hand, and quite thin. Roughly octagonal, it had four sides longer than the others. One edge extended out from the silvery metal and was a reddish color.

The glowing script only appeared on one side, while the other was smooth with no marks. Ardyn looked around, sifting through the dirt of the cave floor to see if there were any other objects like this one, but he found nothing.

Shivering from the cool air in the cave, Ardyn carefully put the object into his pack and slid back into the warmth of his bedroll. Exhaustion hit him, so he settled in to get some much-needed sleep while the storm continued to rage outside. He could worry about the strange object tomorrow.

ENCOUNTER

Ardyn awoke to the sound of chirps and cries of wildlife coming from outside the cave. Based on the light filtering in, it was still early morning, and the storm had finally passed. Blinking the sleep from his eyes, Ardyn sat up and reached into his pack to break his fast when his fingers brushed over the strange object he'd found.

Gingerly grasping it, he took it out of the pack and contemplated it once again. He was sure the words on the face were an archaic form of the Athla'naa script. They only taught those destined to become elders how to read it. Most of his people never even learned how to read. Those who learned were taught a simplified form, and Ardyn had been privileged enough to have been taught.

Why were these ancient Athla'naa words etched into something so technologically advanced? His people only created the tools they needed for survival. Anything as advanced as metalworking was strictly forbidden. Trading for metal tools with the Medellans was enough to be shunned. The Athla'naa favored wood, bone, or stone for everything from weapons to eating utensils.

The Athla'naa elders taught their people to do things the same way, from one generation to the next. Innovation and invention were the product of *weak and lazy minds*. The elders would not tolerate any deviation from those time-honored traditions, always reminding their people it was a slight against the ancestors.

When he was younger, Ardyn had always wondered why the elders were so strict regarding these edicts. He'd found himself punished often for daring to speak out and question their wisdom. Ardyn's curiosity never abated, but he had learned the hard way to keep his questions to himself.

Looking at the strange glowing object in his hand, he worried about how the elders would react upon seeing it. Ardyn was certain he'd seen this script in the ancient tomes the elders were often reading. However, knowing their aversion to technology, he imagined they would likely take it from him and possibly destroy it without explanation. Not being able to reconcile the conflicting evidence he held in his hand, Ardyn once again shoved the thing back into his pack.

After Ardyn had eaten and pulled on his still damp clothing, he packed up his bedroll and left the confines of the small cave. In the storm's wake, Ardyn would have to pick up the beast's trail again. He was certain he had strayed beyond his usual range, into Medellan territory. After running blindly through the storm, he wasn't sure where he was.

The best way for Ardyn to regain his bearings was to go up. Making his way toward a suitably tall tree, he climbed into the lowest branches before taking off his pack, bow, and quiver. He left them secured to a branch before continuing his climb unhindered. Ardyn carefully picked his way through the branches until he could look over the tops of most of the surrounding trees. As soon as he scanned the horizon, his heart jumped into his throat. *Oh no.*

This wasn't Medellan territory he had wandered into. *This was much worse.* He'd crossed into the Aria'una. Ardyn could clearly make out the red leaves of the *bhat'laa'arh* that marked the border, and they were south of his location. He had to get out of here. *Now.*

The elders would already know of his transgression, so he was in a near state of panic as he descended the tree. He wasn't sure how, but they *always knew* when someone accidentally wandered into the area. They had a specially trained group of hunters they would send whenever anyone entered the Aria'una.

Ardyn's heart raced, and his breath caught in his throat as he climbed even faster down the tree, nearly slipping on moss-covered branches. Once he made it back to the lowest tree limbs, he grabbed his gear and dropped to the ground. As he shouldered his pack, he oriented himself towards where he'd spotted the perimeter of the Aria'una before running in that direction. His heart thudded in his chest as he realized that even running at top speed, it would take too long to reach the perimeter.

How did I get so deep into the Aria'una? I know I could not have run that far through the storm. I must have been so intent on tracking the beast, I didn't notice how far north I had wandered. Still, how did I miss noticing the bright red trees lining the perimeter?

Ardyn was a seasoned ranger; he shouldn't have let himself become so distracted by his prey that he had missed seeing the *bhat'laa'arh*. Now, as he fled through the trees, he felt like a complete fool, as Aelrynd's warning rang in his ears.

After running until he was out of breath, Ardyn stopped to rest. He knew he had to make it out of the Aria'una as soon as possible, or face even worse punishment than he knew he was probably already in for.

However, at his current speed, he'd pass out from exhaustion before he'd ever reach the border. Trying to calm his nerves, he took stock of the situation and slowed down, pacing himself. It would be nightfall by the time he'd reach the border this way, but that was better than pushing himself and the risk of lying on the forest floor, passed out for who knows how long.

After traveling at a more moderate pace, Ardyn reached a natural spring by mid-afternoon. He had made good progress, so he sank to his knees by the spring to slake his thirst. He decided it wouldn't hurt to take a few moments of rest as he pulled out his rations and sat himself more comfortably on the ground.

Exhaustion crept up on Ardyn, dulling his senses. He sat idly by the spring, lost in thought, almost missing the sound of a twig snapping behind him. Turning around more slowly than he normally would, he saw the beast that he'd been tracking. The *sar'ora* was now hurtling toward him, fangs bared. An instant later, it was on top of him, knocking him backward on the embankment and lunging for his throat.

Ardyn dodged the first lunge as he twisted to one side and tried to clamber from beneath the beast. As it lunged forward again, Ardyn heard a yell and the distant twang of a bow as it loosed an arrow. In the next moment, the *sar'ora* collapsed onto him, dead. Pushing the massive beast off him, he scrambled free, only to look up and see a tall, dark-skinned Medellan walking toward him.

Standing up slowly, Ardyn remained wary. The man walked up to him brazenly and greeted him in the Athla'naa tongue. *"Yawen uthera'ior. Kerros'nor Jevan."*

Ardyn was stunned for a moment, not expecting to hear his own language from the man. Taking a moment to compose himself, he returned the greeting in the Medellan language.

"Greetings, Jevan. My name is Ardyn. I owe you my thanks."

Jevan's gray eyes sparkled as he regarded him. "You're welcome," Jevan said with a charming smile, his hand extended in greeting. "It's always nice to meet such an attractive elf."

Ardyn shrank away from the outstretched hand, his ears dropping as he took a step back from the tall Medellan. *Oh, no... it's... it's him.* Taking a breath to compose himself, Ardyn's voice still quavered when he spoke. "Y-You... saved my life and felled the *sar'ora* I have been tracking for the past five cycles of the sun. For that, I am grateful."

"You tracked the triwolf for that long?" Jevan asked, lowering his hand and raising a quizzical eyebrow. "Then how'd it get the jump on you like that? Is this the first time out here on your own?"

"No," Ardyn scoffed, squatting down to survey the carcass, impressed by the precision of where the man's arrow struck. "It's a long story, but I lost the trail and was hurrying back to my settlement. This *athla'maakh* had been preying on our children, and Elder Aelrynd tasked me with hunting it down. A lone *sar'ora* is always dangerous, but this one was unnaturally vicious with its kills, so I had to approach it cautiously."

"By rights, the kill is mine now..." Jevan began as Ardyn looked up and scowled at him. "...*But* since it nearly ate you, I *guess* I can let it go. Do you need any help with skinning and preparing the pelt?"

"No. I've been skinning beasts since I was a small child. I don't require the help of an *athla'maakh*," Ardyn spat with more vitriol than he felt. "Especially one that I should kill for venturing into the Aria'una."

Ardyn turned to face the task before him. The *sar'ora* was a sizeable beast, and this was going to take some time. Taking a deep breath, he noticed the Medellan was still there, watching him. Turning, he glared at the man.

Jevan cleared his throat. "I was wondering, why did you say you should kill me? And what does... Aria'una mean?" Jevan asked, carefully pronouncing it as if it were an unfamiliar word.

Rolling his eyes, Ardyn stood to get the tools from his pack. "It means *forbidden place*. Did you not notice the *bhat'laa'arh*... the red-leafed trees?" Ardyn pointed in the general direction of the boundary. "They clearly mark the perimeter. We allow no one to venture past them. The Athla'naa elders even punish our own people for venturing here. For an *athla'maakh* like yourself, it carries a sentence of death."

"Death? For something I wasn't even aware existed?" Jevan scoffed, crooking an eyebrow at him. "So, why are you here? Are you so fond of punishment?"

"No, I am not. I became disoriented during the storm," Ardyn explained. "I did not know I was running into the Aria'una to escape the deluge." He refused to admit to this Medellan *athla'maakh* that he had accidentally wandered into the Aria'una before the storm.

"Well, no one is going to know we were here," Jevan argued.

Ardyn knelt before the felled beast and laid out his tools before responding. "The elders know already. The Triumvirate always knows if someone has breached the perimeter. I'll expect to face a public whipping when I return."

"So, do you plan to kill me?" Jevan challenged him. "Or will you drag me before your elders for execution?"

The faint smirk on the tall man's face should have annoyed Ardyn. Instead, it made him feel oddly at ease. *No! He's Medellan. I can't lower my guard around him... even if he's never posed a threat,* Ardyn reminded himself.

With a shake of his head, Ardyn responded. "I won't do either. You saved my life, and it would be dishonorable for me to kill you, even if you are *athla'maakh*. Just know, your life will always be in danger from now on."

"Are you telling me, if I hadn't saved you, and we had come across each other inside this forbidden place, you would have killed me for being here?" Jevan asked.

Frowning at the thought, Ardyn regarded the taller man with his twinkling gray eyes. *Would I have killed him? For violating some ancient tradition that I don't even understand?* "I... am not sure."

Jevan huffed and gave him a brief smile. "Well, one more thing, if you'll indulge me. It's obvious that you don't like Medellans, but I'm curious how you know my language? You're the first elf I've met who speaks it so fluently."

"I'm a ranger," Ardyn replied, as if that explained everything, before turning and grabbing his sharpest stone knife from among his skinning tools. *Why won't this fool leave me to my task?*

"Well, I've also never met an elven ranger who can speak the Medellan tongue beyond a few broken words," Jevan said in a suspicious tone. "I frequent a couple of settlements for trade, which is where I learned to speak your people's language. Are rangers from your settlement required to learn it?"

"No, but I thought it would be useful to know," Ardyn said with a shrug of his shoulders as he expertly made the first slice into the corpse of the *sar'ora.* "I used to range close to your territories and have occasionally encountered your people, most of whom refused to learn my language."

"Your language isn't easy to learn," Jevan admitted. "Thankfully, I had a very patient teacher."

Looking up at the man again, Ardyn had to ask. "Who taught you?"

"An elder from a settlement I trade with," Jevan replied. "She insisted I learn and set about teaching me. In exchange, I taught her more of my people's language."

Ardyn turned away from Jevan, going back to his gruesome task. Behind him, he could hear as the Medellan walked away. "Well, I'll let you get to it. Enjoy that pelt."

Looking over his shoulder, Ardyn watched as Jevan began walking eastward. Ardyn found he couldn't tear his eyes from Jevan's retreating form while feeling a pang of regret. *I hadn't meant to be so brusque with him. If only being around him didn't make me so nervous, but if he ever found out...*

When Ardyn remembered the object he'd found in the cave, he called out before he could think better of it. "Jevan! Wait a moment, please."

Turning around, Jevan hurried back to Ardyn with a puzzled expression.

"I found something," Ardyn tried to explain. "I found it in the cave I took shelter in during yesterday's storm. Could you look at it? I was wondering if it was made by your people."

"Yeah, sure. I'd be happy to take a look," Jevan agreed with a warm smile.

Setting aside his knife, Ardyn stood and went over to his pack. He reached inside and felt around for the strange object. When his fingers brushed over its smooth metal surface, he grasped it and pulled it out. The object shone softly as he handed it over, but once Jevan held it, the glow faded. *How curious.*

◆◆◆

Holding the strange object, Jevan marveled at how light and smooth the metal was. "Were those symbols glowing?" Jevan asked in awe as he turned it over to study it.

"Yes. They glow every time I touch the thing," Ardyn replied, reaching out and touching it again. As soon as his fingers made contact, the script flared to life with their soft blue glow.

"That's strange. I wonder why it only reacts when *you* touch it. It certainly doesn't seem to glow from my touch," Jevan remarked as he continued to examine it. "What does the writing say? It's elven, right?"

Ardyn nodded. "It's an archaic script, one that only my elders can read."

"Yeah, but they wouldn't take it well if they saw this, would they?" Jevan asked with a frown. "I know enough about your culture to know that you forbid most technology. This metal work is far more advanced than I've ever seen."

"So, you don't think this was Medellan made, either?" Ardyn asked.

Jevan shook his head. "No, definitely not. I'm no smith, but I know we don't have any metalworking techniques that could make anything this lightweight or smooth. We certainly don't have whatever technology would cause it to glow like that."

"That's what I was afraid of," Ardyn said, taking it back and holding it in the palm of his hand.

They both stared at the object as it glowed in Ardyn's hand. Then Jevan had an idea. "Is this area forbidden because of that? Could there be other technology like this that we're not meant to find?"

Ardyn's ears perked up before dropping low as he frowned at the object in his hand. "I don't know. I shouldn't, but since I'm already here, with more questions than answers after finding this... *thing,* I need to explore the Aria'una and see if I can't find some answers."

With his own curiosity piqued, Jevan flashed a bright smile at Ardyn. "And since I'm supposedly marked for execution anyway, would you mind if I came along? This has me intrigued, too. Please?"

The elf regarded him for a moment before nodding in agreement. "I am usually more wary of your kind, but I feel I can trust you. Yes, I would welcome your company. Will you help me skin this beast?"

"Yeah, I'd be happy to. Let me go grab my pack. We can do it faster with the knives I have," Jevan suggested as he turned and hurried away.

After they'd finished skinning the *sar'ora* and prepared the pelt as best as they could for travel, they spent the remaining daylight searching the surrounding area. They searched for caves where more strange objects could be hiding.

When they hadn't found anything by dusk, they opted to stop and camp for the night. They agreed they would take one more cycle of the sun to search. If they still hadn't found anything, they would make their way out of the Aria'una and part ways.

After making camp, Ardyn used what little light remained to hunt for some dinner while Jevan set about building a fire. It didn't take long for Ardyn to return with a couple of fat little jumpers, called *paal'dak* by the elves. It impressed Jevan with how fast Ardyn hunted them down, and soon they were roasting their dinner and eating in companionable silence.

After they had finished eating, Jevan regarded the elf across from him. Ardyn had delicate, fine-boned features. His long, lilac hair complimented his pale skin, made luminous in the light of the moons. The graceful up sweep of his pointed ears, and the flash of fire in the dazzle of his fathomless eyes, only enhanced Ardyn's looks. He was breathtaking and the most beautiful male elf Jevan had ever met.

"Do I intrigue you, *athla'maakh*?" Ardyn snorted, bringing Jevan out of his reverie.

"Yes, you do," Jevan replied honestly. "I find all elves intriguing. Your people are exceptionally beautiful."

"Is that all that interests you? Our looks?" Ardyn huffed with clear disgust.

Jevan laughed. "Not only your looks, no, but I will admit you are even more attractive than most. You are the most stunning elf I've ever seen."

Ardyn scowled at him while scooting farther away. "Keep your perverse interest in my people to yourself. I know how your kind are."

A mix of confusion and disappointment came over Jevan. "My kind? I would never do you any harm, I promise. You can trust me."

"I put my trust in your people once before," Ardyn said with a growl. "I am no longer so naïve."

Needing to understand, Jevan assumed as non-threatening a posture as he could. "What happened? Can you tell me? Please?" Jevan asked quietly.

HISTORY

Ardyn stared into the fire for a long while. What happened was something he'd never shared with anyone, but maybe it was time. At the time, he'd felt like such a fool, and even now, his face flushed hot at the memory.

"My elders always warned us to avoid your kind," Ardyn began. "However, my first assigned range bordered close to one of your villages. It's named Ahren."

"I know it," Jevan said. "It's a village along my trade route."

"In my first season as a ranger, I saw the outskirts of the village often," Ardyn said. "Seeing the cluster of buildings in a clearing, all on the ground, intrigued me. I wondered how your people felt safe living that way."

Jevan gave him a shrug. "Well, our homes are sturdier than yours, and we have locks on our doors. So that helps a lot."

"Yes, but I didn't know that," Ardyn explained. "Eventually, my curiosity got the better of me, and I dared to venture closer to the village. I tried not to be spotted, but eventually, a man caught me lurking behind a building."

"What happened? Did he hurt you?"

Ardyn shook his head and chuckled, his ears raising in amusement. "No, no, he was gracious and kind. His name was Soren—"

"I know him!" Jevan interrupted excitedly. "He's the old schoolmaster."

"Yes," Ardyn nodded. "He knew a few words of my language, enough to get me to follow him. I went with him to his home, and he offered me food and water. Communicating was awkward at first, but eventually, we struck a bargain. Every time I ranged close to his village, I would stop by, and we'd teach each other our languages. He was as excited to learn as he was to teach."

"Yes, he's always had an insatiable curiosity and eagerness to learn," Jevan said. "He was the first one to teach me your language. At least, enough for me to trade with a couple of your settlements. If he learned it from you, then I have you to thank."

I indirectly helped Jevan learn my language? That thought amused Ardyn, and he couldn't help but smile at Jevan. "You're welcome."

"So, what happened that made you so distrustful of my people?"

"I met with Soren for around one cycle of the seasons," Ardyn continued. "As I became more proficient in your language, I also felt emboldened to walk among your people. Many seemed kind, more so than my elders had led me to believe. I was naïve enough that I began to think that all your people were that way."

Jevan frowned at the implication of those words.

Ardyn could still recall the incident as if it had happened yesterday. *It was late afternoon as he approached Soren's home. As Ardyn neared, he could hear raised voices through an open window. As he passed by the window, he heard an unfamiliar voice spit out, "... that elf!"*

Immediately, Ardyn dropped into a crouch below the window, his heart hammering in his chest and his ears fully forward to pick up on the argument inside.

"Ardyn has done nothing wrong," Ardyn heard Soren say. "He merely comes to me to learn our language."

"He's one of them. That's what's wrong. His people nearly wiped us out, and here you are, helping the bastard!"

"That war ended centuries ago!" Soren argued. "His people keep to themselves and leave us be. Ardyn poses no threat."

"You don't know that, old man," another voice sneered. "He could be trying to figure out our weaknesses, while planning to start a new war. Either you tell your little elf friend to stay away from our village, or you will both regret it."

"The Ard wouldn't—" Soren began.

"It's the Ard that sent us," the first voice claimed. "Either you tell that little elven bastard to stay away, or the Ard will send you to the mines and we'll make an example of him as a warning to his elven buddies."

"My mates and I would love to have our way with that pretty little thing before he's dragged to the town square for a proper beating," another man said lasciviously.

Ardyn's eyes had gone wide at the implication of 'having their way' with him. The very thought terrified him, and with tear-filled eyes, he ran back into the woods.

"I never returned to Ahren after that," Ardyn told Jevan, his voice full of emotion. "I even swapped ranges and moved to an area closer to the Aria'una, on the opposite side of Maala'naa."

Jevan stood and paced before the fire. "Well, that explains some things. When Soren was teaching me, I asked him where he learned your language. He always refused to answer, but he got a wistful look on his face every time I asked."

"Do you think he was remembering me?" Ardyn asked. "I thought he'd hate me after that."

"You did nothing wrong," Jevan said, sitting back down. "Those men should have been ashamed for threatening either of you. I wish our peoples interacted more. My people could learn a lot from yours."

"If it weren't for our stupid traditions, I think the Athla'naa people could learn even more from yours. How much do you know about the history between our people?"

"Only what they taught us when I was a child. I know my people came from across the ocean on large ships from a land called Ateria, and that the elves didn't take kindly to our arrival. As I recall, the wars that followed lasted close to a century, until they came to a tenuous truce that has lasted over the past seven hundred cycles of the seasons."

"The elders taught me that the Medellans attacked us as soon as they landed here," Ardyn explained. "They insisted that this land belonged to them and accused my people of intruding on their territory."

"Yes, I remember Elder Syvan told me the same thing. I don't know how my ancestors could claim this land wasn't yours if your people were here first, but at least we eventually learned how to share it."

"We did but I know my elders are still not happy about it," Ardyn said. "They fear the developing technologies you Medellans keep trying to invent."

"Why do your people fear technology so much?" Jevan asked. "I can never get a straight answer."

Ardyn shrugged. "I never understood why, either. They drilled it into us from a young age that technology is unsafe and that it takes us away from the land and tradition. The elders said it would bring dishonor to our ancestors and being close to the land is important for our people. They taught us that our people would die out if we ever became too advanced. That's all I know."

"That's the same thing I keep hearing, but it doesn't make much sense," Jevan said with a sigh. "You're physically not that different from Medellans, and advancement in our technology has never hurt us."

"Maybe this object will answer some of those questions?" Ardyn wondered.

"Let's hope so," Jevan said. "I've always suspected there is more to the story they've been telling us than we're led to believe."

"Do you ever wonder about the land your ancestors came from?" Ardyn asked. "Why have no others come from across the ocean in all this time?"

"Yes, actually. They always reprimanded me for asking," Jevan admitted. "We were taught that our people came here to form a colony, but we aren't taught why we've never heard from those we supposedly left behind. Maybe there weren't any others left?"

"They might have faced some plague or other disaster, and those who arrived here were the last survivors of your people," Ardyn suggested.

"Perhaps. That would be an unfortunate fate if that turned out to be true. I will admit, I've often dreamed of building a ship and sailing to the lands of my ancestors to find out what happened to them."

Ardyn's eyes began to feel heavy as he tried to stifle a yawn, the need for sleep overcoming him.

"Alright, sleepy elf. I think we should turn in and get an early start tomorrow," Jevan suggested. "I'll take first watch. You look like you could use a good night's rest. I promise I'll watch over you while you sleep. I know you haven't known me long enough to really trust me, but I hope to prove to you that you can."

Staring into the fire again, Ardyn considered the sincerity of Jevan's words. The man already had plenty of opportunities to harm him, and he hadn't. While Jevan was much larger than Ardyn, all he had done was make him feel safe. *Maybe eventually I'll tell him...*

"Thank you, Jevan. I appreciate that," Ardyn agreed before he pulled out his bedroll and settled into it. "Wake me later, so you can also get some rest."

DISCOVERY

The next morning dawned with sunny skies. Jevan and Ardyn opted to eat rations to break their fast before packing up and resuming the search for more clues within the Aria'una. The pair spoke little, as they focused on the surrounding landscape. They weren't sure what they were looking for, but they kept scanning the ground for something that might resemble the object Ardyn had found.

Jevan was staring at the ground ahead, looking for some sign, when he tripped over a tree root and nearly fell. He berated himself for being so clumsy. As he stumbled back to his feet, he looked up to get his bearings when a metallic glint caught his eye. Over to his right, the sun was filtering through the trees onto a small hill, glinting off *something*.

He made his way toward it and soon realized there was a small structure, partially buried in the hillside and almost completely hidden beneath an overgrowth of brush and vines.

"Ardyn!" he called. "Look at this!"

"What is it?" Ardyn wondered aloud as the two of them pulled away some of the vines, revealing a smooth metallic wall.

"I don't know," Jevan replied. "Help me clear away more of these vines. There's another knife in my pack."

At first Ardyn hesitated, and Jevan wanted to reassure the elf that no one was going to know he had used a metal tool. Then Ardyn shrugged to himself and bent to grab the knife from Jevan's pack. That small act of defiance made Jevan smile.

Together, they hacked away at the overgrowth and slowly uncovered a small rectangular structure.

"How does this metal not rust?" Jevan remarked as he kept working at cutting away more vines. "This structure has been exposed to the elements for who knows how long. It should have at least some signs of rust by now."

"What is rust?" Ardyn asked.

"If you leave forged metal lying around without cleaning it regularly, it decays as rust forms on the surface," Jevan explained. "The metal changes color, breaks down, and becomes very brittle. We think it's related to how air or water affects the metal."

Running his hand along the side of the structure, Ardyn nodded in understanding. "That sounds like what happens to the wood we build settlements from. Over time the wood changes color and decays. Yet this metal shows no signs of such decay. Do all metals rust?"

Jevan nodded. "All metals we've been able to forge eventually turn to rust. Some turn green, others red, but all decay if not properly cared for."

When Jevan offered the use of his knife, Ardyn couldn't help his hesitation, until he remembered that everything they were doing was forbidden. *What's one more violation?*

After he'd helped Jevan cut away vines around one edge of the structure, Ardyn moved to clear them away from one of the sides, while Jevan worked around the corner from him. After Ardyn slashed away a portion of the vines, he stood back to look at his progress. The side he'd been clearing away wasn't flat and standing back from it, the deep indentations made more sense.

"Jevan, look. There might be a way inside this thing," Ardyn said, stepping back farther to point at the strange-looking portal with a solid metal door. "How does it open?"

Jevan helped him remove the rest of the vines from around the doorway, revealing a small panel to the side of it. "There's more of the same ancient Athla'naa script here," Ardyn said, pointing to the panel.

What did this mean? Was this structure part of an ancient Athla'naa settlement? Had his people once built their homes on the ground?

The questions swirled in Ardyn's mind as he reached out to trace the words with his finger. As soon as he touched them, they glowed like the ones on the object, making Ardyn flinch away. He wasn't sure he'd ever get used to that.

Below the script was a small slot. "What do you make of this?" Ardyn asked.

Looking over, Jevan looked at what Ardyn was pointing at. His brow furrowed in concentration for a moment. "Where's that artifact you found?"

Retrieving the object from his pack, Ardyn handed it to Jevan. Studying it and the slot for a moment, Jevan turned the artifact around a few times, before aligning the protruding side with the slot. It slid in, fitting perfectly, but nothing happened.

Looking at Ardyn, Jevan removed it and handed it back to him. "You try it. It only lights up when you touch it, so maybe only you can make it work?"

Taking it, he copied how Jevan had slid the now glowing artifact into the slot. As soon as it slid into place, they heard the metal groan and hiss as the doors parted. When the strange doorway opened, they both backed away slowly.

"I was right!" Jevan exclaimed. "As soon as I saw that slot, I had a feeling that our little artifact here was a key."

Looking at Jevan, Ardyn felt even more confused. "None of this makes any sense. A metal... *hut*? That requires a key? They must be of *athla'maakh* construction. Athla'naa don't need doors with locks, and we don't build things with metal or whatever all this is. Yet, they have ancient Athla'naa words on them, and why does it take someone like me to... to... open it?"

"All of this is also beyond my understanding. You're right, none of this makes sense," Jevan agreed.

Ardyn looked toward the open doorway. "Let's see what's inside."

Jevan ventured in first, stooping through the low doorway. The interior remained dark until Ardyn crossed the threshold. They both startled when suddenly the entire interior became illuminated. There were no obvious flames, and the light had an eerie, cold quality.

"What kind of structure is this?" Jevan asked in wonder. "There's no rust, and this light? Where is it coming from? How does it even work? Medellans didn't build this. I've seen nothing like this before."

It equally mystified Ardyn. "Like this... key? The interior began to glow when I entered. I never believed in magic but what else could it be?"

"No, I don't think this is magic. It must be very advanced technology. That makes it even more strange, considering how old it must be."

The interior space was small, not much bigger than Ardyn's treetop hut. On the opposite wall there was another doorway, with a larger panel beside it. Even more archaic script surrounded the now familiar slot.

Taking the key, Ardyn slid it into this slot like he had before. They heard a loud metallic groan for a moment before a light above the slot blinked red, but the door remained closed.

"What would a red light mean?" Ardyn wondered.

"I'm not sure," Jevan replied with a shrug. "Maybe it means it's broken? Or maybe this lock requires a different key?"

Ardyn sat down in the middle of the floor, trying to take it all in. Jevan sat down beside him.

"I have to wonder why this is here, in the heart of the Aria'una," Ardyn mused. "Is this why the entire area is forbidden? There must be more structures. Perhaps an entire settlement of them?"

Shaking his head, Jevan replied. "I have as many questions as you. At least finding this structure answered the question of what that artifact is for."

"Yes, but answering one mystery has led to many more questions," Ardyn said with a frustrated sigh. "It goes against everything my elders taught me. The evidence so far tells me one of two things. Either my ancestors were more technologically advanced than they had led me to believe, or both of our ancestors once worked more closely together. That would suggest perhaps your ancestors were also more advanced in the past."

"That wouldn't make sense, either. As far as I know, my ancestors came to this land centuries ago on great wooden ships. I have seen many artifacts that were preserved from back then, and none of them look anything like this," Jevan said, gesturing around them.

Ardyn frowned. "It makes me wonder, does the Elder Triumvirate know of this? If they do, then they have been lying to my people for generations. For what purpose?"

"I suspect the answers we seek lie beyond that door," Jevan suggested. "Although I fear there may also be many more questions as well."

Ardyn nodded in agreement.

"What do you suggest we do now?" Jevan asked. "Since this lies in the heart of your people's forbidden area, I think it's your call."

We've been here for nearly three cycles of the sun now. Would the elders send a hunting party into the Aria'una if we stayed much longer? They never have in the past, but I know they'll certainly be waiting for us when we finally leave. Well, let them wait.

"Let's make camp here for the night. This place will provide sufficient shelter," Ardyn decided. "Then I think we should search for more structures tomorrow. I cannot go back with so many unanswered questions, and I need more evidence before I confront the Elder Triumvirate."

Giving him a smile of encouragement, Jevan nodded in agreement. "That seems wise. Also, if they don't kill me instantly, I can confirm everything you find. They can't ignore both of us, can they?"

The reminder of the danger to Jevan formed a knot of worry in Ardyn's throat. "I had nearly forgotten about that. I could leave the Aria'una first and let them capture me. Then you might have a chance to get back to your village. I... I do not want you to be killed."

"I'll risk it," Jevan said with a shrug. "I've talked my way out of tighter spots than this. Anyway, you said it yourself, I'm officially marked for death, right? At least I can make it count for something."

Ardyn regarded Jevan. The man was full of brash self-confidence and was amiable when most of his people were standoffish, or worse. Jevan's eyes, that were so full of merriment and mischief, had never made him feel threatened.

That made Ardyn realize he was growing fonder of Jevan than perhaps was wise. He worried over the prospect of Jevan meeting his death at the hands of his people. Perhaps the fact that Jevan had saved the life of an Athla'naa would help him, but Ardyn doubted it. The elders were very rigid in interpreting their laws, and they rarely showed mercy. Especially with any *athla'maakh* that violated them.

Taking a deep breath, Ardyn sighed and stood up. "I'll go hunt for some food for our evening meal while you set up camp."

"Good idea. You proved yesterday that you're a better hunter than I am," Jevan said with a smirk as he stood, stashing his pack.

With a roll of his eyes, Ardyn teased. "Yes, because you were such a terrible shot when you saved me from that sar'ora."

Jevan's laughter followed him as he headed into the forest with his bow and quiver. Turning, he regarded their unusual shelter for a moment. Inside the structure there was plenty of room and it was still mostly hidden, tucked into a hillside, beneath the overgrowth they hadn't removed.

I wonder what the purpose of this was? And why keep it a secret from our people? Ardyn wondered before turning back to his task. *At least we'll both be able to get a good night's sleep tonight. We may need it, not knowing what else we may find tomorrow.*

BARRIERS

The next morning, Jevan left his heavy pack inside the structure, only bringing a small pack with rations and water, along with his bow and quiver. It was late morning when Jevan spotted something that could be another structure. "Over here!" he called out to Ardyn, who was investigating around a nearby boulder.

Jevan pulled out his knife and began cutting away the overgrowth. He soon realized this structure was something different. Ardyn joined him in pulling away the vegetation that covered the large object. It took them the rest of the morning to clear away enough to get a better look at it.

It stood three times as tall as Jevan, and it could have been used to travel, with strange wheels surrounded by a continuous track of metal plates with protrusions that looked like they were designed to grip the ground. At one end was a broad, curved metal plate that reminded Jevan of a shovel.

"What is this thing?" Ardyn asked as he stepped back and stared at it.

"I'm not sure," Jevan replied. "See those wheels? I think they would help it move over the ground, and that end looks like it might be for digging. But it's far too large for any person to pull."

"So, not a dwelling like the other structure we found. Assuming that was a dwelling at all. It didn't seem like a cozy place to live."

"You're right, although if we added some furnishings, that could make it livable," Jevan said as he climbed up to get a better look at this unusual thing. There was a small, glass enclosed structure at the top. "There is a small seat, facing a bunch of knobs and levers. Maybe these helped make this thing move, but I have no idea how."

"I don't think trying to make a giant digging machine work will solve the mystery of the Aria'una. Let's move on, while we still have daylight," Ardyn suggested.

In the late afternoon, as they crested over a steep hillside, they saw something that took Jevan's breath away. In the valley below stood a tall tower, all metal and glass, gleaming in the sunlight. Even the ground around the tower shone with a glint of metal. It rose into the sky, taller than any tree. If it hadn't been in a deep valley, they would have easily seen the tower rising above the surrounding treetops.

"What is that?" Ardyn asked with wonder. "How could anyone build a structure so tall?"

"I don't know," Jevan replied as he stared at it in amazement. "I've heard tales of taller buildings in the cities of my ancestors, across the ocean, but I doubt even those could have towered this high. That looks incredible!"

They approached the gleaming tower with caution, descending the steep hillside. As they neared the tower, Jevan spotted a doorway at the base of the tower. "Let's see if we can get inside," he suggested, eagerly striding ahead of Ardyn, when he quite literally walked into a wall.

Falling backward, Jevan landed on his ass. "*Falx!*" Jevan cursed as Ardyn ran over. Having been a few steps ahead of Ardyn, it had thankfully saved the elf from this indignity. Looking up, he saw Ardyn reaching out a hand to help him up.

"Thanks," Jevan said, dusting off his clothes.

"What happened?" Ardyn asked as Jevan cautiously walked over to the invisible barrier he'd collided with. Looking more closely, he held out his hands until they felt something that was less solid as much as *pushing back* against his hand.

"I ran into... something," Jevan replied, his hands running over whatever this barrier was. "It's almost completely invisible, but it's there. Can you see how it makes the air shimmer when I touch it?"

Stepping closer, Ardyn looked at Jevan's hands. "Yes! I see it. How odd." Reaching out, Ardyn tried to touch it as well, but his hand passed right through. However, he could still *feel* it. It was an odd sensation, like trying to push through water without getting wet. Ardyn kept going and a moment later, he stood on the other side of the barrier.

"Why am I not surprised?" Jevan groused. "Everything about this place seems designed to let elves in and keep Medellans out. It looks like I won't be able to go with you into the tower."

Ardyn gave Jevan a wry smile. "I'm sorry you feel so left out," he teased.

Rolling his eyes, Jevan ignored Ardyn's teasing and reached up as high as he could, his hands following the surface of the strange wall. "This wall seems to keep going, higher than I can reach. I wonder if it covers the entire tower."

"This is all very bizarre," Ardyn said, looking at the doorway and then back at Jevan, before taking out the key. "I'll see if I can open that door."

"Good idea," Jevan agreed.

As he was about to turn and make his way toward the tower, Jevan stopped him. "Hey, wait a moment. I just thought of something. The larger Medellan cities along the coast all have high stone walls that were built to protect them from attack. I wonder if this... whatever this is... has the same function? That would explain why it's keeping me out."

"Were the walls around your cities built back during the war with my people?" Ardyn asked. "Why don't villages like Ahren have them?"

"Many of the villages like Ahren and Yanen were built long after they signed the truce," Jevan explained. "That truce allowed my people to build villages in the valleys where your people wouldn't live, and your ancestors promised not to attack us. So, we didn't have a need for such defenses anymore."

"Okay, but why are you telling me this now?" Ardyn wondered.

"Because, with any wall, there should be a door or some way to let people in. In our cities, we have large steel portals that are locked at night. They were also locked whenever the cities were attacked during the war. But doors that can be locked can also be opened. Large doors like that are too heavy to be opened and closed easily. There's a complex mechanism of levers, chains, and counterweights. I was just wondering if there might not be something inside that tower that could bring down this barrier and let me in."

"That makes sense. I will look around and see if there is anything obvious, but if there's more of that ancient writing, I won't make any promises," Ardyn said, before turning and making his way toward the tower.

When he approached the metal ground that surrounded the tower, Ardyn stooped to touch it. It seemed to be made of the same material as that structure they'd found. Taking a cautious step onto the strange ground, Ardyn let out a breath he didn't even realize he was holding when he was fully standing on it. Looking ahead, he began making his way toward the door. Walking on the metal surface felt very odd to his feet, which were more used to the softer ground of the surrounding forest. Even the wooden floors of the huts back home had more give to them than this metal did.

As he neared the doorway, he saw another slot for the key. This door slid open soundlessly, without the groaning hiss the door from their previous night's shelter had made. Ardyn looked back at Jevan and waved before walking into the tower. As he passed through the threshold, once again, the interior came to life. Lights turned on and a variety of strange sounds began emanating from various locations within the large room he found himself in.

The ceiling stretched high above him, with several levels formed by platforms at various intervals. The platforms were all connected by a series of stairs and ladders, which in a strange way reminded him of Maala'naa.

Facing the large, angled windows that stretched high above him, he saw many strange looking... *tables?* The tops were smooth, like glass. He cautiously sat in a chair that was bolted to the floor in front of one. When he reached out and touched the table, it was immediately illuminated, displaying strange images and more of that archaic script.

Maybe these tables control things in this strange tower? I bet it might even open a door in that invisible wall keeping Jevan out, but I can't make sense of anything. I wish Jevan could see this, but I doubt he'd understand any of it either.

Leaving behind the strange table, Ardyn explored further and saw another doorway but decided not to venture deeper into the tower. Instead, he ascended one flight of stairs to find a tasteful arrangement of padded benches and chairs, facing the windows.

Aesthetically, this place was both foreign and beautiful, and somewhere in the back of his mind, it almost felt like home. Shaking himself out of his reverie, Ardyn felt overwhelmed, so he left the tower and sprinted back to Jevan.

"I can't really describe what I saw in there, and I couldn't make sense of anything. I'm sorry, but I don't know if there's any way to get you past this wall."

"Did you see any other doors inside the tower?" Jevan asked.

"Yes, but I didn't feel right exploring without you," Ardyn admitted as he pushed back through the barrier. "It was very strange inside the tower, and I would feel safer having you with me."

"Well, I don't think we'll find anything more fantastic than this," Jevan said. "This tower must be what your elders have been hiding. I think it's time we go confront them about what we've found."

Reluctantly, Ardyn agreed. They made their way back to the first structure they'd found, each lost in thought. There, they stopped to camp for the night. It was too late to travel farther, and they were still at least two cycles of the sun from the perimeter of the Aria'una.

Ardyn found everything they discovered deeply disturbing. He now questioned what his elders had taught him about his ancestors and his heritage. Those questions turned into regrets. Regrets over things they had forced him to do to uphold *honor* and *tradition*. Regrets that made him feel like he had been *used*.

FRIENDSHIP

They made good time over the next two cycles of the sun, working their way back toward the perimeter of the Aria'una. Since leaving the strange gleaming tower, they had spoken little. Jevan could see what they'd discovered had shaken the elf's faith in his people, especially his elders.

Ardyn also seemed worried for him, but Jevan could take care of himself. *If I can't escape execution at the hands of these elves, at least Ard Mathias can't force me into a pair-bond*, he thought, laughing sardonically to himself.

Jevan was more concerned for the elf's safety, although Ardyn reassured him he was in no danger of execution, despite their extended incursion into the Aria'una. Given what they'd found, he still had a knot of worry that sat in his stomach, hard and heavy.

Beyond that, Jevan also worried about the tenuous truce between his and Ardyn's people. After all these centuries, there was still so much hatred and distrust between them, and if Jevan found himself executed by the Elder Triumvirate in Maala'naa, he hoped it wouldn't spark a new conflict.

Jevan's village of Yanen was the closest Medellan settlement to Maala'naa. *I really don't care what happens to me,* Jevan thought to himself. *But I don't want to put my mother and sister in danger. I hope I can charm my way out of this mess.*

To escape his troubling thoughts, Jevan broke the silence between them. "How large is your family?" he asked.

Ardyn scowled at the question. His ears lowered before he replied curtly. "Large enough."

"What's wrong?" Jevan asked in confusion. "I thought your people loved talking about their families?"

Ardyn stopped walking, his fingers fiddling with the end of his long braid. "They do. It's just... *complicated.*"

"If you'd rather not talk about it, then I apologize for asking," Jevan said sincerely.

"No, I'm sorry. With everything we have learned so far, I have had some realizations that have brought up old resentments I've tried to forget. It's partly related to family," Ardyn tried to explain.

Standing silently, Jevan allowed Ardyn the time to think and explain as much as he was comfortable with.

"Maybe I should get this off my chest, but let's keep moving," Ardyn suggested, walking toward their destination once more. Jevan stared at Ardyn for a moment before jogging to catch up with him.

After a few more moments, Ardyn finally spoke. "First, a short answer to your question. My family includes my parents, my two half-siblings, and my three children."

"What about the rest of your family? Most Athla'naa I've met live in large, polyamorous families."

"Yes, but not all of us do. While the elders encourage us to produce many children with multiple partners because it supposedly helps to make each generation healthier and stronger, not everyone wants to be part of a large family. Once my father met his obligation, he and my mother settled into a monogamous pairing."

"So, you and your father only had one child with each mate?" Jevan asked. "Most of your people I've met have a half-dozen or more."

"Yes, my family is regarded as odd because we have so few children. However, in my case... it was... they *forced* me to mate. The first was for my coming-of-age mating ceremony, and then I had to mate with two other females for their ceremonies. The first one was from Maala'naa, and the other two were from other settlements."

"They *forced* you?!" Jevan exclaimed with shock. "Why?"

Ardyn stopped again, pacing back and forth for a few moments before leaning his back against a nearby tree. "I didn't want to mate with them, but my elders didn't give me a choice. I had to, for the good of our people... or so they told me."

That's when Jevan understood. "So, you're worried that if your elders have been lying about your ancestors, what else could they have been lying about?"

Ardyn pushed away from the tree and paced again. "*Exactly*. Maybe... maybe I didn't need to mate at all. I fought against it, but I gave in because of how *necessary* they said it was for me to produce at least three children. They made it sound like the entire Athla'naa civilization depended on it."

"That's a lot to put on anyone," Jevan said. "I'm sorry. You should never have to be forced into something like that." *We're so alike. This makes me wonder why my people are also so insistent on pair-bonding. What difference does it actually make?*

Jevan set down his heavy pack and sat on a nearby log. Taking a swig from his waterskin, he tried to change the topic. "So, why didn't you want to mate with them? Not your type?"

"Something like that," Ardyn replied, sitting down on the ground with his back against the tree. "I would prefer to mate with males, not females."

Jevan's eyes went wide. "You do? But you seemed put off by my terrible attempt at flirting."

"It wasn't the fact you are male that put me off," Ardyn admitted. "It was the fact you're *athla'maakh*."

"So, you're not into tall, dark, and handsome?" Jevan teased, laughing at his own joke.

Ardyn laughed in return, the sound of it bringing Jevan a moment of joy. *I hope I hear that laugh more often.*

"I'm not sure," Ardyn confessed. "Honestly, between the continued tension between our people, and the fact we're so different from each other, I guess I hadn't really thought about it."

"It's okay. I'm happy to enjoy your company as a friend. We don't need to be more than that."

While Ardyn was beautiful, Jevan had enough liaisons with other elves that he felt no need to charm the pants off this one. Especially not under current circumstances.

Ardyn stood and held out his hand. "Alright, friend, let's keep moving and we may still make it out of here before nightfall."

Jevan let Ardyn help pull him up before he grabbed his pack and followed as the elf led the way.

◆◆◆

After walking in silence for a while, Ardyn turned to Jevan. "So, I shared about my family. What of yours? Do you have a mate and children?"

"No. There's only my mother and sister," Jevan replied. "My father passed from an illness a while ago."

"I'm sorry," Ardyn offered his sympathies. "I haven't experienced a loss like that yet. How does your mother manage? Can she mate again?"

"Our pair-bonds last for life. We are only able to pair-bond again after a bondmate passes, but it doesn't happen often. My sister remains with her, at least until she pair-bonds herself. After that, my mother will have the choice to live alone or live with my sister and her bondmate."

Now that Jevan had put the notion into his head, Ardyn took furtive glances at the tall man. *He is good looking, in his own way, Ardyn had to admit to himself.* "Do you plan to pair-bond with anyone?" Ardyn asked.

Jevan let out an exasperated sigh. "No, but my village ard has been insisting I pair-bond within the next season, but I don't want to," Jevan explained.

"Why not? You seem like someone who would enjoy having a mate and children. You're so jovial, and you would make a good father."

"Well, the truth is, I don't like the idea of being pair-bonded to only one person for the rest of my life. Also, there isn't anyone I know I would want to pair-bond with."

"Are all your pair-bonds between males and females?" Ardyn asked. "Do your people put as much emphasis on having children as mine do?"

"No, although most Medellans will pair-bond with the opposite sex, and have children," Jevan replied. "But it's not unheard of for someone to pair-bond with the same sex. I know a few couples like that, scattered throughout the villages I trade with."

Wait, Jevan finds me attractive, right? "Since you flirted with me, are you like me? Do you only enjoy mating with males, too?"

Jevan chuckled at that. "Not quite. I don't care what someone's sex is. The reason I haven't chosen to pair-bond is because I'd much prefer having multiple partners."

Oh. To cover up his disappointment, Ardyn teased. "Then you would fit right in with my people. You just need pointier ears."

That made Jevan laugh. "The thought had briefly crossed my mind once," Jevan admitted. "I'd worry I would never be welcome to see my mother and sister again, but I almost asked Elder Syvan to let me become a member of her settlement."

"Would you be able to give up all your metal tools?"

"Honestly? Yeah, I would," Jevan said. "Although, if ancient elves made all those structures we found, I would have liked to have met them. I'd love to learn how they forged that metal."

Feeling sheepish, Ardyn ducked his head. "Don't tell anyone, but... I would love to know, too," Ardyn admitted quietly. "I have always had a fascination with the technology I've seen your people use, and what we found in the Aria'una makes me want to know more."

Looking up, Ardyn saw the stark white trunks and red leaves of the *bhat'laa'arh* in the distance. Slowing his pace, he pulled on Jevan's arm. "We are approaching the perimeter; keep up your guard."

"Are you sure they are already waiting for us?" Jevan whispered.

Ardyn nodded. After so many cycles of the sun, the elders would have had plenty of time to move hunting and ranger patrols all along the perimeter of the Aria'una. A true breach happened rarely, but he'd been a part of several patrols over the past few cycles of the seasons when the elders suspected an incursion.

As they neared the *bhat'laa'arh*, Jevan stopped and pointed up at something. "Ardyn, have you ever really looked at these?"

Looking at where Jevan was pointing, partially hidden up in the branches, was a small metal box with blinking lights. Along the perimeter, as far as they could see, there were boxes positioned on every tree. "No, I've never been this close to the trees before... well, never this close while paying attention, anyway."

"I was wondering about that. I would have noticed trees like this. It makes me wonder if we both stumbled into your forbidden area through a section where these trees are missing or more obscured by the surrounding brush and vines?"

The thought hadn't even occurred to Ardyn. The elders taught that the *bhat'laa'arh* formed an unbroken perimeter around the Aria'una, but it's possible some may have been felled by a lightning storm. Trees were long lived, but even they weren't immortal.

Jevan walked closer to a tree, setting down his heavy pack and hoisting himself up to get a closer look at the box. "These are made of the same metal as that key," Jevan said. "Come up here and take a look."

Climbing up next to Jevan, Ardyn pulled the key out of his pocket and held it up next to the box. The metal was the same color and smoothness, and the box also had some of that now familiar elven script. When Ardyn reached out to touch the box, the script glowed and a small panel on the side of the box popped open.

"*Ior'kah!*" Ardyn cursed. "You're right!" He looked inside the box and saw a confusing array of blinking lights and things he couldn't describe. "The elders must know these exist and... and... they must use this technology somehow. That would explain how they always knew when a breach of this perimeter happened. They *have* been lying to us. That's the only explanation."

The next moment, a voice called out from below, speaking in the language of the Athla'naa. "Get down from there immediately!"

Looking down, Ardyn recognized members of one of the hunting parties from Maala'naa. *They'd found them.*

JUDGMENT

Once they were back on the ground, the hunting party grabbed them and bound their hands behind their backs. They tethered each to a different hunter, while other hunters carried their packs. What surprised Jevan was that they hadn't killed him on sight. Either Ardyn was wrong about his transgression being an instant death penalty, or the elven elders had other plans for him.

By the next afternoon, the group arrived in Maala'naa. Jevan barely had time to take in the elven settlement as the hunters immediately dragged them in front of the Elder Triumvirate. They were already convened and awaiting them, seated next to each other on a long bench.

"Kneel!"

Jevan did his best to lower himself to his knees while his hands were still bound behind him, keeping his head up and studying the Triumvirate. Each elder carried a staff, signifying their rank within the Athla'naa community. Jevan recognized each of them based on descriptions Ardyn had given him.

Aelrynd was a female elf with short, dark, bluish-purple hair that had a single streak of silver running back from her left temple. She sat in the center as the eldest and the head of the Triumvirate. To her left sat Druyndar, a male elf with long silver hair and a scowl on his dour face. Taeglyn wore his mix of lavender and silver hair in a long braid, like Ardyn, and looked curiously at the tall, dark Medellan who knelt before him.

Aelrynd spoke first. "You both entered the Aria'una during that last storm. We might overlook it as an error because of the weather, but then you remained within the Aria'una for several cycles of the sun. Explain!"

So, Ardyn was right. They knew exactly when they had entered the Aria'una, and for how long they remained, Jevan realized. These elders *must* possess some technology that allowed them to track their movements.

"I'm sorry, Elder Aelrynd," Ardyn began. "It's my fault. I was tracking the *sar'ora*, as you had tasked me to do.

When the storm hit, I didn't realize how close I was to the Aria'una. I ran blindly, seeking shelter."

"You hadn't realized you crossed the perimeter?" the elder asked pointedly.

Ardyn shook his head. "No, Elder, I hadn't. I found a small cave and spent the night there to escape the deluge. It wasn't until the next morning, when I climbed a tree to get my bearings, that I realized where I was. I immediately made my way toward the perimeter, but when I stopped to rest, the *sar'ora* attacked me."

"Yet you live, seemingly unscathed," Druyndar pointed out.

"Yes. This *athla'maakh*, Jevan, saved my life. He killed the *sar'ora* before it could rip out my throat," Ardyn explained. "I brought back the pelt as proof. It's with my pack."

Druyndar pointed to a hunter. "Bring Ardyn's pack and unroll the pelt."

The pelt was laid out before the elders. "After this *athla'maakh* completed the task I gave you, why did you remain for several cycles of the sun?" Elder Aelrynd asked with a frown of disapproval. "Were you injured? Unable to walk?"

"No, Elder Aelrynd," Ardyn replied softly.

"Speak up!" Druyndar commanded.

"No, I was able to walk," Ardyn replied.

"Then why did you remain? Explain yourself!" Aelrynd demanded, growing impatient.

Jevan could feel Ardyn's uncertainty as he hesitated. Looking at him for a moment, Jevan flashed Ardyn a reassuring smile. Nodding, Ardyn squared his shoulders and looked back at the elders.

"I found a strange artifact in the cave where I sought shelter. I showed it to Jevan, thinking it may have been made by his people. He couldn't explain it either, so the two of us searched for more clues. We wanted to understand how such an object could exist."

A brief expression of alarm followed by a dark scowl crossed the face of all three elders. "Where is this object now?" Aelrynd asked.

"In my pocket," Ardyn replied.

"Search him," Druyndar commanded.

A hunter went through Ardyn's pockets until she found the object. In her hand, it glowed as it had for Ardyn, which confirmed Jevan's suspicion. This technology only worked when touched by an elf.

The hunter handed the object to Aelrynd, who studied it and then handed it to Druyndar.

"Curious, but worthless," Druyndar said dismissively. "This hardly warrants you ignoring our laws and turning your back on our heritage."

"It is not worthless! It is a *key*!" Ardyn declared, causing those assembled to gasp. "We found a small structure and a tall tower in the Aria'una, made from the same finely wrought metal as that key. The key opened locked doors, allowing us inside—"

"Enough!" Aelrynd said with a growl. "You blatantly ignored our laws, explored an area that is expressly forbidden, and allowed an *athla'maakh* to stand witness to the same. That is inexcusable!"

The three elders huddled together and began conferring with each other in hushed tones, occasionally pointing and gesturing angrily at the two of them.

Jevan was stunned at how unsurprised the Triumvirate was at Ardyn's revelations. As if they had known about this technology all along. This was another confirmation that the Triumvirate had been lying to the elven people. Perhaps for generations. Jevan's heart pounded in his chest as he tried to process what that meant. He had a bad feeling and feared that his charms and good looks might not get him out of this predicament. Yet, he had nothing left to lose.

"Elders," Jevan addressed the Triumvirate in the elven tongue, catching them off-guard. "I wish to beg you for mercy. I apologize for blundering into your Aria'una, but I never saw the perimeter, and I wasn't aware that the area was forbidden. You must believe me. I had no intention of violating your laws. However, if I hadn't stumbled into the area, I wouldn't have been there to save Ardyn from the *sar'ora* that attacked him. Please, neither of us meant any harm. Our curiosities got the better of us."

The elders rose, ignoring Jevan's plea. Aelrynd stepped forward. "Ardyn, for violating our most sacred laws, and not only entering the Aria'una, but daring to explore its interior, you are to suffer one hundred lashes. You will also lose all your rights and privileges as a ranger and be confined to the settlement of Maala'naa."

Ardyn gasped in shock at the pronouncement of his punishment before bowing his head. "Yes, Elder."

Leveling her gaze onto Jevan and speaking in the language of Medellans, Aelrynd proclaimed her sentence. "As for you *athla'maakh*, upon first light tomorrow, we will execute you for venturing into the Aria'una, as allowed by the treaty agreement between our people."

"That's in the treaty? That you can execute Medellans who accidentally venture into your forbidden forest?" Jevan asked in shock. "Why aren't my people told about this?"

Aelrynd shrugged her shoulders. "That is between you and your ard. If he failed to warn you, it is no matter to us. It is in the treaty, and so you will die for your transgression. Be grateful we will give you a swift, painless death."

Wait, Mathias knows about all this?

Turning to the hunters, Aelrynd instructed them on what to do next. "Secure them in separate huts until tomorrow. The *athla'maakh* may eat a last meal if he wishes, but serve only water to Ardyn."

The hunters nodded and dragged the two off in separate directions.

They stripped Jevan naked and secured him within a small hut that appeared to be used for storage. His hands were bound above his head, forcing him to kneel. As an added precaution, they hobbled his knees. Under different circumstances, Jevan would have flirted with anyone stripping off his clothing, but he didn't find himself in his usual charming mood.

Jevan shivered in the chill evening air and refused any food they offered. The prospect of dying had made him lose his appetite and eating was rather pointless now, anyway. While kneeling there alone, Jevan looked back on his life. His only regret was not being able to say farewell to his mother and sister. A part of him grieved for his mother, to lose her son in this way. It also saddened him that he wouldn't be able to fulfill his promise to his sister. Since their father had passed several summers ago, he was to recite the blessing at his sister's pair-bonding.

Something that surprised him was feeling regret at never having formed a deeper bond with anyone outside of his family. He'd always moved on after a night or two of fun. While he may not have wanted to be forced into a lifelong pair-bond, it didn't mean he never wanted to find love.

As a slight breeze blew in from the open window of the hut, Jevan realized his face was wet with tears. He hadn't cried since he was a small boy and he felt somewhat embarrassed that he did so now. His heart ached, but there was nothing he could do about it.

●●●

As the daylight waned, nightfall darkened his surroundings. Despite his uncomfortable position, Jevan drifted in and out of consciousness. His mind and body were both weary, and he thought briefly that he might almost welcome death come morning.

Suddenly, Jevan heard a sound at the door of the hut he was in, and it opened and closed swiftly and quietly. It startled him into full wakefulness.

Jevan kept still, wondering what was going on when he felt a hot breath by his ear, and someone whispered hoarsely, "remain silent, please."

The next thing he knew, they untied his hands and legs, and handed him some clothing. "Dress, quickly," the voice whispered again.

Complying as fast as he could, with how stiff and numb his limbs were, Jevan pulled on his breeches and shirt before the mysterious figure handed him his boots and cloak. Once dressed, a warm, firm hand grasped his. "Follow me."

Jevan followed without question as they slipped out of the hut as noiselessly as possible. He followed the cloaked figure as they led him across several bridges before they climbed down out of the trees and slipped silently into the surrounding forest. His rescuer took his hand again to prevent being separated, and they ran for what felt like hours until Jevan needed to stop and catch his breath.

"Wait, please," Jevan breathed heavily as he dropped to his knees.

The other figure stopped and turned around. "Alright, let us rest while we can, but then we must keep moving until we are no longer in Athla'naa lands."

Jevan nodded and looked up as his rescuer pulled back his cloak and smiled at him.

Ardyn.

FLIGHT

Ardyn raised a finger to his lips, to let Jevan know to be quiet. He handed over a waterskin and gave him a moment to drink his fill. Then he grasped the hand of the Medellan once more, as they continued to move swiftly away from Maala'naa. Despite the dark moonless night, he guided Jevan effortlessly through the dense forest.

The next time Jevan tugged on his hand, Ardyn stopped and looked around. He heard no sounds of pursuit, so he led them to a nearby log where they could sit and rest. Their panted breaths came out in thick clouds in the chill night air.

Untying a waterskin from his belt, Ardyn handed it to Jevan before untying another for himself. After taking a long drink from the waterskin, Jevan asked in a hoarse whisper. "Why?"

"Besides myself, you are the only one who knows the truth of what we found in the Aria'una," Ardyn responded in a whisper. "Also, you saved my life and you... you're a friend. I couldn't let them kill you."

"Well, I think now we're even," Jevan whispered back teasingly. "What happens now?"

"Which way leads to your village?" Ardyn asked.

"It lies east of Maala'naa," Jevan replied. "I'd need to see the sky from a clearing to have a better idea."

Ardyn nodded. "I know these lands well, so we'll keep moving east for now. We'll stop again when we come upon a clearing. They will discover our escape by sunrise, and I want to be out of Athla'naa territory by then."

Jevan nodded, and they continued until they found a clearing. They stopped long enough for him to get his bearings. Then Jevan took the lead, guiding them toward his village. When they came across a creek, they also stopped long enough to fill their water skins.

"The water is shallow, so let's move upstream for a while, to help cover our tracks," Ardyn suggested. It would mean they would have cold, wet feet, but it beat the alternative of being caught and possibly executed on sight.

"Good idea," Jevan agreed.

They finally crossed out of Athla'naa territory as the sky brightened at the dawn of a new cycle of the sun, and they could slow their pace. As they walked, Ardyn reflected on his actions over the past several hours. After hearing the pronouncement from Elder Aelrynd, his heart clenched at the thought of Jevan losing his life. While it didn't surprise him, it was neither just nor fair, regardless of the laws. Especially considering the centuries-old lies that he and Jevan had uncovered.

Based on the elders' reactions, there was much more going on than either of them had realized. That key, and the buildings it unlocked, was only part of a larger mystery. The lack of surprise regarding their discoveries confirmed the elders knew about everything and were hiding some dark secret.

Helping Jevan escape and fleeing his own punishment also weighed on Ardyn, as he realized he may never return home after this. In fact, he wouldn't be safe in any Athla'naa settlement once the word spread.

"How close are we to your village?" Ardyn asked.

"We should reach there by mid-afternoon."

"Will they welcome me? I doubt I'll ever be able to return home after what I've done, so I hope to seek shelter among your people," Ardyn admitted.

"We tolerate elves well enough," Jevan replied with a smile. "Besides, you'll have me to protect you, in case anyone picks a fight."

Ardyn looked up at Jevan. "I am stronger than I look, *Medellan*," he teased, nudging Jevan with his elbow playfully. "But in all seriousness, would they allow me to stay?"

Looking down at him with obvious sincerity, Jevan replied. "I would insist upon it. You could stay with me. I have a small house. With how much I travel, you'd often have the place to yourself. It would be nice to have someone there to come home to."

"You would have me become your mate, keeping your house for you?" Ardyn asked, raising an eyebrow at the man.

Laughing at the idea, Jevan shook his head. "You may be the most beautiful elf I've ever laid my eyes on, but that wasn't what I was suggesting. It would be less of a wasted resource if the home was actually being used."

"If you're home so rarely, why do you have your own house?" Ardyn asked. "Wouldn't it be easier to just share a space for the brief periods when you are there? My parents and I shared the hut I used when I was back in Maala'naa."

"It belonged to the last trader in our village," Jevan explained. "After he passed, Mathias offered the position to me, which included the house. It's small but suits my needs when I am back home."

"What happened to the previous trader's family?"

"His wife moved back to her village after he passed, and their only child was grown and living with her bondmate. So, the home passed to me when I took the position and is mine as long as I remain a trader in Yanen."

Ardyn contemplated the idea for a moment before responding. "I appreciate the offer, but I am trained as a ranger. I would be restless remaining in one place overlong. Is your village in need of a ranger?"

"That would be a question for the ard. Part of his job is to allocate resources and services both within our village and between other villages in our area," Jevan explained. "So, if someone in our village shows an aptitude toward a profession that we don't require, he will enquire if another village is seeking an apprentice in that profession."

"Hopefully your ard will have some use for my ranging skills then," Ardyn said before lapsing back into silence. He felt no remorse for having exiled himself from his people. He had always felt different and therefore kept to himself, even as a child. Jevan was one of the first people he'd met that he felt completely at ease with.

"Once we arrive, the first thing we should do is speak with Ard Mathias," Jevan declared.

"Are you sure I'll be safe? Your people don't have any laws for executing Athla'naa, do they?" Ardyn asked, still unsure of living among Medellans. "After the villagers in Ahren turned against Soren for befriending me, I don't want that happening to you."

"I'm sure," Jevan replied amiably. "Besides, we have no secret forbidden zones and you haven't broken any laws."

I hope you are right. Taking a deep breath, Ardyn nodded. "Okay then. I'll go with you to meet your ard."

MATHIAS

Jevan told Ardyn more about Ard Mathias as they walked. He was a gruff older man, who was mostly kind and understanding. About most things, anyway. Jevan only grumbled about how Ard Mathias kept pushing to see him pair-bond with someone. *Anyone.* For Jevan, the practice of pair-bonding was archaic at best and a lifelong imprisonment at worst.

Ardyn laughed at Jevan's grousing. "I don't know. It doesn't sound so bad, spending your life with the one person you love."

"That's part of the problem. If we're paired with someone we didn't choose, we're stuck with them for the rest of our lives. That's how it was for my parents," Jevan explained.

"So, once a pair bonds, they cannot go their separate ways?" Ardyn asked. "Even if they find themselves incompatible?"

"They could, and sometimes they do," Jevan said. "I'm not entirely sure why my mother stayed in a loveless bonding for so long. However, once bonded, neither of the pair can enjoy the company of another for as long as their bondmate lives."

Ardyn was about to question that revelation when they crested a rise and saw the village of Yanen in the valley below. It was picturesque, a scattering of homes with red-tiled roofs. Surrounding the village were large tracts of farmland on three sides, and some dense woodlands on the northernmost side.

As they passed by, villagers working out in the fields greeted Jevan with friendly smiles, some asking about his companion. It was clear many had never seen an Athla'naa before, and Ardyn tried his best to give a friendly wave, even as he steeled his nerves.

They approached a road that took them into the village, and Jevan led them toward the largest of the homes near an open market square. Yanen was larger than Ahren, but otherwise quite similar. Ardyn still marveled at how different

Medellan villages were from the tree-top homes of Athla'naa settlements.

Once they stood outside of the door of the large house, Jevan knocked on it with his fist. The door opened a few moments later, and an older man greeted them warmly. His hair and beard were white, and his skin was much paler than Jevan's. The range of skin colors Medellans had was so different to Ardyn's people, who were all the same pale shade.

"Jevan! We were expecting you back several cycles of the sun ago. Where have you been? I see you've also brought a visitor with you. Come in, come in!"

The older man led them inside and into a room that reminded Ardyn of Soren's living room, with cushioned seating, tables, and a fireplace. Even the smell reminded him of Soren's home, a mix of wood smoke and food. It surprised him how welcoming that felt after his last encounter in Ahren. *I guess a part of me missed Soren more than I realized.*

"So, who do we have here?" the man asked.

"This is Ardyn," Jevan introduced. "Ard Mathias."

"Does he speak our language?" Mathias asked.

"Greetings," Ardyn replied and bowed in respect. "Yes, I speak and understand your language. Thank you for welcoming me into your home, Ard Mathias."

"Excellent!" Mathias exclaimed. "Come, sit and tell me what brings you to my door."

Jevan and Ardyn took turns explaining how they met and their ensuing adventures, ending with Ardyn rescuing Jevan and fleeing to Yanen. While they spoke, Mathias said nothing, but as the tale progressed, his expression grew troubled.

After they had finished relating their tale, Mathias rose and paced the room, lost in thought. Then he sat down and looked at the pair of them gravely. "This is bad. *Very* bad. I wish you had not chosen to return here, Jevan."

Jevan seemed surprised by this pronouncement. "It raises a lot of questions about the elves, certainly, but—"

"You don't understand, Jevan," Mathias interrupted. "You broke the treaty between our people by escaping your execution."

"So, you do know about this part of the treaty? Did you also know about this forbidden zone of theirs? Why have you never warned anyone to avoid it?" Jevan questioned with a raised voice.

"Because the perimeter lies within elven territory," Mathias explained. "We're all cautioned to avoid entering the elven lands. If you don't trespass on their lands, then you are in no danger of wandering haphazardly into this forbidden area. There are no settlements to trade with near it, so it never occurred to me to give you any special warning."

"Don't you remember? I told you there is a new settlement I've been trading with," Jevan reminded him. "I came across their settlement about one cycle of the seasons ago and have been trading with them regularly. That's the last settlement I visited before the big storm. They are very near the border of the Aria'una."

Mathias scowled. "The maps I have of the elven territory show no settlements anywhere near there."

The older man rose and went to a large chest that sat in the corner of the room. He pulled out some scrolls and unrolled them on the low table before them. "See? Here's the line of those red-leafed trees that mark the border. Here's Maala'naa. The nearest settlements I know of are all farther south and west."

Ardyn had never seen a map before. He gazed at it, attempting to comprehend what Mathias was pointing out. "If this is Maala'naa," Ardyn said, pointing his finger at the spot Mathias had shown. "Then you're missing several settlements on this map... here... here... and here," he pointed to spots where he thought they would approximately be.

"Yes," Jevan agreed, pointing his finger at a specific spot. "The settlement I mentioned is located here. According to this, it's quite close to that line of trees."

Sitting back in frustration, Mathias ran his hands over his face. "I should have asked you for more details when you told me of the new elven settlement you'd found to trade with. However, something else about this is wrong. Despite the standing order to execute any Medellan who dares step foot inside this Aria'una, they have never carried it out.

"There is a tacit agreement between us and the Elder Triumvirate. In the past, they would send a party of hunters and rangers to locate and escort any Medellan out of the Aria'una that stumble into it by accident. Then they send the

Medellan on their way with a stern warning. It has rarely happened, but they never once carried out an execution."

"Then why did they capture me and threaten to execute me?" Jevan wondered aloud.

"Most likely, because you lingered and saw things you should not have," Mathias speculated. "There is a reason that area is forbidden."

Shaking his head, his ears lowered, Ardyn spoke up. "That's not right. They also forbid hunters and rangers to enter the Aria'una. The Triumvirate would never send us to escort someone out. No one came after us while Jevan and I explored. They were waiting for us outside the border of the *bhat'laa'arh.*"

"I see," Mathias said. "That's not what they recorded in the histories. I can read to you the—"

Making a sound of frustration, Jevan sat forward. "Do *you know* what lies hidden there? Why is it forbidden?" Jevan challenged, an edge of anger in his voice.

"Some of it, yes. Not everything," Mathias admitted. "I didn't know about the structures you found, but their presence does not surprise me."

Ardyn was appalled. *Jevan's village leader had also been lying and keeping secrets? Could none of their leaders be trusted?*

"You knew?!" Jevan yelled, bolting to his feet. "Why are you the only one who knows?"

"It's part of the treaty agreement," Mathias said. "Only the village ards are allowed to know, and we are mandated to prevent our people from finding the truth. It's worked well enough for centuries to keep the peace between our people."

"So, what now?" Jevan asked, sitting down next to Ardyn. "Because I've seen some things that the Triumvirate didn't want me to see, you would have let them kill me?"

"If only it were that simple," Mathias said, standing up and pacing again. After muttering to himself for a few moments, he sat back down and faced Jevan. "No, I won't just hand you over to them to execute. You didn't know the full consequences of your actions. However, this could cause an all-out war with the elves if I don't do *something.*"

"What will you do?" Jevan asked.

"For now, I'll ask you to remain confined in your home," Mathias decided. "Then I will consider my options on how to appease the demands of the treaty without simply sending you to your death. I will hold a public tribunal tomorrow and announce my decision then."

"A tribunal?" Jevan asked, his voice raised in anger. "All because I found out about some strange buildings, hidden in a remote part of the forest? What are you and the Triumvirate trying to hide?"

"I'm sorry, Jevan," Mathias said. "I truly am, but I must follow the law if I want to avoid starting a war with the elves that our people cannot win."

Ardyn looked up at that, his ears raised in surprise. *Why does he think his people can't win against my people?* The Medellans had the use of metal, which surely was superior to the stone weapons the Athla'naa used.

Before Ardyn could speak up and ask, Jevan looked over at him. "What about Ardyn?"

Looking at him, Mathias asked. "Do you wish to return to your people?"

Shaking his head, Ardyn replied. "No. After helping Jevan escape and fleeing my punishment, I fear they may also execute me if I return."

"Then you may remain with Jevan for the time being," Mathias said. "I need to study the treaty and the books of law. I've never had to pass judgment on someone who wasn't Medellan, but I may need to appease your people. Since you cannot return home, you will face the tribunal with Jevan."

Ardyn's ears flattened back as he bowed his head. None of this felt right, but there wasn't much he or Jevan could do about it. At least, not right now.

What aren't they telling us? he wondered.

TRIBUNAL

J evan paced, furious over their current predicament, while Ardyn sat cross-legged on the bed, watching him. He had never felt so outraged in all his life. Out of frustration, Jevan shouted. "Why?!"

"Why what?" Ardyn asked.

"Why are they doing this? Why are they keeping these secrets? What's so damned special about those structures we found that warrant convening a tribunal?" Jevan asked, flailing his hands in exasperation. "I just don't understand."

Ardyn's ears lowered. "Are tribunals that serious?"

"Yeah, they are," Jevan replied, grabbing a chair, facing it away from Ardyn, and then straddling it, so he could lean his arms across the back. "We reserve tribunals for the worst offenses. I only witnessed one when I was a kid."

"What was the offense?"

"A young unbonded man named Valen traveled from Yanen to a village along the coast. He'd gotten drunk and forced himself on a pair-bonded woman, causing her to die," Jevan explained.

Ardyn looked at him in shock. "Why would he kill her?"

"He didn't want to kill her, not intentionally," Jevan explained. "Once Medellans pair-bond, having sex with someone other than your bondmate risks serious illness or death. Valen knew that, but he insisted he never believed in the *old fairytales*. It horrified him that the woman died, but even if she hadn't, what he'd done was inexcusable."

"So, what happened to him?"

"They brought Valen back to Yanen to face the judgment of a tribunal. Mathias had recently become our new ard. He presided over the tribunal, along with the ard from the village where the assault happened," Jevan said. "The ards gave him three punishments to pay for his crimes. First was a public flogging for the crime of having sex with someone in a pair-bond. Second was castration, for the crime of rape. Third was a life sentence working deep in the mines for causing the death of another. He will never see the light of the sun again."

"Why didn't they just sentence him to die?" Ardyn asked, confused.

"Medellan law doesn't allow death as a punishment for any crime," Jevan explained. "But there's nothing we've done that should even warrant a public tribunal. There must be more that Mathias and your elders aren't telling us. Some secret they are desperate to keep hidden."

"You're right," Ardyn agreed. "It makes me wonder what else we could have discovered if we'd spent more time in the Aria'una. I regret not exploring that tower further, but I wish you could have come with me."

A knock came at the door. When Jevan opened it, one of Mathias' sons stood there with a tray of food. Taking it gratefully, he tried to speak to the young man, who fled as soon as Jevan gripped the tray. Bringing it inside and setting it onto the small table he had by the window, he didn't realize how hungry he was until he looked at the bowls of thick stew.

"Come on, we might as well eat," Jevan said, grabbing the chair he'd been sitting on and moving it back to the table. "We should keep our strength up."

Ardyn joined him at the table, and they ate together in silence. Outside, the sun was setting, so after he'd finished his stew, he lit a fire in the hearth, along with a couple of candles. Trying to keep their mind off what fate awaited them, they sat together on the bench before the fire.

While Jevan knew Mathias wouldn't sentence them to death, he still worried that they might wind up in the mines, and that was as good as a death sentence. While those who willingly worked in the mines could take time off and enjoy the outdoors, those sentenced to work there were never allowed back to the surface. It was a fate worse than death.

They'd both grown quiet, staring into the dying embers in the hearth. Ardyn was nervously fiddling with the end of his braid, lost in thought. Watching for a time, Jevan looked at Ardyn's pale, slender fingers, as they twisted and untwisted his hair. Not even thinking, he reached out and grabbed the elf's hand.

Flinching, Ardyn looked up at him suddenly. Jevan was about to blurt out an apology when Ardyn squeezed his hand and gave him a shy smile. "Your hand is very warm," Ardyn remarked, making Jevan relax. They sat there for a while; their hands intertwined. Jevan had to fight the urge to pull Ardyn into an embrace. After everything they had been through together, it made Jevan feel closer to Ardyn than he'd felt to anyone besides his family.

Their long run through the forest earlier finally caught up with him, and Jevan felt his eyes grow heavy. Ardyn must have noticed, as he squeezed Jevan's hand and let go, getting up to stretch.

"I wish I had thought to grab a bedroll in my haste to rescue you," Ardyn groused, looking around the small space.

Jevan stood and walked over to the bed and gave Ardyn a mischievous smile. "Come, join me in the bed. It's large enough."

When the elf hesitated, Jevan folded down the covers. "I'm far too tired to do anything more than sleep, so don't worry, you're safe."

Giving him a wary look, Ardyn finally agreed. "Okay, thank you. I appreciate that."

They prepared for bed and then slipped under the covers. Jevan turned so his back faced Ardyn. He felt Ardyn slowly settle in next to him. When he peeked over his shoulder, Ardyn also had his back turned toward him and was breathing softly, already asleep.

◆◆◆

The next morning, a loud knocking awakened them. When Jevan answered the door, a young man handed him a tray with some porridge and water. "Prepare yourselves. The tribunal begins shortly."

They ate quickly and dressed, trying to make themselves as presentable as possible before several men from the village arrived. Willam, one of the local farmers, scowled at them. "Put your hands behind your backs," he said as two of the others approached them with ropes.

"Is this really necessary?" Jevan asked, complying with the demand, while their hands were bound behind them.

"Ard's orders," was all Willam said, before the three men marched them toward the village square. There was a raised dais where musicians would play during festivals. Ard Mathias stood upon the dais, flanked by two elder members of the community.

The entire village had gathered to bear witness to the tribunal. Jevan spotted his mother and sister in the crowd near the dais and regretted not going to speak with them first when he had returned. Now they would have to hear the accusations against him without being able to explain.

The men brought them before the dais and the crowd closed around them. Looking up at Ard Mathias, the man had an angry scowl upon his face when he looked down at them. It gave Jevan a sinking feeling that this would not go any better than it had for them in Maala'naa.

Stepping forward, Mathias began listing the charges. "Jevan of Yanen, you are charged with trespassing into an area within the elven territory that is forbidden to all, known to them as the Aria'una. You also aided in the theft of an object found within the Aria'una and you escaped the judgment the elves pronounced upon you. How do you plead?"

Looking at Mathias defiantly, Jevan responded. "Not guilty because those charges are absurd. That area should not be forbidden, just because there are—"

"Silence!" Mathias interrupted before Jevan could tell the entire village what they'd found. There was a collective gasp from those in attendance, and Mathias waited for silence before continuing.

"Ardyn of Maala'naa," Mathias addressed the elf. "You are charged with the same crimes. How do you plead?"

Jevan looked over at the elf, and Ardyn gave him a small smile before speaking. "The guilt should fall entirely on my shoulders, Ard Mathias. I was the one who found the object you speak of. If Jevan hadn't come along to save my life, the object would have remained in the Aria'una, along with my festering remains. I also freed Jevan in Maala'naa and helped him escape the judgment of the Elder Triumvirate. Please, don't punish him for my crimes."

Ardyn's plea touched Jevan deeply. He was about to argue when Ardyn looked at him and shook his head. He turned back to Mathias when the Ard spoke again.

"Since you so brashly admit your guilt," the Ard said. "I will now pronounce your sentence. Within a fortnight, we expect the Elder Triumvirate to arrive from Maala'naa to come and bear witness as we carry out your sentence in accordance with our treaty. You are both to be publicly flogged. One hundred lashes. *Each*."

The villagers cried out at the pronouncement of such a harsh sentence for the crimes of trespassing and theft. Usually only those who committed rape or murder received that many lashes. Mathias let the people shout their disapproval for a moment before raising his hands to quiet them.

"They will receive twenty lashings over a period of five cycles of the sun," Mathias continued, and the crowd's protest reduced to a murmur. "After your flogging, we will take you to the mines, where you will live out the rest of your lives performing hard labor."

Jevan tried to remain stoic, despite the rage roiling inside of him. He looked down at Ardyn, who had tried to sacrifice himself for him. Ardyn was tough and would survive the lashings, especially spaced out as Mathias had proclaimed, but Jevan worried how long Ardyn would survive deep in the mines.

As several men led them away, Jevan gave his mother and sister a smile, keeping a brave face despite their horrified expressions. They were being held back from rushing to his side, crying out his name and pleading with Mathias for mercy. On the way back to his home, Jevan's mind raced. They had some time before the Triumvirate would arrive in Yanen. An idea struck him, and he soon had the beginnings of a plan.

They untied them after they were back inside Jevan's home. Two men were to guard the front door, while another would watch the perimeter. They brought meals each morning and evening, and a tub of water for bathing every other cycle of the sun. Otherwise, they were to be left alone until the Triumvirate had arrived to bear witness to their punishment.

Once the guards left and the door closed, Jevan pulled Ardyn away from the door. "I have a plan, but I need you to be in complete agreement," Jevan said quietly.

Ardyn nodded.

"We will escape. Not right away, because it would be too easy to track us if we ran now, and they are too watchful so soon after the tribunal," Jevan explained. "You know that storm we encountered meant we're about to enter the rainy season. I expect another heavy rainstorm soon. We'll make our escape then, so the rain can obscure our tracks."

"If the rain doesn't come?" Ardyn asked.

"If the rain doesn't come, we'll still attempt to run," Jevan said. "They can't do much worse to us than we've already been sentenced to. We just need to wait until their guard is down."

"Okay," Ardyn agreed. "Then what will we do? Where can we go?"

"We cannot seek refuge amongst either of our kind," Jevan said. "So, how about we go back to the Aria'una? As forbidden as it seems to be, I think they may not follow us there. Also, I would really like to see what exactly they are keeping us from finding."

"So would I. Alright, let's bide our time until the next rainstorm, or we leave the night before the Triumvirate arrives, whichever comes first."

Jevan nodded. "Agreed."

CONFINEMENT

While they waited for the next rainstorm, Jevan and Ardyn bided their time, preparing to run at the first sign of a deluge. The morning after the tribunal, Jevan rummaged around in his wardrobe, pulling out various items and placing them on his bed. "Some of these clothes are from when I was younger. See if any of them fit you."

Ardyn looked through the collection of roughspun and leather shirts, breeches, and cloaks. Holding one shirt up that fell below his knees, he laughed. "I think you were always a giant."

Tossing a belt at Ardyn, Jevan smirked. "Just cinch it with this, and you'll be fine."

"You really aren't planning to come back here again, are you?" Ardyn asked as he tossed a shorter cloak over his shoulders, checking the length.

"I don't think it'll ever be safe for either of us, do you?" Jevan replied.

Setting aside the cloak, Ardyn looked up at Jevan. "I'm sorry I dragged you into all this. I'm used to being alone, spending several cycles of the moons away from everyone. You're used to being around people, and now you'll be stuck with only me for company."

"Well, you'll also be stuck with me," Jevan reminded him, handing Ardyn a spare pack he had. Then he grabbed some of the clothing and packed them into another pack. "We should also try to pack some of the food they're feeding us, so we can eat until we're able to make some new weapons for hunting."

●●●

Whenever they could, they tucked away a portion of their meals into their packs, which they kept hidden inside the large trunk Jevan had at the foot of his bed. They also filled some spare water skins Jevan had lying around, so they were ready to leave at a moment's notice.

One morning, after they had been served their breakfast, Ardyn looked across the table at Jevan as he was finishing his bowl of porridge. "You told me they make this porridge from a grain your people grow. How did Medellans figure out how to grow and harvest food like this?"

Jevan shook his head and shrugged his shoulders. "It's something Medellans have always done, as far as I know. From what I understand, the technique isn't that complicated. It merely requires some soft soil, seeds, and water. There's probably more to it, but I'm no farmer."

"Where did the seeds come from?" Ardyn asked. "I've never seen plants like your crops growing wild."

"My ancestors probably brought them with them when they crossed the ocean to get here. They must have farmed these crops in Ateria," Jevan replied.

"It seems like such a natural thing to do. It would make feeding our people so much easier, but planting seeds is one of the many things explicitly forbidden by our elders," Ardyn said.

"Could it be because Medellans are farmers?" Jevan wondered aloud. "Does your Triumvirate hate my people so much that they'd outlaw anything to do with our culture?"

"I am not sure," Ardyn replied, his forehead furrowed in concentration. "The elders taught us that the Athla'naa must be one with the land, and we must survive on what we can gather from it. They also teach that the farming your people do corrupts the land. I often wondered if that was part of the reason our people warred with each other for so long?"

"That's not what Mathias or my school master taught me, but who knows?" Jevan said, gathering their bowls and getting up to hand the tray to one of the men outside.

"What we found in the Aria'una contradicts all I've been taught. How could my ancestors have been *one with the land*, and also built something like that tower?"

"I don't know, but I'm glad we're going back," Jevan admitted. "The answers we need are there. I can just feel it."

One evening, after having bathed, Ardyn straddled the bench that sat before the fireplace, untangling his hair with his fingers as he always did. Jevan watched for a few moments from where he sat at the table, before getting up and retrieving an old hairbrush his mother had given him when he was younger and had worn longer hair.

Walking back to where Ardyn sat, lost in thought, he held out the hairbrush where Ardyn could see it. "May I?"

Staring at the brush for a moment, a look of recognition crossed the elf's face, and he nodded. Jevan straddled the bench behind Ardyn and gently pulled his hair over his pale slender shoulders until it cascaded down his back. Slowly he worked the brush through the damp hair, working out the tangles. He held Ardyn's hair to avoid tugging on his scalp until the brush ran smoothly through the silken lavender strands.

Quiet moments like this made Jevan feel a growing connection with Ardyn. These peaceful moments of companionable silence were becoming a favorite part of his time with the elf. There was no expectation for anything more, just each other's company. Jevan had never experienced this with anyone else, and a small part of him kept wondering *what if?*

Once he was done, he went and put the brush away. Ardyn turned to face him when he walked back, with a quizzical look on his face. "How did you know how to untangle hair like that? Yours has such a different texture, and you keep it so short."

Running a hand over his thick, curly hair, Jevan chuckled. "My sister. I often helped brush her hair after a bath when we were younger. Hers is also curly, but it's much longer than mine."

"You and your sister were close as children?" Ardyn asked. "I was mostly raised with my cousins, but we weren't close because I was so different from them. I was always asking questions that kept getting me in trouble."

"Yeah, we were. Jenira is my only sibling, and we would spend hours exploring the woods together. I taught her how to hunt and fish. She's almost as good with the bow as I am," Jevan said with pride as he sat next to Ardyn again.

Using a finger, he bade the elf turn around, before plaiting Ardyn's hair back into his usual style, tying off the end with a leather tie. Then he turned back toward the fire and stared into it for a while, before bouncing his knee restlessly and then getting up to pace the room.

"I wish the rains would come, because I'm going a little stir-crazy, being cooped up in here. I rarely spend more than two or three cycles of the sun before I head back to make my rounds through the villages and settlements, bringing with me goods from Yanen to trade."

Rising fluidly from the bench and stretching his lithe body, Ardyn made his way toward the bed and gracefully slipped under the covers. "Well, come to bed and try to get some rest," Ardyn beckoned. "You will not accomplish anything by worrying a hole in the floor."

Laughing, Jevan nodded in agreement. "You know you sound like a bondmate," Jevan teased as he went around the room to blow out the candles, before climbing into bed next to the elf. "*Come to bed now, dear,*" he mocked.

Ardyn punched Jevan lightly in the arm before dissolving into laughter. The two laughed until tears streamed down their cheeks. If nothing else, the companionship made this confinement more bearable.

Lying awake, Ardyn watched Jevan fall asleep beside him, as the man's breath evened out and his features relaxed. Ardyn's mind wandered back to the moment they'd shared earlier. *It felt comforting to have someone else help me with my hair, like my father did when I was young.*

Then he reflected on all that Jevan was sacrificing, just for him. *Jevan has a good heart. He doesn't deserve this.* Ardyn had considered slipping away on his own several times, but he couldn't leave Jevan to his fate alone. *We're in this together, no matter what happens.*

A feeling of guilt crept over Ardyn as fleeting memories crossed his mind when he'd first spied Jevan from his treetop hideout, well over a cycle of the seasons before. *I should tell him...* Ardyn thought as he finally drifted off to sleep.

Ardyn awoke the next morning with a disappointed frown because the weather was still clear and sunny. He sat up and watched as Jevan continued to sleep peacefully next to him. Ever since the last time he went to Ahren, Ardyn never imagined he would be comfortable enough to share close quarters with a Medellan, much less share a bed with one.

Since Ardyn's initial rejection, Jevan never tried to force himself on him, and his every touch had been chaste. Ardyn felt safe around him. He trusted the *athla'maakh* not to hurt him, which felt strange. It had been a long time since Ardyn felt he could trust anyone besides his parents.

A knock at the door brought Ardyn out of his reverie as a villager brought their morning meal. Along with their usual porridge, there was also bread and some cups of water. Ardyn thanked the young woman as he took the tray from her, noting how she was trying not to stare at him before she scurried away.

After Ardyn set the tray down on the table, he saw Jevan stir. As he took the bread and stashed them with the other provisions they'd been saving, he called over to Jevan. "Get up and come eat. You know this porridge is not pleasant to eat cold."

Jevan grumbled and buried his head under his pillow. Ardyn had always been one to rise before the sun, but Jevan usually slept until the morning meal was served. Smirking at the grumbling Medellan, he pulled away the man's pillow and blanket. "Up or I'll eat your porridge and you can go hungry until the next meal arrives."

Jevan sat up and gave Ardyn a mock scowl as he rubbed the sleep from his eyes. "Alright, Alright. I'm up already. Are you sure you're not trying to act like my bondmate? I could swear I remember my parents having this same argument every morning."

REMINISCING

Ardyn laughed nervously at the suggestion that he was treating Jevan as a mate. "N-no, I am trying to be your friend and make sure you eat. If you starve yourself, you will be too weak to run when the rain finally comes."

"You're right, as usual," Jevan agreed as he rose with a groan and came to the table.

Sitting down opposite Jevan, Ardyn ate his porridge, which was thankfully still warm. When they were first served this for breakfast, Ardyn made the mistake of letting Jevan sleep in and waited for him. By the time they got around to eating, the porridge had hardened into a cold, lumpy mess that was nearly indigestible.

As they ate, Ardyn thought about everything going on. "Why do you think our leaders have been keeping all these secrets?"

Jevan shook his head and shrugged. "I wish I knew. There's something they're hiding. Something worth punishing anyone who finds out. After everything that's happened, I really want to know what's in that tower. We need to find a way for me to get inside. Maybe we can dig under that wall somehow?"

"That might work," Ardyn replied. "I want you to see it, too. It was unlike anything I've ever seen. There's something else that's been bothering me about what I saw. Nothing was covered in dust. If the place is forbidden and has been abandoned for so long, then what's keeping the dust from settling and covering every surface?"

Leaning forward, Jevan tilted his head. "That *is* very odd. Could your elders be going there and cleaning off the dust?" Jevan wondered.

"The Triumvirate rarely leave Maala'naa, except for their annual pilgrimage. The fact they are traveling here to witness our punishment is highly unusual."

"Where do they go on their pilgrimage?"

"They visit the elders of each settlement. It takes them one cycle of the moons before they return. With as distant as some settlements are, I doubt they would also have time to visit that tower and clean it."

"Then who... or what... is keeping the tower clean? It's all so bizarre. You said you saw things that looked like slanted tables that lit up with symbols and Athla'naa script when you touched them? I wonder if those symbols controlled anything. I'm betting one of them may even control that invisible wall we found."

"That was my thought, but I could not make sense of it. I was afraid if I touched the wrong one, I might turn on something worse than that wall. I will need to take more time to study everything and then maybe I can figure it out and get that wall down so you can join me."

"How will you get back in? Your elders took the key from you," Jevan said with a frown.

A mischievous grin crossed Ardyn's face, making Jevan look at him curiously. Then Ardyn rose and made his way over to the cloak he had been wearing the night he rescued Jevan. Reaching into a hidden pocket, he pulled out the glowing key.

"How did you get it back?" Jevan asked with a look of surprised delight.

"They put it back into my pack and stashed it in one of our storage huts," Ardyn replied as he slid the key back into its hiding place. "Remember, my people don't use locks, and I don't think they expected me to escape and take you with me. They didn't seem to think it was all that important. You saw how quickly they dismissed it."

They lapsed into silence, both lost in thought. To busy himself, Ardyn made the bed while Jevan stoked the fireplace. It wasn't cold, but it was something to do. Once the bed was made, Ardyn wandered over to the window that overlooked the forest. Jevan's small home stood on the edge of the village, right next to the woods.

Ardyn longed to wander the forest again. He missed the freedom that came with being a ranger and wondered if he'd ever be able to do that again. Once they made their escape, he and Jevan would be fugitives from both of their people. Neither of them could ever go home again.

"Hey, what are you thinking about?" Jevan asked as he joined Ardyn by the window.

"I was just thinking about how much we're going to give up, all because of that stupid piece of metal I found."

"Hey, don't talk like that," Jevan admonished. "You discovered a long-held secret, protected by centuries of lies. The truth is there, within the Aria'una. Whatever it is, it's important. I can feel it and we need to see this through."

"I know. Part of me is excited to find out more, but a part of me grieves for everything I'm giving up because of it," Ardyn confessed. "Look at how much our lives have already changed in such a short time, just because of this one little thing. Neither of our lives will ever be the same again, no matter what we do."

"Yeah, I know," Jevan said with a sigh as he sat down on the bench and rubbed his face. "However, being fugitives on the run will be far better than facing that flogging and spending the rest of our lives in those mines."

"True," Ardyn agreed. "Escape is really the only logical option since your ard refuses to speak with you."

Jevan had tried to send messages to Mathias, but the ard denied all requests. There was nothing else to be done, other than to either face their fate or run from it.

As they both became lost in their own thoughts once more, Ardyn went to sit on the bench while Jevan paced the floor. Watching him, Ardyn admired the effortless grace with which Jevan moved, despite his tall frame and the obvious tension that ran through him.

Eventually, Jevan gave up pacing to sit on the floor by Ardyn's feet. "You haven't told me too much about your childhood, beyond some vague references to your extended family, and how you kept getting in trouble for asking too many questions. Would you tell me more, please?"

Shrugging dismissively, Ardyn looked down at Jevan, trying not to admire how his sparkling gray eyes contrasted with the beautiful dark tone of his skin. "It was noisy. I was always surrounded by people. When I couldn't explore the forests around Maala'naa and had finished my assigned chores, I often sat in a corner and just watched everyone. Even as a child, I was not very social. I spent a lot of time thinking about things I shouldn't. Often, I wondered how things worked or came to be. I wanted to make things, and when I tried, I always found ways to improve them, which got me in trouble."

"What kinds of things did you try to make?" Jevan asked.

"Nothing that special. My favorite one was an improved bow design. I worked on it in secret and kept it hidden in a small hollowed-out log outside of our settlement I thought no one else knew about. Changing the shape of the bow helped my arrows fly farther with more accuracy. So, I hid it for a long time, knowing they would punish me for it. They eventually caught me and destroyed my new bow. I was publicly whipped and confined to my family's hut for many cycles of the sun."

"Is that why you eventually became a ranger? To get away from all that?" Jevan asked.

"Yes. I know the elders welcomed that. I was seen as a troublemaker, with an infectious curiosity. Getting me to stay as far away from everyone was a good solution all around. So, what happens when Medellan children have curiosity like I do?"

"When our children show an aptitude toward a certain skill, whether it's hunting, farming, trading, metal working, or building, they become apprenticed with an adult who is a master in that profession," Jevan explained. "The master will teach their apprentices until they master the skill for themselves."

"What if an apprentice finds a better way to do something than how the master taught them?" Ardyn asked.

"Either the master will take the new way into consideration and incorporate it into how things are done, or they will show the apprentice why it's not a good idea."

"What aptitude did you have that led you to become a trader?" Ardyn asked.

"Being a trader requires a certain amount of charm and persuasiveness. There isn't much I can do to improve that other than to be even more charming," Jevan said with a broad smile and a sly wink, making Ardyn laugh. "However, I have seen some improvements in how we approach farming and metalworking since I was a child. Often times these were suggested by an apprentice and improved upon by a master. Ultimately, the improvement is demonstrated to our ard, who decides whether the improvement is worthwhile or not."

"What happens if your ard doesn't approve?" Ardyn asked.

"Then we keep doing things the old way," Jevan said. "It's happened a few times and I know the apprentices who have had their ideas rejected were unhappy about it, but there was nothing they could do to change their ard's mind."

Ardyn contemplated that, while fiddling with his braid absentmindedly. A thought struck him then. "Do you think your ard might also purposely hold back some innovations, like the Athla'naa elders do?"

Jevan frowned at the implication. "If you had asked me that a season ago, I would have said no. I would never have believed such a thing. However, with everything we've encountered, you may be on to something.

"It would certainly explain a lot that I've often wondered about. Why does it seem every question we have leads to more questions? Now I want to go back and figure out what their big secret is even more."

"Yes, as do I," Ardyn agreed.

ESCAPE

The hoped-for rain finally came a few cycles of the sun before the expected arrival of the Elder Triumvirate. At first, the morning had dawned disappointingly sunny, but their hopes rose when the sky grew overcast by late afternoon. By the early evening, the rain began, promising to be another deluge that could last for hours. Ardyn and Jevan waited until it was late at night, when everyone in the village would be asleep and their guards would hopefully be less watchful.

Besides the two guards who were always outside his door, a third patrolled around the house, deterring any escape through the window. However, with the torrential rain, Jevan hoped they'd rethink going on patrol. Since Jevan and Ardyn hadn't attempted to run, they hoped the guards would be more lax in their duties. They also hoped the guards would assume that no one would willingly try to run in the middle of a storm like this.

After their last meal was served, they knew the guards would leave them alone for the rest of the evening. No one would bring them bathwater in the middle of a storm. So, they felt safe enough pulling out their packs and making final preparations. Once Jevan deemed it late enough, they grabbed their laden packs, donned their cloaks, and slipped through the window.

When they reached the edge of the woods, they looked back one last time to make sure no one had spotted them. Then, clasping each other's hand to keep from being separated in the downpour, they headed roughly northwest, straight for the heart of the Aria'una.

The rains didn't let up for hours, and Jevan hoped it would obscure their passage enough to prevent the villagers from following them. Their plan was to go as deep into the Aria'una as possible, and hopefully take shelter in the small metal structure. Once the rains stopped, they planned to scout the entire area as thoroughly as possible.

They ran through the downpour, stopping to rest only when their legs refused to carry them any farther. They were both soaked to the skin and Ardyn's smaller frame began shivering if they stopped for too long. Jevan offered to help warm him by holding the elf close to him. Ardyn appreciated it, although it didn't help much.

When they reached the perimeter of the Aria'una, Ardyn slowed and looked up to locate the metal boxes that would alert the elders of their presence. Carefully, he climbed into two trees, one after the other, and using a rock he'd put into his pocket, he smashed two of the boxes until their blinking lights went out. Even though they were sure the elders would be alerted to the damage, they hoped it would be enough to slow down their ability to track them.

The rain continued unabated. They wanted to head toward the large clearing where the mysterious tower stood, which was easily a journey that would take two cycles of the sun. From there, they could get their bearings before beginning their search. In the meantime, they made their way to the smaller structure to take refuge and rest for a few hours.

Once they found it again, Ardyn used the key to get inside, out of the pelting rain. They stripped themselves out of their wet clothes, unabashed at their nudity. Everything they had brought with them was also damp, but not completely soaked. They laid out their rain-soaked clothes and grabbed their bedrolls, which were still dry on their interiors. Jevan laid his down and then grabbed the other to use as a blanket. Ardyn was shivering again, so Jevan held out his arms to Ardyn. "Come here," he offered.

Ardyn slipped between the bedrolls, letting the larger man pull him into an embrace. "Th-th-thanks," Ardyn said through chattering teeth. Jevan tried to speed up the process by rubbing Ardyn's hands and arms. Slowly, Ardyn's shivers subsided. As he snuggled into Jevan's arms, the feeling of warmth and relative security lulled him into a light sleep.

Despite the damp and chill, Jevan felt more content here, with Ardyn snuggled next to him, than he had in quite a while. He thought back to the last morning he'd woken up feeling content. It hadn't been that long ago since he'd spent the night in the elven settlement, enjoying Taela's company, but it felt so long ago now. Yet, even with everything that had happened, Jevan felt happier with Ardyn in his arms than he had with his most recent lover. It made him realize he was developing feelings for Ardyn. Feelings he usually shied away from. For the first time in his life, the realization didn't terrify him.

Jevan sighed and then allowed himself to relax, drifting off to sleep with Ardyn still nestled in his arms.

●●●

They spent the next couple of cycles of the sun near the small structure, taking time to recuperate. After the rain stopped, they hung all their clothes over low-hanging branches to dry. The food they brought helped to sustain them while they waited, not wanting to venture too far into the woods completely nude. Once everything was dry, they went out into the forest to fashion some spears they could use to hunt. Jevan also made a couple of crude shovels they could use to dig under the wall around the tower.

By the third morning of their self-imposed exile, they headed back toward the tower. "There must be something more out here than what we already found," Ardyn said. "There has to be, or why else would they want to execute anyone finding these things? Nothing of what we've found can justify that."

"Agreed. Well, we have the rest of our lives to figure this mystery out."

When they reached the invisible barrier, Jevan tried again to get through it, but it still repelled him. "Alright, let's start digging and see how far this extends underground."

Jevan dropped to his knees, digging into the ground and removing dirt along the wall. What surprised them both was when Jevan's shovel went past the barrier, causing Jevan to lose his balance and fall against it.

"Oof!"

Ardyn watched Jevan's shovel fall onto the other side of the barrier. "I'll go get it! I guess it is only keeping *you* out, not things you're holding."

Jevan groaned in frustration as Ardyn pushed past the wall and went to get the shovel. As he came back through, he handed it to a sheepish-looking Jevan. "I swear I'm not usually this clumsy."

Laughing, Ardyn grabbed his own shovel and started digging again. "Don't worry, I think it's adorable," he teased.

They began digging in earnest, testing every now and again if Jevan could push past the barrier yet. After digging for the better part of the morning, the top of the hole was nearly as deep as Ardyn was tall. When his shovel hit against something hard, he heard Jevan's shovel hit something as well. Looking at each other, they cleared enough dirt away to see what they had hit.

"It's more metal," Jevan said, slumping in defeat.

Still on his knees, Ardyn stood up and clambered out of the hole before looking up at the gleaming tower. "I wonder, could this be connected to the tower? Does it extend underground somehow?"

Climbing out and standing next to Ardyn, he also looked up at the tower and back down to the bottom of the hole they'd dug. "You know, that's possible, but how far? Between the two of us, I doubt we can find out, especially with these crude shovels."

A sudden realization hit Ardyn. "Could that large dirt... mover... *thing*... could that have been used to help build this place?"

Nodding, Jevan agreed. "Yeah, that makes some sense. I wonder if it still works?"

"Well, there is only one way to find out."

They headed over to where they found the enormous machine and began cutting away the rest of the overgrowth, finishing just before sundown.

"Let's go back to camp," Jevan said, looking as sweaty and tired as Ardyn felt. "Maybe we can catch some dinner along the way and then get some rest. We can figure out how this thing works tomorrow."

⬡⬡⬡

The next morning, not long after they set out, they heard voices coming from a distance. "Climb into the trees," Ardyn whispered. "As high as you can." Once they were both up high enough for the foliage to obscure their presence, they waited silently.

The voices moved closer. The first distinct words they heard were from a male voice, speaking in the Medellan tongue. "Are you sure they came this way?"

Jevan recognized the voice immediately. *Ard Mathias.*

"Positive," another male voice replied, with an elven accent.

From the sound of the footfalls, there were perhaps a half-dozen people walking below them. The elven voice continued. "They had sought to take down our detection grid by destroying two of the markers at the perimeter, but we replaced them. This tracker allows us to detect both Medellan and Athla'naa life signs. According to this, they are still within the Aria'una."

"We must keep searching for them!" an elven female ordered.

For a moment, the footsteps paused. Spying a face between a gap in the canopy of leaves, Jevan recognized Elder Taeglyn. He held something in his hand that glinted like metal, with glowing letters and flashing lights. Something that was undoubtedly related to all the advanced technology they kept finding within the Aria'una.

Jevan flushed with anger at the realization. This confirmed all their suspicions and was the most damning evidence of all. The elven elders were liars and hypocrites. Not only were they aware of this technology, but it was clear they knew how to use it as well.

The people below them continued their search, but thankfully, Jevan and Ardyn were dressed in browns and greens. From their position in the dense foliage, they were difficult to spot as long as they remained still. Eventually, the party moved on. Once they could no longer hear their voices, the pair clambered out of the trees and ran in the opposite direction.

Feeling betrayed by Mathias, Jevan fumed with anger as he ran beside Ardyn, who undoubtedly was feeling equally betrayed. Jevan may not have agreed with Mathias on the necessity of pair-bonding, but until now Jevan had respected the man. *Not anymore.*

They continued to run, but did not know where to run to. They had been followed into the one place they thought was a safe refuge. If they remained in the Aria'una, they would eventually be tracked down as long as the elders possessed the technology to find them.

Outside of the Aria'una, there weren't any options for them either. They could survive in the dense forests, but both Medellans and elves regularly patrolled their lands. There was a high likelihood of them being found, regardless of where they went.

A sense of panic overtook Jevan, not knowing where to go or what to do. He was so lost in thought; he wasn't paying attention to where he stepped. When his boot caught on something, he didn't have the chance to correct his balance before he was falling face-first onto the ground.

Great. Not the best time for my two left feet to get tangled in a tree root.

UNDERGROUND

Ardyn ran to Jevan's side and helped him up. "Are you alright?"

"I'm fine. You know how much of a clumsy oaf I am," Jevan joked, feeling foolish for stumbling on another tree root.

Looking at where he'd tripped, he noticed a glint of metal. "Hey, look at this!"

Crawling over to where he'd seen the glimmer, Jevan cleared away the vines and foliage covering the forest floor, only to find what he'd tripped on wasn't the root of a tree at all. It was a metal handle. As they cleared away more brush and dug the dirt away around it, they uncovered a circular metal plate with hinges on one side.

"Is that a... *door?*" Ardyn asked in wonder.

"I think so," Jevan said. "Look, there's another slot for that key of yours."

Pulling the key out of his cloak, Ardyn inserted it. They heard a whirring sound followed by a loud metallic clang as the door came to life, lights and more of the glowing elven writing appearing on the small panel below the slot.

Jevan tugged on the handle and the door creaked open. Beyond the door was a dark tunnel and rungs of a ladder that disappeared into the darkness. "What do you think?"

Ardyn stared down into the tunnel for a moment. "We might as well see where it leads. What do we have to lose?"

"Good point," Jevan agreed. "You go first. Everything in the Aria'una seems to like you more than me."

"Yeah, good idea."

As Ardyn made his way down the ladder, the tunnel illuminated, which no longer surprised either of them. Jevan followed, reaching up to lower the door over his head. He breathed a sigh of relief when he heard the lock re-engage.

Hopefully, that will slow down the hunting party.

When they reached the end of the ladder, they found themselves in a wide corridor, all white with silver accents and a red stripe running the length of the walls. The corridor was slightly curved and stretched far in either direction.

Jevan noticed Ardyn's ears moving back and forth, as if trying to catch some sound in the eerie silence. "Do you hear anything?"

Ardyn shook his head. "No," he replied in a hushed tone. "That's what worries me. I've never heard this much... *silence.*"

Looking up and down the corridor, Jevan wondered aloud. "Is this connected to the tower?"

"If it is, then this place is larger than any settlement my people have ever built."

"And bigger than our largest city, Tafaran," Jevan said.

"Where is Tafaran?"

"It's on the southern coast of Vestos, where my ancestors first made landfall. I've only traveled there once. It's a thriving metropolis compared to the village of Yanen."

"Do you think anyone actually lived here?" Ardyn asked, as they chose a direction and made their way along the corridor.

Looking around at their sterile, pristine surroundings, Jevan wasn't sure. "This doesn't look very homey to me, but who knows? What I don't understand is why this is underground. Did they build this because they needed a place to hide?"

"But then why build that tower?" Ardyn asked as they approached a junction.

Turning right at the junction, the new corridor was lined with doorways like those of the structures aboveground. Using his key, Ardyn randomly opened one, so they could explore what was inside. What they found was a storeroom stacked with metal crates.

Jevan approached the crates and tried to open one, but the lid wouldn't budge. There was a button on the side and Jevan pressed it with no luck. "It looks like I'm not even allowed to open boxes around here," he said with a sarcastic chuckle.

Ardyn pressed the button, and sure enough, the lid unlocked, and they were able to lift it away. Inside the crate were neatly arranged objects. Jevan couldn't even guess their purpose. They each picked one up and Jevan half expected Ardyn's to glow or do... something.

"Huh, that's weird, that it's not reacting like everything else has. I wonder what they're for?"

"Don't look at me," Ardyn said with a laugh, putting the thing back into the crate.

After unlocking a couple more doors, all they found were more crates with indecipherable objects. "Okay, maybe this wasn't for hiding. It looks like they built this entire place for storage," Jevan speculated. "It doesn't feel like a place anyone could live."

At the end of the corridor, they found a ladder leading down to another level. "Does this go down as far as that tower stands tall?" Jevan asked, gesturing for Ardyn to go first.

"Your guess is as good as mine," Ardyn replied, making his way down the ladder. "At least we lost that hunting party for a while."

The new level they found themselves on had a blue stripe along the corridor walls, and the doors were smaller. Ardyn opened the first one near the ladder. Instead of stacks of crates, there were rows of small tables, each with its own chair, all facing the opposite end of the room, which held a larger table and chair.

Everything was pristine, with the same bright white and silver as they saw in the corridors. "See? No dust anywhere," Ardyn pointed out. "Maybe there are people living here? How else is it all being kept so clean?"

"Yeah, I see that," Jevan replied. "We'll need to be on the lookout for anyone else around here."

When Ardyn approached the larger table and touched it, it flared to life, with strange images and symbols seeming to hover in the air above the desk. Ardyn was so startled he jumped back, knocking into one of the smaller tables. When his hand was no longer touching the table, it all disappeared again.

"What was that?!"

"I don't know, but touch it again," Jevan encouraged. "Maybe there's something here that can help us understand?"

This time Ardyn crept around the table and sat himself in the chair. Jevan noted the chair was the perfect size for an adult elf, and all the other tables and chairs in the room were much smaller, almost as if they were made for children.

"Hey, I know what they might have used this room for," Jevan said, walking around to stand next to Ardyn. "Look how small those chairs are. I think this might be a place for children to learn."

Looking over the room from his vantage point, Ardyn nodded. "You're right. So that means this is where their teacher must have sat. I wonder if we can find a way to learn as well?"

Laying his hands back onto the table, the symbols and images came to life in mid-air once again. They couldn't comprehend the symbols any more than they could any of the archaic elven script. The surface of the table itself glowed with an array of mystifying symbols and scripts as well. "Try touching something," Jevan suggested.

One symbol on the table was shaped vaguely like a head. Ardyn reached out and touched it. Suddenly, the floating symbols and script dissolved. In their stead appeared the face of a female elf. Jevan and Ardyn looked at each other, and then back at the face when it spoke.

"Yaven utera'ior. Kers'nor Cytra."

To Jevan, it sounded like the elven greeting he was familiar with, but in a strange dialect. "Did she say her name is Cytra?"

"I think so, but she's speaking in a dialect I've never heard before."

After Ardyn stopped speaking, Cytra continued, but Jevan couldn't decipher it as easily. "Did you understand that?"

"I think she's saying something about choosing what to teach. Half of it doesn't make sense to me. There are words I've never heard before."

"Ask her something," Jevan suggested.

"What are you?" Ardyn asked in his language.

Cytra paused and turned her gaze toward Ardyn. She replied with more words Jevan didn't understand. "Did any of that make sense to you?" Ardyn asked Jevan, switching back to the Medellan tongue.

Shrugging his shoulders, Jevan replied. "I think I'm understanding about as much as you are."

Turning back, Ardyn tried a different question. "Cytra, where are we?"

This time the dialect was closer to Ardyn's, but it still made little sense to Jevan. "You are on the *rahn'naa*, a *pah'maala*," Cytra replied.

"What does that mean?" Jevan asked. "We're on the *first light*, a *flying settlement?*"

Ardyn shook his head. "You're translating that first one too literally. She used the word *rahn'naa*, which means first light of morning, what you call *dawn*," Ardyn explained. "But I don't know what a *pah'maala* could be. Settlements can't fly."

Jevan laughed at the picture in his head. "Can you imagine my house sprouting wings like a bird?"

Ardyn laughed before he turned back to Cytra. "What does *pah'maala* mean?"

Cytra explained about traveling through *vaara* and Jevan was lost again. Ardyn looked at him, just as dumbfounded. "That didn't help," Jevan admitted.

"Let me try something else," Ardyn suggested. "Cytra, why are we underground?"

"Activating external sensors. Checking mechanical storage. Excavators missing," Cytra said, as her eyes fluttered before focusing back on Ardyn. "You are correct, we are underground. It appears that someone buried the Rahn'naa after it crashed."

Looking at each other, they both asked, "how does the *dawn* crash?"

CYTRA

Ardyn needed a moment to think, mulling over how Cytra was using the word *rahn'naa*. That's when he realized something. "I think... that Cytra isn't talking about the dawn of a new cycle of the sun. She's using it like a name." Looking back up at Cytra, Ardyn asked. "Cytra, is the name of this settlement Rahn'naa?"

"The name of this *pah'maala* is the Rahn'naa," she confirmed, emphasizing *flying settlement*.

"So, it's a name, but there's that word again," Jevan said. "Earlier, she said something about traveling. I wonder if maybe a *pah'maala* is a kind of ship? They travel the oceans and I guess they could crash, but we're too far from shore. Where could it have crashed from?"

"Cytra, where did the Rahn'naa come from?" Ardyn asked.

"The Rahn'naa came from the Athla'naa *aria'maal*," Cytra replied, her dialect continuing to become easier to understand.

"Did she just say that this *ship* came from the Athla'naa... *home... world*?" Jevan asked, sounding confused. "Isn't *this world* your home?"

Ardyn's mind raced at the implication. "I... thought so. I know your people call it Medellus, which doesn't translate at all into our word for this world, Aria'nor. That always seemed strange to me."

"Aria'nor translates to *our world*, right? I'll admit, I always thought that was a bit arrogant when I learned the meaning."

Ardyn smirked at him. "Cytra, what is the name of the Athla'naa *homeworld*?"

"Our homeworld is called Aria'naa."

Jevan looked at Ardyn. "That's close... but doesn't that mean *first world*?" he wondered aloud. "Cytra, are you sure the name of the homeworld isn't Aria'nor?"

The floating head did not react to Jevan's query, and he rolled his eyes. "Let me guess, she won't respond to me."

Giving him a sympathetic look, Ardyn asked. "Cytra, why did you not respond to my friend's question?"

Cytra looked at Jevan before looking back at Ardyn. "I am programmed to only respond to queries from Athla'naa."

"Can you change that, please?" Ardyn asked. "I would like you to respond to both of us."

"Yes, of course," Cytra replied. The glowing shape of an Athla'naa hand appeared on the surface of the desk. "Please place your hand here so I can scan it."

Reaching out his hand, he placed it over the four-fingered outline as best he could. "I'm sorry, my hand is large," he apologized.

A glowing line appeared under his hand and ran down the length, from his fingertips to his palm. After it finished, Cytra looked blankly ahead for a moment, her eyes fluttering, before turning to Jevan. "Please state your name and the name of your species."

"My name is Jevan. My people are called the Medellans," he replied.

"Welcome Jevan of the Medellans," Cytra said. "Your input and queries will now be accepted."

"Thank you, Cytra," Jevan replied.

The glowing handprint remained, and Ardyn reached out to place his palm on it as well. He looked up at Jevan and gave him a shrug. "Can't hurt, right?" he said before looking at Cytra. "My name is Ardyn of Maala'naa. That is the name of my settlement."

"Welcome Ardyn of Maala'naa," Cytra replied, as the table scanned Ardyn's hand as well. "You have both been added to my records. What is your query?"

"You said the name of the Athla'naa homeworld is Aria'naa," Jevan said. "But Ardyn's people call this place Aria'nor. Is this *pah'maala* not from here? From Aria'nor?"

"No," Cytra replied. "The Rahn'naa crashed here. It came from Aria'naa."

Ardyn sighed in frustration. "Then where is Aria'naa?"

Once again, Cytra explained with too many words that neither of them understood. "Cytra, we don't understand," Ardyn said, stopping her in the middle of her explanation. "All this technology you have is more advanced than anything I have ever seen. My people live simply in tree-top settlements. We don't even forge metal like the Medellans do."

Cytra once again switched to a blank stare for a long moment, before looking back at them. "The Rahn'naa traveled here from across the stars."

"The stars?!" Ardyn and Jevan exclaimed.

"How is that even possible?" Ardyn asked. "The stars are very far away."

"I think I'm starting to understand," Jevan said. "We have some learned men in our capital city who study the stars. You know that this world we live on circles around the sun, right?"

Ardyn nodded. "Yes, the Athla'naa elders taught us of the motion of the sun, stars, moons, and planets."

"Good. I think Cytra is saying that your people, the Athla'naa, came from a different world than this one," Jevan said.

"Then... that would mean that the Rahn'naa... it traveled the stars like a ship travels the ocean?!" Ardyn asked incredulously.

"Yes," Cytra confirmed. "The Rahn'naa travels through the *vaara* between the stars."

Now they understood the meaning of *vaara*. It meant space.

Sitting back in the chair, Ardyn's mind reeled as his ears pulled back. This meant that his ancestors had been far more advanced than he could have ever imagined. "Cytra, how long ago did the Athla'naa arrive here?" Ardyn asked.

"According to my records, the Rahn'naa crashed one thousand, two hundred and fifty-three years ago."

"How long is a *year*?" Jevan asked.

It took a few more questions before they understood that a year on Aria'naa was the equivalent to one cycle of the seasons on their world. Once he understood, Ardyn could still hardly comprehend that. He'd believed that his people had always lived in the forests of this land, which is why his ancestors had fought so hard against the invading Medellans.

"Well, that still explains why your people were already here when my ancestors arrived."

"Does the Triumvirate know any of this?" Ardyn wondered. "Why didn't they want us to know we came from another world? I still have so many questions."

"Please state your next query," Cytra said.

Ardyn didn't know where to begin, so Jevan intervened. "Could you explain what those structures are that we saw aboveground?"

"Activating external sensors," Cytra said, fluttering her eyes. "I detect that one airlock, one hatch, and the observation tower of the *Rahn'naa* are still aboveground."

"That structure we've been sleeping in must be the airlock," Ardyn deduced. "Cytra, does the tower control all functions of this ship?"

"Some functions for this ship can be controlled from there, but the control center is in a more heavily protected part of the ship, and overrides everything in the observation tower."

"Cytra, there was an invisible wall around the tower that I could not pass through. Is there a way to allow me to walk through it like Ardyn can?" Jevan asked.

"The forcefield that is active around the observation tower prevents any *athla'maakh* from passing through." Cytra explained, before her eyes fluttered briefly. "Medellans should now be able to pass through the forcefield."

Turning back toward Jevan, Ardyn looked up at him. "This is more than I ever expected to find and it's making my head hurt."

Jevan squatted next to Ardyn and reached out a comforting hand. "Yeah, I know. It's one thing to think your people may have once been more advanced, but that they came from the stars... I never imagined such a thing was possible."

That thought prompted a new question. "Cytra, how far away is the Athla'naa homeworld from here?"

"Aria'naa is approximately eleven point eight seven light-years from this planet," Cytra replied.

Jevan and Ardyn looked at each other, once again, in complete confusion.

REVELATION

Trying to comprehend what this strange floating head was telling them, Jevan asked. "Cytra, what is a light-year?"

"A light-year is the distance light travels for the length of one year on Aria'naa."

Next, Cytra had to explain to them what a year was, which Jevan grasped more quickly. "Oh, she means a cycle of the seasons. Cytra, are you telling us that a year is a measure of time, and a light-year is a measure of distance?"

"Precisely."

"So, it took the Rahn'naa around eleven years to travel here from Aria'naa?" Jevan asked next.

"No," Cytra replied, showing them images of stars and what Jevan assumed must be planets. "The Rahn'naa is only capable of traveling at twenty percent of the speed of light. The Rahn'naa traveled for sixty-one point seven two years before it arrived on this planet."

Laughing, Jevan shook his head. "I'm sorry I asked her that. I'm even more confused now."

Ardyn sat thoughtfully for a moment. "I don't quite understand everything, but I think she means Aria'naa is far away. Too far away for us to be concerned with." He pulled out the key from his pocket and laid it on the table. "Cytra, what is this?"

Cytra's eyes fluttered before she replied. "It is a control access key. It allows access to various parts of the ship to anyone with a recognized biosignature."

"Cytra, is that what the words on the key say?" Ardyn asked. "The script is old, and I cannot read it."

"Yes, that is the meaning. Please, input a sample of your current writing so I may update my database," Cytra offered, as a small tablet rose from the desk, along with something that resembled a writing implement.

Ardyn had learned to write using feather quills on rough parchment made from bark. Because of that, he understood enough to recognize how to use the implements presented to him. Picking up the tablet and strange quill,

Ardyn wrote a brief paragraph in the current elven script, introducing himself and giving a description of the settlement of Maala'naa. When finished, he placed the implements back on the table.

"Please read what you wrote aloud," Cytra requested. "So that I may learn more of your dialect."

Ardyn began reading and Jevan's eyes went wide as he saw the words on the key change into the modern elven script. He couldn't read it as well as he spoke the language, but he understood enough to make out the words *Control Access Key*.

"If you provide more words, I can update all signage throughout the Rahn'naa," Cytra recommended.

"Okay. I think I'll write a fable my parents told me as a child." After he finished and read it aloud, more words on the desk changed, until they were all in the current elven script.

"Can you read all of that?" Jevan asked.

Nodding, Ardyn was reading everything. "Yes, but I do not understand all of it. There are many words I am unfamiliar with, but at least I can read them now."

"That's a step in the right direction," Jevan said.

They turned back to Cytra with more questions. "Why did my people leave the homeworld to come here?" Ardyn asked.

"Do you wish a detailed explanation or a summary?" Cytra asked in response.

"Let's start with a summary," Jevan suggested. "We can learn the details later."

"The population of Aria'naa was increasing, and if trends were going to continue, we would face an overpopulation crisis, along with a strain on resources," Cytra explained. "The leaders of Aria'naa ordered probes to be sent to search for habitable planets with no intelligent life. Our probes found five such worlds within a reasonable distance from Aria'naa. The Rahn'naa was the fifth colony ship built."

"Did she just imply that they didn't consider Medellans intelligent?" Jevan bristled. "Cytra, this world already had an intelligent species living on it."

"This was not the planet intended for colonization," Cytra explained, showing a planet on the screen before zooming out and then zooming in on another planet. "The Rahn'naa was heading to the planet we named Maal'dak Five, which is fourteen point four three light-years from our present location and twenty-six point three light-years from Aria'naa."

Jevan relaxed a bit. "Then how did the Rahn'naa come to be on this planet?"

There was a long pause as Cytra's eyes fluttered. "I cannot explain," she said, her eyes darting back-and-forth. "There are gaps in my memory. Files have been erased. Scanning... scanning... signs of sabotage are detected."

Ardyn felt bad for this strange, floating head, but pressed on with more questions. "Cytra, why would the Athla'naa abandon all this technology when colonizing a new planet?"

"Upon arrival, the colonists would have begun building a city. All materials to build one are part of this ship."

"My people never built a city here, Cytra," Ardyn said.

Cytra looked at them blankly for a moment. "That is because the *baaru'dak* and *laasa'dak* still sleep."

"The *make new* and *make healthy* are... sleeping?" Jevan asked. "I'm missing the context again because that makes as much sense as *flying settlement*. Cytra, what does *baaru'dak* and *laasa'dak* mean?"

"The Baaru'dak are the Athla'naa who build and repair everything you see around you. They are the class of Athla'naa that includes engineers, architects, and other technical specializations. They built the Rahn'naa. The Laasa'dak is the class that includes all the medical and scientific professions."

"Oh, so the Baaru'dak are the Athla'naa who know how to operate all this technology," Jevan said with a glimmer of understanding.

That's when Ardyn seemed to have a realization. "Cytra, you said that these Baaru'dak and Laasa'dak are Athla'naa, and that they are still sleeping?"

"Yes." Cytra confirmed.

Standing from the position he'd been squatting in, Jevan paced behind the chair Ardyn occupied. "I'm not sure I can believe this. I think she's saying there are elves who traveled here on this ship, currently asleep. We certainly didn't see any in the sections we explored earlier. If they've been here all this time, how come we haven't seen any? Cytra, how is that possible?"

"They remain in cryostasis," Cytra replied. "They will remain asleep until I am ordered to awaken them."

● ● ●

Ardyn couldn't quite believe what he was hearing. There were ancient Athla'naa, asleep somewhere on this ship. His mind raced at the implications. "Why are they still sleeping, Cytra?"

Cytra fluttered her eyes and looked back at Ardyn. "The automated wake-up protocol was disabled after the Rahn'naa crashed. I have been waiting for further instruction."

"Disabled? Does that mean what I think it means?" Ardyn asked, turning to Jevan.

Rubbing his face in frustration, Jevan shrugged his shoulders. "I don't know, but it sounds to me like maybe your ancestors left them behind on purpose."

A sense of dawning realization crept across Ardyn's mind. "Could this be why the Aria'una is forbidden? The elders must know that this ship is here, but do they know what it contains? Is that why they keep everyone away, to keep us from discovering the truth?!"

Ardyn looked up at the floating face above them. "Cytra, where are all the sleeping Athla'naa?"

"They remain within their cryopods," Cytra responded. "Would you like me to wake them?"

Turning to Jevan, Ardyn looked at him for guidance, clearly overwhelmed.

Stepping forward, Jevan addressed Cytra. "Is it possible to wake up only one, so we could speak to them?"

"Yes. I would advise reviving Chief Technician Takyra," Cytra recommended. "She leads the colony expedition."

"That sounds like the right Athla'naa to start with," Jevan said, nodding to Ardyn.

"Okay, Cytra, please wake up Chief Technician Takyra," Ardyn instructed.

"Revival process initiated. Please proceed to the cryopod revival chamber," Cytra said.

"Where is the revival chamber, Cytra?" Ardyn asked.

Cytra's face disappeared, and in its place was a map of the ship, with lights blinking in two locations. "The blue indicates your current location. The revival chamber is marked in green."

They hesitated, trying to study the map, when Cytra's voice spoke again. "I have duplicated the map onto the tablet. You may use it to guide you toward the revival chamber."

"Thank you, Cytra," Ardyn said, picking up the tablet. "You've been very helpful. Come on, Jevan, let's go meet this Chief Technician."

TAKYRA

The corridors were a vast maze and even with the map, Ardyn and Jevan made several wrong turns. Thankfully, Cytra was monitoring their progress. Whenever they passed a wall display, she would show an arrow to help direct them.

When they finally arrived at the cryopod revival chamber, Ardyn used his key to open the door. They entered cautiously, not knowing what to expect. The lights came on as they entered, and they both gaped in awe at the size of the chamber they stood in. Numerous lights illuminated as they approached the railing around the small platform they stood on. From there, they saw several levels above and below them, filled with rows and rows of person-sized containers.

"Those must be the cryopods," Ardyn surmised. "How many of them are there? How could my ancestors have abandoned them all?"

"That's a good question," Jevan said. "I can't even imagine how anyone could have built something like this. It's breathtaking."

Before they could even try to count how many pods there were, a loud whirring sound startled them as a gigantic metal arm appeared. It grasped a pod, releasing it from its resting place and carrying it over to the platform where Ardyn and Jevan stood. They backed away to avoid being hit by it.

Moments later, several metallic rope-like mechanisms emerged from the floor around the cryopod and attached themselves to it. Various lights on the cryopod flared to life, along with beeps and whirrs. The frosted window of the pod cleared, and the face of an Athla'naa female appeared. She had close-cropped hair, a dark shade of reddish purple, and ears that were more sharply pointed than Ardyn's.

Despite all the evidence up to this point, it still startled Ardyn to see the sleeping Athla'naa female, and the truth of what they'd discovered hit home. The fact that there were probably hundreds, if not thousands, still asleep after so many centuries, abandoned by his ancestors, tore at Ardyn's heart.

Watching with bated breath, they startled when the pod hissed, and clouds of steam billowed out as it opened. The front split in two before lifting and sliding to the sides of the pod. The Athla'naa inside wore a one-piece, loose fitting outfit made of dark blue cloth cinched with a belt at her waist.

She awakened, blinking her eyes, and looking around with confusion until she focused on Ardyn. Within seconds, a look of recognition and then rage overcame her, and she tried to leap from the pod, launching herself directly at Ardyn. She stumbled out of the pod, almost falling. As she regained her balance, she once again came at him, yelling a word that sounded like *traitor*.

Ardyn backed away from her advance as Jevan stepped between them, holding her at arm's length. She stopped and stared at the tall Medellan, a look of shock on her face.

Approaching warily, Ardyn tried to greet her. "*Yawen uthera'ior. Kerros'nor Ardyn.*"

Her brows knit in confusion as she replied cautiously. "*Yaven utera'ior?*"

Recognizing the older dialect, Ardyn did his best to reply in the same. "*Yaven utera'ior.*"

Her eyes narrowed for a moment and then seemed to come to a decision. "*Toren'ior,*" she said, gesturing them to follow her.

"Well, I understood that, at least," Jevan said as he and Ardyn followed her out of the cryopod chambers. She led them down the corridor, toward a doorway at the end, and placed her palm against a panel on the wall. After a moment, the door opened. It revealed a tiny room, and the Chief Technician motioned them inside before following them.

After the doors closed, she pushed one of an array of buttons on a panel next to the doors. That's when Ardyn experienced the strangest sensation. It felt as if his stomach was trying to rise through his throat. It scared him as he grasped Jevan and laid his ears flat against his head. The Chief Technician studied them as the sensation continued for another moment before halting.

"What was that?" Ardyn asked in Medellan. Jevan looked at him wide-eyed and shrugged.

When the doors in the small room opened again, they were in an area of the ship they hadn't been to yet. The walls were still the same stark white, but there was a stripe of purple painted along the length of each wall. Following her, she led them around a corner toward two wide doors that were more ornate than others they'd seen. The panel beside it read *Primary Control Center.* She stopped and stared at the sign for a moment, before grumbling something and led them through the doors.

The control center was large and reminded Ardyn of the inside of the tower. There were more of the mysterious tables lining the walls, all of which came to life with lights and symbols as they entered. She made her way over to the largest one in the center and her hands flew over the controls as she spoke words in a commanding tone. Cytra appeared before her, and they began to converse.

From what Ardyn could make out, she was asking for something to help communicate with them. A moment later, a small compartment opened on the table near her hand. She took out three small objects. Handing one to each of them, she placed the last one in her ear. Looking at what she'd given him, Ardyn could see how it might fit into his ear, so he mimicked what she had done.

Once they all had one in their ears, she looked at them both. "Now that we can better understand each other, my name is Takyra. I am the Chief Technician of the colonization ship *The Rahn'naa.* Who are you, and why are you aboard my ship?"

Ardyn and Jevan looked at each other in amazement. They both could understand her clearly. "My name is Ardyn, of the settlement of Maala'naa. This is my friend Jevan, from the village of Yanen."

"What are you, Jevan?" Takyra asked. "You're not Athla'naa."

"No, I'm Medellan," Jevan said. "Although sometimes your people call us *athla'maakh.*"

Takyra's eyes widened at that term. "You seem sentient enough to me, Jevan. I don't see a reason to insult you or your people that way."

"That's an insult?" Jevan asked, who looked at Ardyn.

Giving Jevan a sheepish grin, he nodded. "I'm sorry. While it translates to *not Athla'naa,* we generally mean it to refer to beasts, like the *sar'ora.*"

"We're going to have to talk about that later," Jevan said before turning back to the newly awakened Athla'naa. "How should we address you?"

"You can call me Takyra. Chief Technician is my title, but you aren't under my command. There is no need for such formality," she replied, before turning to Ardyn. "I must apologize for attacking you. I thought you were someone else for a moment. Please, tell me why you have awakened me."

Pulling the key out of his pocket, Ardyn handed it to her. "I found this. It was in a cave I sheltered in during a storm. Afterward, Jevan found me and saved my life when I was attacked by a *sar'ora*," he explained. "This object was a mystery to both of us, and we wanted to learn more. So, we explored the Aria'una. That eventually led us inside this structure. Cytra has been trying to explain, but I'll admit I am struggling to understand everything she has been telling us. It was her idea to awaken you."

"The Aria'una? Why is it forbidden?" Takyra asked.

"The elders of my settlement would never tell us exactly why, only threatening dire consequences if we ever entered the Aria'una," Ardyn explained. "After finding this ship and learning so many Athla'naa remain asleep here, I think that's why they made the area forbidden. They didn't want anyone else finding out about it."

Takyra made a noise of angry frustration and then turned to Jevan. "How did your people come to be here? We were attempting to settle on an uninhabited world."

Jevan recounted a brief history of how his people came from across the ocean to this continent eight-hundred cycles of the seasons before, intending to colonize it.

"From what Cytra told us, your people were already here for over four hundred cycles of the seasons, what she called *years*, before my ancestors arrived," Jevan revealed.

"*Ior'kah*! The fools. They told me they had scanned the entire planet." Takyra turned around. "Cytra, how long have I been asleep? When did the Rahn'naa crash on this world?"

"The Rahn'naa crashed approximately twelve hundred and fifty-three years ago," Cytra replied.

"You're kidding?! I've been in cryogenic stasis for over twelve-hundred years?" Takyra shouted in surprise. "We did not design the cryopods to last that long!"

Turning back to them, she looked more closely at Ardyn and Jevan, taking in how they were dressed. "You don't even know, do you?" Turning to Ardyn. "You don't know where you're really from, or the extent of the betrayal of your ancestors?"

Ardyn took a deep breath and shook his head. "No, but Cytra has been trying to explain."

Takyra ran her fingers through her hair in obvious frustration. "Tell me, how many Athla'naa are there, living on this world?"

Taking a moment to think about that, Ardyn gave a shrug. "I'm not sure. I think there may be around five thousand in the main settlement of Maala'naa, but there are many other settlements scattered throughout this continent. We keep to the forests while the Medellans have built their villages on the coasts and in the valleys."

"Well, it sounds like they followed my advice on how to maintain their population," Takyra said mostly to herself, before she turned around, touching several controls on the table. The display replaced Cytra's face with an informational display that Ardyn couldn't begin to understand.

With the lull in conversation, Ardyn asked something he'd thought of earlier. "Why were you still in that cryopod?"

Takyra hesitated before turning off the display and looking back at Ardyn. "That is a long story. However, now that I'm no longer connected to the cryopod, my body's metabolism is reengaging," she began, smirking at Jevan and Ardyn's confused faces. "I haven't had a meal in over twelve-hundred years, and I'm feeling hungry. Let's go somewhere, so I can prepare some food, and I'll explain what I can."

CONNECTING

ollowing Takyra back to what she called the *elevator*, she took them to another level. This one had a green stripe along the corridor walls and was lined with smaller doors than the level with the storage rooms they'd found earlier. Each of these doors had a number next to it.

At the end of the long hallway, Takyra led them toward the last door. The number for this room was simply *one*, and below the number, it displayed Takyra's name and rank. "These are my private quarters, for when I'm not in cryostasis. Please, come in."

They followed her into the quarters. It was a spacious set of rooms, divided by partial walls. On their right was a seating area with a comfortable-looking couch, a couple of upholstered chairs, and a low table. On their left was a small area for food preparation. Ahead of them, behind a half-wall, was a room with a bed large enough to sleep at least two people, and next to it was another small doorway.

While Jevan stared in awe at the pristine luxury of the space, Ardyn spoke up with a question. "I'm curious. Shouldn't there be dust covering everything?"

Walking into the room on the left, Takyra ran a finger along the counter. "We programmed the ship to maintain itself. The ship filters the air to eliminate most dust particles, and the surfaces are self-cleaning. The ship recycles the dust for other purposes."

Walking over to a panel in the wall, she pushed some buttons. There was a brief sound, and Takyra's shoulders tensed for a moment. She made an audible sound of relief when the panel opened. They stared in shock as she pulled out a plate of steaming hot food that smelled delicious.

"Well, I'm glad the replicators still work after all these centuries," Takyra said. "Are you hungry as well?"

"It has been a few hours since we last ate," Ardyn admitted.

"Then you must join me. Let me make each of you a plate."

Soon, there were three plates of food. Takyra handed one to each of them before going into a drawer to pull out some utensils and leading them toward the seating area.

Ardyn and Jevan each took a chair, while Takyra sat herself on the couch. Staring at his plate of instantly appearing food, he had to ask. "How does this all work? That seemed like magic, but I never believed in such a thing."

Giving a brief laugh, Takyra smiled at them. "I can see how this might seem like magic if your technology has not progressed this far, but I assure you it's not. It's complicated to explain fully, but the replicator can take something and make it into something else. There are stores on this ship that contain all the basic components to create anything, from food to clothing."

"That's... incredible!" Jevan exclaimed.

"Now, let's eat and get to know each other. I think I have as many questions for you both as you have for me."

Jevan watched as Ardyn stared at the food in his lap, poking at it with the utensil in his hand. He then took a bite, which made his face light up with a broad smile. "This is delicious!"

Taking a bite of his own food, the burst of flavors amazed Jevan. Humming in agreement, he quickly took another bite before noticing the amused look on Takyra's face. "This was a popular dish on Aria'naa, before we left," Takyra explained. "Since you're a different species, I hope it will not give you any digestive distress, Jevan."

"My people eat a lot of the same food as Ardyn's do, so I'm sure it will be fine," Jevan said, digging into his food.

They were all hungry, so they ate in silence. Once finished, they placed their plates on the low table. Takyra took them and placed them back into the replicator. Sitting down again, she took a deep breath. "Let me start by explaining everything I know."

Takyra reiterated what Cytra had told them earlier, this time stopping to explain things when either of them became confused. She told them how the experts foresaw the eventuality of Aria'naa running low on resources. Their lead scientists tried slowing population growth, but it wasn't happening fast enough.

At the same time, they were at the early stages of interstellar travel, and had detected many habitable planets throughout the galaxy. "That's when we sent probes to find the nearest ones without intelligent life for us to colonize. That way, they could both reduce the burgeoning population on Aria'naa and use the colony worlds to supplement the dwindling resources on our world.

"We populated each colony ship with a mix of people from different backgrounds, especially those of the technician, medical, and agricultural classes. The Baaru'dak were the ones to build and maintain the infrastructure of the colony, the Laasa'dak looked after everyone's health, while the Paahr'dak would keep the new colony fed, clothed, and grew other raw materials that couldn't be mined or otherwise created.

"However, there had been a growing faction within the Paahr'dak, known as the *Aria'asharra*, that didn't agree that the Baaru'dak or Laasa'dak were needed. Many Aria'asharra wanted a colony ship of their own, so they could find a planet where they could *go back to nature* and a simpler way of life.

"The Rahn'naa was the fifth of the colony ships to leave Aria'naa. What we didn't know was that the Aria'asharra had infiltrated our ranks and planned to sabotage our ship, sending it on a course to a different planet, one not charted for colonization."

"So, that's why the Rahn'naa crashed here instead of going to Maal'dak Five?" Jevan asked.

"Correct. The Aria'asharra found this world was along our planned flight path," Takyra explained. "They hoped to stop here temporarily and have someone take them with a shuttlecraft to the surface. After they had left, they planned to let the Rahn'naa continue to the colony world. Unfortunately, something went wrong with their plan. By the time they woke me, the ship had already crashed, and we were all stranded here. I was going to launch a subspace beacon to call for help, but they stopped me."

"Do you know why they chose this world? Didn't they know it was already inhabited?" Jevan asked.

"They assured me they had run their own scans of this world and they showed me the results of a last-minute scan they did as the ship was hurtling toward your world. The scan was only of a single landmass, but it was unoccupied when the ship crashed," Takyra recalled.

"It was," Jevan confirmed. "My people arrived here about four hundred cycles of the seasons after your ship crashed. We sailed across the ocean from another continent."

"Those idiots," Takyra groused. "I am sorry Jevan. We should have never come to this world, although it is far too late to change that now. I can only hope that the descendants of those who left the ship didn't irreparably damage your species' natural development."

"I never thought they interfered, considering our peoples mostly avoid each other since the tenuous truce we established," Jevan informed her. "But Ardyn and I have been finding out a lot of things that the leaders of both our people had been lying to us about."

"A truce? That means that you and the Aria'asharra warred with one another?" Takyra asked, looking deeply troubled. "The Aria'asharra who crashed our ship assured us they were peaceful and merely wanted to return to a simpler way of living. Ardyn, as their descendent, what did they teach you?"

"Our elders shun all but the most basic technology and punish anyone who shows curiosity or questions the *ways of our ancestors*," Ardyn explained. "They emphasize that technology corrupts the land, and we do our best to live in harmony with nature."

"Then why would your people have gone to war with Jevan's people?" Takyra asked.

"The wars were hundreds of cycles of the seasons ago," Ardyn replied. "From what they taught me, Medellans invaded our land and attacked us. My ancestors fought to protect themselves and their way of life."

Takyra looked concerned. "Jevan, how much do you know?"

"My school master taught us that Ardyn's people—my people call them *elves*—attacked us first. They didn't want us colonizing their territory and wanted us to go back to where we came from. My ancestors fought back because they were not able to return," Jevan explained before clarifying. "Our history books don't explain why we could never return, it only warned that we should never attempt to."

"I suspect the truth may lie somewhere in-between, that perhaps neither actually attacked first." Takyra said.

"It's more likely that some misunderstanding led to the hostilities, as is often the case."

Ardyn agreed. "I think you're right, especially since our leaders have been lying to us for all this time. Why did my ancestors only wake you? Why keep everyone else asleep?"

Takyra sat forward, wrapping her arms around herself protectively. "The Aria'asharra forced me to show them how to operate everything. They didn't want to allow anyone outside of their faction to join their new society. They were afraid we'd have a corrupting influence on their children," Takyra said with a growl. "Yet they didn't want to outright murder us, either. Instead, their solution was to abandon us in our cryopods."

Jevan looked at Ardyn and watched as he shrank into himself, his ears going flat in distress. *Oh, no. Poor Ardyn. That's horrible!*

REFLECTION

Staring at Takyra, that revelation confirmed even more of Ardyn's fears. "How can anyone do something like that?"

"I know this must be a shock to you both," Takyra replied. "Looking at your clothing, I suspect neither of your civilizations is very advanced compared to what you're seeing on this ship."

Looking around him, Jevan nodded. "All of this is going to take a lot of getting used to. I'm usually hiking between villages and settlements, trading for goods."

"So, you're a trader." Takyra looked at Ardyn. "And what is your profession?"

"I was a ranger. I would spend most of my time in the forests, protecting Athla'naa territory and hunting down predators that threatened our settlement," Ardyn explained.

"Was?" Takyra asked.

"After I found this key, and we discovered the structures within the Aria'una, Jevan and I headed back to Maala'naa. A hunting party was waiting for us and brought us before The Elder Triumvirate, who sat in judgment against us. I was to be punished and Jevan executed for violating one of our most sacred laws, but we escaped, and I can never return."

"We made it back to my village," Jevan continued. "That's where we learned that the ard of my village knew more about the Aria'una than he had ever told me. He also sat in judgment over us and planned his own punishment, so we ran again. It took several cycles of the sun, but we finally stumbled upon a way into this ship that wasn't protected by that forcefield around your tower."

"The forcefield is still active?" Takyra looked at them, concerned. She sat quietly for a long moment before speaking again. "I need to plan what to do next carefully, so I don't cause conflict between either of your people and mine. However, I have another urgent matter to consider, especially if the forcefield has been active all this time. We did not design the cryopods to be in operation this long. Many may have already failed, meaning the occupant inside would have died. I cannot delay reviving them too long."

"Is there anything we can do to help?" Jevan asked.

"I appreciate the offer, but I need to spend some time analyzing the situation first. You both look exhausted. Why don't you get some rest while I figure out how to best proceed?"

Trying to stifle back a yawn, Ardyn nodded. "We would appreciate that. We've been on the run since early this morning, after we discovered that a hunting party pursued us into the Aria'una. When we were fleeing from them, we stumbled on a hidden entrance into this place."

"I see," Takyra said with a note of worry. "I will monitor for any intruders. You can tell me more after you've both had some rest. Come, follow me."

Takyra led them down the hall to two sets of quarters, showing the doors across the hall from each other. "We designed most quarters to be shared by two, but with many cryopods empty and everyone else still in cryostasis, you're free to each have your own."

Jevan looked at Ardyn with a shrug. "What do you think? You can get away from this annoying Medellan for a while. We've been tied at the hip for so many cycles of the sun now."

That made Ardyn laugh, but when he thought about having to sleep alone inside this strange ship, his heart rate sped up and he shook his head. "I don't think I want to be alone. This has been overwhelming and everything here is so strange," Ardyn admitted, looking at Jevan. "I trust you, and I would miss your familiar presence."

Smiling at him, Jevan agreed. "Yeah, I think I'd miss having you nearby as well. Thanks for the offer, Takyra, but I think we'll share one."

Giving them a knowing look, Takyra led them back up the corridor, closer to her own quarters. "Most of the shared quarters have two single beds in them," she explained. "But I think you'd be more comfortable sharing a larger bed."

Ardyn couldn't deny that, but said nothing. Jevan's little smile told him that the man agreed with him as well.

"Let me have your key for a moment," Takyra requested. Ardyn handed it to her, and she turned to tap a spot on the wall, making a display appear. "While this key will open most publicly accessible doors throughout the ship, the quarters are meant to be private spaces. I am having your key reprogrammed specifically for this door."

Once she finished, Ardyn noted how their names appeared on the display below the number *three*. Handing the key back to Ardyn, she gestured for him to unlock the door. Once inside, they saw these quarters were like Takyra's, although slightly smaller. Takyra showed them how to lock the door, and how to use the food and clothing replicators.

Turning to leave, Jevan stopped her. "We've been on the run so long. Is there a way for us to bathe? Also, what can we use for a chamber pot?"

"Oh yes, I forgot," Takyra apologized. "I'm guessing neither of you have used a toilet or shower before."

Looking at Jevan, they both shook their heads and shrugged.

Leading them to the door next to the bed, she explained what the toilet and shower were and how to use them. Ardyn marveled at both and looked forward to having a chance to wash his hair again.

Stopping by the door, out to the corridor, Takyra turned back to them. "One last thing. When you're near the display in the living area, say Cytra's name and tell her you'd like to talk to me. She will activate the communications system and you can let me know when you're both rested."

"Thank you, Takyra," they both said, in turn.

Once alone, the two looked around them in awe. "Can you believe any of this is real? I feel like I'm dreaming," Jevan said, leaning against the half wall.

"You're right. I knew when I'd found this key, it must be very advanced technology. Yet, I never even imagined the truth it would unlock."

"So... about calling me an *athla'maakh* when we first met..." Jevan began.

Ardyn's eyes darted away from Jevan. "I am sorry. Some of my people mean it as an insult, but I hadn't intended it that way. I... promise I'll never call you that again."

"So, that triwolf that nearly killed you?" Jevan prompted.

"Yes, that would be an *athla'maakh*," Ardyn replied. "The meaning of the term is closer to the word *beast* in your language."

Jevan chuckled. "Well, that brings some new context to certain conversations I've had with your people in the past, that's for sure."

"You're not angry with me?" Ardyn asked, looking back at Jevan.

The Medellan smiled at him warmly. "I know you didn't mean any harm. So, let's make a deal. If you stop calling me *athla'maakh*, I'll stop calling you an *elf*."

"I never thought to ask, but what does *elf* mean, anyway?" Ardyn asked.

Jevan shrugged. "I don't know. All I know is that there are ancient fairy tales with elves, and they had pointed ears, but if there's a meaning beyond that, I have no idea."

"You'll have to tell me these tales some time, but I think I'm almost ready to sleep, after I try out that shower."

"Okay, you do that," Jevan said. "I'll play around with this clothing replicator. I think we both need a clean change of clothes."

"You're right," Ardyn agreed, before heading back toward the shower room. Once inside he unclipped his cloak and removed his leathers, folding them carefully. Then he used the toilet. After spending most of his life urinating in the woods, it still felt odd to do it inside, even after using Jevan's chamber pot for all the time they'd been confined together.

Afterward he stepped into the shower. Ardyn marveled at the concept, having water rain down on him while inside and having the ability to control the temperature. Being able to cleanse himself with hot water was a luxury he'd never imagined. Even when he was stuck in Jevan's house, the water they used to bathe was still often lukewarm at best.

As he stood there under the spray, letting the water rinse away the dirt and stink from his body, Ardyn's mind reeled at everything he'd experienced in the past few hours. All the time they'd been searching the Aria'una, he never imagined everything they had found.

Once he felt clean enough, Ardyn turned off the shower and dried himself with one of the towels that hung on the wall. Walking back into the bedroom, unabashed by his nudity, he went to sit on the bed. He was too tired to take much notice of the shy smile that crept over Jevan's face as he hurried past him.

Ardyn worked his fingers slowly through his long, wet hair, as his exhaustion caught up to him. He caught himself nodding off when Jevan emerged from the shower, still sleepily trying to untangle his hair, and failing.

Jevan presented Ardyn with some clothes. "The replicator suggested these for sleeping," Jevan explained. "Put them on, and I'll help you with your hair."

Taking the clothes, he marveled at the softness of the gray fabric and how tightly woven it was. "Wow, this feels amazing," he said as he slipped on the bottoms first, followed by the top.

"Yeah, it feels so different from the roughspun fabric and leather we usually wear," Jevan said as he slipped into his sleep clothes, before guiding Ardyn to sit down on the couch and turn his back toward him.

"I wish we had brought our packs with," Jevan said, using his fingers to help Ardyn untangle his wet hair. "I'm going to miss brushing your hair."

"Why don't you use that replicator to make a new hairbrush?" Ardyn suggested.

"How'd you get so smart?" Jevan teased as he went over to the replicator again. "Cytra, can you replicate a hairbrush?"

The replicator display showed an array of hairbrushes made from different materials and different styles of bristles. "There are so many to choose from. Which one do you like?"

Ardyn came over and looked through the options with him. "That one, I think," Ardyn said sleepily, pointing to one that had a wooden handle and soft, brown bristles. "That looks like it would feel nice."

Making their selection the replicator created the brush. Taking it out of the receptacle, Jevan admired the craftsmanship. "Good selection," Jevan said. "Although, I still want to get my other brush back, eventually. It was a gift from my sister."

Sitting back down, Ardyn turned, so Jevan could use the brush on his hair. "Yeah, I have a few items in my pack I would like to have, too. Just some trinkets I've collected over the seasons. We should go get them when we have a chance."

Jevan slowly worked the brush through the wet strands of Ardyn's damp hair. He enjoyed working out the tangles until Ardyn's hair was smooth and nearly dry. This was an evening ritual that he would miss, if they ever went their separate ways again.

Once Jevan was done, Ardyn turned. "Thank you. I really enjoy it when you brush my hair. It's very soothing."

"You're most welcome," Jevan said with a warm smile and a wink. "I find it relaxing, and I'm glad you trust me enough to do this for you."

"Right now, you're the only one in this world I *do* trust," Ardyn said honestly.

"That means a lot," Jevan said, looking back at him with a smile. "The feeling is mutual."

Returning the smile, Ardyn crawled under the covers. "Now come, let's go to bed. I feel like I could sleep for at least five cycles of the sun."

Jevan rolled his eyes. "Yes, dear," he teased as he set the brush aside and slipped under the covers next to Ardyn.

ACCOMMODATIONS

Jevan woke, slowly becoming aware of his surroundings. He sat up, startled, unsure of where he was. It took a moment for his sleep addled brain to remember everything that had happened before he'd laid down to sleep. Looking down next to him, he saw Ardyn, usually the first to wake, was still fast asleep.

As silently as possible, Jevan rose and went to enjoy another hot shower. He'd rarely ever had a hot bath in his life, and he'd never seen something like these showers before. It was ingenious, and the hot water helped ease some of the tension he'd been feeling. After he'd finished showering, he picked up his old clothes and realized how rank they were.

Folding his dirty clothes again, he stashed them in a corner of the room and made his way to the clothing replicator. He whispered to it, and it showed him a variety of clothing options it could make. Some looked more practical than others. In the end, he opted for a white shirt, and a simple pair of brown trousers, with a matching jacket and boots. There had been no options for any style of cloak, as he was used to wearing, so the jacket would have to do.

By the time he finished dressing, he heard Ardyn stir behind him. Looking at the bed, he smirked when he saw the elf also startle awake. "Where are we?" Ardyn asked sleepily when he saw Jevan.

"In our *quarters* aboard the Rahn'naa," Jevan replied, the new word still feeling strange on his tongue. "Remember?"

Sitting silently for a moment, Jevan could see Ardyn processing his memories from yesterday. "Oh, that's right. Are you sure I'm not still dreaming?"

Nodding, Jevan smiled. "Yes, I'm sure."

Staring at him more intently, Ardyn squinted. "What are you wearing?"

"I picked out some new clothes from the replicator," Jevan explained. "My old ones are really dirty and after taking another shower, I didn't feel like putting them on again."

"Another shower sounds like a good idea," Ardyn admitted. "I would also love something to eat."

"Go shower and get dressed," Jevan suggested. "I'll figure out how to make us some food."

Making his way into the kitchen, Jevan touched the display next to the food replicator. Cytra helped him navigate the menu and the dizzying array of choices. "Cytra, we just need something simple. What is customary to eat as the morning meal on Aria'naa?" Jevan asked.

This narrowed down the menu and Jevan selected something that resembled a meat stew served with bread. He was pulling two servings from the replicator when Ardyn made his way out of the shower room. Looking at Jevan sheepishly, he tilted his head toward the clothing replicator. "You're right about our clothes. I feel so clean now. It would be a shame to put mine on without cleaning them. Can you help me make some new clothes? I was too tired to process what Takyra explained."

Setting down the plates of food, Jevan came over and showed Ardyn how to use it. "There are a lot of options and color choices. I opted to stick with something that I could wear in the forest once we leave here."

Looking up at him, Ardyn had a quizzical look. "Leave? Where do you think we could go? Back to the woods?"

"That's a good point," Jevan replied. "We should ask Takyra if we can stay here. At least until a better opportunity presents itself."

Ardyn opted for a similar set of clothes to Jevan's, although he chose a forest green color instead. While they sat and ate their meal, Jevan tried not to stare at his elven companion, or the way his new green jacket complemented his slender form.

● ● ●

Ardyn enjoyed the stew and bread that Jevan had prepared with the mysterious replicator. It was delicious, but not as heavily spiced as the meal Takyra had made for them. As he ate, he studied the Medellan, while trying to sort through all his own doubts and fears. "Are you feeling as overwhelmed as I am?"

Jevan nodded. "We knew they were hiding something in the Aria'una, but this?" he gestured at his surroundings.

"How could your ancestors condemn all these people to an indefinite sleep? It seems so... *cruel.*"

"I wish I knew," Ardyn replied with a shrug. "Our whole lives were a lie and I feel so used." A shudder ran through him when he remembered the matings they had forced him to endure, all for the sake of honor and tradition. A tradition based on twelve centuries of lies.

"Now the truth has to come out," Jevan said with a note of optimism, reaching for Ardyn's hand. "I'll make sure no one ever uses you like that again."

It was almost as if Jevan could read his thoughts, making Ardyn blush. He squeezed Jevan's hand, enjoying the warm touch. "Thank you."

Once they had eaten, Jevan went to put the dishes back into the replicator, where they magically disappeared. After putting the small earpiece back into his ear, Ardyn went to the communications panel to contact Takyra. She told them she was back in the control center where they'd been yesterday, and Cytra helped guide them there.

On entering, Takyra looked up from what she was doing to greet them. "I hope you both slept well," she said. "I've made progress on orienting myself to the current situation, but I could use a break. Come and sit."

There were chairs in front of each station around the room. They took a seat in the two closest to Takyra. "I was wondering," Ardyn said. "If all your people on board this ship were sleeping in those cryopods, why does this ship have all those living quarters? Why did you need the cryopods in the first place?"

Takyra swiveled her chair around to fully face them. "It takes a long time to cross between solar systems, even with as fast as this ship could travel. We expected the journey to our colony world to take about one hundred and thirty-five years. We designed the cryopods to keep us alive, without aging, until we reached our colony.

"However, there is always the possibility of running into a problem. In case of an emergency, we programmed the ship to wake us all up. In that eventuality, we would need someplace to live while we made repairs."

"Cytra also mentioned something about building a city using the ship?" Jevan interjected.

"Yes, exactly," Takyra confirmed. "That's the other reason we needed the ship to be so large. We designed it to be disassembled and turned into our first settlement. We planned to convert all the quarters into apartments, and the rest of the ship would be converted into various facilities to serve our new community, including a hospital."

"That's clever," Jevan said. "Bringing the building materials with you so you don't have to manufacture them on the world you are colonizing."

"It was a controversial decision," Takyra admitted. "Considering how scarce the resources were becoming on Aria'naa. However, they decided to give each colony the best start at being successful. The hope was that eventually the colonies could then provide raw materials to the homeworld, which would make the sacrifice of materials to build the colony ships worth it."

"What do you plan to do next?" Ardyn asked. "You said you had made some progress?"

"Yes! Come, follow me back to the cryopod chamber. I'll explain along the way," Takyra said.

They followed Takyra as she led the way. "Since you mentioned you were being pursued by a hunting party, the first thing I need to do is wake a few more of my people, before your pursuers find their way inside. If what you say is true, that they likely know about the ship, then it will be only a matter of time before they come looking for you in here."

Once back in the cryopod chamber, Jevan walked to the edge of the platform and stared at all the rows of pods, stretching farther than his eyes could see. "How many are there?" he asked, still in awe of the size of this structure.

Working at one of the display consoles, Takyra explained. "We were carrying ten thousand colonists. Nearly half were from the agricultural class. The ones that remain in cryostasis are the technical and scientific members of the Baaru'dak and Laasa'dak classes."

"If those who left the ship were mostly farmers, how did they know how to control this ship? Did all your people know how?" Jevan asked.

"No, they would have needed help from someone in the Baaru'dak class to do it," Takyra replied, before giving Ardyn a strange look.

"You know who helped them, don't you?" Ardyn asked.

"Yes," Takyra confirmed, as she turned back toward the console she was working on. Her hands flew over the controls and a moment later, a name and other information appeared with an image. "He was a young Baaru'dak named Kyrael."

TARGET PRACTICE

Ardyn stared at the screen, looking at the face of an ancient Athla'naa whose face was younger than his own. "Who was he?"

"Kyrael was a flight engineer," Takyra replied. "The Aria'asharra probably chose him, hoping he knew how to pilot the ship."

"How do you know he's the one who helped those who crashed this ship?" Jevan asked.

"According to the records, his cryopod is empty. So, he must have left with the Aria'asharra," she explained. "Not that it matters now. What matters is making sure we can defend ourselves. That's why I will revive some of our security techs to assist us."

Jevan watched as Takyra began making her selections. "How many do you plan to wake?"

"I have ten selected, all weapons specialists from the Baaru'dak security subclass," Takyra explained. "I want to make sure we can defend ourselves if that hunting party finds a way into the Rahn'naa. Jevan, please join me in the control center. I need to oversee the revival process from there, and it's best you aren't the first one they see. Meeting a member of an alien species when they first wake may cause them to lash out like I did. Coming out of cryostasis, especially after so long, is disorienting."

"What can I do to help?" Ardyn asked. "I may not look alien, but they won't understand how I speak, will they?"

"Language shouldn't be a problem anymore," Takyra reassured him. "I had Cytra input how our language has evolved into their minds. They will understand you easily enough, even without the translators."

"How is that possible?" Jevan asked.

"While in cryostasis, the mind still requires stimulation, or it will atrophy. Each cryopod has a neural interface that connects to our brains." Pulling down her collar, Takyra showed them a small opening in the side of her neck. "This provides intellectual stimulation to the mind for as long as we're in cryostasis. One of its functions is to teach.

While we were in cryostasis, one goal was to improve our knowledge in our personal area of specialization during the voyage. In fact, while you both slept, I returned to my cryopod for a short period so Cytra could input the linguistic changes to my mind as well. I no longer need to wear the translator earpiece to understand you."

"Can your cryopods do the same thing for us?" Jevan asked.

"I'm not sure if it would be compatible with how your species' brain works," Takyra replied to Jevan. "However, we could outfit Ardyn with a neural interface like I have, if you would like. Until then, the earpieces should work well enough."

Ardyn contemplated having an easier way to learn how all this amazing technology worked. There was so much he wanted to understand. Yet, the idea of getting put into one of those pods and having a small hole like that in his neck made him uncomfortable. "I'll... think about it."

"It's not something we could do until our medical facilities are fully operational, so take your time." Takyra reached out and put a comforting hand on his shoulder. "For now, please greet each person as we revive them. Tell them that Chief Technician Takyra will explain everything once we have revived all of them."

"I can do that," Ardyn replied with a nod.

A few moments after Jevan left with Takyra, the first pod arrived on the platform. The Athla'naa that stumbled out had the light purple hair typical of males but cut short in the manner favored by females. This took Ardyn by surprise, but he still stepped forward with a welcoming smile. "Greetings, my name is Ardyn. Chief Technician Takyra is waiting in the control center. She will explain everything."

"Greetings, Ardyn. I'm Aerys, head of the security subclass and second-in-command of the Rahn'naa," he greeted in return, the tenor of his voice confirming he was indeed male. "How many have been revived so far?"

"Only Takyra and yourself," Ardyn explained, as the next cryopod arrived. "She said she would revive ten security techs."

This made Aerys frown. "What's happened?"

"It's probably best if we wait for everyone to be revived and let Takyra explain," Ardyn replied.

Once the other nine security techs had joined them on the platform, Aerys turned and immediately took charge of the group. "Fall in line and follow me to the control center with Ardyn."

"Yes, sir!" the group replied in unison.

Aerys led them to the control center. Along the way, Ardyn explained that there was an *athla'maakh* waiting with Takyra in the control center. This seemed to alarm the group, but Ardyn didn't ask why.

When they arrived at the control center doors, the entire group tensed as if expecting a fight. Aerys opened the doors and rushed in, only to stop short when he saw Takyra and Jevan.

"Aerys!" Takyra greeted. "It's so good to see you again, my old friend. Let me introduce our new friend, Jevan of the Medellans."

The entire group seemed to slump in disappointment upon seeing Jevan.

"I'm sorry, was I not what you expected?" Jevan asked.

Stepping forward, Aerys greeted Jevan. "My apologies. When Ardyn mentioned an *athla'maakh*, I was expecting a ferocious beast, not a sentient person."

Jevan laughed, shooting Ardyn a look. "Ardyn needs to stop referring to me as that, I think. We've already had this conversation with Takyra."

Shuffling his feet and avoiding Jevan's gaze, Ardyn stumbled over his words. "I am sorry. It's an old habit."

Interceding before this conversation devolved into something counterproductive, Takyra spoke up. "What we all call each other is a discussion for later. Right now, we need to be prepared to defend ourselves in case that hunting party makes their way into the Rahn'naa."

Aerys stepped forward. "What is going on, exactly?"

"A lot has happened. I can't go into all the details now, but we crashed onto the wrong planet, and there may be hostiles who might try to board the ship," she explained.

"I see," Aerys said, glancing at Jevan.

"Jevan is Ardyn's friend," Takyra explained. "We do not need to fear him."

"Okay. Then, let's go to the nearest armory and prepare ourselves. We can discuss the ramifications of what has happened later."

While leading them through the ship, Takyra told Aerys a little more about what was going on, and who Ardyn's people were. Aerys kept looking back at Ardyn with concern but said nothing.

They were led into a large room lined with locked cabinets, that Aerys opened with a key like the one Ardyn found. "Some of our weapons are stored here. There are three other armories like this one and can only be unlocked by the control access keys. I have one, as does Takyra. The other keys belong to the heads of various departments."

Taking out his key, Ardyn hesitated to ask. "Is... this key one of them?"

"Yes," Takyra confirmed.

How did it end up buried in the back of that small cave? Ardyn wondered to himself.

Next to the weapons lockers was a room that was used for target practice. "After being in cryostasis for so long, I think we all need some practice handling our weapons again," Aerys declared as he handed one to each of the techs.

Takyra went back to the lockers and handed one each to Jevan and Ardyn, while Aerys gave her a disapproving look. "I think our two guests should also learn how to handle a *rahn'ora*."

"*Rahn'ora?*" Jevan questioned. "That means deadly light, right? Why is it called that?"

"Watch," Aerys said, as he walked behind a mark on the floor, raised his weapon, and aimed his *rahn'ora* at a target hanging on the far side of the room. For a moment, a bright white light appeared on the target, before a large clean hole burned right through it.

Ardyn jumped back, accidentally into Jevan's arms. Embarrassed, he righted himself and tried to regain his composure. "I see what you mean. That light definitely looks deadly. Isn't that excessive?"

Aerys nodded. "Sometimes excessive force is necessary. However, you can change the intensity. At the lowest setting, it will only stun someone unconscious. At the highest setting, it will disintegrate the target into a pile of ash."

"The hunting party is only armed with bows, arrows, and spears," Ardyn explained. "I grew up with all of them.

Please, can we only use that stun setting? I don't want anyone to die."

"I agree," Takyra said. "From what Ardyn has told me, they are a small party, and the descendants of the *Aria'asharra* live primitively. There is no need for us to murder them, even if they come with less than honorable intentions."

"You're right, Takyra, as always," Aerys replied with a small smile. "However, we need the middle setting at a minimum for target practice. Afterward, we can reset them down to the stun level."

When Aerys handed Ardyn a *rahn'ora*, he studied it. It looked like they made it from the same silvery looking metal that didn't rust. It was sleek and stylish, the handle of it fitting easily into the palm of his hand, with grooves perfectly slotted for his long fingers. Looking at Jevan, he had to hold back a chuckle, because the Medellan's much larger five-fingered hand made the weapon look like a small toy. These weapons were clearly designed for Athla'naa hands.

"Hold it like this," Aerys instructed. "Then straighten your arm and shift your body sideways. Do you see the small tab at the end? Use that to aim at your target. When you're ready, simply press this button with your thumb."

Following the instructions, Ardyn aimed at the target. After pressing the button for a heartbeat, it didn't seem to do anything. Then the bright light lit up the target. Ardyn immediately stopped pressing the button. He'd struck the target dead-center.

"Excellent! I think you're a natural," Aerys praised.

Jevan went next and despite the awkward grip he had, still hit his target with the same precision as Ardyn.

They trained, shooting target after target, testing the various intensity settings to get a feel for each of them. Once Aerys was satisfied that his team was sufficiently warmed up and that Ardyn and Jevan could handle the weapons safely, Takyra led them to a communal area to share a meal. Along one wall was a bank of food replicators, and the room had several large hexagonal tables surrounded by chairs.

"Why is that wall made of dirt?" Ardyn asked, following Takyra to the replicators.

Looking over at the wall Ardyn pointed to, a wistful look came over her face. "The dirt is outside of the observation port. We built this ship in space, and I helped oversee most of its construction. I spent many evenings gazing through that port, to Aria'naa below."

Ardyn tried to imagine but he couldn't picture what it must have looked like, floating high above a planet like that. He suspected it was very beautiful.

They sat together and ate, while Takyra explained everything to Aerys. He scowled but still said nothing. Once Takyra was finished, he pushed away his plate, sat back, and crossed his arms. "This is bad, but there isn't much we can do about it now. Let's inform the others."

Standing up, Aerys got everyone's attention. "Gather around. We have something to tell you."

As Takyra and Aerys informed them of what happened, tensions quickly rose once they understood. Then, without warning, one of the security techs grabbed Ardyn roughly by the arm. "We should make you pay for this, you son-of-a-traitor!"

CLOSE

Ardyn felt a knot of guilt tighten in the pit of his stomach as he tried to pull away from the security tech holding him. At the same time, Jevan turned, towering over them both. He looked like he was about to rip the head off Ardyn's attacker when Aerys called for order.

"Let Ardyn go at once," Aerys ordered. "This is not the time nor place to point fingers. We cannot blame Ardyn for something that happened over twelve-hundred years ago. He and his people have also been the victim of generations of lies and hypocrisy. We should be grateful he found us and helped free Takyra from cryostasis. Don't take your anger out on him. Those who did this to us are long dead. We need to focus on the present and prepare for the future."

Letting Ardyn go, the Athla'naa sheepishly apologized, his ears lowering and going completely flat against his head. "I am sorry. It is hard to imagine that you are so many generations removed from us."

After giving him a slight nod, Ardyn stepped forward to address the group. "Thank you, but I want to apologize to all of you. I may not be personally responsible for this situation, but I feel terrible that it happened. I want to do whatever I can to help make things right between our people."

Takyra came over and placed a hand on Ardyn's shoulder. "Thank you, Ardyn. We wouldn't be here if it weren't for you and your friend Jevan."

There was a chorus of *thank yous* from the group before Aerys stepped forward again. "I want all of you to get some exercise. We've been in those cryopods for far too long. Then spend some more time at target practice. I need all of you in top form. We'll meet back here for an evening meal. Then we'll do patrol rotations of five on and five off, in the corridors between the control center and living quarters."

Jevan and Ardyn joined them, hoping to get to know all of them better. After sharing another meal, Jevan and Ardyn retired to their quarters. Ardyn slumped onto the couch in the sitting area, patting the seat, inviting Jevan to sit next to him.

Ardyn sat forward again. "I know I keep saying this, but everything in our lives is going to be so different."

Relaxing next to him, Jevan nodded. "For the better, I hope. I think both of our people have been stuck in their way for far too long. The influx of all these technologically advanced Athla'naa will shake things up."

"I agree. My people's traditions will have to change," Ardyn said. "Hopefully, with all these new Athla'naa, there will be no need for the ritual *breedings*."

Putting a comforting arm around Ardyn's shoulders, Jevan agreed. "I'm so sorry you had to suffer through that," he said, as his fingers played with some loose strands that had fallen from Ardyn's braid.

Idly playing with Ardyn's hair seemed to be a favorite thing for Jevan to do, and Ardyn happily allowed it. After some time getting lost in their own thoughts, Jevan asked. "Have you thought about it? Your people's homeworld, where everything must be like this ship?"

Letting out a slow breath, he shook his head. "No, I have not. I wonder if they still exist, after all this time? How much more advanced do you think they are, after twelve hundred cycles of the seasons?"

"Good question. I couldn't even imagine all this if I wasn't experiencing it firsthand. Maybe sometime in the future you can travel there and find out. If there was a chance, would you?"

"I'm not sure," Ardyn replied. "I don't like the idea of being stuck in a cryopod for that long. Besides, there is too much uncertainty right now."

"That's true. First, we still need to deal with your Triumvirate and Ard Mathias," Jevan pointed out. "I hope they won't cause too much trouble. They were determined to hide this secret from everyone."

"How long has your ard known about this? It's obvious that he has been complicit with my elders," Ardyn wondered aloud.

"Most likely Mathias learned it from our previous ard before he took over the position," Jevan speculated. "When an aging ard chooses an apprentice, they pass on their knowledge. Much of it is found in the books at the ard's house, and each new ard adds a book of their own, recording the history of their village for future generations."

It was all so much to think about. Letting out a long sigh, Ardyn dropped his head to the back of the couch. The stress from everything was catching up with him. His neck and back were in knots. Reaching around, he rubbed the pain sparking in his neck.

"May I help?"

Ardyn looked at Jevan skeptically. "How?"

"Sit up and turn around. I'll show you," Jevan said, spinning a finger in the air.

Ardyn turned around slowly, not sure what to expect. Jevan took Ardyn's long braid and tossed it over his shoulder. When Ardyn felt Jevan gently grip his shoulders, he couldn't help flinching.

Immediately, Jevan removed his hands. "Please relax. I'm only going to help work some kinks out of your back. Is that okay?"

Trying to relax, Ardyn nodded his consent and Jevan's hands returned. Slowly, the man kneaded the muscles of his shoulders and neck, finding knots of stress and slowly working them out. Ardyn couldn't help the pleasured groan he made as the tension receded from his muscles, making Jevan chuckle.

Ardyn tried not to imagine those wonderful hands wandering elsewhere. "Where did you learn how to do this?"

"Believe it or not, my mother and sister," Jevan explained. "Whenever I came back from a trading run, spending so much time on the road carrying that heavy pack, they would sit me down by the fire and do this."

"It's a shame I never met them when Mathias had us locked in your house. I would have liked to get to know them," Ardyn said.

"They would have loved you," Jevan said with a slight chuckle as he continued to knead Ardyn's back. "My sister would have loved playing with your hair."

"Oh, so that runs in your family?" Ardyn teased, making Jevan laugh.

Once Jevan reached his lower back, Ardyn felt more relaxed than he had in a long time. Turning around, he looked up at the man, happy to see the twinkle back in his eyes. "Thank you."

"It was my pleasure," Jevan assured him.

Relaxing back on the couch, Ardyn posed a new question. "Do you ever wonder what might have been, if things were different between our people?"

"How do you mean?" Jevan asked.

"Well, as you know with the Athla'naa, once we fulfill our mating duties, we are free to... enjoy... the company of anyone we wish," Ardyn said, tentatively. "Do you think our people might have been more open to mate with each other?"

"That's a good question. Pair-bonding is such an ingrained part of Medellan society, and the pair-bond ritual changes something in us. It prevents us from ever having sexual contact with others after we're bonded."

"I forgot about that," Ardyn admitted. "You told me what happened when that young man from your village forced himself on a pair-bonded woman."

"Yeah, it's one reason I never wanted to pair-bond with anyone. If I did, that person would have to be worth it, because we'd be stuck together for the rest of our lives." Shrugging, Jevan slowly massaged a thumb over the back of Ardyn's hand. "I don't think it's something I have to worry about any longer."

Jevan held Ardyn's gaze for a moment, flicking his eyes to Ardyn's mouth more than once. Ardyn's ears lowered, as the pounding of his own heart was all he could hear. Jevan looked as if he were contemplating an action before pulling back, stifling a yawn. "How about we go get some sleep?"

Ardyn took a deep breath, his heart still racing, as he watched Jevan stand and make his way back toward the bedroom. *Was I imagining that?* Ardyn wondered before getting up and following.

After taking turns in the shower and changing into their sleeping clothes, they slipped into bed together. At first, they started as they always did, their backs facing each other. However, Ardyn couldn't turn off the thoughts racing through his mind, and he became restless, flopping over onto his back in frustration.

"Can't sleep?" Jevan asked.

"I have too much on my mind," Ardyn admitted.

Jevan opened his arms and invited Ardyn closer. "Come here."

Sliding closer to his friend, Ardyn curled into Jevan's embrace as he tucked his head under the man's chin. One of Jevan's hands rested on his back, warm and comforting.

"Any better?"

Nodding slowly, Ardyn felt safe, enveloped in Jevan's warm embrace. Finally, he felt slumber overtake him. A moment before sleep pulled him under, Ardyn thought he heard Jevan whisper. "If only..."

CONFRONTATION

Some hours later, Jevan awoke, limbs tangled with Ardyn's, making him smile sleepily. The fact Ardyn had felt safe enough to sleep so close together meant that he truly had won his trust. The thought of that made Jevan's heart rejoice. He had missed the quiet intimacy of waking up entangled with someone. Knowing there'd likely be nothing more between them, Jevan still felt completely content.

Despite almost slipping last night, tempted to kiss Ardyn, Jevan was happy to remain platonic friends. Yet, he kept a spark of hope. The lithe, beautiful elf had captured his heart. Admitting that to himself caused him a mixture of both elation and fear. He'd never expected to care about someone as much as he cared for Ardyn.

A loud chime followed by an urgent knock on the door of their quarters pulled Jevan out of his reverie and startled Ardyn awake. They disentangled themselves and Jevan jumped up to see what was going on. As he opened the door, Aerys met Jevan with a serious expression.

"Hurry and dress. Ardyn's people found their way into the ship. They are making a systematic sweep of the upper decks. Join us in the control center and don't forget to bring your *rahn'ora*."

"We'll be there shortly," Jevan acknowledged before turning to find a sleepy Ardyn getting out of bed.

"I heard," Ardyn said as he stumbled toward the shower room. While Ardyn used the facilities, Jevan changed out of his sleeping clothes. Once they were both ready, they hurried down towards the control center to find everyone else already gathered.

"How many are there?" Ardyn asked.

Takyra pointed at the display that she'd been studying when they arrived. "About six of them," Takyra replied, pointing at a small group of moving dots. "The security cameras showed us three older and two younger Athla'naa, plus one older Medellan."

"That's the same party we saw hunting us in the forest before we stumbled down into the ship," Ardyn said. "If reinforcements have not joined them, they probably think we're still alone, hiding inside this ship. They'll be in for a surprise."

"Indeed," Takyra agreed. "What do you propose, Aerys?"

Stepping forward, Aerys touched the screen to expand one section of the map. "Based on their current heading, we should station half of our people along these points. As this hunting party passes by, the group stationed at this juncture can slip in behind and follow them cautiously." Aerys explained, pointing at the map. "Then Ardyn and Jevan can meet them at this juncture, with the rest of us lying in wait for them out-of-sight, here and here."

"So, you're asking us to lure them into a trap?" Jevan asked.

"Yes. We will have them surrounded, so you will both be safe," Aerys continued. "Try to engage them in conversation and determine their purpose before we reveal ourselves to them. Can you do that?"

Ardyn nodded. "Yes. If that helps us to avoid hurting anyone."

"Alright everyone, you know what to do. Get into position," Aerys commanded.

◆◆◆

The security detail took their positions while Jevan and Ardyn went to the corridor junction where they expected to confront the party hunting them. Once they were in position, Ardyn felt his heart rate ramp up. The weapon he had hidden in his clothing gave him no comfort. He was unsure if he had the heart to fire it at his own people, even knowing it would only stun them. Without even thinking, Ardyn reached out and grabbed Jevan's hand to calm his nerves.

Ardyn hoped no deaths would come from this, but he wasn't sure how far his elders were prepared to go to maintain this damnable secret of theirs. If Ardyn had left things up to the will of his elders, Jevan would be long dead, and his own life would still have irrevocably changed.

Their only advantage was the knowledge that they only had two Athla'naa hunters with them. It betrayed an overconfidence that Aerys was now going to use to their advantage. Thinking about the two hunters in the party, Ardyn was sure they hadn't known about any of this before now. He wondered what they thought about everything they were seeing, being inside such a structure. Ardyn smirked when he remembered that much of the writing displayed within the ship had changed to reflect the current written language of the Athla'naa. That must be a surprise, even to the elders.

The elders had betrayed their people for generations, ever since they had first come to this world. It hurt Ardyn's heart to think about the many generations of lies that had been told. Jevan must have similar thoughts, Ardyn realized. How could life ever go back to normal after this?

Whatever *normal* was.

Footsteps sounded down the length of the corridor, coming from the next junction. Ardyn felt Jevan squeeze his hand for reassurance, and he squeezed back, holding firm. Then the party appeared around the corner. The elders stalked down the corridor, their boots falling heavily, along with the staves they carried. The hunters' steps fell softer, as they remained cautious and lithe on their feet. Ard Mathias had taken up a position in the middle, between the elders and hunters.

As soon as the party caught sight of the pair, the entire group stopped short. A dark scowl crossed over their faces before they moved forward to face Ardyn and Jevan, while the hunters drew their stone knives from their belts.

Stepping forward, Elder Aelrynd looked at them with righteous indignation. "How dare you set foot in the sacred temple of the ancients?!"

Ardyn looked at Jevan, confused. "What sacred temple?"

"You desecrate the temple with your very presence!" Druyndar yelled. "We will execute you both for your crimes!"

Ardyn could no longer contain his anger over the situation. "We have done nothing wrong! *You* should be judged for continuing the generations-old hypocrisy and lies that brought our people to this planet over twelve-hundred cycles of the seasons ago."

The hunters lowered their knives as their eyes widened in shock. Feeling a surge of confidence, Ardyn let go of Jevan's hand and addressed the pair of hunters directly.

"That's right. Our elders have been lying to us for generations. Look around you. This isn't some *sacred temple.*

It's a ship that once sailed among the stars in the sky. Our ancestors built all that you see here. Their technology was more advanced than any Medellan has achieved. Surely you must realize this is true, with all the Athla'naa writing literally on the walls."

Ardyn pointed to a display stating they were on the *Engineering Deck, Navigational Subsection.* The words may have been meaningless to the hunters, as they exchanged confused looks, but it was clear they were written by Athla'naa.

"Seize them!" Aelrynd commanded. "We will return to Maala'naa with these traitors immediately."

That's when Takyra and Aerys appeared, while the security techs surrounded the party. "I don't think so," Takyra said, leveling her weapon at Aelrynd.

Stumbling backward, Aelrynd let out a bewildered cry. "Who? What? Where?!" she stuttered.

Aerys stepped forward, his own weapon raised. Nodding to the security techs who had appeared behind the hunters, he commanded. "Disarm them and escort our guests to the holding cells so we can sort this mess out."

As the security techs tried to take the staves from the elders, Druyndar tried to use his as a weapon, swinging it wildly. Two other techs stepped in and easily disarmed him, securing his hands behind his back as he struggled. "Unhand me! Where have you come from? You're all traitors to the ancestors!"

While the Athla'naa elders were being secured, Mathias looked on in shock. "They... they told me this temple was an ancient tomb, where they buried their honored dead." Looking at Jevan, he shook his head. "You say it's... a *ship*?!"

Before Jevan could respond, they were all led away. Once they could no longer hear the protestations of the hunting party, Ardyn hugged Jevan, relieved that it was over. As soon as he realized what he was doing, he let go and backed away. "Um... sorry," he apologized, feeling awkward.

Smiling down at him, Jevan shrugged. "I didn't mind. Feel free to do that again, anytime," The Medellan said with a wink.

Aerys coughed awkwardly behind them, and Ardyn felt the heat rise in his face.

"Come, follow me. We need to talk to those fools now that we have them secured."

IMPASSE

They followed Aerys to the holding cells. "We set aside some space in case we had any troublemakers after we awoke. I never thought we'd be using them for something like this."

Ardyn smirked at Jevan when they could hear the elders ranting and raving from down the hall. The holding cells were within a large octagonal room containing eight cells, each large enough to hold two or three people.

The Triumvirate were in one cell, while Mathias was alone in his, and the two hunters shared a third cell together. There didn't appear to be any doors, but Ardyn noticed the two hunters pressing their hands against an invisible wall, much like they'd encountered outside of the tower.

After they arrived, Aerys spoke to Takyra loud enough so everyone in the cells could hear. "I think we should leave them to cool their heels for a day before we conduct our interrogation," he stated before turning abruptly and looking at him. "What do you think, Ardyn?"

A smile crept over his face as he understood. "I agree. That is an excellent idea. They are much too emotional right now."

Turning, the four of them walked back out into the corridor when Aelrynd called after them. "Stop! Wait! Don't just *leave* us here!"

"Jevan!" Mathias cried out. "You can't leave me locked up with them. Please!"

Aerys turned, facing the three occupied cells. "Will you calm down enough so we can discuss matters like civilized people, or will you continue to scream like an *athla'maakh?*"

Using that word as an epithet took the elders by surprise, and Aelrynd took several breaths before responding. "We'll calm down."

The rest agreed in unison, with the hunters remaining silent, sulking in their cell.

Aerys smiled, stepping further into the room. "Excellent."

"Let's begin with some introductions," Takyra suggested. "I am Chief Technician Takyra, and this is Chief of Security, Aerys. I take it you know Ardyn and Jevan?"

"They are known. However, I do not know these strange titles you have given yourselves, Takyra and Aerys. I am Elder Aelrynd, head of the Triumvirate of Maala'naa. These are Elder Taeglyn and Elder Druyndar," she pointed to each elder as she named them.

"Under different circumstances, I would say it was good to meet you," Takyra said. "However, I do not appreciate you barging onto my ship and threatening our new friends."

Aelrynd ignored the accusation, making a demand instead. "Name the settlement from where you came."

"I suppose you could say this ship is my *settlement*," Takyra replied. "It is named the Rahn'naa."

An angry scowl crossed Aelrynd's face, but before she could respond, Druyndar spoke. "How dare you call this sacred temple a settlement? Why do you demean this ancient ground so?"

Ardyn rolled his eyes. "Elders, how can you not see you are standing within a technological marvel? This is no *temple*. Even Jevan understood that advanced technology was needed to craft everything you see around us."

After the elders gave snorts of derision, Takyra spoke again. "Ardyn speaks the truth. Perhaps you have been using this as a temple, but this was a ship that could fly between the stars. It brought your ancestors to this world."

"That's impossible." Elder Taeglyn spoke for the first time. "Our ancestors constructed most of this temple underground. It could never have flown like a bird."

"The Rahn'naa crashed and became buried," Takyra explained. "I can assure you we did not construct it where it is now. I *personally* oversaw the construction of this ship before it left the orbit of our homeworld, Aria'naa."

"You... what?" Aelrynd spluttered. "From where? Our world is named *Aria'nor*."

"*Your* ancestors may have named *this* world Aria'nor, but *Aria'naa* is the name of the Athla'naa homeworld," Takyra explained.

"How do you explain all those who are entombed here?" Taeglyn asked. "There are thousands of caskets."

Taking a deep breath, Takyra tried to explain. "They... *we*... weren't entombed. Those aren't caskets filled with the dead. Most, if not all, are still very much alive. Aerys and I slept in them for the past twelve centuries until Ardyn and Jevan helped to wake us."

Aelrynd threw her hands up in the air. "Enough! You speak of nothing but blasphemy! I will hear no more of your lies."

"Alright, then why don't you tell us what you know of your history," Aerys suggested.

Heaving a deep sigh, Aelrynd sat on the bench next to her. "There are truths only the Triumvirate may know. It is pointless to continue, and you all are to be executed."

Jevan smirked at Ardyn, hearing that idle threat.

Taeglyn rolled his eyes. "Well, seeing as they are to be executed, no harm can come from them knowing, can it?"

Then Taeglyn related what the significance of this *temple* was. It became clear that the Aria'asharra must have purposely lied to the next generation, teaching them that the observation tower was a temple that housed their ancient dead. The true history became warped over the course of nearly fifty generations, and now only the Elder Triumvirate even knew of the existence of the tower and what lay beneath.

"Why was this *temple* abandoned? Why don't our people know about its existence?" Ardyn asked, curious how the Elders would respond.

Druyndar glowered at him. "As we have taught you, technology leads to nothing but violence and destruction. It nearly destroyed our ancestors. This temple stands as a monument to the near destruction of our people. It's why we abandoned all technology eons ago."

Standing again, Aelrynd continued. "Our ancestors decreed to never tell our people of the temple, as they may become too curious and attempt to learn its secrets."

Coming to an impasse, Takyra declared an end to their conversation. "We're getting nowhere, and there is much we need to do. We will make sure you are comfortable and given a meal."

"You can't just leave us here!" Mathias cried out as they turned to leave.

Ardyn paused when Jevan turned back to his ard. "I'm sure they'll let you go after we've sorted this mess out," Jevan reassured him. "There is much to consider, and the last thing we want is for a new war to break out between our people. Please, give us some time."

Mathias huffed in indignation, but there was nothing he could do from within his cell, so they left them to join the others in the control center. "They aren't ready to hear the whole truth," Takyra was saying as they entered. "I'm not even sure they can handle that knowledge."

"This has all been a shock to us as well," Ardyn confessed. "But Jevan and I are more open-minded than the Elder Triumvirate is."

Aerys nodded. "I am grateful for that. We will need to find another way to get through to them. However, our priority should be to wake up the rest of the Athla'naa aboard ship. The cryopods have been in continuous use far past the safety limits. It's possible not all within their pods have survived."

"We also need to contact Aria'naa. We don't know what may have happened to our people in the intervening centuries. Tensions were building at the time we left, and there were the rumblings of war. However, we still need to reach out to whoever may still be out there," Takyra said.

"How can you send a message that far away?" Ardyn asked. "How long would it even take to get there?"

Takyra operated the display before her as she explained. "If one of our subspace beacons is still operational, I could launch one into orbit. It can send a message back to Aria'naa within a few days. Subspace communication travels much faster than this ship can."

Jevan and Ardyn looked at each other, dumbfounded. "I guess we'll have to take your word for it," Ardyn said, making Takyra laugh.

BEACON

The next morning, Takyra invited them to join her in the dining hall for a meal while they discussed their options. It was clear that once they revealed their existence to both the Medellan and Athla'naa populations on this continent, it would irrevocably change the lives of everyone. There was always the possibility of factions forming a resistance against their presence that might lead to violence. These were things Takyra was adamant they avoid.

Another issue was the pressure on local resources by adding a population of nearly five thousand new people, all of whom would require food and shelter. The Rahn'naa could sustain them for a time, since it had been running on standby mode for over a millennium. However, once everyone was awake, the ancient equipment may break down and they would run out of resources to repair or replace parts. This meant they would eventually have to venture beyond the ship and build a settlement of their own.

"Wasn't this ship designed to be turned into a city?" Jevan asked.

"Under ideal circumstances, yes," Takyra replied. "However, I don't even have the resources available to assess how much damage the ship took when it crashed. We may not be able to salvage the equipment needed to excavate it after it's been buried for so long. If we could reach out to Aria'naa, they might send us additional resources that would reach us in about sixty years. Perhaps sooner if they've improved the speed of their interstellar travel by now."

"Then our first priority should be to revive everyone before the cryopods begin failing," Aerys pointed out.

Takyra agreed. "Please analyze the viability of all the occupied cryopods and come up with a revised revival plan."

"I'll have a report for you to review by tomorrow morning, Chief."

"Excellent. In the meantime, I'll work on the subspace beacon problem. The sooner we get a message transmitted, the sooner we'll get a response," Takyra said. "Jevan and

Ardyn, you can keep me company while I check to see if any of our subspace beacons are still operational."

●●●

They followed Takyra to the elevator. Stepping out, Ardyn was taken back to the day they had first seen the strange tower in the valley. *I've been here before!*

"Jevan! We're inside the observation tower," Ardyn said, pointing. "That's the door I entered, when you were stuck outside the forcefield."

Jevan looked around, awestruck. "I can see why you were overwhelmed. What is this all for?"

Takyra led them toward one of the many stations lining the windows that overlooked the valley below. "That's right. You told me you'd found your way into the observation tower before. This area functions as our secondary control center. We can control most of the ship's functions from here."

Jevan stared up at the large windows and several levels of platforms above them. "Why do you need two control centers?"

"In the original design, were going to use this as the primary control center," Takyra explained. "However, after the one of our earlier colony ships ran into an asteroid belt and their observation tower was damaged, they had to be rescued because no one could easily access the control center to pilot the ship. All future ships were built with two control centers. The primary one is now located in a secure position within the center of the ship. It relies on external sensors and cameras instead of these windows to navigate."

"Why even build an observation tower, if it's so easily damaged?" Ardyn asked.

Takyra walked toward one of the stations and sat down. "The tower is meant to serve a practical purpose in the colony. It houses all the meeting rooms and the conclave hall where the colony is governed."

Activating the display at her station, Takyra worked over the controls. "Yes, it looks like two beacons are still operational. At least those fools listened to me when I told them to activate the solar panels on this tower before abandoning us to our fate. It helped us conserve our power reserves and I should be able to launch a beacon with no issues. Come, follow me."

They joined Takyra in the elevator again, heading up farther into the tower. While they headed up, she explained how the solar panels helped keep the quark fusion engine that powered the ship stable over all these centuries. The solar power also helped to power some secondary systems, and the ship kept a store of power from the solar panels in case the engine ever went offline. The subspace beacons were part of the secondary systems powered directly by solar.

Exiting the elevator, Takyra led them down a short hallway into a room named *Subspace Beacon Control*. The walls were lined with large hatches, like the one Jevan tripped over in the forest. All had lights, most red, with only two green.

Takyra opened one and slid out a strange-looking object the size of a large boulder.

"That's a subspace beacon? How does it work?" Ardyn asked, staring at the strange object.

While she continued checking over the beacon she'd pulled out, Takyra did her best to explain. "I'm going to launch this into space. It will stay in orbit above us while it sends a message to the homeworld. The signal will travel through subspace, which helps it travel faster than a normal signal would."

"Why does it have to go into space to send this signal?" Jevan asked.

"The atmosphere interferes with the signal," Takyra explained. "Sending it into space guarantees a clearer signal. When we left, Aria'naa also had beacons like these in orbit."

Once Takyra checked over the beacon, she placed it back into its launch tube and pulled out a tablet from a pocket inside of the jacket she wore. "Launching beacon," she declared as she tapped on the tablet.

They heard a rumble as the beacon launched from the observation tower. Running toward the window, they could watch it arc through the sky toward its destination. Ardyn never saw anything like that before, as he stared at the cloud-like trail it left in its wake.

"While we wait for the beacon to get into position, we can work on the message we want to send. I will set it to repeat automatically until we receive a response. Help me compose the message."

Chief Technician Takyra from the Colony Starship Rahn'naa contacting the Aria'naa Leadership Conclave. We were headed for the colony on Maal'dak Five when our ship was commandeered by a rogue faction called the Aria'asharra and taken off-course. The Rahn'naa crashed and the Baaru'dak and Laasa'dak classes remained in cryostasis. We were recently revived by a descendent of the Aria'asharra and...

Takyra looked at Jevan. "How much do you want me to say about your people?"

"Tell them this is the Medellan homeworld," Jevan suggested. "They have nothing to fear from us, as we're too primitive to do them any harm."

Takyra added Jevan's suggestion, while Ardyn thought about what else to add. "How about including the fact that my people don't know the truth of what happened? I hope those on Aria'naa today wouldn't hold us accountable for our ancestors' actions."

"Good idea," Takyra agreed. After she finished composing the message, she read it aloud, recording it into the tablet.

A thrill ran up Ardyn's spine when Takyra finished the recording and pressed send.

INTRACTABLE

The next morning in the dining hall, Aerys handed Takyra the report he'd promised on his assessment of the cryopods. "Thank you. Tell me, have any of the pods failed?" Takyra asked.

Aerys was tight-lipped for a moment before responding. "Unfortunately, yes, and many others are close to failing. I've made my recommendations on the priority of who we revive based on my findings."

Setting the report aside, Takyra frowned. "Thank you, Aerys. I will study your report and complete the revival plans before the end of the day."

"Why don't we meet after the evening meal and discuss the plans then?" Aerys recommended.

"Good idea. Meet me in the control center," Takyra agreed.

Aerys then turned to Ardyn and Jevan. "I have a task I think you are uniquely suited for."

"What kind of task?" Ardyn asked, eager to be of help.

"We cannot let your people go," Aerys began. "Not yet, anyway. Not until they have a better understanding of what really happened to our people. However, I don't want to keep them locked up in the holding cells indefinitely. We have enough room, so I would like them to be housed in the living quarters. They would remain under guard, but be more comfortable."

"Are you asking us to keep an eye on them for you?" Jevan interrupted.

Aerys shook his head. "No. I have assigned security techs to that task. What would be of more use is taking some time to talk to them. Explain to them everything you have learned so far. You understand your leaders better than I do. You may be better at explaining all this information to them."

Taking a long moment to consider it, Ardyn nodded. "Yes, I think that would be a wise approach. Can Cytra help illustrate certain things when words alone may not be enough?"

"Absolutely," Takyra replied. "In fact, I'll make sure you each have a portable tablet that you can give them as a learning tool. They can use them along with the displays within the quarters to help them comprehend. Cytra is connected to each of them and can guide you."

●●●

Early that afternoon, with tablets in hand, Jevan and Ardyn made their way toward the quarters where they were to meet with their recalcitrant leaders. "Are you ready for this?" Jevan asked.

"No," Ardyn replied with a shake of his head. "But we must try to make them understand. Druyndar will be the most difficult to convince. He's always been the most outspoken against any perceived innovation he saw within our community."

The guards that stood outside of the door greeted them before unlocking it to let them enter. The Elder Triumvirate were pacing while Ard Mathias sat brooding, although he perked up when he saw Jevan.

"Let us out of here!" Aelrynd demanded as soon as she saw Ardyn.

"Not until you understand the truth," Ardyn replied. "Please, sit down. We have much to discuss."

"Not until you feed us," Druyndar insisted. "Starving us serves no purpose!"

Ardyn rolled his eyes. "Didn't they show you how to use the food replicator?" he asked, making his way into the small kitchen, before seeing plates of uneaten food on the counter.

"I will not touch anything cursed by... by... *that!*" Druyndar said indignantly, pointing a finger at the replicator.

"It's perfectly fine food," Ardyn said, picking up a plate and eating a bite to show them. "Just because you don't understand how the technology works, does not make it cursed."

"But the ancestors—" Aelrynd began.

Setting down the plate with a loud *clonk*, Ardyn let his frustration have free rein. "Enough about the *ancestors!* Whatever it is you've read in those ancient tomes of yours were lies!"

"How dare you—" Druyndar tried to interrupt, but Ardyn wasn't finished.

"Sit down and listen for once!" Ardyn yelled, pointing at the seating area where Mathias stared at him, his mouth open in shock. "I am done letting you tell me what I should say or believe."

Jevan stood by the doorway, his arms crossed and looking impressed. Reluctantly, the three elders sat down and glared at him.

"I know you have always believed this was a temple," Ardyn continued. "But think about it. Why would a temple have all these places to sleep? There's room enough to house ten thousand Athla'naa."

"This was the last refuge of our ancestors before they nearly destroyed this world," Druyndar replied. "They had to take refuge underground for generations until the world healed itself. After that, they abandoned all technology, creating the Aria'una to avoid their descendants repeating their folly."

That explains a lot. If Ardyn didn't know the truth, he might have believed that. "That was what you were taught. That is not what happened."

"How would you know what happened?" Taeglyn asked, sounding more curious than condescending.

"Because this ship and its abandoned inhabitants told us," Jevan replied. "We first met Cytra, an *artificial intelligence*, that has been maintaining this ship for all these centuries. She told us about the sleeping Athla'naa in their cryopods. After we woke Takyra, she told us the rest."

"Cytra, can you explain where we are right now?" Ardyn asked, activating her and the display on the far wall.

The elders were startled when Cytra responded. "You are in living quarters number four hundred and twenty-nine, on the primary habitation deck of the Rahn'naa."

Mathias' and Taeglyn's mouths hung open, while Aelrynd looked skeptical and Druyndar seemed furious.

Aelrynd demanded an explanation. "What is going on?"

Turning to face Aelrynd, Cytra responded. "Please clarify."

"Who are you?" Taeglyn asked.

"My name is Cytra," she replied. "I am the Artificial Intelligence programmed to facilitate all operations aboard the Rahn'naa."

Druyndar scoffed. "Can you not see? She is the spirit of an ancestor. She tests our loyalty to honor their ways."

"I am *not* a spirit," Cytra insisted. "Chief Technician Takyra and her team programmed me, and helped me learn, as I integrated into the primary computer of the Rahn'naa before we left the Athla'naa homeworld."

Druyndar made a low growl of frustration. "What is any of that nonsense supposed to mean? The ancient texts of our ancestors are very clear about what happened to them. They did not want us doomed to repeat their errors."

"Then why don't you teach any of that to the rest of us?" Ardyn challenged, his ears flattening back in defiance. "Why is this the first time I've ever heard of this?"

"It is the first commandment in the texts," Aelrynd replied. "Only the Triumvirate must learn the truth. If others learn of it, the curious ones may venture forth to discover the temple and defile it. Which is exactly what you have done!"

RECALCITRANT

Ardyn groaned in frustration. Jevan came over and put a comforting hand on his shoulder before looking at the intractable group sitting before them. "Mathias, how much of all this were you aware of?"

Mathias shook his head. "I wasn't aware of anything. It wasn't until after we went to search for you. That's when they began telling me about this *temple* where their ancient dead lay entombed. When I saw the tower... I'd seen nothing like it before."

"Is that how you got inside the ship? Through the tower?" Jevan asked them.

That piqued Ardyn's interest, and his ears moved forward in curiosity. He realized he hadn't thought about how the hunting party could follow them inside. "Do you also have a key?"

Aelrynd reached within her cloak and pulled out a key identical to the one Ardyn had.

"No wonder you were unsurprised by what we had found in the Aria'una," Ardyn realized. "You have been here before!"

"Yes, of course," Aelrynd admitted, tucking the key away again. "We make an annual pilgrimage to give homage to our ancestors and perform the required rituals."

Ardyn furrowed his brow and narrowed his eyes. "Every cycle of the seasons, when you're supposedly visiting other settlements, you were venturing into the Aria'una? What rituals were you performing?"

All three were silent until Taeglyn dropped his ears and responded. "Within the tower, the texts tell us to pay homage to the dead, and then check the power levels and... to readjust the solar collectors."

"*We must look to the sun for light and warmth as we turn our backs on the evils of technology,*" Druyndar recited.

"Druyndar, you must have suspected the truth, as I did long ago," Taeglyn said, placing a hand on Druyndar's shoulder. "There was only one reason this temple... *ship...*

would require power. Look around you. All this technology is wondrous, as Ardyn said. We should listen."

Druyndar angrily pulled his shoulder away from Taeglyn's hand and stood. "No! Do not let them corrupt you!"

Ardyn stomped his foot in frustration. "You hypocrite! You refuse to listen, yet you willingly used this technology to patrol the perimeter of the Aria'una and track any incursions. You even used it to track Jevan and I all the way here!"

Druyndar's ears fell flat despite remaining otherwise indignant. "That... that was a necessary evil. We had to maintain the sanctity of the temple. It was decreed—"

Not letting him finish, Ardyn pointed out another inconsistency. "Also, since when do we entomb our dead? Our tradition has always been to build a funeral pyre and return our bodies to the dust whence we came, or so you have always recited."

Druyndar folded his arms. "Those entombed here were left as a warning of the evils of technology. They were left to rot within the very thing that destroyed our civilization."

"So, you admit that our ancestors left Takyra's people here to rot," Ardyn said, dumbfounded. "You never once thought to question why you were checking the power levels of this place? You were keeping them alive, in an endless slumber."

With a huff of indignation, Druyndar countered his argument. "Their remains were being preserved. No one can sleep for so many centuries and remain alive!"

Taeglyn interrupted. "That's enough! He's right, we are hypocrites for decrying the use of technology, while knowingly benefiting from using technology ourselves. We should listen to what they are telling us."

"We're not getting anywhere," Ardyn said, sighing in resignation. "Thanks for trying Taeglyn. I'm glad you're seeing the truth."

Turning back to the uneaten plates of cold food, he realized these were all unfamiliar dishes to his elders. "Let me prepare you something more familiar to eat," he suggested. "Then perhaps we can talk again tomorrow."

After removing the plates of food, he picked up the tablet and activated it. "Cytra, could you help me replicate four bowls of a simple meat stew, please?"

"Please state which type of meat you would prefer," Cytra replied.

He looked at Jevan and shrugged his shoulders. "There are small animals that we hunt for food. We call them *paal'dak*."

"Oh yes, jumper stew is one of my favorites," Jevan said. "Cytra, are you able to scan the forest for small creatures that can jump? That's the meat we would recommend."

Cytra activated the external sensors and scanned for the described lifeforms. "*Paal'dak* lifeforms detected," she said. "Please indicate the spices to be used in the stew."

"Please keep the stew simple," Ardyn suggested. "My elders may not enjoy too much spice."

A moment later the replicator hummed and when Ardyn opened it, there stood four bowls of steaming *paal'dak* stew. "This is perfect, Cytra, thank you."

All the while, the elders and Mathias were watching them as they interacted effortlessly with the technology, as if Ardyn and Jevan had been born to it. Ardyn tried not to smirk at them gawking as he and Jevan placed the four bowls onto the table in the sitting area before going back to fetch some water. "Now, I suggest you all eat and keep up your strength," Ardyn said. "Even you Druyndar. This food won't kill you. I promise."

"Oh, and Mathias, you must try the shower," Jevan recommended. "I don't know if I'll ever be able to wash myself without hot water ever again."

The man nodded. "I might do that. I haven't bathed in many cycles of the sun," he said, wrinkling his nose. "Although I don't have any hope for these three."

"I will leave these tablets for you. They contain further information and Cytra can add more if you require. If you need anything, ask for Cytra. She will be far more patient than we are," Ardyn said as they made their way to leave. "We'll be back to check on you tomorrow."

Taeglyn and Mathias thanked them while the others remained silent, Druyndar going so far as to turn his back on them entirely. Ardyn sighed and shook his head as he turned to leave.

"I'm glad that Taeglyn seemed to realize what's really going on," Jevan said as they made their way back toward their own quarters. "I'm not surprised Mathias is also willing to listen. You were right about Druyndar, though."

"I think we need to talk to Takyra and Aerys again," Ardyn said. "Maybe they have some suggestions on how we can convince them to listen."

"Let's do that tomorrow," Jevan agreed. "Right now, I need to eat. That stew looked delicious, and I would love a bowl of that myself!"

Ardyn laughed, looking forward to having some as well. Hopefully, tomorrow would work out better.

REVIVAL

The next morning, Ardyn sat on the couch, nursing a cup of tea and fiddling with the key. It still glowed whenever he touched it, and with a small programming change, it now glowed for Jevan as well.

I can't believe how amazed I was by this. After everything we've found here, it seems so ordinary now. Finishing his tea, Ardyn slipped the key into the pocket of his jacket that hung over the back of a chair and went to take a shower. *It's funny how quickly we've become accustomed to living like this. I wish the elders could appreciate all this the way I do.*

They had been living onboard the Rahn'naa for almost ten cycles of the sun, and Ardyn found he enjoyed the quiet time he had in the mornings, before Jevan woke. As he stepped out of the shower and dried himself with a towel, he couldn't help but smile at the thought of Jevan. *I enjoy these moments to myself, but I find I enjoy being in Jevan's company even more.*

Another smile crossed his face when he saw Jevan in the kitchen getting a glass of water. The look on Jevan's face whenever he saw Ardyn naked was adorable. "Good morning."

Flashing him a bright smile, Jevan gulped some water before asking. "Are you ready for another cycle of the sun of dealing with *them?*"

Rolling his eyes, Ardyn began to dress. "Don't remind me. We still need to talk to Takyra first. I don't know what else we can do to convince Druyndar."

"Yeah, maybe she'll have a better idea of what else we can try," Jevan said, heading toward the shower room. "Can you make more of that stew we had last night? That was great."

After they'd broken their fast, they headed toward the control center, finding Takyra and Aerys busy at their stations.

Takyra swiveled her seat around as they entered. "How did it go yesterday?"

Ardyn gave a sigh of frustration. "About as well as I'd expected. Taeglyn and Mathias seemed willing to listen, while

Aelrynd said little. Druyndar will be the most difficult to convince. He's stubbornly refusing to see the truth, even claiming Cytra was the spirit of an ancestor."

"We need to find another way to convince them that this isn't some old temple holding the remains of their ancestors," Jevan said. "We left the tablets for them, but other than Mathias, I doubt they've touched them."

"I think we can help with that," Takyra said. "Aerys and I have completed our plans to revive those in cryostasis. Perhaps we could have them observe the revival process. That should prove that our cryopods contain living Athla'naa and aren't merely a tomb for those long dead."

Ardyn wasn't convinced. "*Maybe* that will work. At least, we may sway Aelrynd, but I have my doubts about Druyndar. He seems to have an explanation for every point we make."

Aerys stood from his seat. "I'll get some security techs to go fetch them and we can meet them in the revival chamber."

After making their way to the chamber, the security techs brought in the elders and ard. As they shuffled onto the platform, Druyndar was still indignant. "What is the meaning of this? Why do you continue to defile the tomb of our ancestors?"

"This isn't a tomb, and we will prove it to you," Takyra said. "We're here to begin the revival process of the Athla'naa still in cryostasis."

When Druyndar did nothing but harrumph, she turned to Ardyn and Jevan. "Aerys' report confirmed my worst fears. Many of the pods are close to the point of failure and over a dozen have already failed. Those inside died within the last year."

"When the pods fail, why don't those inside wake up?" Jevan asked.

"Cryostasis isn't that simple," Takyra explained, making her way over to the control console, selecting those to revive. "This isn't my area of expertise, but to sustain and prolong life, the cryopods placed each of us into a medically induced coma, while they circulated a specially formulated chemical through our systems. It fixes any cell damage that normally would cause aging. The pods also kept us nourished and cleaned out our bodily waste. When the revival process begins, it must purge this chemical from our system before we're brought out of the induced coma."

Ardyn struggled to imagine what Takyra described, but didn't want to interrupt. *I can ask Cytra later to help me understand.*

Takyra continued as she worked the control console. "By making these selections, I am beginning the first stage of the revival process."

Aerys then stepped forward to explain further. "If the pod fails, then the occupant will not have the chemical cleansed from their bodies or given the necessary medication and stimulus to wake. Eventually, they will die of starvation."

Jevan looked shocked. "That sounds horrible. I'm glad we came along in time, or you could have all died."

A shudder ran through Ardyn as he imagined arriving too late, only finding a tomb of the dead. Then he had a realization. "This is what our ancestors had intended all along... for this place to *become* a tomb. They knew the cryopods would eventually fail, didn't they?"

"This is utter nonsense," Druyndar proclaimed. "This has always been a crypt of the dead. Our ancient texts are very clear on that."

Aerys walked up to Druyndar and stated emphatically. "Your ancient texts are wrong. I lived and worked alongside your ancestors. They betrayed you as surely as they betrayed us by writing those lies."

Takyra put a hand on Aerys' shoulder, while addressing the elders. "That's why we're here, to show you the truth. Cytra, please begin the final stage of the revival process for Amyra."

"Right away, Chief Technician Takyra."

Ardyn watched as the giant arm went to retrieve a cryopod, making the elders behind him gasp. When the pod was in place on the platform, they watched and waited as the revival process completed and the doors of the pod opened. Out stumbled a female Athla'naa, and Takyra rushed over to help her.

"What trickery is this?!" Druyndar demanded when Aelrynd smacked his shoulder.

"Do you not believe what you have witnessed with your own eyes?" Aelrynd reprimanded. "I have been skeptical, but even I cannot deny the truth any longer. That wasn't a dead ancestor within that casket... cryopod. She lives and breathes!"

"Everyone, please meet Amyra, Chief Medical Technician of the Rahn'naa," Takyra introduced before Druyndar could respond to Aelrynd.

"I will not stand here and bear witness to more blasphemy!" Druyndar yelled, before turning and pushing his way past the two security techs behind him. As he approached the doors, they opened automatically, and he fled down the corridor.

The security techs looked at Takyra and Aerys for guidance. "Let him go," Takyra said. "If this wasn't enough to convince him, I'm not sure what else would."

"Do we need to worry about him?" Aerys asked the elders.

"Druyndar is full of bluster, but he is only one voice of the Triumvirate," Taeglyn replied.

The recently revived Amyra looked bewildered. "What *is* going on?"

"Oh, don't get me started," Takyra replied before turning to the elders. "Will you remain with us until we can explain everything to you fully?"

"Yes, I think we must," Aelrynd replied.

"Absolutely," Mathias agreed.

ACCORD

Takyra led them all to the dining hall, while Aerys returned to the control center. "Now that everyone is in accord, let's share a meal," she suggested. "I think our guests can all learn something while I get Amyra up-to-date."

Once they were all situated, Takyra explained what had happened so far. Jevan and Ardyn filled in some details from their perspective, although they glossed over some of what happened, giving the elders and ard spurious glances.

It was when Amyra asked questions that everyone at the table became a little tense. "So, after all these centuries, you thought this was some ancient temple filled with your dead ancestors? Not one of you wondered why part of your rituals included checking on the *power levels?*"

Mathias raised his hands in supplication. "My people are innocent in all this. I knew nothing before we followed Ardyn and Jevan into the Aria'una."

The Athla'naa elders both looked chastised, and Taeglyn spoke up. "I had my doubts," he admitted. "But the ancient texts were very clear, and I did not feel I had cause to doubt them."

Aelrynd let out a frustrated growl. "Admit it, you feared Druyndar. We are both guilty of trying to placate him, lest he revolt and fracture the harmony our people have forged."

"Do you think he is capable of that?" Takyra asked with concern.

"I am not sure," Aelrynd admitted. "Our people should know not to listen to only one member of the Triumvirate. The three of us together are considered the voice of reason among our people. However, Druyndar can be *very* convincing when he wants to be."

"I will make sure my techs remain alert," Aerys said. "They are also working on repairing some damage to the external sensors, so we will be alerted if anyone tries to cause trouble."

Taeglyn lowered his ears and hung his head. "I'm sorry that we've caused so many problems. This should be a joyous occasion, being reunited with your people."

Takyra reached out and gave Taeglyn a comforting pat on his shoulder. "What's past is past. Your generation is not at fault for what your ancestors did. They are the only ones to blame for our internment. They knew we would spend a tortured eternity asleep, dreaming one day to waken."

"You were aware of your slumber, all those cycles of the seasons?" Taeglyn asked, taken aback by Takyra's admission.

"Yes. Your ancestors knew what life was like inside those cryopods because they had been in them for around sixty years themselves."

Ardyn couldn't believe what he was hearing. Takyra hadn't told them what it had been like inside the cryopods, and he couldn't imagine experiencing something that sounded like an unending nightmare.

"We've always believed that technology corrupts," Aelrynd said. "However, it seems corruption can happen, even in the absence of technology."

"We have never lived with anything more advanced than stone tools," Ardyn said. "Everything I have learned here shows me that technology is nothing more than a tool to make tasks easier."

Taeglyn smirked at him. "Even after all the times we tried to beat tradition into you, you never lost that spark of curiosity."

Ardyn couldn't stop the sudden well of anger that bubbled to the surface. "Don't talk to me about your damned traditions," Ardyn spat, springing out of his chair. "Now that I know the truth, I am sickened at how you used me, bred me, and for what? So, we could maintain a stable population when our ancestors forced five thousand of our people to rot?"

Jevan stood next to Ardyn, wrapping an arm around his shoulders as he seethed with anger.

Looking shocked, Amyra turned her gaze to Ardyn. "They *bred* you?"

Feeling his face heat from the shameful memories, Ardyn nodded. "Yes. We are forced to mate when we come of age, and every male must impregnate at least three different females to fulfill our duty to *tradition*."

"We still have more females born than males," Aelrynd argued, as she turned to Takyra. "The ancient texts instructed us to mate in this fashion, to maintain the proper balance of sexes within our population. It's one of our most sacred traditions."

Burying her head in her hands, Takyra screamed in frustration. "That's not what I meant! This should never be something that is forced on anyone. The *Aria'asharra* on board the ship had an unbalanced population, with three times as many females as males. After they woke me, and I understood their intentions, I merely suggested that they shouldn't let their new society become monogamous. Their population was small and was cut off from Aria'naa. They needed to make sure that all the females who wished to bear a child would have the opportunity."

"The coming-of-age ritual is very honored among our people," Taeglyn interjected. "Many of our children look forward to it. Ardyn was unusually reluctant."

"That's because I have no desire to mate with females!" Ardyn shouted. "I told you that over and over, but you refused to listen."

"We were well aware of your preferences," Aelrynd said. "We never forbade you from pursuing male partners for your sexual gratification, but you knew you were required to produce children, for the good of the community."

Standing and pounding a fist on the table, Takyra shouted. "Enough!"

Everyone immediately quieted as all eyes turned toward her. "This is not the way of the Athla'naa. This was never the way of our people, and I am disgusted to hear that you devolved into... *this*."

"Our ancestors must have had their reasons for what they did," Aelrynd tried to argue.

"*Your* ancestors were a small radical faction in our society," Takyra said. "We had achieved peace and prosperity, yet they were still discontent, and they tried to spread their discontent to others."

"If you had achieved such prosperity, why did you have to send so many of our people to live among the stars?" Taeglyn argued.

As Takyra took a moment to regain her composure, Ardyn and Jevan sat back down.

"For many reasons," Takyra replied. "Due to all our advances, we lived longer, healthier lives. Every year more children were born than died. As our burgeoning population grew, we foresaw a time when we would overpopulate Aria'naa and run out of resources entirely."

"Our scientists searched for other planets for us to colonize," Amyra added, joining the conversation. "The aim was two-fold. Sending us into space helped to reduce the population by a fraction. Then, once the colonies were established, they could send resources back to Aria'naa, solving two problems at the same time."

"Many of us jumped at the chance to venture among the stars," Takyra said. "The prospect of living on a new world and building our own civilization excited us."

"So, Aria'naa hadn't suffered from an..." Aelrynd paused, seeming to search for the right words. "From an ecological collapse? Our ancient texts explained that was why they took refuge inside this... this... ship."

"No, Aria'naa hadn't suffered from an ecological collapse," Takyra replied. "Not yet anyway. We recognized that there could be problems in the future if we didn't slow population growth and find new resources to help sustain our existing populations. Colonization was one of many ways we were trying to prevent a potential catastrophe."

"From what you've told us, that was centuries ago," Taeglyn interjected. "How do you know Aria'naa isn't a dead world by now?"

"We'll soon find out," Takyra replied. "I sent a subspace beacon into orbit recently and transmitted a message back to Aria'naa. I'm hoping to hear from them within another day or so."

At that moment, Takyra's tablet chimed. Activating it, Ardyn could hear Aerys. "Takyra, please come to the control center. There's been a response to our message."

MESSAGES

They all looked at Takyra. "Well, that's a surprise. Please, everyone, join me."

As they followed Takyra toward the control center, Aelrynd eagerly kept pace with her. "What's this message?"

"It must be the message I was telling you about," Takyra replied excitedly. "The one I sent to Aria'naa."

Ardyn felt his heart speed up as Takyra's palpable excitement rubbed off.

"Do you know what they've said?" Taeglyn asked.

"Not yet," Takyra replied. "The implications of this will affect all of us, which is why I want you there, so we can find out together."

When they entered the control center, they gathered around the console where Aerys was stationed. "What was the response?" Takyra asked.

"It's brief," Aerys replied before touching one control on the console before him.

"We're coming," said a terse sounding voice.

"We're coming?" Ardyn asked, looking at Takyra. "Does that mean...?"

Takyra was suddenly quiet. Unusually so.

"Takyra? Does it mean they are coming here?" Ardyn completed his question.

"Yes, I think so," she replied hesitantly. "If they are coming here, they're sending a ship."

Jevan looked at Ardyn and then back at Takyra. "A ship? Like the Rahn'naa?"

Nodding, Takyra paced excitedly. "I had hoped to exchange messages. I didn't expect them to send a ship so soon. The reply was so abrupt, I'm not sure what to think."

"How do they know where we are?" Taeglyn asked. "I thought this... this... *ship* crashed on the wrong world?"

"When I sent the message, I included our coordinates based on the star positions, taking into account twelve hundred years of stellar drift," Takyra explained. Seeing the confused looks, she added. "Perhaps Cytra can explain it to you later."

Aerys rose from his seat. "The *Rahn'naa* took over sixty years to reach this world and we don't know if their ships can travel faster now. We could have months or years to prepare for their arrival."

Takyra hummed in agreement. "I will send another message. Hopefully, they can tell us how long they expect it will take them to reach us. In the meantime, we need to move forward with our plans to revive the rest of those still in cryostasis."

"Where will all these Athla'naa live?" Aelrynd asked.

"For the time being, right here," Takyra replied. "We designed this ship to house all ten thousand Athla'naa that had been in cryostasis for our journey. There is plenty of room for those still sleeping. Once they're all revived, we'll need to decide whether to remain on this world."

"Are you saying that your people might leave Aria'nor?" Ardyn asked, his ears lowering at the conflicted feelings that brought forth.

"Not only those of us on the Rahn'naa," Takyra replied. "The Leadership Conclave on Aria'naa may decide for all Athla'naa to depart this world."

This declaration took Ardyn aback.

"Are you suggesting that you would force all Athla'naa, including my people, to leave and return to Aria'naa?" Aelrynd demanded.

"No, I meant we could continue toward our original destination, Maal'dak Five. We were never meant to be on this planet," Takyra said, placing a hand on her shoulder. "Who knows what long-term consequences our people's presence has had on the Medellan people? Either way, this won't be my decision alone to make."

Jevan stepped forward. "What if we choose to let you stay? The Medellan people should get a say in the matter, shouldn't we? I can't imagine this world without your people in it," he said as he wrapped an arm around Ardyn's shoulders.

Trying to give them a comforting smile, Takyra grasped each by a shoulder. "Don't worry about it right now. The matter is hardly decided, and we likely have decades before it becomes an issue."

Mathias crossed his arms with a frown. "Do not leave my people out of this decision. Yes, your people's arrival on our world may have disrupted my people's development, but it may have improved us in other ways we don't know."

"You don't resent how much we've asked your people to restrict your progress?" Aelrynd asked, sounding surprised.

Wait, we also put restrictions on the Medellans?

"So, you admit to *purposely* restricting the Medellans' development?" Takyra asked. "This is exactly what I was saying. Our people have already exacted too much influence on the natural development of this world. This *never* should have happened."

"You want to force all the elves to leave, merely because they may have affected our people's progress?" Mathias asked.

Takyra tilted her head and lowered her ears. "Don't you want to have your world to yourselves?"

Mathias paced in a small circle for a moment before turning back to Takyra. "My people came from across the ocean. This land belonged to the elves—sorry, *Athla'naa*—long before we arrived. We interfered with them as much as they interfered with us. It's why we were at war for over a century and why the peace between us has always been tenuous."

"If your people had arrived and found this land empty, as it should have been, your people's development would have been very different," Takyra argued.

"These people have been here for twelve hundred cycles of the seasons, and we've shared this land with them for eight hundred. They are a part of our culture and history," Mathias reasoned. "We have a say whether all of you must leave."

Rubbing her temples, Takyra nodded. "You may have a point. First, we need to deal with current situations at hand. We don't know yet how soon the ship from Aria'naa will arrive, and we have nearly five thousand people to revive. Besides, we don't know what Druyndar might do. We can discuss our options further once we have a better handle on those situations. Agreed?"

Mathias, Aelrynd, and Taeglyn all nodded. Ardyn breathed a sigh of relief, glad they could all agree on something.

"In the meantime, I would suggest all of you watch some of the historical videos we have on record. It will show you what life on Aria'naa was like around the time we left and explain more about our colonization mission." Aerys said.

Taeglyn seemed genuinely interested in this recommendation. "I would love to learn more about where our ancestors came from."

It had been a couple of cycles of the sun since the cryptic communication from Aria'naa had arrived. Ardyn and Jevan were visiting the control center when an alert came from Takyra's console.

"Oh!" Takyra exclaimed.

Curious, Ardyn peered over her shoulder. "What is it?"

Takyra's hands flew over the console, and she let out a surprised gasp before tapping on the button for the communications system. "Aerys, report to the control center *immediately*."

A few minutes later, Aerys arrived. "What is going on? What was so urgent?"

"We received a response to my second message," Takyra said. "Listen!"

She played it for all of them to hear.

The message from the Rahn'naa has been received and is acknowledged. The people of Aria'naa rejoice in the knowledge of your survival. We will ready a ship and send to your coordinates to assess your current condition. According to our calculations, we should be there in approximately thirty of your days. Please be prepared for our arrival.

This time, the voice sounded more welcoming, much to Ardyn's relief.

Aerys was looking at Takyra with surprise. "They can send a ship that fast now?"

"It took the Rahn'naa over sixty years to travel here, right?" Jevan asked. "How are they able to get here so much faster?"

"We'll have to ask them when they arrive," Aerys replied. "It sounds like our civilization not only survived, but thrived, since we left."

Ardyn felt a thrill of excitement, knowing that in a short time he was going to meet even more advanced

Athla'naa than he already knew. "I wonder what other marvels they've developed since then?" he mused aloud, smiling at Jevan.

"I can't even imagine," Jevan said. "But I'm excited to find out!"

PURPOSE

Those who had already been revived aboard the Rahn'naa were abuzz with excitement. The news that their homeworld was still thriving after all these centuries lifted many of their spirits, despite the circumstances they found themselves in.

At first, it took time for them to adjust to the news of being stranded on the wrong world twelve hundred years in their future. However, with a ship arriving so quickly from Aria'naa, there was the possibility of returning to their homeworld for those who may wish to. It may no longer be the Aria'naa they had left, but for some, it was better than the *primitive backwater planet* they currently found themselves on.

With the state the Rahn'naa was in, it would have taken them decades to excavate her before they could repurpose the various ship components into the colony they had planned to build. Now they hoped that they would have help from Aria'naa to help excavate her and set up their colony, either here or on Maal'dak Five.

It had been a few cycles of the sun since the second message had been received. Ardyn and Jevan were in their quarters breaking their fast, and Jevan frowned as he watched Ardyn pick at his food. "Aren't you hungry?"

With a bored shrug, Ardyn pushed the bowl away and took a sip from his tea instead. "I don't know what we're still doing here. Everyone that's been revived so far has an assigned task on board this ship, and there's not much we can help with."

"Yeah, I know. I'm feeling a bit useless myself, but what options do we have right now?"

"That's the problem," Ardyn admitted. "There's no point ranging around the Rahn'naa. There is no danger of attack from a pack of *sar'ora* or anything else. They don't need anyone to go hunting or gathering for food, and I don't have any other skills to offer."

Nodding, Jevan grabbed their dishes and went to put them away. "I have the same problem. They have no need for me trading goods for them, either."

Just then, their door chimed and Jevan rose to find Takyra outside. "Good morning! May I come in?"

Standing aside, Jevan let Takyra enter. "Did you need us for something?" Jevan asked, as he led Takyra to the living area, where there was more seating. Jevan sat on the couch, inviting Takyra to take a seat in one of the upholstered chairs, while Ardyn sat next to him.

"Actually, yes," Takyra replied. "First, I want to say that I am very impressed by both of you. You've taken everything you've encountered in stride. You both also represent your respective people very well and you have a way with all the newly revived. After meeting you, several have told me it has helped them process what's happened. Because of this, I think you would be an asset for helping us get all the newly revived situated."

Jevan beamed at the idea. After the conversation they'd just had, he knew they'd both appreciate having something useful to do. "I'd love to help. What do you think, Ardyn?"

Ardyn's ears rose eagerly. "What would you like us to do?"

Takyra leaned forward as she explained. "After each group is revived, I would like you both to be there to greet them. We'll revive them in groups of twenty-five. After greeting them, you would take them to the dining hall for a meal, and explain to them what's going on, before leading them to their assigned quarters and handing them their duty assignments."

"Wouldn't it be better if they saw you first?" Jevan asked, recalling Takyra's initial reaction to seeing them the first time.

"I have far too many other things to do, including preparing for the arrival of the ship from Aria'naa," Takyra explained. "I have recorded a short video which will play in the revival chamber after we have revived each group, which hopefully will reassure them."

Putting a hand on Jevan's shoulder, Ardyn replied. "We would be honored to help."

They welcomed the next group of revived Athla'naa that afternoon, after spending the rest of the morning being trained on how to manage each group and how best to inform them of the current situation. Jevan was glad to feel useful, and he used all of his charm to help make each Athla'naa feel relaxed in his presence.

However, after a few missteps with that first group, they quickly realized it was best that Ardyn greet them first, before they introduced Jevan. A few in that first group nearly fainted when confronted by a very tall, dark-skinned alien. Thankfully, Jevan's warm smile and patient demeanor won them over.

Each group had many questions for them, after they were presented with the reality of their situation. Kyael, a member of the medical technicians, was especially curious about the planet they were on. "What is it like outside?"

"You should take a moment to go up to the observation tower when you get a chance," Jevan replied. "This land is covered in dense forests. Especially in the areas that the Athla'naa occupy. My people keep to the lowlands and valleys, where it's easier for us to farm our crops. There is also a large mountain range to the west, where we mine most of the material we craft the metal tools we use."

"That's wonderful that your people and ours have learned to live in such harmony," Kyael said. "We tried to avoid colonizing worlds with sentient species on them because we didn't feel we had the right to interfere with them."

Jevan gave Ardyn a look, who took a deep breath before explaining their history.

Kyael and the others were dismayed to hear of the hostilities between the Medellans and Athla'naa, along with everything that had recently come to light. "Oh, that's disappointing. I guess we were right to want to avoid going to planets like this one. I'm sorry the Aria'asharra forced us to come here and make such a mess of things."

Jevan gave him a sympathetic smile. "It's not your fault, and now that we've found you and contacted Aria'naa, hopefully both our people can come to an accord and move forward peacefully together."

Ardyn gave him a pensive look, and Jevan nodded, saying nothing. *Yes, hopefully everything will continue to develop peacefully.*

DISCORD

Once they had revived over half of the Athla'naa in cryostasis, the Rahn'naa felt a lot less abandoned. Jevan and Ardyn were well known by everyone on board, and were always greeted by friendly smiles as they made their way through the various decks and corridors of the Rahn'naa. It gave them a sense of joy to see so many living and working together in harmony.

They had just gotten another group settled when Takyra summoned them to the control center. "I wonder what's going on now? It's too soon for the ship from Aria'naa to have arrived," Jevan wondered.

As they entered, they were both surprised to see Aelrynd, Taeglyn, and Mathias already there.

"You asked to see us?" Ardyn asked.

Takyra nodded. "We felt you needed to know what's going on. This morning we completed the repairs to our external sensors, and after we brought them back online, we detected a large group of Athla'naa life signs heading toward the Rahn'naa. They are surrounding the forcefield around the observation tower."

"It seems we may have underestimated Druyndar," Aelrynd said with a frown.

"We detected his life signs, so we know he's among them," Aerys confirmed.

"How many are there?" Ardyn asked.

"Between two and three thousand," Aerys said sternly. "We can easily keep them at bay, but it would be unwise for us to have a protracted stand-off."

Ardyn was surprised by that number. "Druyndar must have recruited Athla'naa from all the nearby settlements."

"Do you have a plan?" Jevan asked.

Aerys nodded. "The first thing I did was reprogram the forcefield around the observation tower. It will prevent any life form from getting through. At least that will slow them down."

Takyra looked at the elders. "Now that we have blocked them from gaining entry to the observation tower, and all other points of entry are buried or locked down, how would you recommend we proceed with Druyndar?"

After speaking in hushed tones with each other for a moment, Aelrynd looked at Takyra. "If he's gone this far, then Druyndar will not see reason, but many of our people will. Let us try to appeal to them."

"I'll need to reconfigure the shields before you can go out there," Aerys said. "Currently it can block life forms, but not inorganic projectiles, like the arrows they are armed with."

Ardyn remembered when he and Jevan had tried digging under the forcefield, and Jevan's shovel had easily broken through the barrier. "You can block arrows with the forcefield?"

"Yes, if configured correctly," Aerys replied. "When the ship travels through space, the forcefield has to protect the ship from any potential hazards, including any debris or asteroid fields it may fly through."

"Aerys, summon a security detail to meet us in the observation tower, and then reconfigure the shields," Takyra ordered. "Jevan and Ardyn, please accompany us."

Once they reached the observation tower, they had a rough plan. The Athla'naa elders would be the first to appeal to those gathered, using their full authority as members of the Triumvirate. If their words couldn't sway them, then Mathias and Takyra would join in, hoping to appeal to their better natures.

Through the windows of the tower, they could see the throng gathered around the entire perimeter. They were throwing rocks at it, the air rippling with each impact against the otherwise invisible barrier. Some rocks were getting through, but fewer with each passing moment.

Ardyn stopped and stared at them for a long moment. Jevan placed a hand on his friend's shoulder, knowing that among the attackers were those he considered friends and even family. He hoped they could reason with them, and that this wouldn't end in bloodshed.

A few dozen security techs joined them, one of whom approached Jevan and Ardyn, handing each of them a *rahn'ora*. "Here. Aerys thought you might want to defend your elders."

"Aerys, how are you coming with the forcefield?" Takyra asked through a communicator.

"*I have completed the reconfiguration,*" Aerys replied.

Looking again, Ardyn saw that all the rocks being thrown were now bouncing off the forcefield.

"Wait here for a moment," Takyra said before she made her way into a side room. She came back with several devices, handing one each to Aelrynd, Taeglyn, and offered one to Mathias. "Use these when you speak. They will amplify your voices so all gathered can hear you."

Looking at each other, Aelrynd and Taeglyn nodded. "Thank you. We must try to appeal to our people. This cannot continue," Aelrynd said, her head held high, while gripping the staff of her rank as the leader of the Triumvirate in her hand.

"Alright, let's get this over with," Takyra said, leading the group outside. They remained on the metal platform outside the tower, while their attackers were held back by the forcefield at the tree line.

The cacophony of voices as they emerged from the tower rose in volume, with words like *traitors* and *defilers* being hurled at them. As they approached, the Athla'naa who saw them momentarily halted their efforts.

"Athla'naa! Lay down your arms and hear us! Druyndar has misled you," Aelrynd addressed the gathered force, speaking into the device she was given. Her voice boomed through the valley from loudspeakers on the tower. "Despite what Druyndar may have told you, this tower behind me is not an ancient temple honoring our ancestral dead. It is a ship that brought our people to this world from across the stars!"

Aelrynd paused as a hush fell over the crowd.

"Those we thought entombed here are very much alive. They have shown us the truth of where we came from. The truth of why we are on a world where we do not belong. Our ancestors betrayed us all."

Taeglyn stepped forward. "Our ancestors left nearly five thousand Athla'naa for dead inside of this ship. Look at them!" He pointed at the gathering of security techs behind him. "They are our kin. They did not deserve to be abandoned."

Druyndar emerged from the crowd and began screaming. "Do not listen to these traitors. The evil technology within that tower has brainwashed them! I have seen it with my own eyes. It's unnatural and should never have existed! Athla'naa, continue your assault!"

Doubt clouded the faces of those who could hear Druyndar's words. The rest looked at Aelrynd and Taeglyn in confusion.

Aelrynd continued. "You have always relied upon your Triumvirate for guidance. We may be divided, but I assure you, it is Druyndar who is the *traitor* here. He refuses to listen to reason or hear the truth. His personal fear of technology clouds his judgment. Elder Taeglyn and I had our doubts, but they have opened our eyes. We are still your Elders. Put down your arms and listen!"

Jevan saw some step away from the barrier and lay down the spear or bow they held. *Is it working?* He hoped. *Maybe we can end this peacefully.*

After a pause, Aelrynd pressed on. "Our ancestors left Aria'naa looking to build a better life on a new world. This land, that we named Aria'nor, was not the world our ancestors had intended to colonize. A traitorous faction arose and crashed this ship into this planet instead, not realizing that the Medellans existed here on the far continent. This world belongs to the Medellans."

A discontented murmur arose from the crowd.

"Lies!" Druyndar shouted again. "There was never another world. Before our ancestors nearly destroyed this one with their vile technology, they built this temple as a refuge for the last of our kind. They remained within for centuries until the land had healed itself. That is when our ancestors emerged and deemed this part of Aria'nor to be forbidden, so our people would never again destroy this land!"

The crowd around Druyndar became agitated again. Several of those who had laid down their weapons picked them up, and Jevan had a sinking feeling that this was far from over.

ATTACK

akyra stepped forward. "My name is Takyra. You do not know me, but I am the Chief Technician of the Rahn'naa. That is the name of the ship that carried our people across the stars. Your ancestors betrayed our people twelve hundred years ago and left us to slumber between life and death. That is the truth!"

The gathered crowd murmured while Druyndar seethed. "More lies! Do not listen to this traitor!"

"I assure you, I am no traitor," Takyra continued, looking directly at Druyndar. "Your ancestors betrayed us—"

Before Takyra could continue, Jevan heard a strange sound in the distance and saw several of the Athla'naa outside the forcefield look up and point at the sky. Turning around, he saw a strange object flying through the mountain pass behind the tower. "Takyra, look!"

They all turned to see, and Takyra immediately turned on her communicator. "Aerys! There's an aircraft approaching from the northeast. Are you picking it up on external sensors?"

"*Yes,*" Aerys replied before a brief pause. "*Scans of the primitive craft show it's nearly out of fuel and will need to land.*"

"Have you tried to communicate with them?" Takyra asked.

"*Yes, but there has been no response.*"

Turning back to the crowd, Takyra cried out. "Athla'naa! Please, I beg you, lay down your arms. We need to lower the forcefield for the approaching aircraft. Please, do not attack!"

"Do you know who is approaching?" Jevan asked.

"No," Takyra replied. "You said there were other Medellans on the far continent? They may have come from there. Either way, we cannot let them die. Security techs, set your *rahn'ora* to stun and prepare to defend us as they lower the forcefield!"

Jevan watched the aircraft as it flew closer and security techs surrounded them, drawing their weapons. Once they were in place, Takyra spoke into her communicator again. "Aerys, lower the forcefield so they can land safely!"

The aircraft circled around the tower and made its approach, coming in low towards their left. It came in for a landing on the strip of meadow between them and where the forcefield had held back the gathered Athla'naa. As it touched down, it sped past them, slowing and coming to a stop on the uphill rise to the right of the observation tower.

They were about to run toward the craft to greet the newcomers when Jevan heard a roar as the attacking force of Athla'naa was being riled up by Druyndar again. At first, Jevan expected the forces to come at them in a rush, but in the distance, they could hear Druyndar caution them. "Stay back! It's more of their insidious technology. They have corrupted the very air. Archers, attack!"

"No!" Ardyn cried out, even as he pulled out his *rahn'ora*, stepping in front of his elders to protect them.

Jevan followed suit, pulling out his weapon and standing next to Ardyn while pushing Mathias behind him. A volley of arrows rained down and the security techs that stood in front of them took the brunt of the attack, a half dozen falling, wounded or dead.

"Those blasted..." Takyra muttered in frustration before shouting. "Activate your personal shields!"

Once activated, the next volley of arrows bounced off them, and the security techs fired at the arrows, disintegrating them. "Get into tiered formation," Takyra ordered. "Bottom tier, stun the archers. Top tier, widen your beams and stop those arrows!"

The rest of the group drew back to a safer distance, while the security techs changed formation. Some focused their fire entirely on the arrows, with a wider, more deadly beam. The others had their *rahn'ora* set to stun, firing at their attackers. One by one the Athla'naa fell, as they were stunned unconscious. This seemed to anger their attackers, as they did not understand that their friends and neighbors were not being killed.

Another group of security techs poured out of the tower behind them, spreading out and taking a similar formation to the ones already protecting them. As the attackers fell in greater numbers, Aelrynd tried once again to make them listen, to no avail. "Athla'naa! Please cease this pointless attack. These weapons are not killing anyone. Those who have fallen are merely unconscious. Check for yourselves!"

"Your weapons are the only ones causing harm," Taeglyn said, pointing to the techs who had fallen. "You have killed several of our kin."

Jevan saw a few Athla'naa stop their attacks and kneel to check those stunned around them, but too many were attacking in a frenzied rage. "Should we take cover inside the tower?" he asked Takyra.

"Bring your elders to safety. I can't leave those in the aircraft out here to fend for themselves," Takyra replied. "This stand-off has to end."

"No, we will stand with you," Aelrynd insisted. Taeglyn and Mathias nodded in agreement.

With a shrug, Jevan turned back to the fight. They did their best to shield Aelrynd, Taeglyn, and Mathias. Occasionally, an arrow whizzed past their heads, far too close for comfort. Then Jevan saw one coming straight for Ardyn. He pushed his friend to one side, just as the arrow narrowly grazed Ardyn's arm, slicing through his skin. Ardyn cried out but kept firing his weapon, trying to knock out as many of their attackers as he could.

"Are you alright?" Jevan asked.

Ardyn nodded and gave Jevan a thankful smile before turning his attention back to the battle. Jevan tried not to worry as he saw purple blood soak Ardyn's sleeve.

"Try to target Druyndar," Takyra ordered. "Once he falls, it may be easier to convince the rest to cease this madness."

Unfortunately, once the Athla'naa around Druyndar saw what the *rahn'ora* could do, they surrounded their leader to protect him. However, the security techs had the upper hand, as they felled many of the attackers.

When a lull in the battle happened, Aelrynd once again pled with her people. "Please, you must stop this madness. Can you not see that their technology is superior? They could have killed you all by now, but they have not. Look at those felled at the start of the battle! They are already beginning to revive. We need to end this conflict before more are hurt. You cannot possibly breach their defenses, so please lay down your arms!"

Many of them hesitated, already weary of the battle, and likely realizing that Aelrynd was right. Their people had not engaged in any protracted battles since the treaty seven hundred cycles of the seasons earlier. Some threw down their bows and spears, refusing to continue the onslaught against their own people.

Eventually, only a few dozen Athla'naa that surrounded Druyndar were still following his orders. The rest had opted to toss aside their weapons, and either sat down or tended to the fallen around them.

Druyndar seemed to realize he was defeated and called for a retreat. When Takyra saw this, she ordered the security techs forward. "Take out Druyndar and any of those who remain loyal to him. We cannot let them get away and bring back reinforcements from other settlements."

The security techs ran after the retreating Athla'naa, stunning them as fast as they could.

"Thank you for ceasing the attack," Takyra addressed those who had put down their weapons. "Let us take some time to treat our wounded, and then we need to talk."

Putting away her amplifier, she called Aerys. "Bring a team of medical techs up here to treat the stunned and wounded."

Then Takyra turned to face the aircraft that sat at the far end of the meadow. "While the medical techs make their way up here, let's go see who our new arrivals are."

VISITORS

As they walked toward the aircraft, Jevan took the time to study it. It was unlike anything he'd ever seen before. The craft was small, with only room for two. It had two sets of wings, parallel to each other. One crossed perpendicular over the top of the craft, and the other underneath. The entire thing sat on two wheels, keeping it angled up toward the sky, as if it were ready to leap back into the air at any moment.

Two male figures stood next to the craft. One looked like he was taller than Jevan, and the other slightly shorter. The taller one had a warm brown tone to his skin, slightly lighter than Jevan, and he wore his light brown hair shoulder length. The shorter man's skin was much lighter, nearly as pale as an Athla'naa. His dark brown hair, beard, and eyes were striking against his pale skin.

As the group approached, the two men looked at them warily. That was unsurprising, as the pair had been forced to land in the middle of a battle.

"They look Medellan," Mathias said. "Jevan and I should greet them first."

"Agreed," Takyra said, halting for a moment and holding out two small earpieces. "Jevan, when you greet them, give them these."

"Good idea," Jevan said, taking them from her. "I'd almost forgotten that we speak different languages."

As they approached them, Jevan and Mathias moved ahead of the small group. Mathias held out his hand as he was about to greet them when the shorter one stepped forward.

"What in the blue blazes is going on around here?" he asked, taking Mathias aback. "If we had known we were flying into the middle of a war, we wouldn't have bothered to come all this way."

"My apologies," Mathias said. "You have come at an awkward time, but thank you for disrupting their attack. I am Ard Mathias of the village of Yanen, and this is Jevan."

"I'm Tomas," the taller man replied in greeting. "My grumpy friend here is Aron."

"Nice to meet you, Tomas and Aron," Jevan greeted, also shaking the men's hands before holding out the small translators. "I'm sorry you didn't arrive under better circumstances. Could you do us a favor and put these into your ears, please?"

The two of them looked at each other and shrugged as they each took an earpiece. "What are they for?"

"They will help translate the Athla'naa language," Jevan explained. "Most of my purple-haired friends here do not speak the Medellan language yet."

"You mean those *elves*? What... who are they?" Tomas asked as he placed the earpiece into his ear.

Jevan chuckled and gave Ardyn a little reassuring wink before responding. "Yeah, my people call them *elves*, too. Well, I used to, but they call themselves Athla'naa. Our ancestors encountered them when they first arrived on Vestos."

The two men looked up at the tower and back at the Athla'naa. "So, these... Ath... laa... naa? They were here before your ancestors arrived?" Aron asked. "Did they build that tower?"

"Yes, and..." Mathias struggled to find the words.

"It's complicated," Jevan said, not even knowing where to begin.

"Welcome," Takyra greeted after they had put the earpieces in. "Thank you for agreeing to wear the translators. As you saw when you approached, we've been a little preoccupied with a local dispute. My people haven't had time to learn your people's language yet. I'm Takyra, the Chief Technician of the Rahn'naa."

"You're the chief of the dawn?" Aron asked with a scowl, after he heard the translation.

Jevan laughed. "I had the same reaction when I heard that. *The Dawn* is the name of their spaceship that crashed here a long time ago. That is the observation tower of the ship. The rest of the ship remains buried underground."

"That tower as tall as our tallest skyscrapers," Aron said. "If that's only part of the ship, how big is it?"

"The Rahn'naa originally housed ten thousand of my people, when it crashed here twelve hundred cycles of the seasons ago," Takyra explained, using terminology they would understand.

"*Twelve hundred* cycles of the seasons, and your people came from *space*? Well, that explains a lot," Tomas said. "We were sent to investigate after our radar detected something being launched into space from here."

"What you saw was a subspace beacon," Takyra explained. "I apologize if that caused your people concern. We did not know that your people had technology advanced enough to detect it."

"It caused quite a stir," Tomas admitted, turning to Mathias. "It's been centuries since your ancestors left, and we weren't sure they survived."

"Well, we survived just fine," Mathias said with a scowl. "No thanks to your ancestors, I might add."

Aron crossed his arms across his chest defensively. "Well, your ancestors brought it upon themselves—"

"We don't have time for this now," Takyra interrupted. "My apologies, but we just fended off an attack and we need to look after our wounded. You're welcome to make yourselves at home and we'll take time later to sit down and discuss everything."

"I will escort them to the ship," Mathias offered. "I'm not much use out here right now, anyway. Jevan, will you join us?"

The two men grabbed some packs from their craft, and they all began walking back toward the tower.

"I can help them get settled into quarters near you," Jevan offered. "But I don't want to leave Ardyn alone for too long."

Ardyn came over to him and put a hand on his arm. "I'll be okay. You take care of your guests."

"What about our aircraft?" Tomas asked. "Will it be safe here?"

"We had to take down our forcefield when you came in for your landing," Takyra said. "You couldn't have known it was there, and we didn't want you to crash, but we will put it back up once we've finished tending to all the wounded. I'll make sure we extend the forcefield around your craft."

"A forcefield? I know I've heard our science-types talk about such things, but I don't think we've figured out how to create one of those yet," Tomas said, sounding impressed. "Thank you, I'll rest easier knowing the craft will be safe."

"Why did you nearly run out of fuel?" Takyra wondered aloud. "Were you not expecting to make a return flight?"

"We *thought* we had enough fuel," Tomas replied. "It seems the old maps had the distance between Ateria and Vestos dead wrong."

"So, we're going to be stuck here indefinitely," Aron groused.

"Let my engineers look at your aircraft. I bet we can upgrade your fuel system into something more efficient that can get you both home," Takyra offered.

"That would be much appreciated, ma'am," Tomas said gratefully.

As they approached the tower, Jevan joined Mathias and led the two men inside the tower. He turned back for a moment to watch Ardyn following Takyra, as they made their way toward the injured that still lay scattered.

Jevan pushed away a small knot of worry for his friend as he hurried after the others into the tower. *Please, stay safe.*

AFTERMATH

The rest of the group walked back to where Druyndar had made his last stand. Aerys and the medical techs were already moving through the wounded and stunned. They stabilized the more heavily wounded and sent them below to the medical bay to be treated before moving on to treat those with minor injuries.

When they approached Aerys, he turned to them with a grim look. "We found Druyndar. I'm sorry to report that he's dead."

"What? No!" Ardyn shouted.

Ardyn's heart lept into his throat, his eyes scanning until he saw the body of his fallen elder. He ran toward Druyndar, dropping to his knees next to his still form. Druyndar's eyes remained open, staring lifelessly at the sky.

Looking up at Takyra with tears streaming down his pale face, Ardyn shouted. "I thought you said the *rahn'ora* couldn't kill on the stun setting! Why is Druyndar dead!?"

"I am so sorry, Ardyn." Takyra looked equally horrified as she glanced between Ardyn and the two remaining elders. "The techs should have had all their weapons set to stun. Let's get him down to the medical bay so we can figure out what happened."

Two security techs came over with a stretcher, gently placing Druyndar's lifeless form on it, before carrying him away into the tower with Aerys accompanying them. Takyra tried to reach out and comfort Ardyn, but he shrugged away and ran toward the tower, with more hot tears streaming down his face.

When Ardyn ran into the tower, instead of taking the elevator with Druyndar's remains down into the ship, he sprinted up the stairs to the next level. There, he found a corner of the platform that overlooked the valley through the large windows. Sliding to his knees, Ardyn sagged onto the floor.

As much as he had butted heads with the Triumvirate over the seasons, especially with Elder Druyndar, Ardyn had never wished for their deaths. Seeing him lay there, with his lifeless eyes staring into nothing, haunted him. *This is all my fault. If I hadn't found that damned key...*

It took Ardyn some time to calm himself. When he heard people moving on the level below, he looked over the landing to see Aerys and his two security techs return, along with Jevan. "This is most unfortunate," Aerys said. "While Amyra does a full analysis on Druyndar, have every *rahn'ora* inspected for possible failures."

"Yes, sir," said the tech, sprinting ahead.

"I should go find Ardyn," Jevan told Aerys, before he turned and left the tower.

Taking a deep breath, Ardyn composed himself and followed Jevan outside, looking to see where his tall friend had gone. When he found Jevan, Ardyn approached and gave his friend a sheepish smile.

"Hey, are you okay?" Jevan asked.

"No," Ardyn admitted, letting Jevan wrap an arm around his shoulders.

The two stayed back, watching in silence while the techs made their way through all the stunned and wounded. Once they tended to everyone, Aerys approached Takyra. "We have fourteen dead. Druyndar was the only casualty on their side. The rest were our people. *Ior'kah,* what a mess!"

"It's not your fault," Takyra said. "Those shields had to come down or our two new Medellan friends would have needlessly died."

"You're right," Aerys agreed. "It was the right call. I just wish we could have made the other side see reason and prevented this tragedy."

"As do I," Takyra said.

As the techs carefully laid out the dead next to each other, Ardyn watched in shock. Jevan let go of his hand and wrapped an arm around his shoulders, careful of Ardyn's injury. "I'm sorry about Druyndar. It shouldn't have come to this."

Leaning against Jevan, Ardyn didn't know what to do. He ached to scream or cry or... *anything.* All these pointless deaths, and for what? While losing Druyndar had come as a shock, it hit Ardyn even harder to see some of his newfound friends lying dead after having just escaped from a millennium-long slumber. It all felt so senseless.

Jevan squeezed him gently. "Let's go down to the medical bay and get that wound looked at. Maybe they'll know more about what happened to Druyndar by now."

Nodding, Ardyn allowed Jevan to lead him back down into the ship. As they neared the medical bay, there was a flurry of activity in the corridor as the other wounded were still being helped into the bay, which only had eight active beds. Those with less serious injuries had lined up along the corridor and were waiting their turn.

While the Rahn'naa had a full hospital wing on board, it wasn't operational yet. They hadn't expected needing it before Druyndar's forces arrived, and there wasn't enough time to bring the wing online now. So, Amyra had to make do with the smaller medical bay.

Jevan tried to guide Ardyn past the crowd, but Ardyn held back and led Jevan toward the end of the line. "My wound is not that bad. I can wait."

A few of the techs had severe injuries, so it took some time for everyone to get treated and then sent back to their quarters with orders to rest. Meanwhile, Takyra and Aerys passed by them, most likely to check in with Amyra on the status of the wounded. When Ardyn and Jevan finally made it into the medical bay, they found them still speaking to Amyra.

"I'm sorry to make you wait," Amyra apologized.

"I'll be fine. The wound isn't serious," Ardyn insisted. "Do you have news regarding Druyndar?"

"Yes. We've summoned Aelrynd and Taeglyn to inform them. Let's get your injury taken care of while we wait," Amyra suggested.

Ardyn hopped up onto an unoccupied exam bed and Amyra carefully cut away the sleeve around his wound. While it was only a flesh wound, it looked worse than it felt.

Amyra cleaned the area around the wound with something that looked like water but stung, making Ardyn hiss. "I'm sorry. I should have warned you. This removes bacteria from the wound before I close it up."

Close it? Ardyn wondered to himself while Amyra went to fetch a small device. As she held the device over his injury, it emitted a light that she moved slowly over the wound. The light caused a warm, tingling sensation under his skin. Ardyn watched in amazement as the flesh around his wound slowly knit back together. A moment later, his skin looked unmarred.

"That's amazing!" Ardyn exclaimed as he ran his finger over the smooth skin where his wound had been.

Just then, Aelrynd and Taeglyn joined them and Amyra led them to the bed where Druyndar's body lay covered with a thin sheet. "I ran several scans of his body; I can confidently report that Druyndar died from heart failure. He had been under severe levels of stress, and I believe even before he was stunned with the *rahn'ora*, that his heart was on the verge of failure. Being stunned merely sped up the inevitable."

While it still saddened him that Druyndar had died for his misguided cause, Ardyn was relieved to know that whoever had stunned him hadn't been personally responsible for his death. There was enough animosity without having someone to blame.

That's when Ardyn remembered the reason behind this idiotic conflict in the first place. His people's hatred and fear of technology. Turning to his two remaining elders, Ardyn couldn't hold back. "Do you see now? They ended this conflict without deliberately killing our people. Our primitive technology did far more harm! This advanced technology is not *more dangerous* as you have always claimed!"

"You're right. This incident has given us much to think about," Aelrynd agreed. "However, first we should honor the dead and perform the funeral rites. Will you allow us to assist in the rites, Takyra?"

"Yes, of course," Takyra replied. "One of your own is also dead. Regardless of the circumstances, let us come together so our people can heal the rift between us."

FUNERAL

When Jevan woke the morning after the attack, he found Ardyn sitting at the foot of the bed, staring listlessly. "Hey, how long have you been sitting there?"

All Ardyn did was shake his head and shrug.

Jevan scooted down to sit behind him, wrapping his friend in an embrace. "Yesterday was awful, but it's behind us now."

Ardyn turned and buried his head in Jevan's shoulder. "I know. I just wish I didn't feel so damned helpless."

"Takyra said everyone would work on preparations for the funeral rites. Why don't we go up and see what we can do to help?" Jevan suggested.

After taking a deep breath, Ardyn straightened and gave Jevan a nod. "That's a good idea."

They dressed and ate a quick meal before heading up to the observation tower. As they made their way outside, they found Takyra and Aelrynd coordinating the efforts near where some people had begun preparing the bodies of the fallen. He stopped in his tracks when he realized there were more bodies than there had been before. Ardyn tensed beside him when he noticed the same.

"What happened?" Jevan asked as they approached. "Did more die last night? Was there another attack?"

"Oh, no! Nothing like that," Takyra reassured them. "Aelrynd agreed include those who died in their cryopods in the funeral rites."

"Thank goodness," Ardyn said with obvious relief. "I don't think I could take any more bad news right now."

Takyra gave Ardyn's shoulder a comforting squeeze. "Aelrynd and I spoke at length last night about these rites. I was pleasantly surprised to see how little has changed, other than the technology used. We agreed, since most of the dead are out here, to use your people's way of burning the remains. Otherwise, we could have held the rites within the Rahn'naa where we have a more advanced way of sending those who passed to the ancestors."

"How can we help?" Jevan asked.

"Ardyn, you're familiar with preparing the dead," Aelrynd said. "Why don't you help them?"

Those who were already working on preparing the bodies were wrapping them carefully in shrouds of cloth. Ardyn nodded. "Yes, I can do that."

Jevan was about to volunteer to help as well when Takyra suggested another task. "Taeglyn is working with Druyndar's followers to gather the wood needed for the pyre. There are so many dead, so we are building one large pyre. They could use someone tall and strong, such as yourself."

Spotting Taeglyn in the distance, Jevan gave Takyra a small nod. "Okay, I'll see what I can do. Ardyn, will you be alright without me?"

"Go and help Taeglyn," Ardyn insisted. "I'll be fine."

They busied themselves with their tasks, while Athla'naa from the ship would occasionally bring them water and food so they could keep working. It took until nightfall before the pyre was complete and all the dead were laid upon it.

The pyre was built within the forcefield, so it was safe from animal attacks, but they still posted a security detail around the pyre overnight. The funeral rites were planned for the following evening, giving everyone time to get some rest.

That night, Jevan groaned as he climbed into bed. Spending most of the cycle of the sun chopping down trees and carrying logs for the pyre had left his entire body aching. It's when Ardyn didn't tease him for sounding like an old man that Jevan realized his friend was being quieter than usual.

"How are you doing?" Jevan asked, turning to Ardyn, who lay there with his back toward him.

Ardyn gave him a non-committal shrug.

"Today was difficult," Jevan surmised, remembering Ardyn's grim task.

Turning over onto his back, Jevan saw Ardyn's face was wet with tears. "I... I've seen death before, but it's never affected me this deeply."

"Those you've seen die before. What manner of deaths were they?" Jevan asked, hoping that talking about it would help ease Ardyn's mind.

Sitting up, the Athla'naa wiped his face on his sleeve. "Mostly old age or illness. One from an accident falling from a worn ladder. A few who died from *sar'ora* attacks."

"These deaths were different," Jevan pointed out. "A result of senseless violence. It's not something your people are familiar with, are they?"

Shaking his head, Ardyn leaned against Jevan. "Not since our truce with your people, which was so long ago, there is no one alive who remembers what living through that was like."

Jevan wrapped an arm around Ardyn. "Do you remember that story I told you, of the young man who forced himself upon a pair-bonded woman, causing her death?"

Ardyn nodded.

"It doesn't happen often, but unfortunately, sometimes Medellans will commit murder, or worse."

"Like what those men threatened to do to me if I continued my lessons with Soren," Ardyn recalled, a shudder running through his body. "Why would anyone ever do that to another?"

"I don't know. I never understood it, either," Jevan admitted. "How can anyone ever be angry enough to want to bring harm to someone or end their life?"

Jevan leaned back against the pillows, pulling Ardyn with him. "Let's try to get some rest. Tomorrow will be another long cycle of the sun."

◆ ◆ ◆

The next morning, Jevan and Ardyn helped Takyra and the elders coordinate the funeral rites. Takyra and Aerys worked to set up a system from within the Rahn'naa that would broadcast the rites to everyone on board, as there were too many of them to gather outside. Especially with so many from Maala'naa and surrounding settlements still camped around the observation tower.

Mathias had kept Tomas and Aron out of the way, spending most of his time bringing the two up-to-speed on his people's history since they arrived on Vestos. Jevan checked in with Mathias during the afternoon and also relayed an invitation from Takyra to observe their funeral rites.

"I'll be there," Mathias agreed. "I may not have known Druyndar well, but I wish to pay my respects."

Tomas and Aron had looked at each other and a look had crossed Aron's face that Jevan didn't understand. In the end, they declined the invitation. "We've only just arrived, and we don't want to interfere," Tomas said. "Please, send our regards. I think you said we could observe it from here?"

"Yes, that's right," Jevan said, moving toward the display monitor in the sitting area. "You can activate the display by touching the screen or ask Cytra. Takyra said she will broadcast it to everyone, so that's all you need to do."

"I've also shown them how the food replicators work," Mathias said. "So, they'll be fine. You said the rites will begin at sundown?"

"Yes," Jevan confirmed, turning to leave. "I'll see you there."

Near sundown, Jevan and Ardyn met Mathias in the elevator on the way to the observation tower, and they walked together toward the gathering crowd. Ardyn went to take his requested place next to Taeglyn, while Mathias and Jevan hung back a respectful distance.

Aelrynd and Takyra led the funeral rites together. All in attendance around the pyre held hands and sang an ancient dirge as Aelrynd and Takyra took torches and lit the pyre from either end. Then together they recited an invocation.

"We gather here to remember those we have lost. They were our family and our friends. We shall grieve and mourn their loss in the days to come. May they never be forgotten."

The rites continued as they sang more chants of mourning and remembrance. Afterward, those who knew the deceased recalled their favorite memories of them. Aelrynd and Taeglyn spoke for Druyndar, recalling some stories of him from their youth.

Despite the circumstances, it made Jevan's heart glad to see how everyone had come together at this moment. He hoped that would help ease Ardyn's troubled mind, especially with so much uncertainty about what might lie ahead for them.

WAKE

After the funeral, Takyra invited Ardyn to join a private gathering. The revived crew organized similar gatherings throughout the Rahn'naa, each hosted by the friends and family of those who died. There had been discussions of a larger gathering in the dining hall, but the Athla'naa people preferred to mourn in smaller, more intimate groups.

After stopping in their quarters to freshen up, Ardyn asked Jevan to join him. Jevan had been there through everything with him, and Ardyn didn't feel right leaving him out. "I know you're probably eager to talk to Tomas and Aron, but I'd love for you to be there. Please?"

Jevan smiled warmly at him. "Of course, I'll join you. Takyra also invited Mathias. Tomas and Aron can wait. After everything that's happened, I'm sure they'll understand."

When they arrived, Mathias was already there, along with Takyra, Aerys, Aelrynd, and Taeglyn. Takyra greeted them and gave them each a glass of *wah'roh*.

"Be careful, Jevan," Mathias warned. "That stuff packs a punch!"

"Oh, I know! This isn't my first time drinking *wah'roh*. It reminds me of the whiskey they make down in Tafaran," Jevan said, taking a long sip of his. "Oh, wow. This is much smoother than the kind I've tried before!"

Ardyn took a sip. Instead of the strong burn that usually hit his tongue when he drank *wah'roh*, this gave his mouth a pleasant warmth, along with a burst of subtle fruity flavor. "This is delicious!" Ardyn said as he took another enthusiastic sip.

"This is only a replicated version," Takyra said, "but it's close to what we had back on Aria'naa. Our process for making it is probably more refined than yours and made from the native fruits growing on our homeworld. I would love to taste your version of *wah'roh* some time."

"You must come and visit Maala'naa," Aelrynd insisted. "Our people need to put aside our differences and get to know each other again. Especially if we are to coexist."

"Once things settle down here, I would love to come and visit," Takyra said.

"While we're on the subject, I think it's time for Taeglyn and I to return home," Aelrynd announced. "We need to lead our people back to Maala'naa and begin the process of selecting a new elder to join the Triumvirate before we reevaluate our outdated laws and traditions."

That surprised Ardyn. He expected his elders to become more tolerant, but to be open to changing their traditions was not something he'd anticipated.

Mathias hummed in agreement as he took a sip of his *wah'roh*. "I should return home soon myself, but there is much to discuss with our visitors first."

"Why not invite them to visit Yanen with you?" Jevan suggested.

"I did, but they didn't want to travel so far from their aircraft."

"We would love to know more about them, but we need to get our people home," Aelrynd said. "Ardyn, will you represent our people? You have proven to us you have a good head on your shoulders, and I believe your innate curiosity would be an asset here. You can report back to us anything you learn that may affect our people."

A complicated mix of emotions rose in Ardyn. He'd gone from being a pariah and practically an outcast and now he was being asked to represent his people. Ardyn wasn't sure how to feel about that. Still, he hadn't been planning to return to Maala'naa, so he was happy to be given a purpose.

"I would be honored," Ardyn replied. "Thank you for your vote of confidence in me."

Takyra stepped away for a moment, returning with some devices.

"These are long-distance communicators. Please take them, so we can keep you informed of what is happening here." Takyra handed each elder a device. "Will you return when the ship from Aria'naa arrives?"

"At least one of us will, yes," Aelrynd replied. "Whoever we select to join the Triumvirate will require training."

"Aren't there already those who have been training to become members of the Triumvirate?" Jevan asked.

"There are," Taeglyn replied. "However, considering recent events, we're deliberating over a few others. Our old ways need to be reconsidered, and so our Triumvirate should reflect that."

"In fact," Aelrynd said, looking at Ardyn. "We are seriously considering your father for the position."

Ardyn's eyes widened at that news. "But he's always been like me, considered too curious for his own good."

"Exactly why we're considering him," Taeglyn said. "It was your curiosity that led you to find Takyra and her people. Your discovery saved thousands of lives, and you have opened our eyes to so many truths that we were blind to. We could use that kind of thinking in our leadership as we enter a new era of enlightenment."

Ardyn knocked back the rest of his *wah'roh* and went to sit down. *How can they brush off everything that's happened so easily? How can there be a new era of enlightenment when so many have died?*

"Are you alright?" Jevan asked, sitting next to him.

"I... I don't know," Ardyn admitted. "I've been blaming myself for those senseless deaths. If I hadn't been so curious or found that cursed key, those Athla'naa would still be alive."

"Not all of them," Takyra said, walking over. "A dozen of those we mourned today had already died. More would have, if you hadn't found us."

"I know, but it still feels wrong to be praised for something that led to all that senseless violence—"

"Ardyn, you are not responsible for the actions of others," Taeglyn interjected. "They presented us with indisputable facts, and Druyndar willfully ignored them. Instead, he spread more lies to our people. They chose to believe a single member of the Triumvirate, and so their actions will not be without consequences."

Looking up at his elder, Ardyn cocked his head and flattened his ears in curiosity. "How?"

"I recorded the entire battle," Aerys replied. "We can identify every Athla'naa who struck a deadly blow."

"We are working with Takyra and Aerys to determine a just punishment," Aelrynd said. "This cannot bring back the dead, but we will hold accountable those responsible."

An unexpected sense of relief came over Ardyn. "That's... good to know. What will you do with them?"

"I have a few ideas," Takyra said. "But I don't want to decide anything until the ship from Aria'naa arrives. There are too many unknowns for me to make any long-term plans, but it will probably include them working with us on the Rahn'naa."

"How would that hold them accountable?" Ardyn wondered, frowning at his elders. "Whenever they punished me, it usually involved pain."

Takyra gave Aelrynd and Taeglyn a withering look before responding. "If they come and work alongside my people, they will get to know us and see the truth for themselves. Helping us should also help them resolve any remorse they feel over their actions."

"That seems like a very enlightened approach," Aelrynd said. "We will discuss the matter in more detail at the appropriate time."

Aerys handed Ardyn another glass of *wah'roh*. "You look like you need another," he said with a wink.

Ardyn laughed. "Thank you."

After seeing Aelrynd and Taeglyn off the next morning, Jevan and Ardyn went to the dining hall to break their fast. They were about to sit down when Mathias rushed toward them. "Jevan! Ardyn! I have been looking everywhere for you."

"We were seeing the Athla'naa elders off," Jevan explained as he sat down. "I was going to come find you after I ate something."

"Make it quick," Mathias said with a harrumph. "We're gathering in a room up in the observation tower."

"What's going on?" Ardyn asked.

"Mathias is eager for us to meet with Tomas and Aron," Jevan explained. "Apparently, they won't say much unless all the key people are there, which apparently includes both of us."

"Oh, I'm sorry!" Ardyn quickly apologized, getting up. "We can eat later—"

"No, no, my boy," Mathias said, holding up his hands. "Please, finish your meal. I didn't realize how long you'd be seeing those elders of yours off."

"Thanks, Mathias," Jevan said as Ardyn sat back down. "We'll join you as soon as we're finished here. Where is the room we're meeting in?"

"Cytra can guide you to it," Mathias said. "I just know it's up in the tower."

After Mathias left, Jevan laughed, as he saw Ardyn try to inhale his meal. "Slow down," Jevan said. "Mathias gets like that when he's anxious about something, but don't let him rush you. They can wait a little longer."

Swallowing a mouthful of food, Ardyn nodded. "You're right."

"How are you doing now that Aelrynd and Taeglyn are gone?" Jevan asked.

"I don't know. A mix of relief and... something else."

"Are you missing them already?" Jevan teased.

Ardyn stopped eating and stared at his plate for a long moment. "That's not quite it, but... kind of. I've gotten to know them better here than during my entire life growing up in Maala'naa."

After they finished eating, they asked Cytra to guide them to where the meeting was being held. When they arrived, Takyra, Aerys, Mathias, Tomas, and Aron were already there.

The room was located in the upper levels of the observation tower, with large floor-to-ceiling windows along the far side of the room. The view of the valley below and the mountains in the distance was spectacular. Within the room itself, there was a sunken circle in the floor, which served as a seating area, arranged with pillows and cushions. In the center was a low table with a display hovering over the middle.

"Thank you for joining us," Takyra greeted.

"Now that we're finally all here, may we begin?" Mathias asked impatiently.

Ardyn and Jevan made their way down into the circle and found a place to sit. Jevan opted to sit on the stepped seating and Ardyn chose a large pillow on the floor next to his friend.

"I have already caught Tomas and Aron up on the situation they flew into," Mathias began. "Along with as much of our history as I know it."

"You implied there were things about our history that our people weren't aware of," Jevan said, giving Mathias a pointed look. "What was that about our ancestors *bringing it upon themselves?*"

Tomas turned to Jevan. "You really don't know why your ancestors came here, do you?"

"All they taught me was that we came aboard ships to colonize this land, and that it surprised my ancestors when they found it already occupied by the elves." Jevan replied before being nudged by Ardyn. "Oh... I mean Athla'naa."

"Your ancestors weren't exactly *colonists*—" Tomas began before being interrupted by Mathias.

"Wait! Please—" Mathias practically begged.

"*Ard* Mathias, we need to hear the truth. *All of it,*" Jevan interrupted. "Now is not the time for more secrecy or lies."

Mathias looked around at everyone gathered. After a moment, his shoulders merely slumped in defeat. "Alright. Tell them."

Tomas leaned forward, balancing his elbows on his knees, and looked directly at Jevan. "According to our history books, your ancestors were criminals. After our ancestors banished them from Ateria for the crimes they committed, they were forced onto ships and sent to Vestos to establish a penal colony."

Jevan gave Tomas a wide-eyed look before turning to Mathias.

"*That*'s why we never taught that to our people," Mathias said with a growl. "We didn't want you to be ashamed of where you came from, so only the village ards knew the truth."

"A penal colony? Is that why no one else from Ateria ever came?" Jevan asked, his mind reeling at this new information. "And why we never sent ships back there?"

"Based on the written histories, they deemed those who were sent to the penal colony heinous criminals and ill-equipped to survive in the wilderness. The historians assumed that if they didn't perish during their voyage to Vestos, they likely died out centuries ago," Tomas admitted. "There had been expeditions planned to come and find out if there were any survivors, but too many were worried that the ghosts of your ancestors haunted Vestos."

Aron kept quiet, only giving Tomas a brief glare.

Jevan couldn't hold back a hearty laugh, making Aron turn his glare on him. "Your people are advanced enough to build an aircraft, but you still believe in ghosts?"

"Your people don't?" Aron asked with a frown.

"Not anyone I know," Jevan said with a bemused shrug.

"We may be more primitive," Mathias added with a skeptical harrumph. "But we've never been superstitious."

"Before we get too far off-track," Takyra intervened. "So far, we've established that Vestos was a penal colony, a fact which was hidden from most of the descendants. I take it from your flying craft and mention of radar that the Medellans on Ateria are more technologically advanced than those here on Vestos."

"From what Mathias has been telling us of his people, yes," Tomas acknowledged. "However, he wouldn't tell us why his people's development has been as stunted as it is."

Next to Jevan, Ardyn cleared his throat, looking a bit abashed. "That would be my people's fault. We recently learned that when we made the peace treaty with the Medellans centuries ago, it came with the agreement that the Medellans would not advance their society."

The scowl on Aron's face deepened, but Tomas seemed undeterred. "Interesting. In all honesty, our technology didn't really take off until the past century. We've only had the technology of flight for a couple of decades. When we saw your beacon launch, we had to come see if your people had survived and progressed farther than we had. As you can imagine, we are quite shocked to find you haven't been alone here and that your elven friends are clearly far more advanced than we are."

"It's quite a mess that we're still figuring out," Takyra agreed. "As I explained, a large part of our people have been asleep in cryostasis for centuries, and we're still trying to assess what to do about this situation we find ourselves in."

Aron made a snort of derision. "I don't believe you. No one can sleep for that long."

"I understand it's difficult to believe," Takyra said. "One of our technicians who specializes in that area could explain it better than I can. Also, a tour of our cryopod facility can be arranged. You are welcome to observe as we revive more of those still in cryostasis."

"First, I would like to understand more about my ancestors' history, and how Vestos became a penal colony," Jevan said. "Clearly, the Medellans on Vestos know as much about their actual history as Ardyn's people did. It's time for all of us to be honest with one another."

ANNALS

Tomas explained as much as he knew about the history of the Vestos penal colony. "In school, they taught us that the Chancellor of the Grand Council of Ateria had tired of the many uprisings and problems within the prisons.

"He ordered the prisons emptied and put the prisoners on ships to be sent to Vestos. The prisons in our capital city of Donarvon held enough prisoners to fill two ships. The prisons were filled twice more after the first ships were sent, and twice more the prisoners were sent to Vestos."

"Why were only six ships sent?" Jevan asked.

"Not long after the Chancellor sent the last two ships, the people deposed him. History isn't clear on why he was deposed, but the new Chancellor deemed banishment too harsh," Tomas replied. "Instead, he instituted both criminal and prison reforms and he made sure they only incarcerated the most hardened criminals."

"Yet, after that regime change, your people were too *afraid of ghosts* to come check on us," Mathias added sarcastically.

"Basically, yes," Tomas replied with a shrug. "Over the centuries, Vestos and its inhabitants have been largely forgotten, beyond the brief mention in our student history books. Our historians may know more, but most of our people don't really give Vestos a second thought, other than a few fables and ghost stories."

"Now that we know your people have survived, we would love to know what happened when your ancestors first arrived," Aron said. "Do you have any historical records we could look at?"

Burying his face in his hands, Mathias let out a deep sigh. "Truth be told, what we teach our people, and what actually happened, is not the same story," he admitted. "Damn, I need a drink."

"So, more lies?" Jevan asked, exasperated.

Mathias nodded.

"Then tell us what really happened, Mathias," Jevan demanded. "We all deserve to know the truth."

"Fine, but you owe me a drink later," Mathias grumbled, getting up to pour himself a glass of water from a nearby table. "This is going to take some time to explain, so settle in."

"Before we do that, why don't we take a break?" Takyra suggested. "We can get some food and drink and meet back here in a couple of hours."

Putting the glass of water back down, Mathias nodded, looking relieved at the reprieve.

As they all stood and headed for the door, Takyra pulled Tomas and Aron aside. The last thing Jevan heard as he and Ardyn left the room was Takyra telling the two men about the tour she'd promised to arrange for them.

◆◆◆

Jevan and Ardyn went back to their quarters to freshen up and eat something. "I swear my people are just as bad as yours," Jevan groaned as he flopped down onto their bed. "It's not nearly as bad as finding out that we were hiding several thousand people and a fancy spaceship, but I've had it with all these secrets."

"Agreed," Ardyn said, sitting next to him. "At least it's all coming to light now. Hopefully, we can prevent them from ever making it all secret again. Now that they're reviving everyone on the Rahn'naa, that's one secret that isn't going away."

Jevan sat up and studied Ardyn for a long moment. "You know, I think that you're the only one who has ever been completely honest with me. From the first time we met, you trusted me with the truth, even when you had no reason to. Right now, I'm grateful to have at least one person in my life I can count on."

Ardyn ducked his head as his ears dropped and flattened. "Thank you. I feel the same. I'm glad you saved me. That feels like many cycles of the seasons ago now, doesn't it?"

"It does!" Jevan agreed as his stomach rumbled, making him laugh. "I guess we should eat something."

◆◆◆

Once they were all reconvened, there were snacks and more pitchers of both fruit juice and water laid out on the low table.

"Mathias said this could take a while, so I arranged for us to have some refreshments to sustain us," Takyra said, as they all took their seats.

"Mathias," Takyra said, picking up a bottle of amber colored liquid. "I believe you stated earlier that you needed a drink, correct?"

"Yes! This is going to be a stressful discussion. Is that a bottle of your *wah'roh*?" he asked hopefully.

"This isn't the replicated *wah'roh* we had last night," Takyra replied. "I have a personal stash that was distilled on Aria'naa before we left. Are you up to tasting some twelve-hundred-year-old *wah'roh*?"

Takyra was already pouring a glass when Mathias nodded enthusiastically. A smile crossed his face as he savored the first sip. "Oh, that is smooth. Even better than the stuff you replicated. Yes, this will do nicely!"

They passed the bottle around the table so everyone could pour themselves a measure of the drink, and they all settled into the pillows scattered around the table.

"Alright, I might as well get this over with," Mathias said before taking another drink, sounding somewhat less grouchy than he had earlier. "Everything I'm about to tell you is what I remember from the histories kept in Tafaran. Only the Council of Ards has ever been granted this knowledge and they swore us to secrecy."

Jevan leaned forward and frowned at Mathias. "Why were the actual accounts kept secret?"

"Those who wrote the histories believed that if their descendants knew the truth, it would cause an uprising," Mathias explained. "All the colonists agreed they would never teach their children what really happened, because if our people knew the whole truth, it might incite another war with the elves—"

Takyra cleared her throat at the mention of *elves*, giving Mathias a look.

"Oh, I'm sorry. The Athla'naa," Mathias corrected himself.

Jevan shifted uncomfortably. "All these lies, on both sides, have hurt all our people. We need to know the whole truth."

"Yes, I know you're right," Mathias replied before taking another long sip. "According to the histories kept in the

Tafaran archives, when the first two ships landed, they didn't immediately encounter the Athla'naa. Many aboard came from larger cities and had never lived in the wild. Instead of exploring farther inland, they stayed near the coast. They deconstructed the ships and used the timber to build the first structures in Tafaran. While they had shelter, they were not prepared for the coming winter and nearly a quarter of them had died by the next spring."

"Why were they sent to establish a penal colony without adequate provisions?" Takyra asked, sounding baffled.

"They weren't willing colonists, just criminals being shipped off as a way to be rid of a problem," Tomas explained. "They wouldn't have been given much beyond the bare necessities to survive."

"The following summer is when our ancestors first came across the Athla'naa," Mathias continued. "Out of desperation, they began learning how to hunt and fish. It was a small hunting party that came across an Athla'naa settlement. According to the journal of the first Ard of Tafaran, that encounter did not go well."

When Mathias hesitated and took another drink, Jevan leaned forward again. "What happened?" he asked impatiently.

"The journal wasn't clear about who attacked first," Mathias admitted. "Later, historians speculated it could have been a misunderstanding because of the language barrier, but there were deaths on both sides. The only detail the journal was clear on was the number of dead. Only three Medellans died, while eleven Athla'naa were killed."

Takyra gasped. "If they were only a small hunting party, how were they able to kill so many?"

"They had different weapons back then," Mathias explained. "They were called pistols and rifles. These weapons weren't very accurate, but were deadlier than the bows and arrows we use now."

Jevan's mouth dropped open. "Are you telling us that our ancestors once had weapons more advanced that we have now?"

Mathias nodded. "Yes, and at first, the Athla'naa didn't stand a chance against them. After being banished from Ateria, they were intent on claiming this land as their own, and weren't willing to let some *strange, pointy-eared freaks* run them off the only other land their people knew existed."

Takyra gave Mathias another pointed look.

"My apologies," Mathias replied. "That was how our ancestors described your people."

"Regardless of how the first conflict began, it sounds to me that perhaps your people were the more aggressive ones," Aerys pointed out.

"You're not wrong. The journals of that first ard were quite unkind to the Athla'naa people," Mathias admitted. "Initially, they reached a tenuous truce because the colonists realized the Athla'naa outnumbered them and didn't have the manpower to sustain a long conflict."

"I thought the war lasted for nearly a century?" Jevan asked.

"Oh, it did," Mathias confirmed. "When the other ships came, that brought reinforcements and more weapons. By the time the last ships arrived, Tafaran was a bustling town, and a few more villages had been established. The colonists began farming and could sustain themselves through the winters. They'd also began mining for metals to create even more weapons. That's when the occasional skirmishes between them and the Athla'naa became a full-blown war."

"This war lasted nearly a century?" Takyra asked, "How did it end?"

"Once our ancestors had reinforcements and more weapons, they decimated the Athla'naa population, but they kept fighting back," Mathias said. "Especially whenever our forces got too close to their forbidden zone. The Elder Triumvirate at the time were desperate to keep Medellans from finding what was hidden here. As for the truce—"

"The Triumvirate was always vague about how the truce came about," Ardyn interrupted.

"The schoolmaster in Yanen and Soren in Ahren were also vague about that truce, which is why I didn't know the Aria'una even existed," Jevan added.

Mathias let out a long sigh and looked at them both. "There was a reason for that."

CANDOR

Ardyn sat forward, intrigued to hear more from Ard Mathias.

"After a century of constant fighting, our ancestors were gaining the upper hand," Mathias said. "They developed better weapons that were more accurate and could kill more efficiently. I never understood everything described in the historical texts, but they had a plan to eradicate every Athla'naa on Vestos."

"Then how are my people still here?" Ardyn asked. "How did they ever agree to a truce?"

"There was a decisive battle that happened about one cycle of the moons before the Medellan forces were ready to move forward with their plan for eradication," Mathias revealed. "In that battle, the Athla'naa slaughtered every Medellan on the field, wielding some strange weapon that shot beams of light at them. I believe you call them *rahn'ora*?"

Takyra's breath hitched at the revelation.

"The Aria'asharra resorted to using our weapons? That goes against everything they believed in," Aerys said, sounding bewildered. "After Takyra revived us, I had my techs do a full inventory. None of our *rahn'ora* are missing."

"The histories say that they returned them as part of the treaty agreement," Mathias explained. "With those weapons, they nearly wiped out my ancestors, instead of the other way around. Those who survived surrendered in defeat. The Triumvirate wrote the treaty and gave our ancestors no choice but to agree to all terms. That included destroying their weapons."

"So, my ancestors made them destroy the technology they already had?" Ardyn asked, unsure how to feel about that revelation.

"Only the weapons," Mathias replied. "That was part of the treaty. Both sides agreed to stop using advanced weapons of any kind. The Triumvirate returned all their weapons to where they found them, and my ancestors agreed to melt ours down. The treaty specifically states that neither side could use weapons more advanced than bows and arrows or spears. However, we were able to use metal for anything else. So, we still make many things out of metal, from the buttons on our shirts to the pots we cook in."

Ardyn stood and made his way over to the windows and stared down at the valley as the tower cast a long shadow in the late afternoon. "Aelrynd admitted the Triumvirate had been purposely restricting the Medellans from advancing their technology, but..." Sighing deeply, he hung his head, folding back his ears. "Maybe Takyra's right. Maybe the Athla'naa people should leave this planet so your people can finally develop the way you were meant to."

"Don't you start with that nonsense," Mathias said with a growl. "Why don't you ask us what we want first? Stop trying to decide for us. It was our ancestors on both sides that agreed to that damned treaty, and they're long dead. We're the ones here now, and we should get a say in the matter."

Takyra came over to where Ardyn stood, placing an arm on his shoulder and turning him to face everyone still seated. "All of you are still like children—" she began.

"Children? How can you call us children? We're all adults here," Tomas protested.

"I meant technologically, Tomas," Takyra clarified. "Your people are more advanced than those on Vestos, but from the look of your flying craft, your people are still centuries away from the level of technology used to build the Rahn'naa."

Looking around the room they were in, with its pristine walls and digital displays, Ardyn wondered how different the ship coming from Aria'naa might be. "Aren't you also centuries away from the technology the people on our homeworld use?"

Takyra nodded, patting Ardyn's shoulder. "You're not wrong. Although at least we would still understand certain scientific principles that I think your people would struggle to grasp."

Cradling his head in his hands, Jevan grumbled. "I think I've had about enough for today."

"Why don't we change the subject?" Takyra suggested, walking back to the seating area and pouring herself another drink.

Ardyn followed suit, settling himself next to Jevan once again.

"As Ardyn just reminded us, the Athla'naa are about to be reunited with members of our homeworld," Aerys said, speaking up. "Along that vein, I think we should celebrate the historic reunion of your people."

"Yes, this is indeed historic," Tomas said, raising his glass, and everyone followed suit.

After everyone took a drink, Tomas turned to Takyra. "I have been meaning to ask, would you be able to set up a means for us to communicate with our people in Ateria? We sent a brief radio message from our aircraft before we landed, but your mountains are blocking our signal and we haven't been able to reach them."

"Yes, of course," Takyra replied. "I'd be happy to."

"Thank you," Tomas said. "We have much to update them on. Now that we know Medellans survived on Vestos, we should let them know. Perhaps they'll even let your people return home to Ateria. I think your people have been banished long enough."

Home? It was difficult for Jevan to think of Ateria as home. Vestos and his way of life here had always been home to him. Now he realized why Ardyn hadn't been eager to visit his people's homeworld. The idea of leaving behind everything he'd ever known was both exciting and terrifying.

"How will they take the news of the Athla'naa presence here?" Takyra asked.

Tomas shrugged. "I'm sure the Grand Council will want to meet you."

Ardyn leaned forward. "Do you think they would want our people to leave your world, or would they be amenable to having some remain if they chose to?"

"The ship that brought your people here crashed twelve hundred cycles of the seasons ago, and your people have developed their own society here, right?" Tomas asked Ardyn, who nodded in response. "I don't think it's up to my government to decide what happens on Vestos, although I can't speak for them. They'll probably send a representative to assess the situation first."

"Thank you. That is good to know," Takyra said. "I will take that into consideration. Our crashing here twelve hundred years ago complicated so many things, but it is a moot point until the ship from Aria'naa arrives. Once they are here, it would be wise to have representatives from each group on this world meet with the captain of that ship. Then we can all discuss what we should do to move forward."

"When do you expect them to arrive?" Aron asked.

"According to the last message we received, another seventeen days," Takyra replied.

"Okay. We'll have to include that in our report back home. It will take a long time for us to explain and I don't think they'll believe everything at first. We certainly found a lot more than we bargained for."

Ardyn looked at Jevan and let out a genuine laugh. That was one of the truest statements they'd heard in a long while.

BURNOUT

When Ardyn woke the next morning, he made his way to the shower, intending to follow his usual routine. After spending a few moments under the warm spray, Ardyn leaned his back against the wall and slowly slid down. Huddled on the floor, everything that had happened over the past many cycles of the sun hit him all at once.

Ardyn didn't realize how long he'd been staring blankly at the shower wall when Jevan gently shook his shoulder. "Ardyn? Are you alright?"

Looking up at Jevan's concerned face, Ardyn shook his head. "I don't know."

Turning off the shower, Jevan gently helped Ardyn up and wrapped him in a towel. "I think you're clean enough, at least," he teased, trying to lighten the mood. Without even thinking, Ardyn leaned into his friend's embrace while being led back to the bed.

"If Takyra wasn't expecting us at breakfast soon, I'd suggest we just stay in bed for an entire cycle of the sun," Jevan said as he took another towel and worked on drying Ardyn's hair. Ardyn leaned into the touch and gave Jevan a half-smile.

"I don't think I've ever spent an entire cycle of the sun in bed," Ardyn admitted. "Why didn't we do that when we were locked in your house?"

"Force of habit," Jevan said, getting up to get the hairbrush. "It wasn't that long ago, but it feels like it's been many seasons, doesn't it?"

Nodding, Ardyn agreed. "It does."

After Jevan finished brushing out his hair, Ardyn took a deep breath and looked at his ever-present companion. "Thank you. Now go get ready. I'll be fine, and we shouldn't keep Takyra waiting."

●●●

As they sat in the dining hall with Takyra and their guests, Ardyn barely picked at his food. He had tried to gather himself together, but he was struggling.

"Are you feeling okay?" Takyra asked, her voice filled with concern.

Looking up, his ears flattened as he shrugged. "Not really," Ardyn admitted. "Everything that's been going on hit me harder than expected this morning."

"Takyra, would you mind if Ardyn and I didn't join you for the tour today?" Jevan asked. "I think the both of us need to go out and get some fresh air. What do you think, Ardyn?"

When Ardyn thought about being back out among the trees, a small thrill ran up his spine. "Yes, I think that's exactly what I need."

Giving them both a sympathetic look, Takyra nodded. "I think we can spare you for the day," Takyra said with a warm smile. "If anything comes up that pertains to your people, Ardyn, I'll brief you after you return. Please check in with me once you get back, so I know you're both safe."

"Thank you," Jevan said as he stood. He stacked Ardyn's tray with his and put them away before leading Ardyn back to their quarters.

"You didn't eat much, so why don't you replicate some snacks for us?" Jevan suggested. "I'll replicate a couple of small packs for us to carry them in."

"Good idea," Ardyn said, heading into the kitchen. "Can you replicate some waterskins, too?"

"I'll see what I can find," Jevan replied.

In the end, they each had a small pack they could carry on their backs, with a blanket, food, and sealed metal containers filled with water. They headed out from the observation tower, the weather sunny and warm. Ardyn paid little attention to where Jevan was steering them, as they walked in companionable silence.

Looking around him, Ardyn thought back to his life before he'd found that key and met Jevan. Life had been simple, spending most of his time roaming the forests around Maala'naa. After they had reassigned him to a range that didn't come close to Medellan lands, his only duty had been to protect the settlement from wild beasts. The hunters that came through his range could take care of themselves and often wanted nothing to do with the troublesome ranger.

A tightness settled into Ardyn's chest, knowing that his entire life had changed. Everything he'd learned since discovering the Rahn'naa and its inhabitants had shattered whatever innocence he'd had left. While a part of him reveled in all this new knowledge, another part of him mourned the loss of the simpler life he once led.

"How are you handling everything so well?" Ardyn asked, looking up at his tall companion.

Jevan stopped and burst into laughter for a moment, making Ardyn smile.

"Maybe I'm better at hiding it, but I don't feel like I've been handling anything well at all," Jevan admitted. "I have struggled between anger and this overwhelming sense of loss. Don't get me wrong, I'm excited about everything we've discovered and learned... but my life will never be the same."

Ardyn hummed in agreement. "That is exactly the same struggle I have been dealing with. This morning my mind couldn't focus on what's ahead. I kept thinking about the past, and what I've lost. Especially because of all the lies and secrets that were kept."

"If they had forced me to endure what you had, all because of those damned secrets, I don't know where my head would be at. Mathias was close to forcing me into a pair-bond. I'd struggle even more with all of it, if I were in a forced pair-bond right now," Jevan admitted. "I should ask Tomas and Aaron if they know anything about pair-bonding. I noticed neither of them have a bonding scar on their palms, so maybe his people don't even practice it anymore?"

"They've had eight hundred cycles of the seasons to develop unimpeded by my people," Ardyn said regretfully. "Their flying machine is a wonder I would never have imagined if I hadn't seen it with my own eyes. It would have shocked me even more if I'd seen it before we'd discovered the Rahn'naa."

"I wasn't even sure there still were people alive in Ateria," Jevan admitted. "I wondered about it sometimes, but I always assumed they were living the same way we were here in Vestos."

"Not knowing how much your people's progress had been repressed, I can see why you would assume that," Ardyn said, looking up at the sky through the canopy of leaves above them, while some of the tension he'd been feeling eased. "Thank you for suggesting this. It's all been too much, too fast. It feels good to be back outside again."

They continued in companionable silence for a long while, each lost in their own thoughts, when Ardyn recognized where they were heading. A moment later, he spotted the small structure they had first found when exploring the Aria'una.

"I thought we could grab our old packs and bring them back with us," Jevan said, pulling the old key out of his pocket and handing it to Ardyn with a sly grin. "There are a couple of things in mine I'd like to have, like that hairbrush my sister gave me."

Ardyn opened the door and saw that everything was still exactly how they'd left it. "What did Cytra call this? An... airlock?"

"Yeah," Jevan replied. "I asked Cytra to explain that to me once. When this ship is in space, the airlock is a way for the crew to get outside and make repairs without letting all the air out of the ship. That's why there's that other door inside."

"So, we could get back inside the ship this way?" Ardyn asked, realizing that the Rahn'naa extended out this far into the forest.

"If that inside door worked, we could," Jevan replied. "I don't think they've started repairs on this part of the ship, but try the key."

Sliding the key into the slot, they heard the same groaning noises as the last time they'd tried it, and the door remained closed. "I guess not," Ardyn said.

Jevan knelt down to gather up some of his belongings and stash them into his pack. "It's understandable. There are more important things for them to do than fixing this one door."

"You're right," Ardyn agreed, joining Jevan on the floor, picking up and packing items into the spare pack Jevan had given him. "I would rather walk back through the woods, anyway."

After they finished packing, they stashed all their packs by the entrance and sat in the middle of the airlock for a moment, sipping on the water they had brought with them.

When Jevan absentmindedly wrapped an arm around his shoulders, Ardyn looked up at his tall companion. "Why—"

Pulling away apologetically, Jevan looked mortified. "I'm sorry, I shouldn't have—"

Ardyn shook his head and reached for Jevan's hand. "No, let me finish. There are so many others you could have had relations with by now. I see how they look at you. Instead, you spend all your spare time with me. *Why?*"

Putting down his water and grasping Ardyn's hand in both of his, Jevan looked down at Ardyn with a wistful smile. "We've survived a lot together, you and I. We've shared experiences that no one else has. After everything, you mean a lot to me," Jevan explained, looking deeply into Ardyn's eyes. "I've come to care for you deeply, more than I ever have for anyone else."

The look of utter devotion in Jevan's eyes nearly took Ardyn's breath away. "Is what we have now enough? Don't you want more from me? For us?"

A sad look crept into Jevan's eyes, that he quickly blinked away. "I'd be lying if I said I'd never thought about it," Jevan admitted, reaching out to play with the end of Ardyn's braid. "But I promise you, I am happy as we are, and I will never push for more. I am so happy to have you in my life and to call you a friend. Sharing the burden of everything we're learning has made it easier to bear."

"I am glad you followed that *sar'ora*. Not just because you saved me, but because it brought you into my life."

Jevan's face flushed darker as he flashed a bright smile at Ardyn. "And I'm very happy that you have let me be in your life, little ranger."

Ardyn ducked his head, laying his ears flat, while his heart fluttered in his chest. Not knowing how to respond to that, he opted to lean over and bury his head in Jevan's broad chest, letting the man wrap his strong arms around him.

After a few moments of companionable silence, Jevan added. "I almost wish we could stay out here, just the two of us."

"Me too. Everything is changing so fast, and we cannot unlearn what we know."

"Very true. Unfortunately, I think Takyra would send an entire security detail after us if we don't return," Jevan said with a chuckle, giving Ardyn a quick hug. "We should head back soon."

They gathered their packs and closed the airlock. Ardyn looked at it wistfully for a moment before taking Jevan's hand in his as they walked back through the forest, enjoying the serenity surrounding them.

After a time, Jevan squeezed his hand. "So, what about you? Why do you spend so much time with me? Besides my obvious charms and good looks, of course."

Looking at Jevan, the Medellan gave him a wink and a smile, which made him laugh. "As you've said, so much has happened, and it forced us together. We've shared so much and you're a comforting presence. You make me feel safe," Ardyn admitted.

Stopping and facing him, Jevan smiled at him. "I do? That makes me glad to hear. All I want is for you to feel safe when you're with me," Jevan said with all sincerity. "No matter what happens, let's make a promise to always be there for each other."

"Yes, no matter what," Ardyn agreed with a smile, before they continued heading back.

Ardyn wondered if he'd ever be ready for a more intimate relationship with Jevan. The man was so patient, and his kindness seemed to know no bounds. Ardyn once again cursed his elders and their ancestors who forced the sexual trauma on him, which kept him from seeking a more intimate connection with someone he cared so much about.

Maybe in the future...?

CATCHING UP

Ardyn awoke the next morning feeling more rested than he had in a long while. Getting away from everything helped, especially learning that Jevan was equally overwhelmed.

Looking over at the still sleeping man, Ardyn contemplated their relationship. While circumstances had forced them together, he couldn't deny that his feelings for Jevan were deepening. It didn't hurt that Jevan was always so sweet and understanding. *Don't forget charming and attractive,* Ardyn reminded himself with a smirk.

Ever since they'd forced him to mate with Cylaen and the others, Ardyn had avoided sexual relationships. *Well, there was that one ranger,* Ardyn recalled. After the incident in Ahren, Ardyn became friendly with a ranger named Laedyn, whose range bordered his new one.

Ardyn had spent little time with Laedyn in Maala'naa, as their families lived on opposite ends of the settlement, but they struck up a friendship as they crossed paths during their patrols. Soon they deliberately ranged so they could spend every few nights eating their evening meal together.

Unfortunately, one night, when Laedyn made intimate advances toward Ardyn, it didn't go well. Ardyn found Laedyn attractive, and at first enjoyed the man's touch. It's when Laedyn offered his body to Ardyn that it triggered memories of his forced matings. Without thinking, Ardyn pushed Laedyn away and fled into the woods, half dressed.

Since then, Ardyn had been too embarrassed to let anyone else get that close to him. Not until Jevan. The Medellan had such a charming, easy-going way about him, he always put Ardyn at ease.

Shaking his head, he gave Jevan one last glance and a soft smile. *There is too much going on right now for me to indulge in such thoughts,* Ardyn reminded himself as he rose and readied himself.

●●●

"Good morning!" Takyra greeted them as they entered the elevator on the way to the dining hall. "How are you feeling today, Ardyn?"

"Much better, thanks," Ardyn replied with a smile before turning to Jevan. "Yesterday was exactly what I needed."

"I'm glad," Takyra said. "You've both been thrown into an overwhelming situation. It continues to amaze me how well you've been handling it. Please, never hesitate to let me know if you need a break like that again."

As they entered the dining hall, everyone else was already seated at one of the larger tables in the corner. After replicating some food, Ardyn joined them. "Good morning," he greeted. "I hope yesterday was productive."

"It was very enlightening," Tomas replied. "The cryopods are a true marvel. I can still hardly believe those things kept your people alive for so many centuries!"

Ardyn agreed. "You can imagine how we felt, when we saw Takyra emerge from one. It was incredible to watch."

As Takyra and Jevan joined them, Jevan asked. "Were you able to contact your people?"

"Yes," Aron replied. "The communications system on this ship is amazing. Clear as a bell with no static! It sounded like they were in the next room, and not far across the ocean."

"So, what did they say?" Jevan asked.

"It took time to explain everything we had learned," Tomas explained. "Because the presence of the Athla'naa it makes the situation more complex than we had expected. They are sending a larger delegation to assess the situation first-hand."

"You have more of those flying craft?" Takyra asked.

Aron nodded. "A few, but this was the only one designed for longer distances. Before we left, they were almost ready to begin test flights of a new, larger long-distance model, but it wasn't ready yet. It will take them some time to finish the safety tests and select who to send, but they should arrive in less than a cycle of the moons."

Ardyn looked over at Jevan, who was clearly excited to meet even more of these intriguing Medellans. "Why are they sending a delegation?" Jevan asked.

"Aron and I are only trained for scouting missions," Tomas explained. "We hadn't expected to find all of you, along with this complicated situation. They are going to send one of our diplomats, a historian, and likely at least one scientist and engineer."

"A historian?" Jevan asked. "That's great. I have so many questions about our people's history. Especially regarding some rituals my people still insist on following, that no one has been able to explain."

Mathias harrumphed at that. *He's still not planning to force Jevan to pair-bond, is he?* Ardyn wondered.

"I'm sure whoever they send will be happy to answer all your questions," Aron said. "I have little knowledge beyond the basics of our history that I learned in school."

"Neither of us are much in the way of academics, which is why we joined the military," Tomas admitted.

"Why do you need a military?" Mathias asked, setting down his fork to give the men his full attention.

"To keep the peace in Ateria," Tomas explained.

"So, something similar to my security techs," Aerys said, understanding.

Before Ardyn could ask, Jevan spoke up. "Protect from what?"

Tomas shot Aron a look, and the man clamped his mouth shut. Taking a deep breath, Tomas replied. "There are people in Ateria who believe that there are forces that may threaten our land. They never explain exactly who they are or where they might come from, but..."

"But the Athla'naa presence here may have just confirmed some of their fears," Aron said, putting his hands up defensively when Takyra frowned. "Don't get me wrong, you seem friendly enough. With your ship buried underground, I don't think you're much of a threat, but with another spaceship on its way, it's raised alarms within the Grand Council."

"Your delegation will be most welcome," Takyra said. "I hope we can show them we are a peaceful people."

"Well, at least most of the time," Ardyn added with a small frown.

"That's what the delegation will need to determine," Tomas said. "Seeing all these technological marvels, I think it would be good for us to be friendly with your people."

"I think we all have much we can learn from each other," Takyra agreed. "Especially if we decide to remain on this world."

After breakfast, they relocated to the tower meeting room to discuss plans on how to prepare for the Medellan delegation. Quarters had to be assigned and Takyra wanted to better understand Aterian customs and cuisine so they could program the replicators accordingly.

They were about to break for the evening when a message came through the communications panel in the room. "Chief Technician Takyra, please come to the control center. We are receiving an incoming subspace message!"

DENYRA

akyra stood and acknowledged the message. "I'll be right there!" she said before dashing out of the door. Everyone looked at each other before hurrying after her, wanting to know what was going on. Once they reached the elevator, Takyra looked at the group gathered around her. "I don't want too many people in the control center. Can we agree for only one or two Medellans to join us for this?"

Mathias stepped forward. "Since he's been here from the beginning, I'll trust Jevan to represent our people. Tomas and Aron, care to join me for a drink?"

"Jevan *does not* speak for the people of Ateria," Aron protested. "We should be there as well."

Tomas put a hand on Aron's shoulder. "You're right, although we don't both need to be there. I'm the senior, so I'll represent Ateria. You go and have that drink with Mathias."

Aron begrudgingly agreed.

Once that was settled, Ardyn followed everyone into the elevator. A sudden knot of concern settled in his stomach as the elevator began to move. *I should be excited about more subspace communications, shouldn't I?*

Mathias and Aron stepped off on the crew quarters deck, and the elevator continued on to the control center deck.

When they arrived in the control center, Takyra quickly made her way to the main communications station and replaced the tech who sat there. Her hands flew over the controls as she opened up a communications channel to listen to the message.

"*This is Captain Denyra of the Star Cruiser Pah'ora, signaling the Colony Starship Rahn'naa.*"

"This is Chief Technician Takyra of the Rahn'naa," Takyra responded. "We are receiving your message, Pah'ora. When do you estimate your arrival here?"

At first Ardyn thought that would be the end, as the subspace communications always seemed to take several cycles of the sun, but it surprised him when they immediately received a response.

"We expect to arrive within fifteen standard Aria'naa days," Captain Denyra responded. *"Please collect all members of the Aria'asharra faction before our arrival."*

With a look of confusion, Takyra looked back at the group gathered behind her. "There are no Aria'asharra on this world," Takyra responded. "Only their descendants remain. Those descendants live in scattered settlements across the continent, and many are a month or more distant."

"Are your shuttles not operational?" Captain Denyra asked with a huff of annoyance.

"Our shuttles were not damaged, but in the twelve-hundred years since the ship crashed, it has been buried underground," Takyra explained. "The shuttle bays are entirely blocked, and we have no means to raise the ship."

There was a long pause.

"Understood," Captain Denyra finally responded. *"It is imperative that you gather as many of these Aria'asharra descendants as you can before our arrival."*

"Why do we need to gather them?" Takyra asked.

"We will explain when we arrive," Captain Denyra said curtly. *"We will contact you again with further instructions."*

The communications link was severed and Takyra sat speechless, staring at her console for a moment. Shaking her head, she turned around. "That was very odd. I wonder why they are so insistent on having all of your people gathered here. I was sure we would only need to convene the leaders of each group to discuss how to move forward."

Concern rippled through Ardyn. Something about that exchange felt very off to him. "It has been a long time, and there is much we don't know about what's happened on Aria'naa. I think we should be cautious."

"You're right," Takyra agreed. "However, we should inform your elders of the request and let them decide for themselves what to do."

Ardyn flattened his ears. "I'm not sure that is wise, but you're right. We should tell them."

Takyra sent a message to the communicators she gave to Aelrynd and Taeglyn and waited. A few moments later, they responded. *"Takyra? Is that you?"*

"Yes. We have received word from the ship arriving from the homeworld." Takyra relayed the message from Captain Denyra. "I would advise caution. The entire exchange felt strangely hostile. It would be wise for only appointed representatives to meet with this Captain Denyra until we can determine what her plans for your people are."

There was silence from the communicators for a moment before Aelrynd spoke. "*I understand your concern, but we will let our people decide. Word has spread and many of our people from other settlements are now encamped around Maala'naa, intrigued by the news and demanding answers. We will share this information with them, along with your note of caution, and let them decide if they wish to comply with the request.*"

Ardyn spoke up. "Elder Aelrynd, while it gladdens my heart that you want to be more truthful with our people, the exchange we just heard makes me uneasy. I agree with Takyra that we must proceed with caution. Appoint representatives to meet with this Captain Denyra, and once we understand her intentions, then you can freely share everything we know with our people."

"*We will take your words under consideration,*" Aelrynd said before ending the conversation.

Typical, Ardyn thought before wondering aloud. "Why were we able to exchange a conversation with Denyra? The last message took time for us to receive."

"They must be close enough for there to be no delay in response," Aerys surmised. "My techs and I will have many questions when they arrive. Something else is also off about that entire exchange. She said she was arriving in *fifteen standard Aria'naa* days."

Ardyn wasn't sure what was wrong with that, when a look of realization came over Takyra's face. "You're right. I had Cytra calculate the difference in our days. Fifteen days on Aria'naa is approximately fourteen days here. That's a day earlier than we were told to expect them."

Jevan came over and placed a hand on Ardyn's shoulder. "Also, doesn't the name of that ship, the Pah'ora, sound ominous to you?"

Pressing his lips together in a thin line, Aerys nodded. "Yes. Naming it *the flying death* means it must be a warship. I think it would be prudent to increase the strength of our forcefield, just in case."

"Yes, good idea," Takyra agreed.

Ardyn flattened his ears. "What about those in the settlements? They won't have the protection of a forcefield. Will they be safe?"

Takyra looked at Aerys and they both flattened their ears as they turned back to Ardyn. "Good question."

SUSPICIONS

Several cycles of the sun later, Athla'naa began arriving with Taeglyn leading the way. They built an encampment around the perimeter of the forcefield. Ardyn went out to greet him with Takyra while Jevan remained behind with Mathias, Tomas, and Aron.

"Elder Taeglyn, if your people insist on being here, please ask them to camp within the perimeter of the forcefield," Takyra said. "We've recalibrated it to allow you to pass through."

"Thank you," Taeglyn said with a slight bow. "I was hoping you would welcome us, despite your misgivings."

"I'm not pleased by the turn of events," Takyra admitted. "However, since they clearly wish to be here, I would rather keep them safe within the forcefield. If necessary, we also have room within the Rahn'naa."

"How have you been getting on with the visitors from Ateria?" Taeglyn asked Ardyn.

"It's been fascinating to learn about how their people have developed," Ardyn replied. "Please, join us for dinner. We can catch you up on everything we've discussed."

Takyra made a sound of distress. "No! Not another dinner meeting."

"I meant with Jevan, Mathias and the Aterians," Ardyn clarified. "You are always welcome to join us, but I know you've been incredibly busy."

Taking a deep breath, Takyra looked a little sheepish at her outburst. "I'm sorry. There has been too much happening between completing the crew revivals, the delegation coming from Ateria, and Captain Denyra getting on my nerves. She has been contacting me several times each day, demanding to know how many of your people we've *rounded up*, as if you were all some domesticated *athla'maakh*."

"She makes me nervous," Ardyn agreed before looking at Taeglyn. "I wish you had not been so willing to let our people gather before we could determine her motives."

"You showed us how dangerous it is to hide the truth from our people," Taeglyn reminded him. "What do the Aterians say on the matter, Takyra?"

"I wanted to inform them of the arrival of the ship from our homeworld, but Tomas advised against it," she revealed. "He confided in me that there are xenophobic elements within his government that might cause a panic among his people."

"They didn't even know about the Athla'naa until recently," Ardyn said, confused. "How could Tomas know his people might fear us? Was there something they said?"

"From what Tomas explained, there has been a faction among their people who have feared an *alien invasion* for some time now," Takyra explained. "Tomas always believed it to be nothing but conspiracy theories until he met us."

"Hopefully, we can assuage their fears," Ardyn said as Takyra's communicator beeped.

Rolling her eyes, Takyra responded. "Takyra here. What is it?"

"*Captain Denyra requests to speak with you,*" came a voice over the communicator.

With a sigh, Takyra replied. "Tell her I'm on my way," she said before turning to Ardyn. "Would you like to accompany me? I could use the moral support."

"Yes, of course," Ardyn agreed.

"I will also accompany you," Taeglyn declared. "I would like to hear what this Denyra has to say."

They made their way down into the Rahn'naa. In the control center, Takyra took a seat while Ardyn and Taeglyn stood behind her. Aerys was already there, and enabled communications once Takyra nodded.

"Chief Technician Takyra speaking."

"*It's about time. I am sending you a schematic for a device I need you to replicate. It is imperative that you make sure all the gathered Aria'asharra are wearing one.*"

As she spoke, Ardyn saw an image appear on Takyra's console displaying the device. "*It is to be worn on the wrist. You can replicate them to fit everyone, from the smallest infant to the largest adult.*"

Ardyn looked at Takyra with alarm, but she placed a finger to her lips and shook her head. "What is the purpose of these?" Takyra asked. "Why do you only want the *descendants* of the Aria'asharra wearing them?"

"*Do not concern yourself with that. This is a direct order from the Leadership Conclave,*" Denyra replied. "*It is imperative that you comply.*"

"They are going to question why they have to wear them," Takyra argued. "Please at least explain the purpose of them to me."

"*Just get it done!*" Denyra insisted before the communication abruptly ended.

Takyra downloaded the schematic onto a tablet before standing. "Join me in my quarters. I think I need a drink."

Ardyn's heart raced as he followed Takyra back to her quarters. It troubled him that Denyra was singling out his people. For what reason, he couldn't even fathom. They passed Jevan in the corridor and Takyra gestured for him to follow as well. Ardyn shrugged his shoulders when Jevan gave him a questioning look.

Once they were all sitting down in her quarters, Takyra explained the latest request from Denyra and handed Aerys the tablet with the schematic. He studied it for several long moments. "I'll have an engineering tech confirm, but it looks like they designed these devices to emit a low-frequency signal, making them trackable."

"They want to track our people?" Taeglyn asked. "Why?"

"Your guess is as good as mine," Aerys replied. "However, even if we comply with her request, I worry we don't have the resources to replicate so many devices. Denyra seems almost obsessed with your people, and it doesn't sit right with me."

"Agreed, but it's a direct order from Aria'naa," Takyra reminded him. "If we don't comply, are we prepared to alienate ourselves from our homeworld? Not to mention the fact that their technology will be twelve hundred years more advanced than ours. If they have become more militant, we don't stand a chance if they want to force us to comply."

Looking at Takyra in shock, the worry in the pit of Ardyn's stomach tightened. "Are you concerned they might attack us?"

Takyra nodded. "I don't like it, but I don't think we have a choice. Until we know what they are planning, it's best we comply. Once their plans become clear, we can better decide our course of action.”

"While we don't have the weapons to fight back, I have been working on strengthening the forcefield and extending its range," Aerys said.

Taeglyn gave Aerys a pat on the shoulder. "That's good to know. Then, I will coordinate my people to move their encampment within the forcefield. I do not regret being honest with our people, but I can see now why you cautioned us."

"We will prepare everything here so we can temporarily house your people within the Rahn'naa, if necessary," Takyra said.

Looking at Aerys, Ardyn nodded. "I hope it doesn't come to that."

Taking his hand, Jevan squeezed it. "So do I."

SEPARATED

On the morning they expected the Pah'ora to arrive in orbit, anxiety was running high. Ardyn and Jevan rose early to prepare, knowing Takyra expected them to be there when she went to greet the new arrivals.

Now that every Athla'naa on the Rahn'naa had been revived from cryostasis, Aerys was able to reroute the extra power to the forcefield. That gave him the power to reconfigure it to allow people to pass through while strengthening its ability to repel energy weapon blasts.

As the encampment continued to grow, with more Athla'naa arriving daily, Aerys also extended the perimeter of the forcefield. It now extended nearly half the length of the buried ship, allowing the encampment to extend into the surrounding forest. Aerys also made it visible, with a faint blue tinge, so they could show any newcomers where to set up camp within its protective canopy.

When the long-range scanners detected the Pah'ora entering orbit, Takyra signaled for Jevan and Ardyn to accompany her and Aerys to the surface. "It should take a shuttle some time to arrive," Takyra explained as they exited the tower. "It's unlikely they would try to land the Pah'ora, because interstellar ships are too large. Instead, they would have at least one smaller shuttlecraft to bring them down to the planet's surface."

The device Ardyn now wore on his wrist made Jevan frown. Ardyn reluctantly agreed to wear one, to reassure his people that they were safe. As he feared the purpose of these devices, Jevan begged him not to, but Ardyn agreed with Takyra. She argued it was best to make a show of compliance until they better understood what Denyra's motives were, but it didn't mean Jevan had to like it.

After they emerged from the tower, Jevan saw a young Athla'naa child run toward them shouting "Papa Ardyn!"

Scooping the child into his arms and swinging her around onto his hip, Ardyn turned toward Jevan, looking up at him with a bright smile on his face. Jevan was about to introduce himself to the child, when a bright light flashed, making Jevan squint and flinch away.

When the light faded, Jevan blinked, not believing his eyes. The entire Athla'naa encampment was suddenly deserted. All the Athla'naa wearing those damnable bracelets, including Ardyn and the child he'd been holding, had disappeared. In their stead stood a handful of Athla'naa dressed in black armor, aiming weapons at them.

"Ardyn!" Jevan cried out in distress, before shouting at the newcomers. "Where are they?!"

In the center of the new arrivals stood an Athla'naa with gold markings on her armor. Takyra and Aerys glared at those pointing weapons at them, daring them to fire as they marched toward the one Jevan assumed must be Denyra.

"Hold your fire," Denyra ordered. "They appear unarmed."

After they lowered their weapons, Jevan marched forward as well, standing behind Takyra and Aerys.

"Where are our people?!" Takyra demanded.

"Your people? You mean those filthy *Aria'asharra*?" Denyra said with a sneer. "My people beamed them to holding cells aboard my ship. I am pleased that you complied and placed trackers on so many. My people will deal with the rest later."

Takyra seemed livid as she screamed at Denyra. "Beamed? Holding cells? Why are they in holding cells? What gives you the right? How were you able to make them disappear like that?!"

"I forget that you're nearly as primitive as the *Aria'asharra*," Denyra scoffed. "We beamed them into the holding cells using our transmat system, pending their executions. This is a direct order from the Leadership Conclave on Aria'naa."

Without thinking, Jevan pushed past Takyra and Aerys, towering over Denyra. "Executions?! No! You can't execute them when they have done nothing wrong!"

Unfazed, Denyra glared up at Jevan. "And what exactly are you?"

"My name is Jevan, and my people call ourselves Medellans," Jevan introduced himself. "Now bring back those Athla'naa immediately!"

"Are your people also like the Aria'asharra? Shunning technology at all costs?" Denyra asked, narrowing her eyes at Jevan, making him glad he wasn't wearing his old leather and roughspun clothing.

"We aren't very advanced technologically, but we don't shun it either," Jevan responded with exasperation. "Now please, let Ardyn and his people go!"

Denyra merely let out a dismissive snort, turning to Takyra. "I don't have time to deal with this *athla'maakh*. Tell him to go back to wherever he came from. This is none of his concern."

Ignoring any further pleas from Jevan, Denyra turned toward her troops. She ordered them to usher Takyra and her people into the observation tower, leaving Jevan staring after them. He ran to catch up, but as they approached the tower, Tomas, Aron, and Mathias were emerging from the doorway.

"Ugh, there are more of them?" Denyra said with exasperation. "I want no *athla'maakh* allowed near the Rahn'naa!"

Takyra faced Denyra with an angry scowl. "You do not give the orders here! I am Chief Technician and the Rahn'naa is *my* ship. You do not dictate who can enter. I have welcomed Jevan and his people into my circle of confidants, and they may accompany us. Whatever it is you are planning will affect them as much as it will affect my people."

Rolling her eyes, Denyra capitulated. "As you wish. I will allow it, *for now*."

As they made their way inside, Jevan worried over Ardyn. This was the first time since their judgment by the Elder Triumvirate in Maala'naa they'd been forced apart. The thought he might lose his dear friend caused a knot of fear tightening in his chest.

Takyra led them one of the meeting rooms in the tower, instead of down into the main part of the ship. After the doors closed behind them, Jevan couldn't contain himself any longer. "You can't execute Ardyn or his people with no cause. It's not right!" Tears stung his eyes as they crested and slid down his face, exposing his deep emotions for Ardyn. What he really wanted to do was hit something, but he knew that wouldn't solve anything.

"Why do you wish to defend this Aria'asharra?" Denyra said with a scowl. "You should be grateful we're disposing of them for you."

"Why should we be grateful to you for murdering innocents?" Aerys spoke up. "I don't understand how you could want to execute your own people."

"They are not *our* people. The Aria'asharra aren't even Athla'naa. They are lower than the lowest *athla'maakh*," Denyra said, glaring at Jevan. "And they are nothing but *traitors*."

Takyra clearly had enough when she stepped in front of Denyra. "They have been on this world for over twelve hundred years. Their ancestors may have been traitors, but these Athla'naa are innocent! You will explain to me *exactly* what is going on and *why*, before you even think about executing any of *our* people," she demanded.

Walking over to the large picture window, Denyra stood for a moment with her hands clasped behind her back. "Perhaps you are right," she conceded. "There is much you are not aware of."

As the tension in the room faded, everyone sat down around the table, while Denyra remained standing. "According to our historical records, the Aria'asharra had been at the height of their treachery around the same time the Rahn'naa launched."

"Yes, their faction had been very outspoken back then and involved in many protests on Aria'naa," Takyra admitted as she sat down.

"It was long suspected that members of their faction were the cause for the disappearance of the Rahn'naa," Denyra continued. "Our ancestors assumed the ship had been purposefully crashed, destroyed to send a message to the Leadership Conclave. When the public heard the news, violence erupted across Aria'naa. That emboldened the Aria'asharra, who openly attacked those who did not side with their faction, especially members of the Baaru'dak class."

Denyra crossed her arms, taking a pause, and looking at them all smugly as she allowed her words to sink in before continuing.

"Civil war broke out the year after your ship went missing. It was bloody and brutal. The Aria'asharra targeted innocents, including small children, trying to unnerve the rest of the population. After several years of trying to quell the violence, they decimated our population, forcing the Leadership Conclave to make a radical decision. *Total genocide.*"

Jevan felt a cold chill run through him, despite not fully understanding. Clearly, he wasn't the only one not grasping the implication as Takyra stood in shock. "You can't mean...?"

"I meant exactly what I said," Denyra replied. "We wiped every single Aria'asharra off the face of Aria'naa and then purged them from every colony as well. Those alive here are the last known group. Once we exterminate this last pocket of filth, we will have finally completed the edict from the Leadership Conclave."

"Must I remind you *again*, these are the *descendants* of those Aria'asharra?" Takyra said with a growl. "They are forty-eight generations removed from a war that happened over twelve-hundred years ago. You speak as if those atrocities happened yesterday!"

"Our people have a very long memory," Denyra said dismissively. "These so-called descendants kept all your people imprisoned in your cryopods for twelve hundred years, didn't they? While maintaining their idiotic fear of technology, no less. I'm willing to bet they also repressed the technological progress of these *athla'maakh* as well." Denyra gestured toward the Medellans.

"They didn't even know where they came from!" Jevan argued. "Not until Ardyn and I discovered what they hid within the Aria'una. Only the Elder Triumvirate knew, and they only knew the lies that had been passed down from their ancestors."

"Ignorance is no excuse!" Denyra shouted. "Their ancestors nearly destroyed our world. They cannot be allowed to live! I would have thought you would understand, after what they did to you and your people. I regret making that assumption."

While still beside himself with worry over Ardyn, Jevan was also livid over Denyra's complete disregard for innocent life. "You say that these Athla'naa have to die because their *ancestors* decimated your population and deliberately attacked innocents, but can't you see that's exactly what you're doing now?" Jevan argued. "How can you justify the murder of the innocent descendants from a war that ended centuries ago?"

Ignoring Jevan, Denyra turned to Takyra. "This is why I didn't want these *athla'maakh* included. This does not concern them."

Before Jevan could react to the insult, Mathias spoke up. "This very much concerns us. This is *our* world, and both our cultures have shaped and influenced each other over the past eight centuries."

Denyra hesitated for a moment, a scowl crossing her features.

"Before we continue to debate this matter, give us some reassurance that those you took are still alive and well," Jevan insisted, before pleading quietly. "Please? Please, let me speak with Ardyn."

Looking none too happy, Denyra scanned the room and finally nodded. "As you wish."

ABDUCTED

Within the blink of an eye, Ardyn went from standing outside, about to introduce his daughter Myria to Jevan, to standing inside a large, enclosed space filled with only the people from his settlement. He pulled Myria close when she shrieked in shock and began to cry. "Hush, little one," he said as he smoothed some of her dark purple hair from her face. "It will be alright, I promise. Be brave for me, okay?"

Looking at him with wide, frightened eyes, she nodded through hiccupping sobs. "Okay, I'll try, Papa Ardyn."

Giving her a quick hug, Ardyn set the girl down when he saw her mother appear through the crowd. Myria turned and ran to her. "Mama!"

Picking up her daughter, Cylaen glared at him. "What's going on, Ardyn? What's happened?"

Throwing his hands up, he shook his head and gave her a shrug. "I don't know. You know as much as I do at this point."

"I don't believe you. You have been away for many cycles of the moons, living with those... what did the elders call them? Baaru'dak? Now look where that's gotten you! Where that's gotten all of us?!"

Ardyn's ears dropped at being unfairly admonished. "You can't blame this on me," Ardyn replied with a huff of frustration. "I have absolutely no idea how we ended up inside this... whatever this is."

"Ardyn!" a familiar voice rang out from across the large space they found themselves in.

"Mama Saelyn?" Recognizing her voice before he saw her, dragging his father along behind her. His ears shot up in surprise when he saw he wore the robes of a member of the Triumvirate and carried the staff that Druyndar once held. "What are you doing here?"

"We only arrived this morning, with Elder Aelrynd," Saelyn replied. "I was worried about you and finally convinced your father to join the others who were venturing into the

Aria'una. Maala'naa is practically unoccupied now and our people need their elders."

"Well, look at where we are now," Taesys groused. "You should have listened to me! You'd think now that I bear the title of Elder—"

"Where are we, Ardyn? Do you know what's going on?" his mother asked, ignoring Taesys' ramblings.

What is going on? Ardyn also wondered as he began pacing nervously in front of them. Were they under attack as Aerys had feared? Were his modifications to the shields he'd made holding? Why were only the Athla'naa from the settlements here, and none from the Rahn'naa? *I hope Jevan is safe.*

"I'm honestly not sure," Ardyn replied before looking down at the bracelet on his wrist. He tore it off and threw it to the ground, smashing it under the heel of his boot with a cry of frustration. "*Ior'kah!*" *I knew we shouldn't have complied with Denyra.*

Before his parents or Cylaen could question him, a disembodied voice boomed through the large space. "*All descendants of the Aria'asharra are hereby sentenced to be executed for the war crimes committed by your ancestors. Make peace with each other during your last hours. As a mercy, we will give you one last day to spend with each other. Executions will commence tomorrow.*"

Everyone in the crowded room took a collective intake of breath, followed by angry objections. "You have no right to do this!" Ardyn cried out, hoping they were listening, but the speakers remained silent. Pacing furiously, Ardyn screamed in frustration, causing those around him to shrink away.

Ardyn made his way through the crowd, with his parents, Cylaen, and Myria following close behind. He looked to see if he could spot any other familiar faces when he saw Taeglyn and Aelrynd huddled together in a corner, conversing. Aelrynd looked up and recognized him. "Ardyn! We had hoped you had remained with the others on the Rahn'naa. What is going on? How did we get here?"

Shaking his head, Ardyn shrugged his shoulders. "I am not sure, but I think it's because of those damnable bracelets. I destroyed mine, although it's probably too late to prevent whatever Denyra has planned for us."

Looking at their wrists, the two elders immediately removed them and smashed the bracelets with the staves they still carried. "I am shocked that our kinsmen would harbor so much hate against our people after all these centuries," Aelrynd said before glowering at Taeglyn. "Why did you insist we wear these things?"

Dipping his ears in apology, Taeglyn slumped against the wall. "I am sorry. I felt if we welcomed those from the home world with open arms and complied with their request, that it would allow us some leverage to negotiate terms amenable to our people."

"What were you hoping to negotiate?" Taesys stepped forward to ask.

"Many of our people are not ready to embrace all this advanced technology," Taeglyn admitted. "They certainly don't wish to reintegrate into modern Athla'naa society on Aria'naa. If Denyra had insisted we leave this world, I had hoped to convince her to allow us to go to the world the Rahn'naa was meant to colonize."

"I knew there was another reason you were being so agreeable about wearing those damnable bracelets," Taesys growled in frustration. "Ardyn, I thought you would have had better sense."

"Aerys and I tried to talk Takyra out of it, but she felt it was safer to comply as a sign of trust. Takyra had hoped to find out what Denyra was planning before anything like this happened. None of us expected them to have this kind of technology."

"I am sorry. This was not how I pictured any of this," Taeglyn admitted. "I don't understand what's happening."

"Neither do I. How can they justify executing their own people? Why should it matter who our ancestors were? Because we have repressed our technology for all these centuries, we're not even a threat to anyone on Aria'naa," Ardyn said as he began pacing again. "They could have just taken those from the Rahn'naa and left us here. This isn't right!"

"No, it's not right, but I don't see how we're going to get out of this situation," Aelrynd said, sitting down against the wall. "We're no match against all their technology."

"I can only hope that Takyra can do something," Ardyn said.

Feeling restless, Ardyn kept pacing for a long while. He wasn't used to being confined around this many people in the same place. Within the Rahn'naa, he'd only spent time around larger groups when they dined together or when he and Jevan had been helping to settle in the revived Athla'naa. Even then, that was by choice.

Thinking of Jevan, Ardyn knew the Medellan must be beside himself with worry. He only hoped that his friend wouldn't try a rescue attempt that could get him killed. Ardyn missed the tall man's calming presence. If he'd been there, they would likely sit in a corner while Jevan played with Ardyn's hair. Reaching up to toy with the end of his braid, the memory of all those quiet moments with Jevan caused a pang in Ardyn's chest. *I hope I am reunited with you, my friend.*

That's when a familiar voice boomed through the room. *"Ardyn? Hey, Ardyn! Are you there? It's me, Jevan. They're letting me talk to you. How are you? What's going on up there?"*

Up? Ardyn asked himself as he pushed through the crowd to get closer to where the voice was emanating from.

"Jevan?!" Ardyn shouted. "Jevan, is that you? We're confined in a large room. Many of those from my settlement are here, including Taeglyn and Aelrynd."

"Good, I'm glad to know you're okay. Hang in there, alright?" Jevan sounded relieved. *"We're trying to talk them into letting you all go."*

Relief flooded through Ardyn, and he heard a collective sigh from those around him.

Another voice came through the comm system. *"Please clear the middle of the room immediately."*

They all looked around at each other in confusion, but quickly complied. *Now what?*

EXECUTION

Once the middle of the room was clear, a large table laden with food and refreshments appeared. A cheer rose as they gathered around the table to help themselves to food.

Ardyn escorted Cylaen and his daughter to the table, where her mother handed the child a piece of fruit. "How are you both doing?" Ardyn asked.

Staring at him for a long moment, she gave him a little shrug. "We're holding up alright," she replied. "Why did Jevan ask for you specifically, and not for our elders?"

Ardyn's ears dipped and his face heated. "He's a friend of mine. Jevan is the Medellan that explored the Aria'una with me. We've saved each other's lives and have become very close."

"Tell me more about him," Cylaen said as she helped herself to some food.

While they ate, Ardyn related the story of how he and Jevan met, and all their adventures together. Cylaen appeared genuinely interested in everything Ardyn had learned and asked many questions.

Even Myria occasionally interrupted with questions of her own. "Are there any children on the Rahn'naa?"

Looking down at her, Ardyn shook his head. "Everyone we revived are young, unmated adults. Takyra told us that children don't do well in the cryopods, so colony ships recruited younger adults who would mate and produce children once they had established their colony."

"Oh," Myria said, her ears drooping sadly. "I was hoping to meet new friends to play with."

"I'm sorry, little one," Ardyn smiled, ruffling her hair.

"Where do you think we are?" Cylaen asked.

"I have no idea how we got here, but based on what Jevan said, I think we may be on board the Pah'ora," Ardyn said. "That was the name of the spaceship they were sending from Aria'naa."

"They named it *flying death*?" Cylaen asked. "That wasn't enough to keep you from cooperating with them?"

"I didn't want to," Ardyn admitted. "Taeglyn and Takyra were both convinced it was best to cooperate until we knew more of their intentions. None of us knew they had this kind of technology that could take us like it did. I know Aerys was worried that they might try to attack, which is why he had been working to strengthen the forcefield around the Rahn'naa. We were not prepared for this."

"It seems our people have come far in their development of technology since our ancestors left their homeworld," Cylaen said, looking down at a yawning Myria. "Now I think it's time this little one takes a nap. I'll speak with you later, Ardyn."

Watching Cylaen lead Myria off to a quiet corner of the room, he realized, with a pang of guilt, that was possibly the longest civil conversation he'd ever had with her.

Knowing that Jevan was well, and that they were working on a plan to get them released, allowed Ardyn to relax. He followed Cylaen, who found her family huddled next to Ardyn's parents. Ardyn joined them, curling up on the floor, intent on getting some rest. Wrapping his arms around himself before drifting off, thoughts of how much he missed Jevan crossed his mind.

Ardyn woke abruptly when he heard a scream come from across the room. He hadn't even blinked the sleep from his eyes when two sets of hands roughly grabbed and pulled him upright and tied his arms behind his back. Struggling against those who sought to restrain him proved futile, and he was soon dragged out of the room and down a dim corridor of the ship, along with the others.

"What is going on?" Ardyn demanded to know, only to be punched in the gut, making him double over in pain.

"Be quiet or I'll vaporize you where you stand," one of the armed men threatened, pointing a nasty-looking *rahn'ora* at him. Based on the indicator, it was on the highest setting.

Shutting his mouth, Ardyn allowed himself to be led with the others down the long corridor. *This means Takyra must have failed to get us released. Are they still alive?* Ardyn wondered. *Would they kill Jevan as well, or let him go?*

The armed Athla'naa made them line up along the corridor in small groups, before herding them into a smaller room. Along the far wall was a platform with five circles. They dragged the five people in front of Ardyn onto the platform, each one on a separate circle, forced them to their knees, and then secured them in place with a forcefield. Once the field was active, it seemed to immobilize them.

Those on the platform looked terrified as the armed Athla'naa stepped away from them. Their gaze turned up toward a control booth that overlooked the room and faced the platform. Another Athla'naa wearing a black uniform had stepped up to the controls and a moment later, the platform was ablaze with light. Those trapped within the forcefields screamed in agony for a brief second before turning into piles of ash, which were quickly suctioned away into the floor below.

Dropping to his knees, Ardyn screamed as tears streamed down his face. He had known two of the people since childhood. Still crumpled on the floor, the armed men dragged Ardyn and four others up onto the platform, kicking and screaming. They forced him back onto his knees before immobilizing him with the forcefield.

Ardyn's heart hammered in his chest, terrified of what was about to happen. So many regrets flashed through his mind, as his eyes flicked up to the figure on the platform above who was about to murder him.

I am so sorry, Jevan, he thought.

Jevan, that kind, patient man, who would never see him again. The man who would never know the depths of how much Ardyn had come to care for him. He wouldn't even be able to say goodbye.

After all of them were confined into their forcefields, the armed Athla'naa backed away and Ardyn watched as the one above approached the controls. Tears continued to streak down his face as he braced himself for the end.

SERENDIPITY

After Denyra allowed Jevan to talk to Ardyn, she reassured them that those taken were going to be fed and wouldn't be harmed, *for now*. However, after several hours of nothing but arguments, Denyra seemed unwavering in her determination to exterminate every Athla'naa who descended from the old Aria'asharra faction.

During a break, while waiting for refreshments to arrive, Aerys pulled Takyra aside. Jevan overheard him debating. "We should throw her into a holding cell until she lets them go," Aerys argued.

"You know as well as I do, we can't hold someone with her level of technology for long," Takyra reminded him.

After more pointless arguments, they finally agreed to break for the night and return to the negotiations the next morning, after everyone got some rest. They escorted Denyra and her people to some quarters after she once again promised not to proceed with her plans for executions until they had completed their discussions.

"I'm stationing some of my people to keep an eye on your quarters," Aerys said, explaining the security techs standing outside the door.

"I have my own guards," Denyra sneered. "They will serve me well enough."

"They don't know our security protocols," Aerys reminded her. "If it's all the same, let your guards rest. This is our ship, after all."

Not looking pleased, Denyra reluctantly agreed, and they all went their separate ways for the night. When Jevan entered their quarters, it hit him how large and empty they felt without his friend. While speaking to Ardyn earlier had helped calm his worries, Jevan still felt anxious for his safety.

I hope Denyra will come to see reason tomorrow, Jevan thought as he flopped down onto the bed without bothering to change his clothes. Closing his eyes, he tried to sleep, but tossed restlessly until he grabbed Ardyn's pillow and hugged it tightly to his chest. Breathing in Ardyn's scent, Jevan couldn't help the tears that pricked his eyes until he finally fell into a restless slumber.

◆◆◆

What felt like only a few minutes later, the door chime awakened Jevan. Stumbling out of bed, he rubbed his eyes as he made his way to the door, greeted by Takyra with a horrified look on her face.

"I had to come tell you in person," she explained. "It's Denyra. She and her people are gone. She left a note stating that she plans to begin the executions as soon as she returns to her ship!"

Steadying himself by grasping the doorframe, Jevan looked at Takyra in shock. "Is there anything we can do?"

"I'm afraid not," Takyra apologized. "We didn't build this ship for combat and the weapons we have are buried too deep underground. The same goes for our shuttles. They are similarly stuck, and we don't have this *transmat* technology she is using to travel to her ship. We're trying to hail them now, but so far there has been no response. I will let you know when I have any news."

"Thank you," Jevan said, before Takyra hurried off. Stepping back into his quarters and letting the door close behind him, Jevan slumped against the wall and slid down to the floor. *No, no, no, no...*

◆◆◆

Ardyn was gritting his teeth, waiting for his inevitable end, when alarms suddenly sounded. Still immobilized, Ardyn could only look as far as his eyes could move. Flicking his eyes up toward the control platform above them, the person who had been about to murder them was gone, and the Athla'naa who had brought them into this room scattered. One cried out about the prisoners and was told to ignore them. "Leave the traitors. They have no way to get off this ship. We need to man the defenses, now!"

A moment later, the entire ship rocked, shuddering beneath Ardyn's knees. If he hadn't still been immobilized by the forcefield, he'd have fallen over. Those who were not on the platform all lurched or fell to the floor. *What is going on?*

The ship rocked again, and the next time it knocked Ardyn over as the forcefield holding him in place disappeared.

Ardyn's arms were still secured behind his back, but he was free. Doing his best to get his feet under him, he rose and ran toward the others, away from the deadly platform. Everyone followed him back out into the corridor, and they realized that all the armed guards were nowhere to be seen.

"What's going on?" someone asked Ardyn as they worked together to free each other's arms.

The ship rocked again, knocking them against the nearest wall. "I don't know, but I think the ship we're on is under attack."

That's when Cylaen ran up to him, holding a sobbing Myria. "What do we do? How do we get out of here?"

"First, we need to see if anyone else is still being held," Ardyn proclaimed. "I'm sure they brought up everyone that was wearing one of those bracelets. Let's go back the way we came and find them. Then we can worry about how to get off this ship and back down to the surface."

Cylaen blinked at him in confusion. "Surface? The surface of what?"

"The surface of our world, Aria'nor," Ardyn explained. "We're currently in a spaceship orbiting above the planet."

"Wait... we're in what?" Cylaen asked, dumbfounded, putting their wriggling child down. "What does any of that mean?"

Grabbing her arm and pulling her along with him, Ardyn continued. "I do not have time to explain everything right now, but we are far up in the sky, above the Aria'una."

"We're really up in the sky, Papa Ardyn?" Myria asked as she ran alongside her mother.

Picking up his daughter, he nodded at her. "Yes, we are. I need you to keep being brave while we find a way home, okay?"

Myria nodded and ducked her head into his shoulder. "Okay, Papa Ardyn. I'll be brave."

Jevan found Takyra in the control center. He knew there wasn't much he could do, but he needed to know what was going on. Even if all he could do was watch helplessly, knowing that Ardyn and his people were being needlessly slaughtered inside the ship hanging in the sky far above them.

Standing off in a corner to keep out of the way, Jevan watched as Takyra and Aerys ran scans of the ship in orbit, trying to figure out what was going on. An outline of the ship appeared on the screens above Takyra's head. "We're tracking all the life signs," Takyra explained, pointing at the dots scattered throughout the outline of the Pah'ora. Jevan's heart ached when he realized that one of them was probably Ardyn.

"They appear to have them locked in several holds of their ship," Takyra said aloud, pointing out the concentrations of dots on the lower decks.

"But look here," Aerys pointed to a long line of dots. "They are lining some of them up and leading them toward this part of the ship."

Jevan moved closer. "Do you know what's located there?"

"It could be anything," Aerys replied. "I'm not familiar with this class of ship and beyond basic life signs and energy signatures, our sensors are too outdated to make much sense of the interior."

"Look, what's happening there?" Jevan asked as five dots broke off from the long line.

They held their collective breath when the dots stopped moving, and moments later, vanished entirely. Before Jevan could even react, Takyra bowed her head. "They've begun the executions."

"What! No!" Jevan let out a wail of anguish. *Did I just witness Ardyn's death? I should have been there with him.* His eyes burned with emotion as another set of dots moved into the same place as the ones that had just disappeared.

Then other dots began to move chaotically when the entire sensor image shook, and a bright flare appeared on one side of the ship. Immediately Takyra's hands flew over the controls as she zoomed away from the Pah'ora and refocused the sensors in the direction of the disturbance. The shapes of three new ships appeared and surrounded the Pah'ora, with bright flashes appearing around the ship, shaking its sensor outline.

"The Pah'ora is under attack and taking heavy damage," Aerys reported from his console. "Their shields won't hold much longer."

No! What if Ardyn is still alive? Jevan's thoughts careened between a sense of hope and dread.

Jevan watched as Takyra opened a communications channel to the new ships. "This is the Colony Ship Rahn'naa, hailing the attacking ships," Takyra said with urgency. "Please, do not destroy the Pah'ora. She is holding many of our people prisoner on board!"

They watched helplessly as the ships ignored their hail and continued to fire.

TRAPPED

Ardyn stumbled as the ship rocked, the surrounding lights flickering. He led everyone back down the corridor to the cargo hold, because they wanted to retrieve any personal items and to gather the remaining food. Standing before the door, Ardyn looked for a slot where he might try using his control access key, but he didn't see one. Instead, there was a simple panel next to the door that was about the right size for an Athla'naa hand. Placing his hand over the panel, it scanned his hand, and the door opened.

"I can't believe that worked!" Ardyn said to no one in particular. Turning around, he saw Taeglyn and Aelrynd approaching. "Elders, we should check the other holds on this deck to make sure no one else is being held. Spread the word. To open the doors, they only need to place a hand on a panel like this one."

Nodding, the two made their way through the crowd, telling others what to do. Soon there were more Athla'naa spilling out of the holds, filling the corridor. Others went to retrieve their items and gather up any uneaten food, passing it out to anyone who was hungry.

Cylaen remained close with Myria, realizing Ardyn had a better understanding of what was going on than anyone else. Ardyn tried reassuring Myria they were still safe, even as the ship kept rocking every few moments, making the lights in the corridor flicker and dim.

"You're being very brave," Ardyn told her. "I'm proud of you."

"Thank you, Papa Ardyn, but when can we go home?"

"That's an excellent question, little one," Elder Taeglyn said, as he, Aelrynd, and his parents gathered around them. "What can we do now? How do we get out of here?"

"That is going to be more difficult. We're far up in the sky above the planet," Ardyn explained. "I think our best bet is to contact the Rahn'naa, which means I need to find a communications console."

Ardyn opened every doorway they came across, but most doors led to stores of equipment or machinery. In one room, they found crates filled with lengths of metal pipe. "Everyone! Arm yourself with one of these. We may need to fight our way out of here."

At first, they hesitated to touch the metal implements, but the three Elders gave their blessing. Ardyn felt less vulnerable as he gripped the pipe firmly in his hands. Leading the way through the maze of corridors, it surprised Ardyn to encounter so few of their captors, given the size of the ship they were on. His people's sheer numbers easily overpowered those they encountered.

After he was sure they had incapacitated all of their captors on this level, Ardyn called out to those around him. "Grab their weapons! They're more effective than these metal pipes."

Several hunters and a couple of rangers each grabbed a rahn'ora and then gathered around Ardyn. "How do we use them?"

These *rahn'ora* were a different design than those on the Rahn'naa, but Ardyn had trained enough with Aerys to figure out the basic mechanism. After a quick explanation of how they worked, he also made sure to set each one to the stun setting.

Next, Ardyn looked around for any kind of display panel they could use to communicate with the Rahn'naa, but saw none. "We need to find an elevator so I can get to their control center. That's our best chance to find a communications panel and send a message to the Rahn'naa. Everyone, look for a door that leads to a tiny room."

After some moments, someone called out, and the word traveled to Ardyn. "They think they've found an... *elevator?*"

Ardyn made his way through the crowded corridor, still followed by his family and the Elders. Once they reached the elevator, he turned to his family. "I need you to stay here. The elevator isn't large enough, and I need some hunters to accompany me. We may need to fight our way to the communications console."

"Stay safe," Ardyn's mother said, pulling him into a hug.

"I'll try, mother," Ardyn said, hugging her back.

The Elders had gathered a few hunters to accompany him. He led them into the elevator, and once inside, he saw all the words were written in the ancient script that he still couldn't read.

"Elders, can you read this script? Do any of these buttons say something useful?" Ardyn asked.

Taeglyn stepped inside and looked. "Yes, here at the top. *Primary Control Center.*"

"Thanks. That is where I need to go. Taeglyn, please remain here and keep them calm. These hunters can protect me as I try to contact Takyra or whoever is attacking this ship."

Nodding, Taeglyn stepped back out and joined the others.

Ardyn turned to address the hunters. "They will have energy weapons. If there are any in the corridor outside the elevator, we may need to overwhelm them as soon as these doors open. Be ready."

Then Ardyn touched the panel where Taeglyn had shown him, and the doors closed. Ardyn's stomach lurched as the elevator moved.

⬢⬢⬢

Watching helplessly as some of the life signs scattered onboard the Pah'ora, Jevan worried about Ardyn. *What if Ardyn...?* Shaking his head, he didn't dare think of Ardyn dying like that. *Not yet.* Then the life signs that had been lined up along a corridor, presumably awaiting their execution, formed a group as they moved back toward the holds where the other prisoners were being kept.

"Look!" Jevan pointed out. "Do you think they're locking them up again?"

As the group of life signs approached the other holds, one by one, the life signs within each hold emptied into the corridor. "They're releasing the prisoners!" Takyra exclaimed, immediately opening a communications channel. "This is the Rahn'naa hailing the Pah'ora. Please, come in!" When there was no response from them, Takyra tried once again hailing the attacking ships with a similar lack of response.

"What is going on up there?" Takyra growled in frustration. "How are their shields holding up?"

"The shields on the Pah'ora are down to forty percent," Aerys replied. "Their weapons haven't damaged the shields on any of the other ships."

The large group of life signs they had been watching were now making their way through various corridors, pausing every now and again. At the same time, there was a smaller group of life signs concentrated at the other end of the ship, on a higher deck.

"I think those are Ardyn's people," Jevan pointed at the larger group. "They look like they are trying to find a way out of the ship."

"If Ardyn still lives, surely he knows there is no easy way to leave that ship right now," Takyra said. "What if he's looking for a means to communicate with us?"

Hope bloomed in Jevan's heart. *Could it really be Ardyn leading them?* Nodding, Jevan agreed. "You're right. Ardyn wouldn't know how to get back down here, so his best option would be to send us a message."

"My scans have picked up several shuttlecraft here," Aerys said, pointing at the rear of the ship. "They won't all fit on those craft, but if they took several trips, they could use them to get back here."

"None of them would know how to fly something like that," Jevan pointed out, fearful of his friend attempting to fly a strange craft.

"True, but we could guide them," Takyra replied. "Their only other option would be to figure out how to use that transmat technology Denyra used, but we couldn't help with that."

Aerys nodded, working the controls at his workstation. "I've opened all communications channels in case anyone up there tries to reach out. Until then, all we can do is watch."

RESCUED

Ardyn readied himself for a fight, gripping his *rahn'ora* as he waited for the elevator to stop moving. When the doors opened, Ardyn stopped short. He had expected to see a corridor. Instead, the elevator had taken them directly to the control center.

After a moment of hesitation, he rushed out, followed by the hunters who accompanied him. He barely made it more than a half-dozen steps when he stumbled as the ship was rocked violently.

The control center was in chaos, with Athla'naa already fighting each other. Ardyn didn't know what was going on, so he stood there staring for a moment as he saw those in black uniforms grappling with others wearing shades of gray and purple.

"Ardyn, what do we do?" a hunter named Laeyla, asked.

"I don't know," Ardyn replied before the blast of a *rahn'ora* fired past his head, making him duck. "Get down!"

Ardyn crouched and moved toward a console, indicating to the others to stay down and cover him. Whatever was going on, Ardyn still wanted to get a message to Takyra and Aerys. Once he reached the console, Ardyn stood to see if he recognized anything familiar. Without realizing it, the fighting had stopped.

When he felt a hand on his shoulder, Ardyn swung around and pointed his *rahn'ora*, intent on fending off whoever was about to attack him. The Athla'naa immediately held his hands up to show he was unarmed. "Are you the captives they were holding?"

"What!? Who are you? What do you want with us?" Ardyn demanded.

"I am Commander Keryth of the Star Cruiser Wah'kah'ria," he replied, giving Ardyn a reassuring smile.

Looking around, Ardyn saw the fighting had stopped and all the black uniformed Athla'naa were either disarmed or stunned unconscious. Only those wearing the gray and purple uniforms remained standing, including Commander Keryth.

"A message from the Rahn'naa said this ship contained people kidnapped from the surface," Keryth explained. "Our communications were being jammed. We received their message but could not reply."

"So, you're here to help us?"

"Where are the rest of your people?" Keryth asked, turning back to Ardyn.

"We were being held on the cargo deck. Everyone else is still down there, but we freed everyone we could find."

"Well, let's get you all home first, and then we can talk about what happened," Keryth said before turning to the other men in the control center. "Two of you come with me. The rest of you throw this trash into the holding cells and sweep the ship for stragglers."

Once back down on the cargo level, Ardyn introduced his elders to Commander Keryth.

"Follow me. I know the fastest way to get you all home," Keryth said. "This old ship has taken heavy damage, so it's not safe for you to remain here."

They followed him down several corridors, but when Keryth approached the execution chamber, Ardyn's heart raced. At the doorway, Ardyn stopped cold, refusing to step inside that cursed room. "What is the meaning of this? Why are you luring us to our deaths?"

Keryth's ears dropped, and he cocked his head to one side. "This is the ship's transmat system. It will send your people back to the surface."

"No!" Ardyn shouted. "Don't lie to me. I saw what it does! It killed my friends!"

That's when Keryth's eyes widened, and his ears completely flattened. "Tell me exactly what you saw."

While his heart hammered in his chest, Ardyn recounted what he had seen happen to the others who went before him on the platform, including the immobilizing forcefields, the shrieks of agony, and watching in horror as it sucked away their ashen remains.

"Wait here," Keryth said, as he ran out of the room. A few moments later, he emerged before the control console in the area above the platform. After studying the controls for a moment, Keryth swore loudly. "*Ior'kah!* They've modified the transmat platform into an execution center. Thank you for warning me. This system is no longer safe to use for transport. We could use the transmat system on my ship—"

"No!" Taeglyn said emphatically. "We've been traumatized enough. Isn't there another way to get us back to the Rahn'naa?"

"The only other way back down would be to use the shuttles," Keryth replied. "It will take some time, but we can also use the shuttles from my star cruisers to help get everyone down. Will that be acceptable?"

"What are shuttles?" Taesys asked.

"They are smaller ships, Papa Taesys," Ardyn explained. "Takyra told me they use the smaller ones to travel from larger ships in orbit down to a planet's surface, because they take less energy and can maneuver more easily."

"So, they're like that Medellan aircraft Taeglyn and Aelrynd told me about? That sounds acceptable," Taesys said, the other two elders nodding as well.

"Okay, we can use the shuttles," Ardyn shouted up to Keryth.

After Keryth returned, he led them all to the shuttle bay while Ardyn kept asking questions. "Why aren't you trying to execute us? Don't all the people from Aria'naa hate the descendants of the Aria'asharra?"

"No, not at all," Keryth replied. "Although it would be tempting to execute those imposters. What they did was inexcusable."

"So, the Leadership Conclave did not send Denyra to execute us?" Aelrynd asked.

"No, they did not," Keryth confirmed. "There is a lot you don't know, but now isn't the time to explain everything."

When they entered the shuttle bay, there were four shuttles. "These are an older style of shuttle," Keryth explained. "Each can hold ten adults. I brought three star cruisers with me, and we each have a complement of six shuttles that can hold fifteen people each. Even then, it will take us some time to bring everyone back down, so please be patient."

Keryth assigned three of his men to pilot the other shuttles, while the commander piloted one himself. Ardyn rode with Keryth, along with Taeglyn, Aelrynd, Cylaen, Myria, and his mother. His father remained behind to help coordinate getting everyone home safely, along with providing reassurance that the shuttles were safe.

"My men will coordinate the other shuttles to bring everyone else down, while my engineering team does their best to make repairs to that heap of junk."

"Can you let the Rahn'naa know we're on the way?" Ardyn suggested.

"Yes, good idea," Keryth agreed. A very relieved sounding Takyra responded to their communication. "We'll be waiting for you outside the observation tower!"

Ardyn was about to launch into more questions when Keryth raised his hand. "Please, hold your questions until we arrive. There is a lot to explain and no need for me to repeat everything twice."

Lowering his ears, Ardyn nodded and settled back into his seat. "You're right."

As the shuttle landed next to the observation tower, Jevan ran out ahead of the others. He bounced on his toes as he waited for the shuttle doors to open. As they did, his eyes darted into the interior, looking for Ardyn, who was the last one to emerge from the craft. As soon as he did, Jevan ran toward his friend with a wide grin.

"Ardyn!" Jevan cried out as he swept his small friend into an embrace and swung him around, making Ardyn laugh. Without even thinking, Jevan bent close and whispered, "I thought I'd lost you," before pressing a kiss to Ardyn's lips. Ardyn stiffened and Jevan immediately put him down and backed away. "I'm... wow. I'm so sorry," Jevan said, his face heating with embarrassment. "I didn't mean to do that. It's just... I was so worried about you and—"

Tears slid down Ardyn's face as he leaped back into Jevan's arms, burrowing his face into the large man's shoulder. "It's okay. I was so close to dying and all I could think about was never seeing you again," Ardyn confessed.

Jevan held Ardyn in his arms as they both cried with relief. "It's alright, you're back, and you're safe," Jevan soothed.

It wasn't until someone cleared their throat behind them that the pair remembered they weren't alone.

KERYTH

Jevan was elated to have Ardyn back, safe and sound, although he was still a little embarrassed by that unintentional kiss. *I hope that doesn't make things awkward between us.*

A moment later, a young Athla'naa child came running toward Ardyn. He bent to scoop the child into his arms. "Since we were so rudely interrupted last time... Jevan, I'd like you to meet Myria," Ardyn introduced. "She's my eldest. Tell Jevan how old you are."

The young Athla'naa looked up at him with wide eyes. "He's *so* tall, Papa Ardyn!"

"Yes, he is," Ardyn agreed with a chuckle. "Jevan is of the Medellan people."

"Oh!" she exclaimed before looking up at Jevan again. "Hello, Jevan of the Medellan people. My name is Myria, and I am almost ten!"

"It's nice to meet you, Myria," Jevan said, marveling at the small child. *I keep forgetting how slowly Athla'naa people age. She looks like she shouldn't be older than four.* "Your papa told me about you."

Ardyn waved over a few other Athla'naa, introducing them, including Myria's mother and his parents. "It's a pleasure to meet you," Jevan said. "I'm glad you all made it back safely."

"So, you're the Medellan that befriended Ardyn," Saelyn said, looking him up and down for a moment before giving him a warm smile. "Thank you for looking after my son. I always worried about him, spending so much time alone."

"Mama Saelyn!" Ardyn protested, making Jevan chuckle.

Cylaen took Myria from Ardyn's arms. "Come, little one, you've had enough adventures for today. I think it's time for your nap."

"Papa Ardyn, can I go inside the tower?"

"Not right now," Ardyn replied. "You heard your mother. It's time for a nap. I'll make sure you both get a tour later, okay?"

The child pouted and hid her face in her mother's neck. "Okay."

Aelrynd laughed at the child's protestations as she and Taeglyn joined them. "If there weren't so much to discuss with our rescuer, I'd be joining that little one for a nap."

Takyra gave Aelrynd a knowing smile as she gestured toward the tower. "If everyone will follow me, there are refreshments waiting for us. You must be hungry, so I had an assortment replicated."

"Your replicators are still operational?" Keryth asked as he gazed up at the tower. "I must admit, they sure built these old ships to last."

"We designed this entire ship to be deconstructed and used to build the first settlement of our colony," Takyra replied. "Everything was designed to last, although the engineers didn't expect the Rahn'naa to be buried underground, much less for twelve centuries."

"It is impressive," Keryth said as they stepped into the elevator.

Takyra led them to the tower room where they'd been meeting. The low table in the sunken seating area held pitchers of water, fruit juices, and bottles of wah'roh. There were also platters of food and a variety of fresh fruits.

"Please, make yourself at home," Takyra gestured. "I also invited some others to join us. We recently received visitors from the far continent of Ateria, and we should include them in this conversation."

That was the first time Keryth acknowledged Jevan. "I was meaning to ask who your tall friend was," Keryth said, approaching the Medellan. "I'm Commander Keryth of the Star Cruiser Wah'kah'ria."

In his best Athla'naa, Jevan replied. "*Yawen uthera'ior. Kerros'nor* Jevan."

"You speak our tongue!" Keryth seemed suitably impressed. "It is an older dialect, but still understandable. I'll admit, it surprised the Leadership Conclave to hear that the Rahn'naa crashed on a world populated by another sentient species."

"It's a long story," Takyra said, pouring herself a glass of *wah'roh* as the three other Medellans entered the room. "Commander Keryth, this is Ard Mathias from the nearby village of Yanen, and Tomas and Aron, who recently arrived from Ateria."

After the pleasantries were complete, they all took a seat, and Keryth addressed the group. "Let me apologize for what happened. We tried to respond to your last message and warn you about Denyra, but she was jamming our signals."

"I wondered about that," Takyra admitted, as she pulled up a display over the table and showed Keryth the transcribed messages. "The first one was so curt."

"That first one was from Denyra's people. They aren't a very chatty bunch." Keryth leaned forward, reading the other message, and nodded when he finished. "The second one was the official message from the Leadership Conclave."

"We should have been more wary, after having been out of touch with Aria'naa for so long," Takyra admitted. "Especially after Denyra began making demands to round up the descendants of the Aria'asharra and make them wear those bracelets. Why were they necessary?"

"Those bracelets are outdated tech," Keryth explained. "Our older ships required them so the matter transmitter system could properly lock on to someone's coordinates. Our upgraded transmat no longer requires them."

"I suspected they might track the wearers," Aerys interjected. "If we had known that you could transport people like that, I wouldn't have spent all my time reinforcing the strength of our forcefield."

"You couldn't have known all the advancements we've made over the past twelve hundred years," Keryth reassured them. "I'm only sorry we couldn't get here in time to prevent those unnecessary deaths. Do you know how many of your people they killed?"

Ardyn shook his head. "I only saw five members of my settlement killed before they placed me on the platform myself. I don't know how many more they murdered before we arrived."

"Even five is too many. We should have arrived sooner. I am so sorry."

"Who is Denyra, and what did she want with the Aria'asharra? She seemed determined to murder tens of thousands of innocent lives," Takyra asked.

"She's a high-ranking member of a radical faction that the Leadership Conclave thought we'd wiped out," Keryth explained. "After your ship disappeared, tensions increased, and eventually civil war broke out. Millions died on both sides. Ultimately, we defeated the Aria'asharra, and restored peace to Aria'naa."

"This all happened because the Rahn'naa disappeared?" Takyra asked, leaning forward with interest.

"It was the final provocation. The Rahn'naa became a legend and a rallying cry. According to historians, they believed that the Aria'asharra had infiltrated the colony population on board and sabotaged the ship," Keryth said. "There were many conspiracy theories about what happened. Everything from the Aria'asharra taking the Rahn'naa to a different planet and subjugating those not part of their faction, or outright destroying the ship to send a message to the Leadership Conclave."

"Well, the former theory is close to the truth," Takyra said. "They diverted the Rahn'naa to this planet, and had planned to take shuttles down to this world and let the Rahn'naa continue on its way to Maal'dak Five without them."

"What happened?"

Takyra let out a frustrated sigh. "They were bumbling fools. By the time they'd woken me, they'd already crashed the ship. The Rahn'naa remained intact, but it was built in space and not designed to take off from a planet. It's too large to achieve escape velocity. So, we were stuck here and the Aria'asharra wouldn't let me send a subspace signal back to Aria'naa for help. So, instead, they shoved me back into my cryopod and left the rest of us to rot."

Keryth poured himself a glass of water. "There were ships sent out to look for you. When they didn't find the Rahn'naa along its planned route, they had to break off the search. As the civil war escalated, the Leadership Conclave needed all resources for defense and so they recalled the ships back to Aria'naa."

"So much tragedy and death." Takyra took a long drink of her *wah'roh*. "Do you have any records of who was lost during that war? I would love to know what happened to the friends and family I left behind."

"The records exist, but they are in the archives back on Aria'naa," Keryth said. "You would have to travel back there to review them."

Aerys changed the subject. "Let's get back to this *radical faction* that Denyra is a part of. If the Aria'asharra were defeated, why was Denyra trying to wipe out their descendants here? They had nothing to do with your civil war."

"They call themselves the *Maara'dahl*."

Jevan did not like the sound of that name. *The Death of All.*

MAARA'DAHL

Putting his glass of water down, Keryth sat back and looked around the room, letting the meaning of Maara'dahl sink in before he continued. "After the war ended, the Leadership Conclave allowed the remaining Aria'asharra to live in peace. Many of them settled on a remote unpopulated island on Aria'naa and some built settlements on our colony worlds, away from the established colony settlements. Their leaders were the only ones who faced consequences for the war."

"Some of our people weren't happy about that, were they?" Takyra speculated.

"There were rumblings of discontent," Keryth admitted. "Based on the historical records, most of the population was happy the war was over. However, there were small, but vocal groups within the Baaru'dak that had wanted to see all the Aria'asharra executed as war criminals."

"That seems extreme," Jevan said, wrapping a protective arm around Ardyn at the very notion.

"What our people didn't realize at the time was that the discontent of these groups continued to fester from one generation to the next, as they slowly became radicalized," Keryth explained. "Some four hundred years after the war, the Maara'dahl emerged. They've been bent on exterminating every pocket of Aria'asharra that remained. They almost succeeded, too. The Aria'asharra descendants on this world may be the largest population left."

"Why did they find it necessary to murder the descendants of the Aria'asharra?" Aelrynd asked.

Keryth took a deep breath and stood, going to the window overlooking the valley for a moment. Turning back to face everyone, he lowered his ears. "The Maara'dahl believe all Aria'asharra are a devolved off-shoot of our species, and if their faction comes into contact with members of other factions, they will somehow *infect* the rest of the Athla'naa people, causing our people to devolve back into simple-minded animals."

Ardyn leaned forward, his ears fully up and forward. "Our people have been here, cut off from Aria'naa for over twelve hundred cycles of the seasons. How could we possibly infect anyone?"

Keryth was about to respond when Taeglyn chimed in. "Exactly! Most of our people are still wary of technology, and we aren't advanced enough to be a threat to anyone on Aria'naa."

"And if our people are no longer welcome on Aria'nor," Aelrynd added, looking at Tomas and Aron. "Then I think our people will happily resettle on Maal'dak Five. We wouldn't want to *infect* anyone."

Once again, Keryth tried to speak, but then Mathias held up his hands. "I don't see why your people need to go anywhere. Do you Tomas?"

"It's not up to us," Tomas said with a shrug. "If you ask me, I see no harm in the Athla'naa staying, if they promise to stop interfering with the progress of the Medellan population. However, the Grand Council of Ateria may have an opinion on that. It will depend on what the delegation recommends."

"Well, I think our people need to stop shunning technology, once and for all," Ardyn said.

"You're right, of course," Aelrynd agreed. "Our ancestors were foolish, and it's time to rid ourselves of these notions. However, not all our people will adapt as easily as you have, Ardyn. Your innate curiosity has served you well here."

Jevan smirked when he saw Ardyn's ears drop at the compliment. *We've come a long way from when we knelt in judgement for daring to explore the Aria'una.*

"Thank you, Elders," Ardyn said. "I hope it continues to serve me well here. I... I don't know if I can ever go back to the life I had before."

"Well, before anyone makes any life-changing decisions," Keryth interrupted as he sat back down and poured himself a glass of *wah'roh*. "We need to make sure this world remains safe. Denyra may be in custody and the immediate threat neutralized, but the Maara'dahl are not a small faction. They will be back in greater numbers, and they may be more direct in their approach next time."

"What kind of *direct approach*?" Takyra asked.

"On the colony worlds where some of the Aria'asharra resettled, the Maara'dahl systematically destroyed them," Keryth revealed. "They would amass a small fleet of ships and bombard all population centers, leaving behind nothing but rubble. By the time the Leadership Conclave knew what was happening, it was too late for them to mount a defense. You're the only remnants of a colony to survive."

"Why would they destroy entire colonies?" Aerys asked. "I thought you said the Aria'asharra built their settlements away from the main colony populations?"

"They did, but the Maara'dahl were convinced that the Aria'asharra had *infected* the entire colony with their beliefs and thought it was only a matter of time before they found a way back to Aria'naa to start more trouble," Keryth replied. "The Leadership Conclave tried to protect the colonies after the first one fell, but the Maara'dahl found ways around the defensive blockades."

It horrified Jevan to hear this, knowing that Ardyn had been in the clutches of such monstrous people. "Would they attack our people as well?"

Keryth nodded. "That's what I'm afraid of," he admitted. "They were unusually lenient by not attacking the Rahn'naa or any of the settlements on this continent outright. Perhaps knowing that the Baaru'dak and Laasa'dak have been in cryostasis all this time made them worth saving."

"Denyra seemed disappointed that we would even ask for mercy for the descendants of the Aria'asharra," Takyra said. "I think she had hoped to find an ally in us, but she was sorely mistaken."

Tomas leaned forward. "What about our people in Ateria? They have had no contact with the Athla'naa. Would they be in danger of attack?"

"The Maara'dahl might leave your people alone, assuming they scan your life signs and realize there are no Athla'naa anywhere on your continent," Keryth replied. "However, they might decide that all life on this planet is forfeit, now that Denyra failed to convince Takyra to join them in their cause."

"If these Maara'dahl were determined to exterminate the Aria'asharra, why did it take them so long to search for this colony?" Tomas asked. "They've had over a thousand cycles of the seasons, so why now?"

"When the ships that were sent to search for the Rahn'naa didn't find any trace of the ship, the Leadership Conclave assumed that it was destroyed," Keryth said. "There is a large nebula between this planetary system and ours. The nebula obscured our ability to see this solar system clearly, so our scientists overlooked it."

Pouring herself another drink, Takyra flattened her ears as she had a realization. "They would never have known we were here if I hadn't sent that subspace message. I alerted them to our presence."

"So, it's your fault we're in this situation in the first place," Aron said with a snarl.

"She couldn't have known this would happen," Tomas admonished his companion. "Remember, they've been asleep for over twelve hundred cycles of the seasons."

Aron made an indignant huff, but didn't say anything further.

"What can we do to prepare?" Aerys asked. "Our forcefield is still operational. Would it be able to hold up against your current weapons?"

Turning to Aerys, Keryth replied. "If we had more time, I'd recommend implementing a planetary defense grid. As it is, the best we can do right now is assess your current defensive capabilities on the ground, while my star cruisers help to defend the rest of the planet from space."

Jevan leaned forward with interest. "What does a planetary defense grid do?"

"They were only theoretical in my day, but the idea was to have a network of satellites in orbit around Aria'naa that could project a forcefield around the entire planet, along with being armed with weapons to repel any hostile spacecraft," Takyra replied, turning to Keryth. "Is that what you've put in place?"

"That's exactly right," Keryth replied. "We've upgraded the technology a few times now. The first grid took decades to build, but we can now deploy one in less than a year. Still not fast enough in this situation, but something to consider for the future."

"This defense grid could protect all of Ateria and Vestos?" Tomas asked.

"Yes, it would surround your entire planet," Keryth confirmed.

Aron looked at Tomas. "The Grand Council would be very interested in something like that."

"Once we've finished bringing everyone back down to the surface and have secured the Pah'ora, I will assign some of my engineering technicians to assess your forcefield," Keryth replied. "If they're compatible, we could upgrade many of your systems to help withstand a direct attack. The fact most of your ship is buried underground also gives you some protective advantage."

"How much time do you think we have?" Takyra asked.

"It depends on if the Pah'ora could send off a message before we blocked their communications," Keryth replied. "It could be a matter of days, but they will come. More ships from Aria'naa are also on the way, but we don't know how large of a force we'll have to deal with yet."

"You might want to call off that delegation until we have a better idea of what we're dealing with," Aerys said to Tomas and Aron.

Tomas sighed and shook his head. "It's too late for that. When we spoke to them yesterday, they said the delegation was to take off early this morning. They are already well underway."

"Fascinating," Keryth exclaimed. "Your world has such a wide variety of technology. I'm sure there are some historians back on Aria'naa who would love to study your world sometime. First, I'd like to know how the people in cryostasis were awakened after all these centuries."

"It all began when I found this key," Ardyn said, pulling it out of his pocket.

Ardyn and Jevan had Keryth's rapt attention as they related their story, with input from the others in the room. When they finished, the commander leaned back, his hands intertwined behind his head. "This is a more complicated situation than we originally thought. I'll need to confer with the Leadership Conclave before we decide anything."

Finally finding the courage, Ardyn asked Keryth. "Will you make our people leave this world?"

With a shake of his head, Keryth smiled with a small shrug. "It's not really my call, but your people have lived here for so long, I don't think it would be right to force you to leave.

I think Takyra's people are potentially more disruptive to this world. It's more likely they would be ordered to relocate."

Ardyn wasn't sure how he felt about that, after having become accustomed to living on the Rahn'naa. *Could I really go back to my old life, if given the chance?*

REGROUP

After the meeting with Keryth concluded, Jevan led an exhausted Ardyn back to their quarters. Yet, once there, Ardyn wasn't as ready to collapse as Jevan had expected he would. Instead, his friend began pacing and mumbling to himself.

"Hey, what's going on in that pretty head of yours?" Jevan asked.

"I'm sorry. So much has happened over the past couple of cycles of the sun," Ardyn made his way to the replicator. "I wanted to keep a clear head when we spoke to Keryth, but now I need a drink. Do you want anything?"

"Yeah, I could use one myself."

Jevan plopped himself onto the couch and watched as Ardyn brought two drinks with him. Settling himself next to Jevan, Ardyn handed him a drink as he took a sip from his, before leaning back and letting Jevan wrap an arm around his shoulders.

"I'm so glad I didn't lose you," Jevan confessed. "When you and all your people just disappeared like that, I was beside myself with worry. I thought all of you had died!"

Next to him, Ardyn took a long, steadying breath. "It was so close. I was up there on the execution platform. They were about to turn me into a pile of ash. All I could think about was you when I was bracing myself for the end."

An ache bloomed in Jevan's heart, and he hugged Ardyn closer to him. "How did you escape from that?"

"The alarms rang, and those who captured us ran off as the ship began to rock and shudder. That must have been when Keryth arrived and attacked. He and his crew saved my life." Ardyn turned in Jevan's arms, looking at him, his eyes brimming with emotion. "I didn't want to die. I wanted to see you again... to tell you..."

Jevan reached over and cupped his friend's face in one hand, as Ardyn leaned into the touch. "What did you want to tell me?" Jevan prompted.

Leaning back, Ardyn looked away from him for a moment, taking a big gulp of his drink before setting the glass down on the table. "I wanted you to know... how much I care for you, Jevan. It made me sad to think I would die without you knowing that."

The ache in his chest grew, now accompanied by a sense of pure joy. Jevan couldn't hold back the bright smile that crossed his face. "I hadn't dared hope, but a part of me knew you were beginning to... also care for me, in the way I've felt for you."

Ardyn's eyes grew wide, and his ears twitched. "We haven't really spoken of it, but when? When did you know?"

"When you saved me from your settlement," Jevan confessed. "That's when I knew I would always care for you."

"So many things are still uncertain. I don't even know where our futures lie. I just know I don't want to be separated from you. For the time being, that's enough."

Taking Ardyn's hand in his, Jevan nodded. "Agreed. Until we sort this mess out, it's enough for me as well."

Ardyn snuggled back into Jevan's embrace, his eyes closing, and ears drooping. They sat in companionable silence while Jevan finished his drink. When he looked down and saw Ardyn drool on his chest, Jevan chuckled.

"Alright, come on sleepy one," Jevan said, putting down his glass and helping Ardyn up. "Let's get you to bed."

●●●

While Takyra was busy preparing for the Aterian delegation, and Aerys worked with Keryth's engineers to upgrade the systems throughout the Rahn'naa, Jevan and Ardyn split up. Ardyn worked with the Elder Triumvirate to calm the frazzled nerves of their people, while Jevan went to spend time with Mathias, Tomas, and Aron.

After what happened, Jevan didn't like being apart from Ardyn for too long. However, with everything going on, they could not stay as attached at the hip as they had been. Today, Jevan was taking Mathias and the Aterians into the surrounding forest to show them the discoveries he and Ardyn had made before finding their way into the Rahn'naa.

"So, you both came back into this forbidden forest after escaping your village?" Tomas asked as they made their way through the trees. "Why would you risk such a thing?"

"Where else should we have gone?" Jevan asked. "The Athla'naa marked me for execution, and any Medellan village would have sent me back to Yanen for judgment. If we were to live out our lives in the wild, it was best to head to the only area where we were sure we'd not encounter anyone. Plus, we wanted to understand what it was about the Aria'una that made it worth a death sentence."

"I wasn't going to let them execute you," Mathias argued.

"You were going to send us to the mines," Jevan reminded him. "A slow death is less merciful than a quick one, if you ask me."

Mathias looked as if he were about to argue when Jevan changed the subject. "How did your trip back to Yanen with Keryth go yesterday?"

"You can imagine the shock on people's faces when Keryth set his shuttle down in the middle of the village square," Mathias said with a mirthful smile. "They were more surprised when I was the one walking out of that flying contraption!"

"Will the Aterian delegation be able to land there?" Jevan asked as the group of them continued to make their way through the forest.

"Yes," Aron replied. "One of your fallow fields will work as a place to land. They just need to smooth the dirt, so the landing won't be as bumpy."

"I've tasked all the young folks in the village to create this *runway*. They didn't understand the purpose of it, but seemed excited that another flying machine was going to land nearby. Keryth will scan for their arrival and meet them in Yanen with one of his shuttles.

"Oh, and your mother and sister send their regards," Mathias said, patting Jevan on the shoulder. "I meant to tell you this morning, but you seemed a bit preoccupied with your little elven friend."

"*Athla'naa*," Jevan reminded him. "They aren't the mythical *elves* from our fairy tales, so we shouldn't keep calling them that. Especially if we expect them to stop calling us *athla'maakh*."

"Yes, yes. You're right, of course," Mathias replied dismissively. "While I was there, I wrote several missives. I had messengers take them to nearby villages, with the directive to copy them and spread the word until all Medellans on Vestos knew what was happening. I instructed them to prepare and take shelter in case those Maara'dahl decide to return."

"Let's hope it doesn't come to that," Jevan said. "Keryth said they have reinforcements coming to help protect us."

"None of our people are prepared to repel an attack from advanced alien spacecraft," Tomas said. "So, I hope they send their entire fleet."

A moment later, they turned into the small clearing where the large machine still stood, where Jevan and Ardyn had uncovered it.

"What is that?!" Aron asked, staring up at it, slack jawed.

"Takyra confirmed these machines were designed to move large quantities of dirt," Jevan said as he walked toward the enormous machine and climbed up the ladder to the control cabin. Looking down at the three below, he continued his explanation. "We think Ardyn's ancestors used them to bury as much of the Rahn'naa as they could. That's why the only part of the ship still above ground is the tower."

"That explains the strange shape of the valley," Tomas said. "The ship must have carved it out when it crashed, making it easier for them to bury."

"Yes, exactly," Jevan agreed. "Ardyn and I were going to attempt to use this machine to dig under the forcefield. At the time we found it, it would only allow Ardyn to pass through the barrier. They configured it to keep any other lifeform out."

Tomas climbed up after him and Jevan made room for the man to move past him into the control cabin. "I still marvel at how advanced this all looks, knowing how old it is," he said as he looked over the controls. "Even a machine like this is far beyond what we've yet achieved."

The tall man dwarfed the seat that was clearly designed for a smaller person, and Jevan couldn't help smirking at the sight. "If you think this is impressive to you, can you imagine how it all looks to someone who didn't grow up with anything more advanced than a water wheel?"

As Tomas made to exit the cabin, Jevan climbed back down to the ground. "Good point. How are you handling all this so well?" Tomas asked, after climbing down himself.

"It's been a lot, I'll admit, but so much has happened. I haven't had a chance to really process it all. Ardyn has been struggling more than I have with it, as you can imagine. His people live even more primitively than ours do and to discover your own ancestors were this far advanced? Their entire society is going through a massive upheaval right now."

"So will ours," Mathias pointed out. "You don't think our people will come away from all this unchanged, do you?"

"No, I guess none of us will," Jevan agreed.

DELEGATION

It surprised Ardyn when he found Jevan awake before him, already dressed and sitting on the edge of the bed, putting on his boots. Crawling over to him, he couldn't help but tease. "You're really excited about today, aren't you?"

"Is it that obvious?"

"I can't remember the last time you were up before I was," Ardyn said with a laugh, getting out of bed. "Have they arrived yet?"

"I haven't heard anything, but I wanted to head to the control center to see if there was any news," Jevan admitted. "I'm sorry if I woke you."

"Give me a few minutes and I'll join you."

Ardyn was pulling on his pants when Cytra relayed a message to them. "The Aterian Delegation has landed in Yanen, and the shuttlecraft will leave shortly."

"Just in time!" Ardyn said as he pulled on his boots.

They hurried down the corridor to the elevator and found Takyra and Aerys already there. "I hope you two didn't have to rush too fast to get ready."

"Jevan woke before me this morning, for a change. I had to skip washing my hair or we wouldn't be ready."

Takyra laughed. "You're really excited to speak to that historian."

"Yes! I have so many questions," Jevan admitted.

"Well, let's go meet them," Aerys said as the elevator doors parted.

Upon emerging from the tower, they could see the shuttle in the distance, flying over the trees toward them. "Where are Mathias and the other Aterians?"

"They went with Keryth to greet the delegation," Takyra explained. "We also sent along a couple of security and engineering techs to watch over their aircraft and make sure it doesn't require any repairs after its long flight."

A small crowd from the Athla'naa encampment had also gathered. Ardyn saw the Elders and a few hunters keeping them back from the area where the shuttle was to land. He smirked as he watched his father holding people back with the

Triumvirate staff in hand. *I still can't believe they allowed Papa Taesys to join the Triumvirate.*

Then the shuttle landed between them and the encampment, obscuring the other Athla'naa from view. It kicked up a small cloud of dust as it settled on the ground, making Ardyn realize why Takyra stayed back as far as she did.

After the dust settled, they approached the shuttle as the door opened. Ardyn found himself excited to meet the newcomers as well. Keryth and Mathias were the first to exit, followed by a tall, older Medellan. His complexion was as dark as Jevan's, but his hair had a shock of white and his eyes were a deep color of blue.

Behind him was a younger female Medellan, only slightly shorter, with paler skin and hair the rich red color of the leaves of a *bhat'laa'arh*. There were two other dour looking males, followed by Tomas and Aron.

Takyra stepped forward, introducing herself, and those who accompanied her.

The older man smiled and held out a hand in greeting. "Nice to meet you, Takyra. My name is Andreesen. This is Marta, a historian from the Aterian Central Archives. Those two grumps behind us are Nels and Oren. They're observers sent by the Grand Council. We left our pilot behind to stay with the aircraft."

"Welcome to the Rahn'naa," Takyra said. "Won't you follow me?"

"If it's all the same to you, I'd rather stretch my legs first," Andreesen said. "We can chat and walk at the same time, can't we?"

"Yes, of course," Takyra agreed as she led the group around the shuttle. "We could take a stroll in the forest if you like."

As they rounded the shuttle, Andreesen made his way toward the gathered Athla'naa. "When Tomas and Aron told me they'd met *elves*, I didn't want to believe them. Yet, here you all are. Goodness, we have much to discuss."

"How much did Keryth fill you in?" Aerys asked.

"The shuttle flight was short, so not much," Andreesen admitted.

"I gave them a summary of what's been happening," Keryth added. "But I'm afraid I left them with more questions than answers."

When they approached the gathered crowd, the elders came forward to greet them. "Welcome. We are the Elder Triumvirate, and we are the leaders of the Athla'naa."

Andreesen narrowed his eyes and the other Aterians with him looked confused. "I thought Takyra was your leader?"

"My apologies," Takyra said. "I'm the Chief Technician of the Rahn'naa, which is the ship that crashed on this world. I lead the ship and its crew. The Elder Triumvirate lead the Athla'naa people who established settlements throughout this continent."

Marta stepped forward. "So, there are two separate populations of Athla'naa?"

"It's a little more complicated than that," Takyra replied. "Elders, you're welcome to join us. Andreesen wanted to stretch his legs, so we're taking a short walk before we head inside."

As they walked, Takyra turned to look at Ardyn. "Why don't you start at the beginning, when you found the key?"

Everyone's attention turned to him as he related his story once again. "Elder Aelrynd had sent me to hunt a beast that had been preying upon our children when I was caught in a rainstorm. I found shelter in a small cave and that's where I found this." Ardyn pulled out the control access key that he still carried with him and held it out to Andreesen.

"This is a key? Why is it glowing?"

"It's an electronic *control access key*," Aerys explained. "This key opens most doors throughout the Rahn'naa. It's programmed to activate when someone touches it. Keys like this can be programmed to only respond to specific people."

"Fascinating. May I see it?" Marta asked. Taking it from Ardyn, the glow faded. "I see what you mean. I assume this end slides into a slot by the door it's meant to open?"

"Yes," Aerys replied. "I'd be happy to have our engineers explain our technology in more detail later. Please, Ardyn, continue."

Ardyn told them how he'd met Jevan and their discovery of the airlock and tower. "A forcefield that can be programmed like this key protects the tower. When we first approached it, Jevan ran into the forcefield. He couldn't get through it, but I could."

"It took us some time, but eventually we found a hatch within this forest that wasn't inside the forcefield, and that allowed both of us into the ship," Jevan added.

"How large is this ship?" Andreesen asked.

"They buried most of it beneath the ground we're walking on," Takyra said. "Did Keryth explain how long ago the ship crashed?"

Andreesen stopped for a moment. "Yes, and I still can't believe it. Twelve hundred cycles of the seasons, and that tower still stands with no sign of decay? I look forward to asking your engineers how that's accomplished!"

They continued walking and related the rest of the story, up to the battle with the Maara'dahl. Takyra had kept their wanderings through the Aria'una strategic, and they emerged back at the observation tower a few moments after they'd finished.

"Now that you're caught up on most of the details," Takyra said. "May I show you to your quarters where you can freshen up? Then you're welcome to join us for a meal where we can answer your questions. Later, I plan to take you on a tour of the ship and show you our cryogenic systems."

"Oh, I'd love to learn more about that," Marta said enthusiastically, while Andreesen merely gave a nod of assent.

PEJORATIVE

It was early evening when they gathered again. This time, Takyra had them escorted to a part of the ship that they hadn't seen before. "Where are we?" Jevan asked.

"We designed this part of the ship to convert into shops and markets for the new colony," Takyra explained. "I thought everyone here would enjoy sharing a meal in what would have been an eating establishment."

As they entered the establishment that Takyra unlocked for them, the lights came on. Instead of the typical bright lights throughout the rest of the ship, the lighting here was dimmer, with a warm tone. It was tastefully appointed with a variety of different sized tables. Takyra went toward the largest one in the center of the establishment.

Around the large oval table were pillowed seats that engulfed the Athla'naa among them and were large enough to accommodate the larger frames of the Medellans. As Jevan sat down, he felt almost weightless. "These are very comfortable!"

Takyra snuggled back into her chair with a happy sigh. "These pillowed chairs were all the rage when we left Aria'naa. When dining out, our people loved to be comfortable. One of my favorite restaurants on Aria'naa inspired this establishment."

"This is very quaint," Keryth said with a smirk. "I've seen chairs and tables like these in the museum. This is an early version of a replicator table, isn't it?"

Takyra gave him a little side-eyed glance, while her ears came forward. "Yes, it was the height of fashion in a public eating establishment."

Lowering his ears, Keryth gave her a chastened look. "I'm sorry. I keep forgetting that Aria'naa having this level of technology was only a couple of months ago for you."

Touching the table, a display rose, and Takyra entered some commands. "There, I've reprogrammed the table to recognize both Medellan and Athla'naa. Everyone, please place your hands on the table for a moment."

Curious, Jevan reached out and placed his hands palms down as Takyra demonstrated. That's when Jevan noticed that there was a slight oval depression on the table before each seat. Takyra then gave a few commands to Cytra, and a moment later, a plate of food and a beverage appeared on the table before each of them. Each dish appeared different. For Jevan, it was a plate of rich meat stew and a slice of hearty bread, along with a glass of what looked like ale.

The Aterians were all slightly startled at the sight before gingerly reaching out to see if the plates were real. "That's incredible!" Marta exclaimed. "How is that possible?"

"As Keryth said, this is a replicator table," Takyra explained. "It works similarly to the food replicators in your quarters, but it includes the capability of determining the best meal for each person. When it scans your palms, it can detect your general meal preference and replicates what's likely to be a favorite dish."

"Historically, these only existed in eating establishments because the technology was difficult to manufacture," Keryth explained. "Today, this is the norm in any Athla'naa home."

"So, no one on your world cooks anymore?" Marta asked.

"Some still cook, if they have the skills and desire for it," Keryth explained. "Although, most of those become professional chefs and operate eating establishments such as this."

"People go out to eat cooked meals on Aria'naa now?" Takyra asked. "Back then, not everyone could afford even the simplest replicator, which is why establishments like these were popular."

"After the war with the Aria'asharra, our leaders realized that our way of life was not sustainable," Keryth explained. "We had the technology and resources to feed everyone but had done nothing about it. Poverty still existed, and some people starved. Within a decade after the war ended, everyone had a replicator in their home. Now many homes are much like the quarters on this ship, with only a replicator in the kitchen. If people want a freshly cooked meal, they can go out to an eating establishment instead."

"Isn't it fascinating how trends change?" Marta pondered aloud. "Not to mention how the cultural implications of people from different eras meeting like this is unprecedented."

As they all began eating, Andreesen only picked at his food with a frown. "Is the meal not to your liking?" Takyra asked.

"This is very close to my favorite dish, but I was hoping to sample some of your cuisine," Andreesen said.

"I can change that," Takyra said with a smile, bringing up the display again. "Please put down the utensils for a moment."

After he put them down, Takyra made some selections on the display and Andreesen's meal disappeared. The replicator replaced Andreesen's meal with a sampling of several Athla'naa delicacies.

"Try the red one," Jevan said, pointing it out. "They're called *asharra'laa*. Those are my favorite."

With a smirk, Takyra made a few more selections on her display and everyone had a couple of pieces of the bright red oblong delicacies on their plates. Jevan couldn't describe the taste, but the burst of exotic flavor when he bit into one always made him smile.

Jevan watched Andreesen as he sampled the food and smiled at the man's reactions. Earlier, Andreesen had said little, only asking a few questions for clarification as they related their story to him. He was clearly a studious man, spending more time listening than speaking.

Andreesen then turned his attention to Jevan, and he felt that perhaps he'd been staring at the man too intently. Instead, the older man gave him a bright smile. "Jevan, you were a trader before you stumbled upon all this. Is that right?"

"Yes, sir," Jevan replied. "I would take goods from my village and trade them for other goods from nearby Medellan villages and Athla'naa settlements."

"Ah, so you enjoy traveling?"

Nodding, Jevan replied. "Yes, sir. I've never been one to stay in one place for too long. This has been the longest I've ever stayed anywhere since I was a boy."

"Is that why you haven't pair-bonded yet?" Andreesen asked, narrowing his eyes at Jevan.

Flushing with irritation, Jevan tried not to raise his voice. "It is one reason, but how could you tell?"

"Tomas mentioned it when we spoke over the radio," Andreesen explained. "It's not right, a young man of your age without a family yet. We have a lot of fine people in Ateria if no one on Vestos suits your fancy."

Jevan was getting angry. *Why does everyone want me to pair-bond so badly?* Boldly grabbing Ardyn's hand, he glared at Andreesen. "With all due respect, *sir*, but I think I can handle my own affairs in matters of the heart and family."

Andreesen's eyes went wide. "Are you telling me you'd rather pair-bond with this... elf... Athla'naa... *person?*"

"What I am telling you is that I don't wish to pair-bond *with anyone*," Jevan said, anger rising in his voice. "Ardyn and I have become close, but neither of us wishes to be defined by whatever relationship we have."

"No one is going to force you into a pair-bond," Ardyn reassured him with a squeeze of his hand. "Not if I have anything to say about it."

Aelrynd put down her utensils and leaned her elbows on the table. "What exactly does this pair-bond entail? I always assumed it was merely a pledge of commitment between two Medellans."

"Oh, no, it's far deeper than that," Mathias replied. "The ritual binds the pair together for life."

"Binds them how?" Aelrynd asked, her curiosity piqued.

"It's our understanding that it binds our hearts and minds together through a chemical process," Andreesen explained. "After two Medellans have undergone the ritual, it's impossible for them to enjoy intimacy with anyone other than their bondmate. To do so is often fatal."

"That's right," Ardyn said. "I remember Jevan telling me about a case where a young man forced himself sexually on a pair-bonded woman, and it led to her death."

"Yes, that was a terrible thing," Mathias confirmed.

After Mathias and Andreesen discussed the case in detail, there was a lull in conversation.

"Why don't you wish to pair-bond?" Marta asked, a wrinkle of concern on her forehead.

"I don't want to be bonded for life to the wrong person and wind up as miserable as my parents were," Jevan responded.

Mathias sighed. "I know your parents were an ill-matched pair, but many bondmates learn to love each other."

"I just don't understand why you're all so concerned about whether I pair-bond or not," Jevan grumbled.

Andreesen wiped his mouth with his napkin and leaned back, giving Jevan an odd look. "What I want to know is why you're so determined to die young?"

BIOLOGISM

Jevan wasn't sure he'd heard right. "Die? What do you mean? Are you saying that if I don't pair-bond, I could die?"

"Yes, that's exactly what I'm telling you, dear boy," Andreesen replied in complete seriousness. "Why else do you think we made it one of our most sacred traditions?"

"I don't know," Jevan admitted. "But then, why did Ardyn's ancestors forbid anyone from venturing near the Rahn'naa? Some *sacred traditions* are merely there to cover up generations of lies. What exactly happens when a Medellan does not pair-bond?"

"The last documented case happened about a century ago," Marta said. "What happened was horrible."

"Wh-what happened?" Jevan hesitated to ask, his heart already sinking at the thought.

Seeing the distress on Marta's face, Andreesen patted her hand and related the story. "The case involved a young woman. An elder sibling had horribly abused her as a child, so she dreaded having to go through the pair-bond ceremony and be compelled to be intimate with someone in that way. So, she refused, and her parents allowed it."

"Forced to be intimate?" Ardyn asked as his ears flattened back. "I didn't think your people did that."

Jevan squeezed Ardyn's hand, knowing how traumatized his friend was over his own forced matings.

"It's a required part of the ceremony to make sure the bond takes," Andreesen explained matter-of-factly. "Although most couples enjoy that part. Especially when it's a love bond."

"Please, what happened to her?" Jevan asked.

"At first, nothing. Then, a few cycles of the moons after her thirtieth birthday, she aged rapidly," Andreesen replied. "Within a few cycles of the seasons, her body was bent with age, barely recognizable. She died before she turned thirty-five."

"If I don't pair-bond before I'm thirty, I'll die before my thirty-fifth summer?" Jevan couldn't help the lump of fear that lodged in his throat, and Ardyn reached out to put a comforting arm around him.

"Unfortunately, yes," Marta confirmed.

"My goodness, I didn't know," Mathias said, looking equally horrified. "I knew there was a strict mandate to maintain the pair-bond ritual, but there was nothing written about why. Jevan is the first one in my village to even consider refusing to pair-bond, so it's never been an issue before."

Jevan leaned back in his chair, defeated. *What sort of fate was that? Forced to be bonded for life to one person or die young?* Without thinking, he stood and moved away from the table. "Excuse me, but I need some time to think."

Jevan headed down to the cargo deck, where he wouldn't encounter many others as he wandered the corridors, trying to clear his head. For seasons Jevan had fought against the idea of the pair-bond, because Mathias had never given him a good reason. Sacred traditions be damned. *But now...*

After wandering for a while, Jevan made his way back to their quarters. His disappointment at not finding Ardyn there yet surprised him. His heart clenched in his chest, and he recalled their recent conversation when Ardyn confessed his feelings. Too much was going on for them to pursue a relationship right now, but knowing he could die if he didn't pair-bond made Jevan rethink that decision.

He realized recently that he'd lost interest in being intimate with anyone, a stark contrast to all his randy adventures over the seasons. There had been plenty of newly awakened Athla'naa who had shown an interest in him sharing their bed, but he'd turned all of them down.

Making his way into the kitchen, Jevan replicated himself a drink. As he sat down, he asked himself, *would Ardyn even want to bond with me?*

◆◆◆

When Ardyn arrived back at their quarters, he found Jevan on the couch nursing a drink. The normally jovial man looked so defeated, it made Ardyn worry. "Are you alright?"

"I don't know," Jevan replied with a shrug of his shoulders. "It's just... we've dealt with so much already, and now I find out that if I don't pair-bond with someone, I'll die young?"

"We have both been through a lot lately, but you're only twenty-five, right?" Ardyn asked, sitting next to him.

"Almost twenty-six," Jevan replied.

"Then you still have over four cycles of the season before you must be pair-bonded. That gives you time to get used to the idea and... and find another Medellan you might enjoy spending the rest of your life with. Maybe Andreesen was right? You could go to Ateria and find someone there."

A sad smile crossed Jevan's face as he reached out and took Ardyn's hands. "I already found someone, but he's a different species."

Ardyn felt his face flush. "You would want to pair-bond... with *me*?"

Nodding, Jevan reached out to caress Ardyn's face. "You're the only one I would even consider it with, but you're Athla'naa. I don't know if the pair-bond ritual would even work between us."

Is this something I want? Ardyn wasn't sure. As his heart hammered in his chest, he tried to give Jevan another option. "What about any of your past lovers? Are you sure none of them were acceptable?"

"Many of them were also Athla'naa," Jevan reminded him. "The other Medellans probably have pair-bonded by now. Even if one was still free, there are none that I would want to spend the rest of my life with."

Ardyn's heart hammered even harder as he ducked his head and flattened his ears. "Are you saying that you want to spend the *rest of your life* with me, if you could?"

"Yes, I would, if you were okay with the idea," Jevan admitted. "Assuming it would even work between our species."

Ardyn stared into Jevan's beautiful storm-gray eyes for a moment, feeling slightly overwhelmed at the surge of emotions he felt. Ducking his head back down, Ardyn took a breath. "Fate has drawn us together from the moment we met. I don't know if it's possible either, but... if it would help extend your life, I would consider it. I don't want to lose you."

"You would? But your people prefer open relationships with many partners. If it is even possible, could you be happy being stuck with me for the rest of your life?"

Without hesitation, Ardyn nodded. "Yes. I care for you deeply. Being with you feels like home to me, and I trust you more than I've ever trusted anyone."

A warm smile brightened Jevan's face as he brushed some stray hair away from Ardyn's eyes. "You're right. I have some time. There's no need for us to decide all this tonight, but... thank you. I feel better knowing you would be open to a pair-bond."

Standing, Ardyn reached out for Jevan's hand. "Come, let's get some rest. I'll fill you in over breakfast on what happened after you left last night. I think tomorrow is going to be another long cycle of the sun."

Ardyn couldn't have been more right.

NEGOTIATIONS

Jevan and Ardyn broke their fast in the privacy of their quarters the next morning. "So, what happened last night after I left?" Jevan asked as he sat down with a bowl of porridge.

After taking a sip of tea, Ardyn replied. "From the look on Andreesen's face, he was not pleased. He said little, but from some off-hand remarks, I have the feeling he is not happy about the Athla'naa presence here."

"What did he say?"

"He continued to call us *elves*, even after Takyra politely informed him we are called Athla'naa," Ardyn replied. "A few times, he also mumbled something about *alien interference*."

"What about Marta? I got the impression she was very excited to meet you and learn about your culture and technology."

"She gave Andreesen disapproving looks a few times last night," Ardyn recalled. "And those other two? Nels and Oren? They stayed true to their titles and merely observed without comment."

"Yeah, I couldn't read either of them. They're the most stoic men I've ever met," Jevan admitted, as he finished his meal. "What's the plan for today?"

"Takyra told me to meet them in the tower room this morning," Ardyn said, standing and taking Jevan's bowl to place back into the replicator for recycling. "Are you ready?"

"As ready as I'll ever be," Jevan replied, with his usual jovial smirk.

When they arrived, Ardyn had to tilt his ears back because Andreesen was shouting at Takyra, towering over her. "I sat quietly and listened to all your explanations yesterday. Today I will say my piece. You do not get to dictate terms to me!"

Taking Jevan's hand, Ardyn led him further into the room and they took their seats in a far corner around the sunken table. *What brought this on?*

Meanwhile, Takyra gave a frustrated sigh. "I am not trying to *dictate* anything. We are merely asking you to cooperate until this matter with the Maara'dahl is settled."

Keryth stood and faced Andreesen. "As we explained yesterday, the Maara'dahl would kill every single Athla'naa born of Aria'asharra ancestry here. Until we subdue them, it would be too dangerous to transport them back to our homeworld right now."

From where he sat, Mathias spoke up. "They've been here for over twelve hundred cycles of the seasons, and we've had a peace treaty with them for seven hundred. These people are not a threat to us."

"They are the reason for the threat," Andreesen pointed out. "Also, you and your people do not get a say in this. You're the descendants of criminals and ne'er-do-wells."

Mathias' face turned red, and it looked like he was about to argue when Marta interjected. "Well, actually..."

"What is it, Marta?" Andreesen groused.

"Sit down first, you old grump, and I'll explain."

With a growl, Andreesen sat down into the cushioned seating, crossed his arms and glared at Marta. Everyone else standing also took a seat.

"That's better. You know I've been researching the history of the *Vestian Outcasts*," Marta began. "I found an archive of old records dating back over eight hundred cycles of the seasons, and I found some startling information."

"What information? Why is this the first I've heard of this?" Andreesen asked, uncrossing his arms, and leaning forward.

"I wanted to have everything properly documented before presenting it to you, but I think it applies to this debate. You need to know this—"

"Well? Out with it already!" Andreesen said with obvious frustration.

Rolling her eyes, Marta explained. "As you know, the Vestian Outcasts were prisoners that were loaded onto ships and exiled. People assumed that the prisoners were a mix of murderers, rapists, and other such ilk. Criminals judged too irredeemable to be set free. However, the records I found tell a very different story. They may not have been criminals at all."

"If they weren't criminals, why were they in the prisons?" Andreesen asked.

"For the same reason they were exiled. If those records are authentic, then most were political enemies of the government," Marta revealed. "The chancellor of that era was cruel and not well-liked. Some people tried to stage a coup that led to a war that lasted for three cycles of the seasons. Each cycle of the seasons, as the prisons filled, the chancellor would ship off a boat full of his political enemies that his forces had captured."

"Is that why the boats stopped coming after three cycles of the seasons?" Mathias asked.

"Yes. They finally defeated the chancellor's forces and deposed him," Marta replied.

"I don't remember learning about any of that in school," Tomas said. "How do we not know about all this?"

"They contained the conflict to the capital city of Donarvon," Marta replied. "The rest of Ateria wasn't involved, and attacking forces kept the news from spreading outside the city. They didn't want the provinces who supported the chancellor to send reinforcements."

"So, they kept the rest of Ateria from learning the truth?" Andreesen asked. "How did they keep his supporters from voting for him again?"

"They didn't include his name in the next election, and it seems few people questioned it. The whole thing was soon forgotten, even within Donarvon," Marta replied.

Next to Ardyn, Jevan leaned forward. "Then why did no one ever send a ship to Vestos after that? Wouldn't Ateria have welcomed our ancestors back if they had supported the coup?"

"I'm not sure," Marta replied apologetically. "There's no further mention of the ships that were sent, but it's possible that they had a difficult time holding on to control of their new government and by the time the region stabilized again, the ships sent to Vestos were all but forgotten."

"Not completely forgotten, or we would have never learned of the Vestian Outcasts in school," Tomas pointed out.

"That's easy to explain," Andreesen said. "Our entire history of the Vestian Outcasts came from a ledger found in the prison warden's safe. It contained a manifest of each group of prisoners sent to Vestos, but it didn't include a record of their crimes. Unfortunately, no one had any empathy for a group of exiled prisoners."

"Including you," Jevan said.

Nodding, Andreesen looked at them for a moment. "You're right, I apologize. Still, your people only represent a fraction of the Medellan population. Why do you think you get a say over what these... these *aliens*... are proposing?"

"This is our continent you're on, and you're currently in the minority here," Mathias pointed out. "Our people have shared this land with the Athla'naa for centuries. They are as much Vestians as we are."

"So, you're in favor of letting their people put a cage around our planet?" Andreesen asked with an irritated huff.

"It is not a cage. The grid is merely for your protection, to keep factions like the Maara'dahl from destroying this world," Keryth stated firmly. "Your people will have as much control over the grid as those here on Vestos. We're just trying to protect all of you."

"There would be no need for protection if *they* weren't here," Andreesen said, pointing at the Triumvirate and Ardyn, who had sat silent all this time. "Just resettle them somewhere else and put your grid around that."

Before any of the Athla'naa could protest, Mathias sprang to his feet. "No! You have no jurisdiction here. Ateria does not get to dictate who we share Vestos with."

"Please, it's unfair to uproot all these people," Takyra argued.

"I thought you were adamant about having us relocated?" Aelrynd questioned, breaking her silence. "Why are you arguing against this now?"

"Because you were right. After speaking at length with Keryth, I have come to see it is not fair to uproot and relocate your people against their will," Takyra replied, looking back at Andreesen. "They have established a society over many generations, while my people have been asleep all this time. Those of us aboard the Rahn'naa could still leave and resettle onto the colony world we were heading for, but please don't force these people to leave."

Before Andreesen could respond, Keryth stood, putting up a placating hand. "Hold that thought. I have an idea. Will you trust me? Please, everyone, stand up."

Everyone in the room looked at each other and gave a cursory shrug before standing. Keryth tapped on the communicator in his ear. "Keryth to *Wah'kah'ria*. Please beam myself and the others I am with onboard."

Beam? Ardyn thought. "No! Wai—"

Before Ardyn could finish his protest, he no longer stood in the tower room next to Jevan. He was standing on a large platform that reminded him of the execution chamber from the Pah'ora. He immediately shrank next to Jevan, who placed a comforting arm around his shoulders.

They all looked stunned. Andreesen kept feeling himself as if to see if he was still alive. "What?! Where are we?"

Stepping off the platform, Keryth gave them a disarming smile. "Welcome aboard the Star Cruiser Wah'kah'ria. Please, follow me."

Keryth led them out of the room, down a corridor and into a large elevator. "How did you get us here?" Andreesen demanded to know.

"The transmat can convert matter into pure energy, beaming that energy through subspace to a specific location, and then converting that energy back into its original form," Keryth explained as the elevator doors opened and they walked onto what looked somewhat like the control center of the Rahn'naa, but much larger. There was also a large window on the far wall with a view of the stars and a planet.

"Is that Aria'nor?" Aelrynd asked in a hushed whisper.

"You mean Medellus?" Andreesen corrected.

"Same thing," Jevan said. "What we call Medellus, the Athla'naa call Aria'nor."

Andreesen scowled at Jevan. "They can't just—"

Before Andreesen could finish his protest, an alarm sounded.

"What's going on?!" Andreesen demanded as the ship shuddered.

Springing into action, Keryth ordered the ship to turn about and the view out of the window changed. As they turned away from the planet, on their viewscreen they saw several other spacecraft, firing at one another. One was firing directly at them.

"The Maara'dahl have returned," Keryth responded. "We are under attack!"

Attack? Not again. Ardyn braced himself as the ship rocked and it threw him into Jevan's arms.

SACRIFICE

Takyra turned toward Keryth. "Commander, we need to return to the Rahn'naa immediately!"

"I'm sorry, but that's impossible," Keryth said as he ran to the control panel and shouted more orders to his crew.

"Why not?" Takyra demanded.

"When we are under attack, we have to divert all auxiliary power to the shields," Keryth explained. "That means we have to take our transmat system offline."

Takyra made a frustrated sound. "It's also far too dangerous for us to take a shuttle. Can I communicate with my crew?"

"Yes, use the secondary communications station over there," Keryth said, pointing out the unmanned station to his right.

As the ship rocked again, Keryth shouted. "Everyone, brace yourselves! This is going to get bumpy."

Ardyn crouched near the entryway, pulling Jevan down with him. The rest of the group followed their lead, crouching low against the walls as best they could while energy blasts continuously rocked the ship. Ardyn didn't understand the commands Keryth was shouting at his crew, so he focused on what he could see out of the forward viewport.

There were two spacecraft facing them and firing their weapons in an unending barrage. "How many are there?" Keryth asked.

"Six of them, Commander," a crew member replied. "They outnumber us two-to-one."

"Forward shields are down to twenty percent, Commander!" another crew member announced.

"Return fire!" Keryth ordered. "Try to take out their weapons systems."

A moment later, the entire ship shuddered harder than before, throwing Ardyn into Jevan's arms, before everything was still. Looking at the viewport, the two spacecraft had stopped firing. "They breached our shields, Commander. Our main weapons are offline."

Keryth looked back at them. "Get in the elevator and take it down to the lowest deck. Now!"

They all scrambled to their feet, but before they could make it to the elevator doors, several Athla'naa beamed onto the bridge, with weapons aimed at them.

"Don't move!" one of them ordered.

"Who are you?" Keryth demanded.

"I'm Commander Galaeron, and I'm here to finish what Commander Denyra started," said the one pointing a *rahn'ora* directly at Keryth. He looked at them all with a sneer. "We're here to execute every Aria'asharra and their sympathizers."

"You are violating Aria'naa law," Keryth said with a frustrated snarl.

"The Maara'dahl do not recognize Aria'naa law," Galaeron said, waving over a couple of his people. "Cover him."

Galaeron stalked over toward the elevator doors. "Who are you?" he asked, approaching them. "You stink like Aria'asharra."

Aelrynd was about to say something when he gave her a hard, back-handed slap to the face, making her stumble backward. "I didn't give you permission to speak, *athla'maakh*."

Hearing that insult used against Aelrynd had Ardyn seeing red. He was about to lunge at the disrespectful brute when Jevan held him back and whispered in his ear. "Don't. He has a weapon."

Trying to calm himself down, Ardyn nodded.

"Look here, what's the meaning of all this?" Andreesen asked, stepping forward, straightening to his full height.

"What are you? You're not Athla'naa," Galaeron said. "But you stink worse than the Aria'asharra."

"My name is Andreesen, from the continent of Ateria of the planet Medellus," he introduced himself. "Why are you attacking our world? We have no quarrel with your people."

"Your world harbors the last fugitives from justice," Galaeron said, pointing his *rahn'ora* directly at Andreesen. "All Aria'asharra must die, along with anyone giving them shelter."

"We aren't giving them shelter!" Andreesen argued. "We only found out about their existence recently ourselves."

"Enough prattling," Galaeron said. "Your world has been polluted by their kind, and we will not tolerate it."

When Galaeron raised his weapon and aimed it at Andreesen, Elder Aelrynd pushed the Medellan out of the way, and took the full blast. She screamed and crumpled to the ground, dead. It all happened so fast that Ardyn looked at Jevan, confused for a moment before he cried out. "No! You murdered Elder Aelrynd!"

Before he even knew what he was doing, Ardyn leaped at Galaeron, tackling him to the ground and knocking the weapon out of his hand. Jevan grabbed the *rahn'ora* and pointed it at the fallen attacker, even as Ardyn kept him pinned down.

The rest of the Maara'dahl were in shock and turned to each other, not knowing what to do, so Jevan spoke to them in their tongue. "Drop your weapons and leave, or your commander is dead."

A moment later, they all disappeared, including Galaeron, causing Ardyn to fall a short distance to the floor beneath him. Jevan was by his side immediately. "Are you okay?"

Kneeling up and seeing Aelrynd's remains next to him, smoke still rising from the corpse, Ardyn shook his head. "No. I'm not." Ardyn grasped Jevan's hand as his friend helped pull him to his feet.

Keryth hailed the other star cruisers. "Status report."

"We disabled the weapons of those attacking us and were about to come to your aid when they all turned and fled. Should we pursue?"

"Yes, and send word to the fleet from Aria'naa that's on its way," Keryth replied. "They might be able to intercept them."

"Yes, Commander."

There was a collective sigh of relief from the control center crew.

"We have a casualty on the bridge," Keryth said into his communicator. "Send medical techs up here immediately."

Everyone was still in shock over what had happened when Andreesen asked. "Why did she do that?"

Taeglyn laid a hand on the man's arm. "Aelrynd acted on instinct. She was a mother to many in our community. While she was often strict, she cared for all. When she saw someone threatened, she would always do what she could to protect them. That was her nature."

"I would like to help prepare the body," Ardyn offered.

Stepping forward, Andreesen seemed mournful. "May I also assist? She gave her life for mine and... I need to do... *something*."

Taeglyn nodded. "Thank you. We would appreciate your assistance. You would also be welcome to speak a few words before her funeral pyre, if you wish."

"Yes, I would. Thank you."

The elevator doors opened and two Athla'naa with what looked like a floating bed stepped out. Gently, they placed Aelrynd upon it and the entire group returned to the Rahn'naa, the mood more somber than it had been that morning.

●●●

They held the funeral rites that evening before a small pyre. The encampment all gathered to pay their respects for their fallen elder. It saddened Ardyn to have lost yet another person, but the haunted look on Andreesen's face broke his heart.

Afterward, Takyra gathered everyone together. "Please, take time to grieve, while Aerys and I prepare, in case there are any more attacks. I know it doesn't feel like it, but we were lucky this time."

While everyone else went back inside, Ardyn took Jevan's hand and led him to the hillcrest, where they had first spotted the observation tower. He sat down and looked over the valley, softly illuminated by the light of their two moons. "After events like this, I just want to run back into the woods and disappear."

Jevan wrapped an arm around him and made a small nod in agreement. "I know exactly how you feel, but I don't think we can run away from this."

"Do you think the Aterians would really force all my people to leave Aria'nor... Medellus...? Ugh. This *planet*, whatever we call it."

Chuckling, Jevan shrugged. "I hope not. The sacrifice Aelrynd made seemed to really move Andreesen. Maybe it will change his mind?"

"I hope so. I would hate to see my people uprooted from the only home they have ever known." With a sigh, Ardyn leaned his head against Jevan's shoulder and just stared up at the night sky, trying to calm his mind.

MED'NOR

rdyn was visiting his mother and daughter in the encampment when he received a call from Keryth. "*I am asking everyone to gather on the Wah'kah'ria. May we beam you aboard?*"

"Could we meet down here, please?"

"*There was a reason I brought you all up the last time, before we were so rudely interrupted. I promise it will be safe. I have launched several long-range scanning beacons. They won't surprise us like that again.*"

"What is it, Ardyn?" his mother asked.

"I have to go," Ardyn apologized. "You be good for your grandmother, okay, little one?"

"Yes, Papa Ardyn. I will!" Myria said, rushing over to give him a quick hug.

He gave them a last wave and then touched his communicator again. "Okay, Keryth. I'm ready."

In the blink of an eye, he again found himself on the transmat platform. Ardyn immediately leaped off without even thinking, stumbling a little. "I'm sorry. These things still terrify me."

Jevan had been waiting for him and helped steady him. "After what you witnessed on the Pah'ora, it's understandable. Come on, everyone else is here already."

Ardyn followed Jevan, who seemed to know exactly where he was going. "Keryth brought us to his ship's observation deck this time. There's more room and an even better view."

As they entered, Ardyn gasped as he saw the large viewport that overlooked their planet. In front of the viewport was a line of benches. He and Jevan took their seats while Keryth stood before them and addressed the group.

"Now that you're all gathered, let me explain why I brought you here. Before the Maara'dahl attacked us, my intention was to show you your world from a different perspective. Both of your continents have been very insular for the past few centuries, and each of your societies has different perspectives."

Turning, Keryth pointed at the planet below. "I hope that by viewing your world from this vantage point will help shift your perspectives. You have a beautiful world that is now home to two different species. Yes, there are other worlds out there, but this world still has more than enough room for both of your societies to flourish."

"You're absolutely right. After what happened, I've seriously reconsidered my previous stance," Andreesen replied. "However, I need to know more before I can put the proposal before the Grand Council for consideration. It would require their approval before our people would agree to such a thing."

"Understood," Keryth said. "Unfortunately, my star cruisers lost track of the Maara'dahl after they went to warp, and the fleet heading our way wasn't able to intercept them. We will need to be vigilant until the fleet arrives."

"How long would it take to build this planetary defense grid that you were proposing?" Andreesen asked.

Takyra looked at him, surprised. "I thought you were against it?"

Andreesen nodded. "You're right, I was. However, Aelrynd's sacrifice caused me to reconsider everything. Since the funeral, I've also taken time to talk with Mathias. He has convinced me that, beyond this Maara'dahl faction, the Athla'naa are no threat. I will recommend to the Grand Council to accept the proposal of putting a defense grid around our planet."

That news made Ardyn smile.

"Thank you for changing your mind," Elder Taeglyn said. "Many of our people did not wish to leave this world. There was even talk of resisting if it came to that."

"To answer your earlier question, it will take several months to build a fully operational defense grid, although we could have some alternative defense mechanisms in place sooner. I'll have my engineers put together the specifics for you to review."

"What can we do in the meantime?" Andreesen asked.

"My star cruisers will remain in orbit and soon you'll have an entire battalion from our fleet here to help defend your world until the defense grid is in place," Keryth replied. "Which brings me to something else we should discuss. The name of your planet. Having a single, unified name we could refer to would be less confusing."

Chuckling, Andreesen nodded. "You're not wrong about that. Before, I would have insisted on our planet be referred to as Medellus by everyone. It is our planet, after all. However, in light of Aelrynd's bravery, I would like to make a proposal in her honor."

"You're not considering changing to the Athla'naa name, are you?" Marta asked. "I don't think the Grand Council would approve of that."

"No, no, I wouldn't go that far," Andreesen reassured her. "I thought perhaps a compromise, blending the two names of Medellus and Aria'nor together. How do you like the name *Med'nor?*"

Ardyn couldn't suppress a small giggle at the name, and he saw the other Athla'naa also holding back smirks.

"Don't tell me that *med* means something amusing or offensive in your language?" Andreesen asked.

"It's not offensive, no," Takyra replied. "The word *med* means a sphere, like a ball. A child's toy."

Andreesen laughed. "Oh my, that is a bit too on the nose, isn't it?"

"I quite like it," Taeglyn said. "Med'nor. I like how it sounds."

"So do I," Aerys agreed. "What do you think, Keryth?"

"Well, it certainly makes this world sound like fun," Keryth replied. "But it's up to you to decide what your planet should be called."

"I think the Grand Council might be open to a compromise like this. Especially since it puts the emphasis on *Med* first," Andreesen said. "What do you think, Marta?"

"I love it. I hope the Grand Council approves."

Andreesen smiled. "Excellent. Then I will include the suggested name change in my proposal. If accepted, it probably won't take long to be adopted, as our people refer to themselves as Aterians more often, anyway."

Mathias quirked an eyebrow at that. "How interesting. No one I know refers to themselves as *Vestian*, although I suppose the name applies to us as much as Medellan would."

As the group broke off into separate conversations, Ardyn stood and walked closer to the viewport and looked down upon his home. That may have just been renamed Med'nor.

"That's quite the view, isn't it?" Jevan asked as he stepped up next to him.

"You know, from up here, it looks like a giant ball, doesn't it?" Ardyn asked, still smirking at the name.

Jevan tilted his head. "Yeah, I guess it does," Jevan agreed. "But it's beautiful. I never imagined seeing our world from this vantage point."

"I'm glad Keryth is here to help us protect it," Ardyn said, watching the slow swirl of clouds move across Vestos. "Where do you think the Rahn'naa is?"

"Based on the maps I've seen of Vestos, I'd say it's up here," Jevan pointed at the northern section of the continent. "Do you see that mountain range there? The Rahn'naa has to be west of those."

"Oh, yes! I can almost imagine the line of *bhat'laa'arh*, just south of there."

Jevan pointed. "And our biggest city is down by that open coastline."

"You said you visited there once? How long did that take you?" Ardyn asked.

"One-and-a-half cycles of the moons," Jevan recalled. "Do you see that long stretch of valleys? We have a road that stretches the length of the Medellan lands, from Yanen to Tafaran. There are several villages along that road, and I would stop and rest along the way."

"With one of Keryth's shuttles, I bet you could be there in a few minutes," Ardyn said.

"I'm sure you're right, but where are you going on my shuttles?" Keryth teased as he came up from behind them.

"We were just speculating how much shorter of a trip Jevan would have if he took your shuttle from his village to the city of Tafaran down on the southern coast. A trip that took him well over a cycle of the moons on foot."

Keryth looked shocked. "You travel on foot? Do you not have any beasts you could ride or that could pull a wagon?"

Ardyn and Jevan looked at each other, trying to picture themselves riding a *sar'ora*. The idea was equally hilarious and horrifying.

PLANNING

Jevan gently placed a hand on Ardyn's shoulder as he guided his friend through the busy corridor of the hospital wing that was recently brought online. Because Keryth's engineering and medical techs were still upgrading some systems, it wasn't fully operational yet.

However, with all the revived Athla'naa aboard the Rahn'naa, along with the growing encampment around the tower, the smaller medical bay could not accommodate everyone's medical needs anymore.

"I have been wanting to come down here ever since I heard they were bringing it online," Ardyn said with a gleam of excitement in his eyes. "I know they explained that a hospital is a larger version of the medical bay, but I've never seen a hospital before."

"Neither have I, although Marta was telling me they have hospitals in Ateria," Jevan said, as they approached the main doors into the hospital wing. "She and Andreesen are getting a tour tomorrow, but I couldn't wait."

The first thing he noticed was a lack of a key slot or touch interface to open the doors. When an Athla'naa who had been walking behind them pushed past, the doors opened as soon as she approached them. Looking at Ardyn, Jevan gave him a shrug as they followed through the now open doorway. Once inside, the doors closed behind them of their own accord.

Before them was a large desk with several Athla'naa behind it, facing them. Jevan recognized the young Athla'naa, who waved them over. "Jevan, Ardyn! Welcome to the hospital wing. Is there something we can help you with?"

"Hello, Kyael! Takyra said we should come and ask for a tour," Ardyn replied. "If it wouldn't be too much trouble."

"You're in luck. Takyra and Aerys are overseeing some upgrades this afternoon," Kyael said. "It's not too busy right now, so I can show you where they are."

They followed the young Athla'naa through another set of doors and down several long hallways. Everything was a pristine white, from the floors to the walls, ceilings, and even the sparse furnishings they saw.

"This wing is enormous," Jevan remarked, as they kept walking.

"We designed it to be the first hospital in our new colony," Kyael said. "Not only does it have the capacity to handle the existing population on board the ship, but we also designed it to have the space for the expected population increase after we'd settled on Maal'dak Five. I still can't believe we ended up here instead."

"We all have had a lot to adjust to," Ardyn agreed.

Finally, Kyael led them into a large room where they saw Takyra and Aerys, along with several others. "There they are," he said, pointing. "I must get back to my post. It was good to see you both!"

"Come join us," Takyra said in greeting. "Were you getting a tour of the hospital wing?"

"Kyael led us to you," Jevan admitted. "All we've really seen are the corridors so far."

Takyra made a bemused noise of disapproval. "Typical. Well, you're just in time to see some of the surgical upgrades come online."

Before either of them could respond, there was a bright flash as Keryth joined them.

"Excellent timing! We were about to—"

Keryth held up his hands to interrupt her. "I have urgent news. Our operatives have finally infiltrated the Maara'dahl leadership, and they have confirmed that the rebels are amassing a large attack against Med'nor."

"How much time do we have?" Aerys asked.

"That is the good news," Keryth replied. "We have enough advanced warning this time, and our fleet will arrive here before they will."

"That is something, at least," Takyra said. "We should inform the others, so the medical bay upgrades will have to wait."

◆◆◆

They found themselves back in the meeting room in the tower. Ardyn and Jevan sat silently in the corner and merely watched, neither feeling they had much to contribute to the current discussion.

Andreesen was pacing by the window. "You're sure that Ateria is in danger of attack?"

"According to our operatives, yes, I'm afraid so," Keryth replied. "According to their reports, the Maara'dahl have amassed a sizable fleet. Possibly large enough to get around our planned blockade and target the planet."

"What can we do? We need to protect our people. We're not equipped to defend against an attack like this," Andreesen said with growing concern.

"Without the planetary defense grid in place, we need a two-pronged approach," Keryth replied. "The battalion arriving from Aria'naa will do its best to prevent their ships from heading toward the planet. However, I'm concerned some may get past them."

Aerys handed Keryth a tablet. "Takyra and I have been going over the logistics. With your upgrades to our forcefield, we can protect a larger encampment and we have space inside the Rahn'naa as well. Although we could use your help to transport people from the nearby villages and settlements. It would take them too long to travel here on foot."

"Yes, excellent idea," Keryth agreed. "With the extension and reinforcement of your shields, you could support a sizable encampment. How many do you think you can also accommodate within the ship?"

Moving toward a display by the wall, Takyra brought up a schematic of the Rahn'naa. "We have enough space to accommodate around five thousand in quarters, and if we have enough time, we could put another ten thousand into the cryopods. However, due to physiological differences, only Athla'naa could be housed in them."

"How about your cargo holds? My star cruisers could use their transmats to move the cargo," Keryth suggested. "The cargo holds on the Pah'ora could also be used to house a couple of thousand people."

"Would they be safe when you engage the Maara'dahl in battle?" Andreesen asked.

"It's an older model that the Maara'dahl must have salvaged from our derelict shipyards, so we wouldn't use it in battle. I've already had my engineers upgrade its shields and my star cruiser can protect it. Anyone on board should be perfectly safe."

"That is all well-and-good," Andreesen said. "However, we have nearly a billion people on Ateria. How do we protect them?"

"Haven't we been building bunkers throughout the provinces for just this eventuality?" Tomas asked. "They won't hold everyone, but they're better than nothing."

"You're right, I'd forgotten about them," Andreesen said. "We haven't completed construction on all the bunkers, but I will recommend to the Grand Council that we shelter as many people as we can in those that have been completed.

"Which reminds me. Keryth, could you help me send Oren and Nels home? It would be best if they addressed the council directly regarding this matter."

From the corner of the room, it looked like Oren wanted to protest this, but then he seemed to think better of it.

"Yes, of course. If you can help me with the coordinates, we can set them down anywhere you want in Ateria," Keryth agreed.

They spent the next several hours calculating exactly how many they could protect within the ships and with the shield around the encampment, and then prioritized which villages and settlements they could most efficiently evacuate.

"Would sending people down into the mines protect them?" Mathias asked.

"Yes, I believe so," Keryth replied. "Our sensors are unreliable at reading life signs deep underground, and would be nearly impossible for the older ships the Maara'dahl are using."

"Wouldn't the mineshafts collapse if they hit them with your energy weapons?" Tomas asked.

"Yes, that is a possibility," Keryth admitted. "However, if any ships get past our battalion, they will center their attacks on larger population centers. Besides, there would be no reason for them to attack your mines, as their sensors wouldn't be capable of detecting life signs underground."

In the end, they figured they could protect around fifty thousand on Vestos, and the bunkers on Ateria could protect another half-million. Only a fraction of the population, but it would have to do.

JEALOUSY

They may have had advanced warning, but the operatives could not give them a precise time of when to expect the attack. So, tensions ran high as everyone helped to resettle as many as they could.

Everyone was giving up their privacy and doubling up on accommodations. Many of Ardyn's people were reluctant, and the Medellans were unable to make use of the cryopods. Many of those either joined the encampment, were housed somewhere in the Rahn'naa, or sent up to the Pah'ora. To make room for more refugees, any non-essential members of the Baaru'dak and Laasa'dak returned to their cryopods, which had also undergone extensive upgrades.

After several cycles of the sun, the tensions frayed the nerves of even the usually jovial Jevan, who became short and snappish. It didn't help that they now shared their quarters with Ardyn's mother and Jevan's sister.

Jevan's mother, Asha, had refused to be relocated to the Rahn'naa, which weighed heavily on Jevan's mind. Asha insisted she'd be safe enough in her root cellar if *worse came to worse*. So, Jenira's bondmate, Micah, remained in Yanen to protect her, while he insisted Jenira go to the Rahn'naa to be with her brother. So, here they all were, crammed together in their quarters and constantly getting in each other's way.

"Don't roll your eyes at me, *elf*!" Jevan snapped at Ardyn. That was the fifth time in as many cycles of the sun that Jevan had called him that.

"I wasn't rolling my eyes," Ardyn said, exasperated.

"Do I need to separate you two again?" Jenira asked, crossing her arms at the two of them.

Before either of them could respond, Cytra chimed in with a message. "Jevan and Ardyn, please report to the control center."

"Now what?!" They both snapped at the AI just as her face disappeared from the display. They both looked at each other and broke out into laughter.

"I'm sorry," Jevan apologized. "Everything has just been—"

"Too much," Ardyn finished for him. "Yes, I know. Hopefully, we can get through this without killing each other and doing the work of the Maara'dahl for them."

Shaking his head, Jevan headed for the door. "Come on, let's see what they want."

When they arrived, Takyra and Keryth were waiting for them with a new Athla'naa they hadn't met before. "Thank you for joining us," Keryth greeted. "Jevan, Ardyn, meet Commander Aramys, leader of the Seventy-First Battalion. They just arrived and are ready to help defend Med'nor."

Commander Aramys was lithe and winsome. Her hair was a shade of purple so dark it was almost black. She wore it long, piled neatly upon her head in an elaborate hairdo.

"I am pleased to meet you both," Aramys said.

Ardyn watched as Jevan put on his brightest smile when greeting the new commander. "The pleasure is all mine, Commander Aramys."

A frisson of jealousy stirred when Aramys ducked her head and lowered her ears when looking at Jevan with appreciative eyes. Then Jevan winked at her, and Ardyn felt his face flush as a wave of unfamiliar emotion hit.

"Keryth has been briefing me about what's been going on here and has spoken of you both often," Aramys said, breaking the tension. "Aerys tells me you two would be excellent guides to show me around the Rahn'naa while he completes his briefing of the preparations."

"It would be our pleasure," Jevan said, inclining his head. "I'm so glad you arrived in time."

Jevan led Aramys out of the control center and answered her questions while Ardyn trailed silently behind. The commander seemed quite taken by the tall, handsome Medellan, and a knot of jealousy grew in the pit of Ardyn's stomach.

Stop being so jealous, Ardyn reprimanded himself. *Jevan's always like this. Isn't he?*

As they continued their tour, Ardyn watched as Jevan's easy smile was back as he clearly flirted with Aramys. With tensions running high, he hadn't seen that smile from Jevan in a while. It hurt to see someone else bring it out in the man he had grown to care for so deeply. Eventually, Ardyn couldn't take it anymore, and he slipped away.

Ardyn kept himself busy assisting others, trying to avoid Jevan and Aramys as much as possible. Occasionally, he'd catch a glimpse of them, and it hurt his heart to see them together, as Jevan smiled and laughed so easily in her presence.

While he'd had plenty of opportunities to have multiple bed partners, until now, Jevan hadn't shown interest in anyone other than Ardyn. *Is he finally tired of me?* Ardyn wondered as his heart sank. Eventually, his dark thoughts got the better of him, and Ardyn returned to their quarters. Thankfully, neither Jenira nor Saelyn were there.

After gathering some of his belongings, Ardyn left with his old pack slung across his back, wearing replicated leathers and a new cloak. He'd packed some provisions and a bedroll, because he decided to return to the woods for some peace and quiet. He also brought his *rahn'ora*, just in case.

I need some time to think, Ardyn told himself. However, what he really didn't want to face was sleeping in their bed alone that night. Especially when he kept picturing Jevan and Aramys in an intimate embrace.

When Ardyn reached the lower level of the observation tower, he made his way toward the exit. That's when he saw Jevan returning from somewhere outside.

"Hey! Ardyn, where are you off to?" Jevan asked, nodding at the pack Ardyn had slung over his shoulder. "I've been looking for you everywhere. Why aren't you wearing your communicator?"

Ardyn kept making his way toward the door. "I am heading out for a few nights."

"Ardyn, stop!" Jevan begged, running in front of Ardyn to block his path. "It's too dangerous to go out there now. You know the Maara'dahl could attack at any time."

"I need to get out of here," Ardyn said with a scowl. "Why don't you spend more time with Commander Aramys?"

Jevan gave him a confused look. "I finished giving Aramys the tour of the Rahn'naa a while ago. She's busy being briefed by Takyra, Aerys, and Keryth over the defense preparations. That's why I've been looking for you. Why did you abandon us when we were supposed to escort her together?"

"You looked like you had it well enough in-hand," Ardyn grumbled, trying to get past Jevan.

Once again, Jevan seemed confused, before a look of understanding shone on his face. "Are you jealous of Aramys?"

"Jevan, please let me go."

"Ardyn, don't leave," Jevan pleaded again. "I couldn't live with myself if something happened to you. I'm sorry if you thought I was paying too much attention to Aramys, but I was trying to be a good host."

"So, you weren't trying to flirt with her?" Ardyn asked, quirking his ears.

"No, of course not!" Jevan insisted.

Before either of them could argue further, they heard a shipwide announcement. *"The Maara'dahl fleet has been detected. They'll arrive within the hour. Everyone, please take your stations!"*

STANDOFF

Everyone around Jevan and Ardyn scrambled to get to their assigned stations, and the crewmembers already at their stations sprang into action.

"Ardyn, I'm sorry," Jevan tried to apologize, realizing how Ardyn might have seen his attempts at being friendly with Aramys as flirtatious.

"Now isn't the time," Ardyn said, stepping back and heading toward the elevator. "We both have our assignments. Go. We can talk after this is all over."

Nodding, Jevan agreed, following Ardyn. There were a few moments of awkward silence as they rode the elevator down into the bowels of the ship. When it stopped, Jevan moved to leave before turning in the doorway. "Stay safe, Ardyn."

"You too. See you later."

Jevan hurried to meet with those who were transporting up to Keryth's ship. Despite the potential danger, Jevan, Andreesen, and Taeglyn were going to witness the battle firsthand in the hopes together they would provide an accurate account of events.

Ardyn stayed on the Rahn'naa to observe everything in the control center, while his father remained in the encampment to watch over their people.

Despite their stupid argument, Jevan was reluctant to leave Ardyn's side. However, he made a promise to Mathias to represent their people on the Wah'kah'ria. The ard felt his place was with his people who had ventured to the Rahn'naa for safety.

Jevan sprinted along the corridor toward the agreed meeting place, his heart hammering in his chest. So much had the potential to go wrong, despite all their preparations. Jevan feared that Med'nor would be doomed if the battalion failed to stop the Maara'dahl fleet.

"There you are!" Taeglyn said with a note of relief as Jevan approached them. "We were worried that you wouldn't make it."

"I'm sorry, but I'm here now," Jevan said. "Is Keryth ready to bring us onboard?"

Andreesen activated his communicator. "Commander Keryth, Jevan is here. We're ready."

A moment later, a bright flash of light enveloped Jevan and between one blink and the next he stood on the transmat platform of the Wah'kah'ria. A crew member was waiting and escorted them to the control center. As they entered, the room was abuzz with activity.

Keryth turned to greet them. "You three can take a position in that corner and strap yourselves in," he pointed. "Please stay out of the way and let us do our jobs. I'll do my best to get us through this."

"How much time until they arrive?" Taeglyn asked as they made their way to the designated corner that had a bench with three seats and safety harnesses. The bench and harnesses looked like someone recently modified them to accommodate larger Medellan frames and didn't quite match the pristine aesthetic of the rest of the control center.

"They could arrive at any moment," Keryth said. "One of our operatives tried to warn us ahead of time, but they were caught before they could tell us when the Maara'dahl fleet was departing. So, we had to rely on our subspace sensor array, which is set up to detect ships at warp within a radius of one light-year."

"How do you know the operative was caught?" Andreesen asked, as they were strapping themselves into the safety harnesses.

"All our operatives have a specific communications protocol they must follow," Keryth explained. "The operative used their call sign, but the signal cut off before they used their sign-off phrase."

"Do you think the operative is okay?" Jevan asked.

Keryth's ears lowered. "No. If they were caught, they're most likely dead. The Maara'dahl do not hold prisoners for long, but they probably tried to extract information from the operative before killing them."

"They risked their lives just to help us?" Andreesen asked.

"In part, but we've been trying to insert operatives into the Maara'dahl organization for years. By attacking you,

Denyra finally gave us an opportunity to infiltrate their ranks. Our operatives all knew the risks."

A wave of emotion crossed his face, and Andreesen had to clear his throat as he tried to school his features. "If we make it through this, I'll recommend we hold a tribute in your people's honor for their sacrifice. I'm not sure my people would have done the same."

Before Jevan could say something, Keryth swung his chair around as he tapped the communicator in his ear, and then tapped a few commands into the console before him. A moment later, Commander Aramys appeared on the viewscreen.

"According to our subspace sensors, the Maara'dahl will drop out of warp momentarily."

"Shields up," Keryth ordered. "Everyone buckle in, we may be in for a rough ride. Someone make sure the Pah'ora has also been alerted."

"Yes, Commander."

Jevan glanced over at Andreesen and Taeglyn. They both looked as terrified as he felt. Looking at the forward view screen, Jevan gasped when the dark backdrop of space filled with ships emerging from warp. Almost immediately, the ships were on the attack, concentrating their fire on the lead ships of the battalion.

"Close in and provide cover fire," Keryth ordered, and the Wah'kah'ria moved toward the attacking fleet. "Make a detailed scan of every ship we get close to. I want to get a better idea of where the Maara'dahl are getting their ships from."

As the Wah'kah'ria entered the fray, some of the Maara'dahl turned their weapons on them. Every blast rocked the ship, and Jevan gripped the straps of the harness to keep from being shaken like a rag doll.

A tech turned toward Keryth. "Those are *definitely* our decommissioned ships, Commander. Several are Mark One Star Cruisers."

The Wah'kah'ria strafed a line of fire along the hull of one ship before changing course. Then they spotted an even larger ship through the fray. "Aramys, are you seeing this? That's the Ora'laa!"

"You're right," Jevan could hear the voice of Aramys coming through the internal speakers in the control center.

"That confirms it. They've been looting decommissioned ships from the old shipyard."

"That is a security breech that needs to be fixed as soon as this mess is over with," Keryth said. "Hail that lead ship and then give the Rahn'naa an update."

After a moment, the communications tech spun his chair toward Keryth. "The Ora'laa is ignoring all hails, Commander."

What Jevan saw next made his heart stutter in his chest. The enormous ship began firing its weapons, but instead of aiming at the battalion, the energy beams flew past and directly at the planet below.

"They are firing all weapons on Med'nor!" a security tech cried out. "The Ora'laa is concentrating its fire on the Rahn'naa."

Ardyn!

The other Maara'dahl ships increased their attacks against the battalion, trying to prevent them from retaliating against the Ora'laa. "Divert more power to the shields. Evasive maneuvers!" Keryth cried out.

The Wah'kah'ria flew down and around the ships, only taking a few hits, before coming around and firing all weapons. "Try to disable as many of them as possible. Aim for their weapons and propulsion systems."

When the first barrage of weapons fire pierced through the shields of a Maara'dahl ship and their weapons exploded, the entire control center erupted in cheers. They took out the other two that had been attacking them, but then Jevan's mind turned to what was happening down on Med'nor.

As if reading his mind, Keryth ordered. "Check on the Rahn'naa. Did they get their shields up in time?"

"Yes, Commander!" came the reply.

Jevan breathed a small sigh of relief, and then a powerful blast shook the Wah'kah'ria forcefully. "Shields are down to ten percent!" someone called out. "What did they just hit us with?"

Before anyone else could respond, they hit the Wah'kah'ria again, causing the ship to shudder violently, while consoles sprayed sparks everywhere and the command center filled with smoke. The shaking snapped Jevan's head up and he noticed the bulkhead above Keryth give way.

Immediately, he sprang into action, unbuckling his harness and running toward Keryth, pushing him off his chair. Keryth cried out at being violently shoved, but Jevan had no time to apologize as the bulkhead came crashing down on him. Intense pain wracked his body before his entire world went black.

HELPLESS

When Ardyn arrived in the control center, he found a scene of barely controlled chaos as techs were shouting out updates, while Takyra and Aerys were busy in front of their display screens. Aerys was in front of the tactical display, showing the various ships in orbit, while Takyra's display had numerous charts and graphs of data that Ardyn did not understand.

One display that caught his eye showed a visual of the ships as they closed their formation over Med'nor. "How can we see the ships?" Ardyn asked aloud to no one in particular.

Without turning to face him, Takyra responded while continuing to work the controls on the console before her. "Keryth launched a satellite a few days ago that gives us a visual feed of what's going on. Please take a seat at that station and monitor the display for me."

Ardyn hesitated. "Shouldn't one of your techs be doing that?"

"You have eyes and a mouth," Takyra said with an edge of frustration. "Just describe what you're seeing. I'll be watching the other displays."

Taking a seat, Ardyn looked at the display. "Which one is the Wah'kah'ria?"

"Ask Cytra," Takyra replied, before going back to her task.

"Cytra, which of these ships is the Wah'kah'ria?"

A moment later, names of each of the ships appeared on the display, with the one labeled Wah'kah'ria standing out with a blue aura surrounding it. "Thank you, Cytra."

Now Ardyn could watch the ship Jevan was on, while also helping monitor what was happening. For the moment, everything seemed quiet. *I wonder how Jevan is doing,* Ardyn thought, when suddenly new ships blinked into existence.

"The Maara'dahl fleet just arrived," Ardyn called out.

"Yes, I see them. Thank you," Takyra said before giving an order to one of her techs. "Transfer all auxiliary power to the shields. We need them at maximum strength. Now!"

Ardyn tapped on his communicator. "Elder Taesys. Father. They're here."

"Thank you, Ardyn," Taesys replied. *"In case we don't get to speak again, I want you to know… I'm very proud of you, my son."*

That small compliment brought a smile to his face and Ardyn lowered his ears in respect, although his father couldn't see it. "Thank you, Papa Taesys."

Tracking the movement of the ships on the visual display, Ardyn saw the Pah'ora hang back while the Wah'kah'ria approached the Maara'dahl ships after they began firing their weapons at the battalion. That's when another, much larger, ship arrived. "Takyra, are you seeing this?"

"Yes! What is that?" Takyra replied.

"A message just came from the Wah'kah'ria," a tech called out. "They want to make sure our shields are up."

"Send them a confirmation, and ask them what that ship is," Takyra said.

Before they could send the response, Ardyn saw beams of energy come from the enormous ship. Instead of hitting any of the battalion ships, they kept going, aimed directly at Med'nor. "Takyra, I think that ship is firing on us!"

A moment later, the Rahn'naa shook violently and the lights in the control center flashed on and off several times. "Can we route any more power to the shields?"

"I can route power from the replication system," Aerys said on the other side of the control center.

While orders were being given, Ardyn saw the Wah'kah'ria fly around some of the attacking ships, firing on them. One hit penetrated the attacker's shields and Ardyn saw an explosion disabling the ship. Ardyn whooped out a cheer.

"The Wah'kah'ria just disabled one of their ships," he explained when Takyra turned to him.

"No time for that now. Ardyn, please send a shipwide announcement that the replicators will be offline."

Hitting his communicator and switching it to a shipwide signal, Ardyn conveyed the message. "Everyone, please remain calm. We had to take the replicator system offline to give the shields more power."

Ardyn switched his communicator back to a single signal. "Papa Taesys, how is everyone in the encampment doing?"

"Terrified!" Taesys replied. "The sky was so bright and loud. What's happening?"

"A large ship is firing their weapons directly at us," Ardyn explained, his eyes still tracking the movements of the Wah'kah'ria as it continued to exchange weapons fire with other ships. "We just gave the shields more power. Try to keep everyone calm."

The enormous ship fired another barrage. Moments later, the Rahn'naa rocked violently enough that some consoles in the control center sparked. "Shields are down to fifty percent," a tech reported. "Whatever they are hitting us with is deliberately draining power from our shields. We can't take more than a couple more blasts."

Another tech spoke up. "The power drain is cascading throughout our systems. The ventilation system is at critical and even some cryopods are on the brink of failure!"

"Get a medical team down there and have them pull out anyone in a failing pod," Takyra ordered. "They can take them to the hospital wing."

That's when Ardyn noticed another ship fire on the Wah'kah'ria. Instead of being absorbed by the ship's shields, the energy beams hit the ship directly, and one part of the Wah'kah'ria exploded.

Oh, no! Jevan!!

HELPFUL

Ardyn paced in the control center, unable to sit still as his eyes remained glued to the continued feed coming from the satellite in orbit. Two ships from the battalion flew to the rescue and disabled the Maara'dahl ships after they fired on the Wah'kah'ria a second time.

Worried for Jevan, all Ardyn could do now was stare at the display, monitoring the ship highlighted in blue. Several other ships from the battalion put themselves between the Wah'kah'ria and the Maara'dahl ships, protecting her from further damage, while another group of ships broke off to engage the large ship that had been attacking the Rahn'naa.

Those explosions looked bad. Ardyn thought back to the last time he saw Jevan. *I was foolish for being jealous. Jevan has always been charming with every new Athla'naa he meets. Why would I expect this time to be different?*

Takyra, Aerys and the rest of the crew were busy maintaining the shields and coordinating teams of techs to work on repairs and get wounded to the hospital wing, while the battle raged on far above them.

"Ardyn, what's going on up there?" Takyra asked without taking her eyes off the console and display in front of her.

Taking a breath, Ardyn sat down and studied his display for a moment. "The Wah'kah'ria was damaged, but it's still in one piece. Some of the battalion appear to be protecting it, while others are attacking that large ship that has been firing on us."

"Good, they're buying us time," Takyra said. "Thank you. Let us know immediately if you see anything change."

"Yes, Chief," Ardyn replied, using Takyra's title, something that felt appropriate in that moment.

Time seemed to drag as Ardyn watched the battle. At first it looked like the battalion was pushing the Maara'dahl back, and then the Maara'dahl would press forward again. The ships that had broken off to focus their weapons on the largest ship thwarted two attempts of attacks against the Rahn'naa, intercepting the energy beams before they reached Med'nor.

However, Ardyn didn't think they could keep doing that indefinitely.

"Our shields are back up to seventy-five percent," Aerys informed Takyra.

Ardyn felt a glimmer of hope when one of the ships intercepting another barrage exploded. "No!"

"What happened?" Takyra asked.

"One of... of the ships that was putting itself between us and the energy blasts. It's been destroyed!" Ardyn replied, with a lump of emotion in his throat and his ears completely lowered. "All those people..."

"They sacrificed themselves for us," Takyra said. "We will take time to mourn them later. Communications, inform the battalion that our shields can withstand another blast."

With the message conveyed, Ardyn saw the ships taking the brunt of the damage withdraw, followed immediately by another wave of energy beams aimed directly at them. He braced himself just before the Rahn'naa shook violently.

After the dust settled, Ardyn tried to reach out to his father via the communicator, but all he heard was the soft crackle of static. "Takyra! I can't reach Elder Taesys!"

"They damaged our communications array," the communications tech informed them.

"Why can I still see what's going on up there?" Ardyn questioned, as he watched the battalion continuing to fight the Maara'dahl fleet.

"That feed is coming in through a new array that Keryth's engineers installed," Takyra explained. "It must be able to withstand the blast more than our twelve-hundred-year-old array could."

Turning back to his display, Ardyn noticed two ships flying around the much larger ship. "I think they're planning to do something," Ardyn said, as Aerys and Takyra switched their displays to the same satellite feed he had been watching.

Moments later, the back end of the large ship erupted in several explosions that set off a chain reaction traveling the length of the ship, destroying it. The control center erupted in jubilation as everyone jumped out of their seats, hugging each other and cheering. For a moment Ardyn reveled in their joy, although still worried about his father and Jevan.

Once the clamor died down, Takyra immediately went back to work, turning to one of her techs. "Find some engineers and get that communications array repaired," she ordered, and then turned to another tech. "Run to the hospital wing and bring me a status report."

"Yes, Chief!" they both said before sprinting out of the room.

Ardyn looked back at the display, and the rest of the Maara'dahl fleet appeared to have surrendered. Those not disabled now gathered into a small group with the battalion surrounding them. The Wah'kah'ria hadn't moved from the same spot it had been, although it looked like there were now shuttles flying between her and the battalion ships that had been protecting her.

"Takyra, I can't watch this anymore," Ardyn said. "Is there anything else I can do to help until we restore communications?"

For the next few hours, Ardyn ran throughout the ship, conveying messages and orders, before going to the surface to check on his father and the encampment.

Approaching the encampment, it was so still, Ardyn at first feared the worst, until someone peeking out of a tent spotted him. Slowly, people emerged, and eventually Ardyn spotted his father. Running over to him, he gave him a hug.

"I'm so glad you're safe," Ardyn said, relief flooding through him. "How is everyone?"

"We're rattled, but otherwise okay," Taesys replied. "Those shields did their job and kept us safe. However, we saw some explosions outside of the forcefield. I fear they also hit some settlements and villages, but I can't be sure."

"As soon as the repairs are complete, they'll be able to scan the area and determine how much damage there is," Ardyn said. "I'm just glad you're all safe."

"Any word from your friend, Jevan?"

Ears drooping, Ardyn gave his father a tight-lipped head shake. "They are still repairing the communications array at the top of the tower. Until it's repaired, we won't know anything."

Taesys reached out and placed a hand on Ardyn's shoulder. "He'll be fine. Why don't you go check on his sister and your mother?"

"Good idea. Thank you, Papa Taesys."

◆◆◆

It was when Ardyn was sitting with Jenira and Saelyn, catching them up on the events he'd witnessed, that his communicator came to life with a message from Takyra. *"Ardyn, we've reestablished communication with Commander Keryth. He wants to transport you to his ship immediately. It's Jevan. He's badly hurt."*

Ardyn sprang from his place on the couch, his heart leaping into his throat. "Thank you. Please tell them I am ready to be transported."

"What's going on?" Jenira asked.

"They have restored communications," Ardyn informed her. "They want to transport me to the Wah'kah'ria. Jevan's been hurt."

Jenira immediately stood up. "Take me with you, please!"

"Ardyn? We're ready to transport you on board the Wah'kah'ria," a voice came through his communicator.

"Can you transport two of us? Jevan's sister would like to come, too," Ardyn replied.

"Yes. Stand by."

"Okay, hang on. This is going to feel really weird, but don't be afraid," Ardyn said, trying to sound more confident than he felt.

"Afraid of—?"

JENIRA

In the blink of an eye, Ardyn's world shimmered out and back into existence. When he rematerialized on the Wah'kah'ria, he reached out to steady Jenira, whose mouth hung open, still mid-sentence.

Jenira looked around, startled. "Wh-where are we?"

"We're on the Wah'kah'ria," Ardyn explained. "This is how their transportation system works. One second, you're on Med'nor, the next, you're up in space."

"You were right, that was very weird," Jenira said, wobbling on her feet. "I don't know if I could ever get used to that."

The transmat tech cleared her throat. "Your friend is in the medical bay. It's three decks up from here. Follow the hall from the elevator and you can't miss it."

"Thank you," Ardyn replied before helping a still bewildered Jenira off the platform. "Come on, let's go check on Jevan."

The mention of her brother's name seemed to snap Jenira out of it. "He better be okay," she said with a huff, before swaying on her feet.

Ardyn reached out and steadied her. "Are you okay?"

"I'm *fine*," she insisted. "That... whatever that was... just messed with my head."

Ardyn kept an arm around Jenira's shoulders as he guided her toward the elevator down around the corner from the transmat room.

Jenira shrugged away from him as he placed his hand on the wall to summon the elevator. "Jevan promised he was going to be fine, and said these ships were completely safe," she groused.

"He didn't want you to worry," Ardyn admitted, leading her into the elevator. "But all the ships were part of the defense against the Maara'dahl."

"So, you knew there was a risk? Why did we send so many people to take shelter in this place?"

"They weren't aboard *this* ship. The refugees took shelter on the Pah'ora," Ardyn explained. "That was the ship

Denyra used to abduct my people. Keryth had his techs reinforce the shields, and the Pah'ora stayed out of the fight. The battalion made sure of that."

"Why couldn't Jevan witness this battle from *that* ship?" Jenira asked.

Ardyn shrugged. "I was told it was because they wanted to have witnesses of the command decisions being made. Because of this, the battalion was going to take the brunt of the attack and keep the Wah'kah'ria and the Pah'ora safe."

"If Jevan's injured, then they didn't do a good job then, *did they?*" Jenira said with a growl, her voice raising in volume, as tears of frustration slid down her face.

The elevator doors slid open, and Ardyn led Jenira down the corridor. Taking hold of her hand, he squeezed it. "I'm worried about him, too."

Sliding her hand out of his, Jenira stopped. "He's always been so brash..."

Ardyn quirked a smile at that. "That's part of his charm. The way he rescued me from that *sar'ora*. If his arrow had missed, we'd both have been dead."

"He's always been everyone's protector, for as long as I can remember," she recalled, fiddling with a loose curl of her hair.

"Jevan is also remarkably gentle for such a large man," Ardyn said. "He told me he often helped brush your hair when you were growing up. He... he also enjoys brushing mine."

Jenira reached out and stroked Ardyn's hair. "I can see why. Your hair is such a pretty color, and it's so soft. Having someone else brush it is comforting, isn't it?"

"Yeah, it is."

"I need to get Micah to help me brush my hair when I see him again," Jenira said, speaking of her bondmate. "I still miss Jevan doing it for me."

"Once he's recovered, I'll tell him to visit and brush your hair. It can be penance for making his little sister worry so much about him."

"I'd like that," she said, taking Ardyn's hand and moving forward once more. "Thank you."

The corridor curved, and they found themselves in front of two large glass doors that slid apart as they approached, reminding Ardyn of the main entrance to the hospital wing on the Rahn'naa. As they entered, they saw many medical techs swarming around various beds, each one occupied by an injured crew member. Scanning the room, he looked for Jevan, spotting him in the far corner.

"Over there," Ardyn pointed, leading Jenira to where he saw Jevan's feet propped up on a small cart, his tall frame too large for their medical beds.

As they approached the bed, Ardyn had been expecting to find a smiling Jevan, joking with the medical techs tending to him. Instead, he saw Jevan lying still as death. His face was ashen and barely visible under something that covered his nose and mouth. There was an array of tubes and wires attached to his head and arms. They had swathed Jevan's head in a bandage and had encased his torso in something solid.

"Jevan!" Ardyn cried out, rushing to his friend's side.

Jenira rushed over next to him, staring at her brother. "Is... is he...?"

Before she could finish her question, she fainted. Ardyn barely caught her and slid down to his knees to soften her fall. Cradling her in his arms, he tried to wake her. "Jenira? Jenira! Can you hear me?" When she wouldn't wake, he looked desperately around at the medical techs tending to other patients. "Someone, please, help!"

The medical techs ran over and checked on Ardyn and Jenira. Someone brought a hovering gurney, and several of the techs gently lifted the Medellan woman carefully onto it. She was not as tall as her brother, so thankfully, she fit on the gurney.

Others helped Ardyn up, and they led him to a seat next to Jevan's bed. It took a moment for Ardyn to orient himself when a tech approached him. "You must be Ardyn. I'm Tamaryn, the chief medical technician on the Wah'kah'ria."

Ardyn's eyes darted from Tamaryn to Jevan and Jenira. His voice caught in his throat when he asked. "I-is Jevan... i-is he?"

"Jevan is severely injured, but he is still alive," Tamaryn reassured him. "Unfortunately, he's too tall for any of our medical beds, as you can see. We've stabilized him, but we need a larger bed for him before we can treat him properly."

Before Ardyn could ask for clarification, one of the medical techs checking over Jenira called out. "Tamaryn, I need your assessment."

Ardyn followed Tamaryn over to where Jenira lay, still unconscious. "What's wrong with her?"

The medical tech was running a hand-held scanner over her and focused on her abdomen. "Am I understanding these readings correctly?"

Tamaryn looked at the scanner's display and nodded. "Yes. Their species are anatomically different, but I believe she is pregnant."

Pregnant?

In that moment, Jenira came awake, suddenly sitting up. "Did you just say I'm pregnant?!"

WORRY

Later that afternoon, Ardyn accompanied Jenira down to Med'nor in a shuttlecraft. She was too scared to take the transmat again, especially now that she knew she was pregnant. As they approached Yanen, Ardyn was glad to see the village looked undamaged. "It looks like the Maara'dahl spared Yanen. Do we know if they hit any village or settlement?"

The pilot shook his head. "Based on preliminary scans of the planet, the Maara'dahl concentrated their attack on the Rahn'naa."

Jenira's mother and bondmate were waiting for them as they exited the shuttle. As soon as she saw them, Jenira ran into her bondmate's arms, hugging him tight. It made Ardyn smile to see they were a happy pair, considering Jenira's condition.

After hugging her mother as well, Jenira happily informed her family. "I'm so happy you're all here because I have news. I'm pregnant! Micah, we're going to have a child!"

"That's wonderful!" Micah said, giving her a warm hug. Ardyn smiled to see how happy the two were together.

"That *is* good news, dear one, but what of Jevan?" Asha asked.

Ardyn's ears lowered at the thought of Jevan lying on that small medical bed. "He... he is badly hurt. During the battle, a support beam fell. It was going to hit Commander Keryth and Jevan pushed him out of the way, and the beam hit him instead."

A look of concern crossed Asha's face. "How bad?"

With a sheepish look, Ardyn replied. "The beam broke his back, hips, and cracked his skull. Unfortunately, the special medical beds they use to repair injuries like these are too small for a Medellan his size. Tamaryn had to put him into a deep sleep until they can fly Jevan down to the Rahn'naa safely. They have been working on adding Medellan sized beds to the hospital wing, and one is almost ready to use. Then they can heal him."

"With a broken back, how?" asked Micah.

"I know you have seen little of their technology, but I believe it's possible," Ardyn replied with more confidence than he felt. "After I was injured, they used a device on me to close my wound right before my eyes. If I didn't know better, I would have thought it was magic."

"Will they let me see him?" Asha asked.

"Once they have transported him to the hospital wing, I'm sure they'll let you visit," Ardyn reassured her.

"How soon will that be?" Micah asked, putting a comforting arm around his bond-mother.

"The Wah'kah'ria is a mess right now, but they were hopeful within the next cycle of the sun they could coordinate moving him," Ardyn replied. "Jenira has a communicator, so I will let you know as soon as he's settled in, and a shuttle is available to take you."

"No," Asha said. "I think I would prefer to walk. How long is the journey?"

"I don't expect you to run the entire way like Jevan and I did, so I think about three or four cycles of the sun," Ardyn replied. "If you leave in the morning and travel northwest from here, you will reach the *bhat'laa'arh* that marks the perimeter of the Aria'una before nightfall. Then continue due north until you reach the valley, and you will not miss it. In fact, you will probably find the outskirts of the encampment before you even reach the valley."

A hand on his shoulder made Ardyn turn to see the shuttle pilot next to him. "We should go. After I drop you off at the Rahn'naa, I need to shuttle more of the refugees back to the surface."

"Yes, of course," Ardyn said before turning to make his farewells. "I will be in touch as soon as I know anything, so please keep your communicator on."

"Thank you, and take care of yourself, Ardyn," Jenira said as they waved at him.

●●●

Ardyn sat next to the pilot and watched as they flew over the tops of the trees that he and Jevan made their way through earlier in the summer. It felt like a lifetime, with how much their lives had changed. *Please be okay, Jevan.*

As they approached the Rahn'naa, Ardyn saw the extent of the damage to the top of the tower. There was an entire section missing, a hole rent in the side of it. Thankfully, it was the side facing away from the encampment, so the debris likely fell into the ravine next to the tower. Looking at the encampment as they landed, he realized that things could have been a lot worse.

After checking on his parents, Ardyn returned to the control center. As soon as he entered, Takyra rose from her station and pulled Ardyn into a hug. "How is Jevan?"

"Not good. They put him into a deep sleep until they can bring him down here. His injuries were severe. When will the larger bed be ready for him?"

"Aramys sent down several of her engineers to help complete the construction. It should be ready by tomorrow. Why don't you go back to your quarters and get some rest?"

Nodding, Ardyn agreed. He hadn't rested since this all began and the exhaustion was catching up with him. "You should do the same," Ardyn said, noting the dark circles under Takyra's eyes.

"I know, and I will, soon."

"I keep telling you, I have it under control," Aerys said from behind her. "Go, rest."

"Alright, alright, I'll go already," Takyra said with a chuckle. "I'll walk with you, Ardyn."

They took their time as they returned to their quarters, Ardyn catching Takyra up on everything that had happened. "Jevan's going to be an uncle? Oh, I'm sure he'll be excited about that news when he wakes. I think he'll make a wonderful uncle."

Ardyn stopped, as the worry he'd been holding back overwhelmed him. "Do... do you really think he'll be okay?"

Placing a hand on his shoulder, Takyra tilted Ardyn's face up. "Yes, I do. What they're able to achieve is nothing short of miraculous. I've seen what their medical beds can do. Given enough time, Jevan will be fine."

"Thank you. I cannot help worrying," Ardyn replied. "The injuries he has would have killed him if it were not for your medicine. I wish there had been more you could have done for Druyndar, Taeglyn, and all the others that lost their lives."

"So do I," Takyra agreed as they continued walking. "Unfortunately, once someone is dead, we do not have the means to bring them back. Jevan was fortunate to have survived long enough for them to stabilize him. Now, it's only a matter of time. You'll see."

They approached Ardyn's quarters, and Takyra took her leave. "Please, try to get some rest. If you need to, replicate some *kala'dak* tea. It can help you sleep."

"I'll try that, thank you," Ardyn replied before opening the door to his quarters and giving Takyra a wave before the doors closed behind him.

Staring at the empty quarters, with only Jenira's belongings still cluttering up the living space, it hit him how alone he was. There was a time he cherished being on his own, away from those who didn't approve of him and his endless curiosity. Yet, after all this time spent with Jevan, he couldn't fathom life without him anymore.

Takyra's reassurances ran hollow as Ardyn looked around the empty quarters. *How much will our lives have changed when he finally wakes? Our world is changing around us so fast.*

Ardyn slumped against the closed door and let himself slide to the floor, unable to take another step. Everything that had happened since he'd found that key swirled through his head. Especially the events of the past few cycles of the sun. His heart hurt in ways he never thought it could, when images of Jevan, laying so deathly still on that medical bed, flashed before his mind's eye.

As tears flowed unbidden down his face, Ardyn made a silent plea. *Jevan, come back to me.*

HEALING

Ardyn paced the length of the hallway outside of the hospital room. Jevan's family was still making their way on foot, and it would take them a couple of cycles of the sun to arrive. For now, Ardyn was alone.

As soon as they told him that Jevan was in the hospital wing, he rushed to be at his friend's side, only to be told to wait. They still needed to get Jevan properly set up in the medical bed and monitor his condition to make sure he remained stable before anyone could see him. So, now all Ardyn could do was pace.

Finally, after what felt like an eternity, a medical tech peeked his head out from Jevan's room. "Hey, Ardyn! You can come in now."

His heart skipped a beat when he approached the door of Jevan's room, afraid of what he might see. In his mind's eye, Ardyn still saw Jevan on that too-small bed with all those wires and tubes attached to him, encased in that awful body cast. As he walked in, what Ardyn saw amazed him. The room was stark white, but lit warmly. Across from the door was the bed, more than large enough for a man Jevan's size.

Jevan was now dressed in white, loosely fitted clothes, and there were no wires or tubes attached to him. His face was no longer ashen, and he looked peacefully asleep. "Is he... healed already?"

The medical tech who had called him in gave him a sad smile and shook his head. "No, he's only just begun the healing process. He will remain unconscious for a while yet, but you may sit with him as long as you would like."

There was a chair positioned next to the bed and as he approached, Ardyn noticed a faint blue forcefield surrounding Jevan. "Will I be able to hold his hand?"

"Yes, of course," another medical tech replied. "You may feel a slight tingle when you reach inside the healing field, but it won't do you any harm. Just make sure that Jevan's hands always remain inside the field."

"Okay, I can do that," Ardyn said. "Thank you."

After the techs left, Ardyn sat and took Jevan's hand into his. "Jevan? It's me... Ardyn. I don't know if you can hear me or not, but... I've missed you. I hope it's okay I talk to you for a while."

Ardyn wasn't sure if he'd imagined it or not, but he could swear Jevan's hand moved, just a little. He smiled and continued, telling Jevan everything that had happened since the last time they'd seen each other.

●●●

Later that afternoon, Keryth and Aramys came by to visit.

Keryth seemed less sure of himself than usual, with his ears down. "We wanted... I... I needed to see how he's doing. He saved my life."

Grasping Jevan's hand possessively, Ardyn frowned at them. "I still don't understand why he risked his life for you. You could have been healed much faster because you would have fit on the healing bed."

A pained look crossed Keryth's face. "The way the bulkhead came down, it would have struck me worse than it hit Jevan. He is also larger and stronger. My engineers tell me that I would have been killed instantly. I truly owe Jevan my life."

Unable to hang on to any anger, Ardyn looked at Jevan with a bemused smile. "He has a habit of saving people, doesn't he? Jevan will be happy to know he helped."

"How are you doing?" Aramys asked. "You look like you need some rest."

Flattening his ears, Ardyn shook his head. "I can't rest. Not until he wakes and I know he's okay." Unable to look at her, Ardyn ducked his head and continued. "Also, I must apologize, Commander Aramys. I had some unkind thoughts about you when we first met."

Ardyn heard a knowing chuckle that made him look up.

"I had a feeling something was going on when you wouldn't speak to me during the tour and then disappeared. Jevan was very informative *and*... I will admit he is *quite easy* on the eyes," she teased.

A flush of anger rose as he shot her a look, making Aramys laugh. "Sorry, I shouldn't tease. I have no plans to steal this Medellan from you. I am happily mated, and I have no desire to add another mate to my family."

The sudden flush of anger turned to embarrassment upon hearing that. "I... I am sorry. I was jealous of the attention he gave you. Before the attack began, I almost walked out on Jevan, determined to sulk in the woods. You must think me very foolish."

"Not foolish, no. It's a natural reaction when you're deeply in love," Aramys said. "Please be sure to thank him for that tour he gave."

Love? Ardyn knew he cared deeply for Jevan, but love? That hadn't crossed his mind until now. *I am not ready to explore that. Not until I know Jevan is okay.* Annoyed at Aramys for complicating his feelings again, he brushed it off. "You can thank him yourself when he wakes. I promise I won't be jealous."

"Unfortunately, I won't be here. One of our operatives managed to send us the coordinates to the Maara'dahl base. So, I am taking the battalion and going after them. I want to put a stop to all this violence, once and for all."

Looking up at Aramys, he felt a mix of relief and regret. "That's good to hear. Good luck. I hope we never have to face something like that again."

"Take care of yourself, Ardyn, and know this. Jevan cares for you as much as you care for him. He wouldn't stop talking about you during the tour," she said with a wink, before turning to leave.

Ardyn's face heated as his ears lowered again, making Keryth laugh.

"I'll talk to Amyra on my way out," Keryth said, becoming more serious again. "You really need to rest. I'm sure they can fit a small bed in here for you to sleep on."

Before he could disagree, Keryth held up a hand. "Don't argue. You will be no good to Jevan if you pass out from exhaustion."

"Okay, good point," Ardyn agreed.

That evening they brought in a small bed, so Ardyn could get some sleep. The room was already equipped with a food replicator and an adjoining shower room, so Ardyn had everything else he needed. The medical techs came in to check on them regularly, monitoring Jevan's condition and admonishing Ardyn gently for neglecting himself.

The healing process for Jevan was going slower than usual, but Amyra told him it was to be expected because of how extensive Jevan's injuries were and the fact he was a member of a completely different species. The delay in getting him inside the healing stasis field of the medical bed also hadn't helped any. However, she reassured him that Jevan *was* healing and would make a full recovery.

For now, Ardyn focused on Jevan's slow, steady breathing to reassure himself that he hadn't lost him. Eventually Ardyn would have to share his time with Jevan's family, so he kept mulling over a confession he'd held back since the day Jevan saved his life. Finally, he worked up enough courage. "Jevan, if you can hear me in there, please do not laugh when I tell you this. I have something to confess. I should have told you sooner, but we've been so preoccupied, I nearly forgot about it until now."

Ardyn took a breath before he continued. "I'm sure you remember when you saved me from the *sar'ora*. What you don't know is... that... that wasn't the first time I ever saw you. I first spotted you in the woods one cycle of the seasons before. I heard you and that noisy pack of yours from a mile away, and I hid up in the trees to watch you."

Ardyn ducked his head, flattening his ears as he felt his face flush hot. "I felt an inexplicable attraction to you, despite my fear of your people. So, I merely followed you to make sure you were not heading toward Maala'naa. After that, I often listened for the clank of your pack, and the sound of it made me smile. Wasn't that silly of me, Jevan?

"Jevan... *please* wake up and forgive this silly old *elf*. *Please*."

FAMILY

Ardyn startled awake when a hand reached out and touched his shoulder. For a moment, his sleep-addled brain thought *maybe*, "Jevan?"

"No, I'm sorry. It's only us."

Blinking the sleep from his eyes, Ardyn looked up to see Jenira, Micah, and Asha. "Oh, hey, you made it."

"They told us you haven't left his side since he was brought down," Asha said, eyeing the small bed in the corner of the room. "We're here now. You can go get some rest."

With an adamant shake of his head, Ardyn shifted in his seat, but did not stand. "No. I will remain at his side until he wakes."

"You're such a good friend, but we're his family," Asha argued. "We'll let you know when he's awake."

That was the first time that being called Jevan's *friend* felt... wrong. "No, *please*..."

A knowing look came over Jenira's face, followed by a smile. "You're not *just friends*, are you?"

"Well... um..." Ardyn stammered, his ears completely flattening against his head.

"Mother, I think Ardyn here may soon be considered family as well," Jenira said with a smile. "You better let him stay."

It took Asha a moment to process what was just revealed before she gave Ardyn a warm smile. "Are you in love with my Jevan? Does he know? Oh, come here and let me give you a hug!"

Ardyn finally stood, allowing the woman to envelop him in her arms and squeeze him. He returned the hug gratefully, having missed Jevan hold him like this. "We have talked, but the subject of love hasn't come up. Not yet. But we do care about each other a great deal."

"Your people don't pair-bond though, do they?" Micah asked, walking around to the other side of Jevan's bed. "Are you even capable of pair-bonding?"

Shaking his head, Ardyn responded. "I don't know. It's something we should ask the medical techs. Maybe they can find out if we're compatible."

"Jevan's been avoiding the pair-bonding for so long. I hope you're compatible," Asha said, before turning to Jenira. "Just make sure you two have a couple of extra babies since Jevan won't be having any with this one."

"Mother!" Jenira admonished, her face darkening.

"I already have three children," Ardyn informed them. "Would they count?"

Asha and Jenira exchanged looks, and then Asha beamed at him. "Of course! If you pair-bond with Jevan, then any family of yours is a family of ours."

"Hey," came a hoarse whisper from beside Ardyn. "Don't go planning my pair-bonding without me."

"Jevan!?" Ardyn cried out for joy, turning to see Jevan's eyes blink open, a cheeky little smile on his face.

Before Ardyn could say or do anything else, a couple of medical techs rushed in. "We were just alerted that Jevan is awake," they explained. "Please give us some room to examine him."

They all stepped into the far corner of the room while the technicians ran scanners over Jevan's body. Ardyn's heart pounded in his chest, happy beyond words that Jevan was finally awake.

When the techs were done, the one Ardyn knew as Faelan turned to them. "Jevan is doing well, but he's not done healing yet. He woke up a little too soon, but I'm sure you're all eager to speak with him. We'll give you an hour, and then we need to place him back in the state of deep sleep he was in, so he can finish healing."

Ardyn had a mix of relief and disappointment wash over him.

"How long until the healing is complete?" Asha asked.

"Jevan is responding better than we expected to the healing stasis field," Faelan replied. "At the current rate, it should completely heal him within a few more days. Three, maybe four at the most. After that, he will require another eight to ten days of physical therapy."

"Physical what?" Micah asked.

Faelan explained the process of physical therapy, helping Jevan to strengthen his muscles after lying in bed for so long, without damaging his newly healed body.

"I still can't believe that you can do all this with just a floating bed," Micah said. "Are you sure this isn't magic?"

"No, I assure you, this is all based on science," Faelan replied. "We have some excellent learning programs you can view, if you would like to learn more about how the technology works."

"No, that's okay," Micah said, taking a step back. "My head already hurts thinking about it."

"Well, if you change your mind, I'm sure Ardyn can help you find the learning programs. I'll be back in an hour."

After the techs left, everyone looked at each other, unsure who should speak to Jevan first. "Alright, all of you, get over here already. We only have an hour!" Jevan called out to them.

Approaching the bed, Ardyn took a place by Jevan's head, while Asha stood next to him and Jenira went with Micah to the other side.

"It's so good to hear your voice again," Ardyn said, reaching out to stroke Jevan's face gently. "I was so worried."

"I'm sorry," Jevan said, leaning into Ardyn's touch. "I don't know what I was thinking. All I know is I had to do *something*."

Ardyn smiled at Jevan. "Commander Keryth was here the other afternoon. He sends his thanks for saving his life. That bulkhead would have killed him if you hadn't pushed him out of the way. You're a hero."

"I'm glad he's okay," Jevan said. "So, how long have all the rest of you been here?"

They caught Jevan up on everything going on with his family since he last saw them. He beamed at the news that he was going to be an uncle. "I can't believe you found out like that," he said with a laugh. "Welcome to the new world!"

"I can't believe you've been living like this for so many cycles of the moons, and haven't invited us here," Asha teased. "Keeping all this luxury for yourself!"

Jenira came around and gently pulled Asha's arm. "Come on, mom, time is almost up. Let's give Ardyn and Jevan a moment to speak privately. Then perhaps we can tear Ardyn away from Jevan long enough to show us where we might sleep."

It hadn't even occurred to Ardyn that they might stay for a while, and he felt foolish for not leaving Jevan's side earlier. He watched as they left the room, before turning back to Jevan, taking his hand. "I am so glad you're going to be okay."

"Thank you for staying with me," Jevan said. "I know I was supposed to be in a deep sleep, but I still knew you were with me all this time. Knowing you were waiting for me made me want to wake and speak to you so much. I've missed you."

Emotion stung Ardyn's eyes. "I... I've missed you, too. So much. I'm sorry for having been such a jealous fool. I should have known that you weren't actually interested in Aramys."

"Well, you were being a *silly old elf*," Jevan teased. "But since you asked me so nicely to come back to you... here I am!"

Ardyn laughed, wiping away the tears stinging his eyes. "Wait, you heard that?"

"Every word," Jevan confessed. "I wish you had told me sooner, but I understand. We've had so much going on, things like that get forgotten sometimes. I'm flattered that you found me so intriguing that you watched for me every time I came through your range."

Ears flattening again, Ardyn ducked his head as his face heated. "I'm... sorry. I should have greeted you the first time I saw you. We're supposed to discourage your people from walking through our lands, especially that close to Maala'naa."

"So, why didn't you?"

"I don't know." Thinking back to when he first spotted Jevan, humming a cheery tune while his pack clanked loudly with his brisk footsteps. "Maybe because you seemed so full of joy. You had this big smile, walking so brashly through our land. I found you fascinating."

Jevan smiled at that. "So, about this pair-bonding I heard you planning with my mother—"

Before Jevan could continue, Faelan returned. "Time's up. You need to go back to sleep, Jevan."

Heaving an exaggerated sigh, Jevan squeezed Ardyn's hand. "Sorry, I guess we'll have to talk about it after I wake up again."

"Sleep well," Ardyn said before Faelan pressed some controls that pulled Jevan into a medically induced slumber. Watching Jevan's eyes flutter closed, Ardyn squeezed his hand back. *We will have much to discuss when you wake.*

RECOVERY

Several cycles of the sun later, Ardyn was still at Jevan's side. After the medical techs deemed Jevan healed enough, they allowed him to sit up and even get out of bed if he could manage it. This morning, Ardyn helped Jevan walk back from the shower room to his bed. Jevan's body was stiff and sore, but his broken bones had fully healed. He just had to work all the kinks out of his muscles after laying still for so long.

"Let me sit in that chair of yours for a while," Jevan said, trying to steer them away from the bed. "I'm tired of laying there all the time."

Ardyn guided him over to the chair. "When are you starting with that... *physical therapy?*"

Jevan sat down slowly, still feeling twinges in his hips and back where the bones were repaired. Once seated, he glanced up at Ardyn, who looked a bit rough around the edges himself. "This afternoon. You better get your pack ready, because I'm going to want to go on a long hike as soon as I'm able."

That made Ardyn smile and Jevan seized the moment, pulling Ardyn down onto his lap. Laughing, Ardyn made a mock protest. "Hey!"

"It's good to hear you laugh," Jevan said, pulling Ardyn closer. "I missed hearing that."

Snuggling against his chest, Ardyn nodded. "So much has happened, and I was so worried about you."

Jevan wrapped his arms around Ardyn. "I know, but you don't have to worry anymore. I'm going to be fine."

"Until the next disaster," Ardyn grumbled into his chest.

"I'm hoping that things calm down."

"With the Maara'dahl still a potential threat, I don't know if that's possible," Ardyn said. "If they try to attack us again, we may have to bring everyone back. Takyra wanted them all to stay after the battle ended, but most of the refugees insisted on going home. The encampment is half the size it was."

"No one should put their lives on hold forever," Jevan pointed out.

"True, plus my people are also having an existential crisis. Our way of life will change forever, that much is certain. This has destroyed all our deeply held traditions, and I'm not sure how I feel about that."

"You told me you always questioned those traditions," Jevan said, idly playing with the end of Ardyn's braided hair.

"I did, but seeing how lost some of my people seem after all this, I sometimes think I should have left well enough alone."

"Hey, look at me," Jevan said, shifting in the chair as much as his sore back would allow.

When Ardyn lifted his head and turned his fathomless eyes to him, Jevan gave him a warm smile. "How many people's lives did we save when we found the Rahn'naa?"

"But how many did we put in danger?" Ardyn countered.

"How many died during the attack?" Jevan asked, having not wanted to broach that subject until now.

"I'm not sure," Ardyn admitted. "I know at least a dozen died when the Ora'laa damaged the top of the observation tower, but I don't know how many were killed in the battle. Takyra and Aerys have been meeting with Keryth and the Aterians, but they haven't included me in any of the discussions. I've tried to ask, but Takyra told me to focus on you and not worry about it."

"I'm sure we'll find out what happened. In the meantime, you could tell me how much my mother has been pestering you about pair-bonding with me," Jevan asked with a laugh. "Don't tell me she hasn't. I remember that conversation you were having when I first woke up."

"Not too much," Ardyn said, ducking his head a little. "We don't even know if we're even compatible. From what Jenira has explained, it's quite an involved process."

"It is. I don't even know everything that goes into the ceremony. Only a village ard knows the full process."

"That's what Jenira said. She suggested we get Mathias to meet with Amyra and show her the pair-bonding process, so she can analyze how it works. Maybe either Amyra or Tamaryn can figure out how to make it work between our species?"

"Good idea. Where is Mathias keeping himself? Still lurking around here, or did he finally go home?"

"He returned to Yanen to help settle people's nerves after the attack. I heard he's coming back tomorrow to attend these talks Takyra has been having."

The door suddenly opened and Keryth entered. "Jevan! It's good to see you up, with a lap full of Ardyn, no less. I'm not interrupting anything, am I?"

Jevan laughed as Ardyn slipped off his lap and scurried to stand behind him, his ears fully flattened.

"No, Commander, we were just talking," Ardyn said shyly.

Keryth gave them a dubious look and then smiled. "Jevan, I wanted to give you my personal thanks for saving my life. I would not be here now if you had not taken the brunt of that beam. It's good to see you are recovering."

Shrugging, Jevan tried to brush off the praise. "I would have done the same for anyone."

"How soon until you're up on your feet again?" Keryth asked.

"They said at least ten more cycles of the sun, maybe more. I need to continue to sleep on this bed and get physical therapy. I start this afternoon," Jevan replied.

"Amyra also said I should start taking Jevan on walks around the ship soon," Ardyn added. "Once he's had a couple of physical therapy sessions."

"So, how would you two feel about visiting Aria'naa?" Keryth asked, changing the subject.

The thought had crossed Jevan's mind, but the idea of visiting another planet was somewhat terrifying. It's certainly not something he'd consider without Ardyn. "Perhaps someday. Not until the Maara'dahl are no longer a threat, and we figure out how our people move forward after everything."

"Agreed," Ardyn said. "Since the trip no longer requires sleeping in cryopods, it would be interesting to visit my ancestor's homeworld."

"Speaking of the Maara'dahl, has there been any word?" Jevan asked.

"No. The battalion had to go silent to avoid alerting them of their location and heading. We may not hear from them until after it's all over."

"I hope that is soon," Ardyn said. "I do not know how much longer we can live like this."

Keryth nodded in understanding. "It is difficult to plan for the future, when you are worried about being alive tomorrow. This has dragged on long enough."

"I couldn't agree more. There are so many other things I would rather do than constantly worrying about this," Jevan said.

"Like visiting our homeworld with Ardyn, perhaps?" Keryth asked, returning to the previous topic.

Why does he keep asking? Jevan wondered. "The opportunity to visit another planet does seem exciting, but as we said earlier, as long as the Maara'dahl are still out there, it's not something we're willing to risk."

"Fair point," Keryth conceded before finally changing the subject. "I hear that you two may undergo a Medellan pair-bond. Is that right?"

"We've discussed it," Ardyn admitted. "We don't know if it will work because we're different species, so we want to ask Amyra and Tamaryn to meet with Mathias and discuss what goes into the ritual. Hopefully, they can analyze it and find out if we're compatible or not."

"That's an excellent idea. It surprised me when I heard that your species only had a lifespan of around thirty years if you don't undergo this ritual. That is far too short of a life."

"I recently passed into my thirty-fifth autumn, so I agree. Jevan still has so much more life left to live," Ardyn said, putting his hand on Jevan's shoulder.

Reaching up to cover Ardyn's hand with his, Jevan nodded. "I am glad I finally found someone I honestly feel I can spend the rest of my life with."

Ardyn squeezed Jevan's shoulder at those words, and he looked back at him as Ardyn flattened his ears again.

"I must get going," Keryth said. "Once you're fully recovered, the council would like you both to appear before us."

Jevan's eyes went wide as he turned back to Keryth. "The... *council?*"

RITUALS

Ardyn and Jenira were fussing over Jevan when Faelan came into the room. "Are you up for a walk?"

"Where to?" Jevan wondered.

"Amyra and Tamaryn are meeting with Mathias in the main lab," Faelan explained. "They thought you might want to be there."

Looking over at Ardyn, he smiled when he saw his ears raise. "This should be interesting."

It had been a few cycles of the sun since Jevan had awakened from his healing slumber. Between the physical therapy and frequent walks with Ardyn and his family around the ship, the aches in his back and hips had almost disappeared. There were still twinges of discomfort, but he was moving a lot better already.

Jevan leaned slightly on Ardyn, mostly to let him feel like he was helping. "Join us, Sis."

They followed Faelan to the lab, and Jevan was trying not to get his hopes up. *We're probably not compatible and then I'll be back to the same problem again. Still, if we are compatible, what would being bonded to Ardyn be like, I wonder?*

"... then I'd like to get a *sar'ora* as a pet. Wouldn't that be nice, Jevan?"

"What?!" Jevan asked, coming out of his reverie, only to see his sister sniggering at him. He realized he'd been so lost in thought that Ardyn was saying nonsense, but he played along. "Oh, yes, that's a wonderful idea. It could sleep at the foot of the bed and keep those icy feet of yours warm."

At that, Ardyn slapped Jevan's arm and gave him a mock growl of frustration before they both broke out laughing.

"If I didn't know better, I'd think you two were already an old, bonded pair," Jenira teased, and they all laughed as they entered the lab.

"Well, it sounds like you're feeling better," Mathias said, coming over to greet him. "Remarkable that you're up on your feet again. I'm sorry I haven't been by to visit, but Takyra has been keeping me busy."

Jevan was about to ask about this council that Keryth had mentioned, but Mathias raised a hand. "Save your questions until you're fully recovered. There's much to discuss, but it can wait. I've been asked to bring all the pair-bonding ritual items for them to analyze. I hear that you and Ardyn are thinking about becoming bonded. Is that true?"

"Yes," Jevan affirmed, hugging Ardyn to him with one arm. "We're just not sure if the bonding will work between our species, which is why they need to know what is involved in the ceremony."

"It would have never occurred to me to wonder about that," Mathias admitted. "Still, I've never heard of a Medellan and Athla'naa pair-bonding either."

They made their way over to Tamaryn and Amyra, who were standing by a table laid out with the pair-bonding ritual items. "Please, tell us what the ritual involves."

"During the ritual, each partner cuts their non-dominant palm before squeezing it into the chalice, which is made from a unique alloy. Then I take the chalice and mix the blood together using the quickener," Mathias explained, picking up the chalice, along with a metal rod. "As part of the ritual, I must stir the blood to the count of one thousand. Then the pair must carefully massage the blood into each other's wound. Afterward, I apply an herbal poultice on each wound before they wrap each other's hand with a strip of ceremonial cloth."

"Why do you make the chalice of this specific alloy?" Tamaryn asked, taking the chalice from Mathias, studying it.

"The ancient texts don't explain it, but perhaps Andreesen or Marta know? All I know is they pass the specific formula for this alloy down from one ard to the next, and that the ritual won't work without it."

"Do you use this alloy for anything else?" Tamaryn asked.

"No. The metal is too soft," Mathias replied.

Jevan had witnessed several pair-bondings and could picture each step as Mathias explained. "I always wondered why the ritual had to include blood. It never seemed very pleasant."

"It's not!" Jenira said, holding out her hand to show her bonding scar. "It hurt worse than I was expecting it to."

"Are these all the herbs you use in the poultice?" Tamaryn asked, picking up a bundle of plants.

"Yes. They must be dried before I can grind them into a fine powder and mix them with some of the oil in that jar," Mathias explained. "It makes a paste that's applied to the wounds."

Tamaryn and Amyra both picked up scanners and used them to scan each of the items. They also took samples of the oil and each herb, placing them into small, clear receptacles and sliding them into slots next to a large display panel on the wall.

Then Amyra came over to Jevan with another tool. "I'll need a sample of your blood for analysis. Also, I'd like to take a sample of blood from Jenira. I need to understand the changes between someone who has undergone the pair-bond ritual with someone who hasn't," Amyra explained. "Then I'll take a sample of Ardyn's blood so we can determine if it's safe for him to undergo this ritual."

"If you are, this will be a momentous occasion," Mathias said, looking like a proud papa. "I'm glad you found each other and have grown so close. Although, I now wonder what you two were up to during your confinement."

Ardyn's ears immediately went flat as his head ducked.

"We were too busy plotting our escape to think of much else," Jevan said with a wink.

Mathias squared his shoulders and took a breath. "I... should have said this a long time ago. I'm sorry for everything I put you through. The sentence I pronounced was unjust. If I had known even half of the truth, I would have never—"

"Thank you," Jevan said, stopping him. "We forgave you ages ago. You have more than redeemed yourself since then."

"We have all been through too much to hold grudges against each other now," Ardyn added.

Amyra walked over to them. "We have everything we need. Why don't you get in some more walking while Tamaryn and I analyze everything? We'll let you know when we have the results."

As his stomach rumbled, Jevan nodded. "How about we head to the dining hall?"

"Glad to see you have your appetite back," Ardyn teased, ready to support Jevan again.

"Let me walk on my own this time," Jevan said as they headed out. "I can't lean on you forever."

Ardyn moved away and mumbled something that Jevan couldn't quite hear. "What was that?"

Sighing, Ardyn looked up at him. "I said, if you needed me to, I'd gladly let you lean on me always."

Jevan reached out and pulled Ardyn close to him, as a flood of emotion rose in his chest. "Come here, you. How about we just lean on each other?"

As they continued down the corridor toward the exit of the hospital wing, Ardyn leaned his head against Jevan as they walked arm-in-arm, while Mathias chuckled beside them.

CUSTOMS

When they arrived in the dining hall the Aterians were sitting down to eat and waved them over. "Jevan! It's good to see you up on your feet," Andreesen said. "How is your recovery coming along?"

"Slower than I would like, but even with all this amazing technology, some things just take time. May we join you?"

"Please, have a seat!"

After the long walk to get there, Jevan's hips and back were aching. "Thank you."

"I'll replicate some of that stew you like," Ardyn said as Jevan slowly sat down.

"That would be great, thanks!"

Mathias and Jenira went with Ardyn to the bank of food replicators, leaving Jevan with the Aterians.

"So, we hear you want to attempt a pair-bond with your Athla'naa friend," Marta said. "Have other Medellans on Vestos ever pair-bonded with them before?"

"No, not that we know of," Jevan replied. "That's why Amyra and Tamaryn are analyzing everything involved in the ritual. Mathias gave them his chalice and quickener, along with a sample of all the herbs that go into the poultice. They also took samples of our blood."

Marta's face lit up. "Oh, that's wonderful. Maybe they'll be able to figure out how this ritual works exactly. Our scientists have been studying it but haven't completely figured out how it helps us live longer."

"Do you have any idea why we make the chalice with that special alloy?" Jevan asked, as the others returned to the table and Ardyn sat a tray before him with a bowl of stew and a cup of herbal tea.

"Yes, we were just wondering about that," Mathias said, sitting down with a tray filled with an array of colorful Athla'naa delicacies. That made Jevan smirk. "The previous ard taught me the precise formula for the alloy to make the bonding chalice, but he didn't know why that alloy was necessary."

Marta wiped her mouth and leaned closer. "You still use a chalice? Wow, I shouldn't be surprised, but we have not used those in decades."

"You don't use a chalice anymore? Then how do you perform the ritual?" Mathias asked.

Andreesen sat forward before explaining. "It is important to take blood from both bondmates and mix it in a receptacle made of that alloy with a quickener before they put the mixed blood back into each of the bondmates. However, the ritual part was painful and unnecessary. We now take the blood from each bondmate with a needle and use a machine to do the mixing. Then, the mixed blood is put back into each bondmate with a syringe."

"So, bondmates in Ateria don't have bonding scars?" Jenira asked, showing the palm of her hand. "How can you tell who is in a pair-bond?"

Tomas pointed to one of his fingers. "We wear a ring."

"Oh, so those aren't just decorative?" Jevan asked. He turned to Andreesen and Marta in confusion. "Why aren't you wearing rings?"

They both looked uncomfortable at the question and Andreesen had a momentary look of anger that he schooled before replying. "Normally, that would be a rude thing to ask, but I will forgive your ignorance. In my case, it is because my bondmate died."

Jevan felt mortified as his face flushed hot. "I am so sorry. I didn't mean to be impolite."

Marta cleared her throat, trying to break the tension. "I've been uncharacteristically choosy about whom to bond with. I still have a few cycles of the seasons, but I know I must make a choice soon."

"So, if those steps are still necessary, do you know why the alloy is so important?" Mathias asked.

"Our scientists have found that the combination of quickening metal and that alloy changes the blood from both bondmates in a fundamental way as they are mixed together," Marta explained. "However, they don't understand exactly how it's changing it yet."

"Well, maybe Amyra and Tamaryn can solve that mystery," Jevan said before drinking the last of his tea. "You can join us back in the hospital wing to hear the results when they're ready."

Andreesen shook his head. "Marta can join you for that. Tomas, Aron, and I have other matters to attend to."

● ● ●

When they were summoned back to the lab, Jevan was finishing up his daily physical therapy. "Oof, I'm not sure I can make it all the way back there. That lab is on the far side of the hospital."

"I have just the thing for that," Jevan's physical therapist said, disappearing into an adjoining room before coming back with what looked like a floating chair. "This new anti-gravity technology is incredible, isn't it? Please, sit down."

As Jevan settled himself into the floating chair, Ardyn walked around it. "I saw something like this on Keryth's ship. They had beds that floated. They used it to lift Jenira up from the floor when she'd passed out."

Jevan sank into the padding of the chair, enjoying how incredibly comfortable it was. "This is great!"

"You can use these controls here to move on your own, or you can let Ardyn push you."

Looking at the right arm of the chair, there was a little stick that stood out from the arm. It wasn't in the best position for his longer arm, but he could reach it by pulling his elbow closer to his body. He pushed the stick, and the chair moved forward. "Oh, this is going to be fun!"

After practicing for a few minutes to get the hang of the controls, he was ready to go. "Thanks again. I'll see you tomorrow," Jevan said as he steered the chair out into the hallway. It didn't move too fast, so Ardyn could walk alongside him at a comfortable pace.

"You've got to try this thing later," Jevan said as they rounded a corner. "This is so much fun!"

Ardyn laughed. "I haven't seen you smile like that in a long time. That's all the fun I need."

"Are you as excited as I am to find out the results of their analysis?" Jevan asked.

"Honestly, I'm a little nervous," Ardyn admitted. "What if my species is not compatible with this bonding process? What will you do then?"

Jevan had tried not to dwell on that possibility. "I don't know. I haven't thought that far ahead yet. Let's see what the results are before we worry about it."

When they arrived, everyone was already gathered. "Late as usual," Mathias teased. "What's that you're riding in?"

Jevan did a little spin in the chair before hopping off and pushing it into a corner. "I was a little sore after my physical therapy today, so they gave me that. I think they called it an anti-gravity chair."

"Yes. Anti-gravity technology was developed a few centuries ago. One of the many uses is to help the mobility of people who would otherwise struggle to get around."

"With all your medical advances, you still have people with disabilities?" Amyra asked.

"Yes," Tamaryn admitted. "There are still conditions we cannot cure and injuries we cannot fully heal. However, we've made sure that anyone with a disability has the same level of access to all public spaces. What our medicine cannot do, our engineering can."

"Fascinating. You'll have to tell me more," Amyra said as she led everyone to a large display with a dizzying array of charts, graphs and images. "But first, let's discuss what everyone is here for."

Jevan stared at it for a moment, not comprehending anything he saw. "So, are we compatible? Can we pair-bond?"

Amyra laughed at his eagerness. "The short answer is, yes, we believe so."

Embracing Ardyn, Jevan couldn't suppress a big smile, as he felt a weight lift from his shoulders. "That's wonderful news."

"If that is the short answer, what is the *long answer*?" Ardyn asked.

Tamaryn pointed at one part of the display. "Well, to begin, I believe I know why the Medellans require this ritual. Your people have severely damaged DNA."

Ardyn looked at Jevan and they both shrugged at each other in confusion. "DNA?"

EVOLUTION

T amaryn looked at their confused expressions and chuckled. "I am sorry. Let me explain. When you told us that a Medellan's lifespan is only about thirty years, I immediately thought there must be a problem with your telomeres."

"What is a *tele... mere?*" Jevan asked.

Amyra began inputting something into the display console. "To put it as simply as possible, your telomeres help to protect your chromosomes from becoming damaged or breaking down."

When Amyra saw Jevan about to pose another question, she raised a hand. "Before you ask, your chromosomes make up your entire genetic structure. They make you who you are. Everything from your height and your gray eyes to those silly round ears of yours. Let me show you."

Amyra changed the large display and brought up an image of something that reminded Jevan of four sausages tied together in the middle. "This is a Medellan chromosome. It's made of that DNA I mentioned before. This contains all the information your body needs to make you what you are."

Jevan looked at Ardyn, beginning to understand. "So, these chromosomes are why Ardyn has such pale skin and mine is so dark?"

"It's a little more complicated than that, but yes," Amyra confirmed before pointing to the four ends of the chromosome, making them change color. "The very end of each chromosome is where your telomeres are. The longer the telomeres, the longer your lifespan is likely to be. In most species, telomeres eventually shorten. That causes us to age and eventually die. When we show signs of advanced age, it is because our telomeres have shortened so much, our chromosomes break down."

"So, the Medellan lifespan is so short because we are born with shorter telomeres?" Jevan asked for clarification.

"Yes, much shorter and also very damaged," Amyra replied. "Because of this damage, once they've shortened, they deteriorate rapidly, which is why any Medellan who remains unbonded will age and die so young. The ritual that you perform when you pair-bond fixes the problem. From our analysis, it looks like there is a naturally occurring bacterium on this planet that is in your blood. They remain dormant until they are introduced to the alloy in the chalice. That's when they go into a frenzy of reproduction and hyperactivity. A side-effect of that hyperactivity causes them to repair the telomeres."

Furrowing his brow, Jevan wasn't sure he understood that correctly. "If putting the infected blood of one person in contact with that special alloy fixes the problem, why must we bond with another?"

"That's the complicated part," Tamaryn admitted. "While the bacteria repair the telomeres, it requires the genetic code of two people to make the repairs work. The bacteria need to take parts from the telomeres of each person to build new, longer telomeres."

"So, once the pair washes each other's hand in the mixed blood, it introduces these new hyperactive bacteria into both of their bodies, and that's what increases our lifespan?" Marta asked, clearly grasping the concept faster than Jevan was able to.

"Precisely!" Amyra confirmed.

"You've also said that there is some sort of bonding that occurs at an emotional and possibly sexual level?" Tamaryn asked. "I think I can explain that as well. Once the hyperactive bacteria have been introduced into the pair's bloodstream, they affect other systems besides fixing the telomeres. I suspect they affect parts of the brain as well, specifically the ones related to sexual and emotional attraction."

"After bonding, why does having sex with someone other than a bondmate cause death?" Mathias asked. "It doesn't happen often, but I've seen it within my lifetime."

"We're not sure," Amyra replied. "That will require more analysis and samples from a larger population."

"However, one thing we found is that the bacteria eventually stop being hyperactive, but they don't return to their previous dormant state, either. Instead, they remain active. I have some ideas about what might cause that, but I'd need to run further tests to confirm it," Tamaryn added.

"What we haven't figured out yet is how the bacteria go from the state of hyperactivity to the lower-level activity we detected in Jenira," Amyra said.

Mathias cleared his throat and looked at Ardyn nervously. "There... there is one other part of the ritual I forgot to mention. Perhaps that might explain why?"

Everyone looked at Mathias expectantly. Taking a deep breath, he continued. "The last part is more private. The pair *must* consummate the union within two cycles of the sun. I never understood why, but the ancient texts deem it absolutely necessary. In fact, as ard, I'm required to witness the coupling to ensure it occurs."

Jevan noticed Ardyn's demeanor change. *I forgot about that part, and I think Ardyn did too. A part of me hoped one day we could be intimate, but I would never want to force myself on him.*

Amyra put that additional information into the computer and ran another simulation with the blood samples she'd taken earlier. "Yes, that's it! The release of hormones during copulation puts the bacteria into a more normal state of activity. That is truly remarkable."

That gave Jevan an idea. "Can these *hormones* be released in any other way? Would it require a traditional coupling?"

"There are usually several ways to achieve the same result, at least within our species," Tamaryn replied. "I would bet that should also be possible for yours as well."

At that, Ardyn seemed to relax a bit, and Jevan breathed a small sigh of relief. *Good.*

"But how is any of this compatible with Athla'naa physiology?" Marta asked. "Your species isn't born with these broken telomeres, are you?"

Tamaryn shook his head. "No, our telomeres and DNA don't show this level of species-wide damage. Since our species evolved on a different planet, our genetic structure differs somewhat from yours, but it all operates on the same principles. Our telomeres are also longer than the ones we saw in Jenira, which explains why our lifespans are longer than pair-bonded Medellans.

"The good news is that based on the simulations we ran, we see nothing that would show this would be harmful. Since our telomeres are intact, the bacteria would have nothing to repair. In fact, we predict that by merging Medellan and Athla'naa DNA, it may add even more years to both of their lives."

Marta clapped her hands together excitedly. "This is all fascinating. It's well-known that the pair-bond is necessary, although none of the historical records explain why. I wonder how our ancestors discovered this longevity process?"

"Do you know what's more puzzling to me?" Tamaryn pondered aloud. "How did the Medellan genetic structure develop this flaw? I cannot imagine you evolved that way naturally. Something must have damaged your DNA."

"There is a lot of our ancient history we don't know," Marta admitted. "It's one of the research projects I plan to work on when I return to Ateria."

Amyra brought up some images from outside the Rahn'naa, including a triwolf and some jumpers. "I still have more research to do, but I took some samples from your local wildlife and none of them exhibit any damage to their DNA. It's quite the mystery."

"Well, I'll leave that mystery for you to solve," Jevan said. "Because I think we might have a pair-bonding to plan, right, Ardyn?"

That's when Jevan noticed Ardyn had moved some distance away from him. *Wasn't he right next to me?*

Ardyn gave him a half-hearted smile. "When the time is right. There is much to discuss first, I think."

The room grew silent and Jevan stared at Ardyn. *Wait, did I do something wrong?*

THE COUNCIL

Ardyn withdrew from Jevan after they found out the results in the lab. He felt foolish for pulling back, but he wasn't ready to talk to Jevan about everything going on in his head right now. At least, not until he could make sense of it himself.

Jevan's family was still there, and he let them have more time with him. It gave Ardyn the time he needed to think about everything, while Jevan continued to finish his recovery. Instead, Ardyn retreated to their quarters, spending most of his time alone.

When he couldn't make sense of his own thoughts, Ardyn would spend hours watching the historical archives from Aria'naa. The videos ranged from interviews of the various Rahn'naa crew members and colonists to videos featuring life on Aria'naa during that time period. They included public hearings, news clips, and even some fictional programs that were part of their popular entertainment. It was all fascinating and took Ardyn's mind away from his own concerns, at least for a while.

Could life here on Med'nor look like this in the future? Ardyn wondered. *I guess it depends on how many people will accept this technology.*

●●●

Ardyn hadn't realized how much time had passed when one afternoon someone knocked on the door. It surprised him to see Jevan standing in the corridor, looking uncharacteristically unsure of himself.

"May I come in?"

Confused, Ardyn moved aside. "Of course you can come in. These are your quarters, too."

"Thanks. I... wasn't sure."

As he watched Jevan move with his usual grace toward the living area, he realized Jevan must be fully recovered. "Did you finish all your treatments and physical therapy early?"

After Jevan sat down, he tilted his head and quirked an eyebrow. "What do you mean, *early*?"

"I thought you still needed to sleep in that healing stasis field for a few more cycles of the sun?"

"I did. I completed that last night."

"How long has it been since we learned of our pair-bonding compatibility?"

"That was about five cycles of the sun ago," Jevan replied. "Did you lose track of time? Is that why you haven't been by to visit me?"

Ardyn sat on the chair across from Jevan, staring at him, dumbfounded. "It has been that long?"

Nodding, Jevan looked bemused. "After you pulled away from me when I teased about planning our pair-bonding, I thought you were having second thoughts. Are you?"

"I... I'm not sure," Ardyn began. "There are so many things to consider—"

Suddenly, Cytra appeared on the wall display. "Jevan of Yanen and Ardyn of Maala'naa, you are being summoned to appear before the Council of Vestos."

◆◆◆

Cytra guided them to a section of the tower they hadn't been to before. After exiting the elevator, they walked down a corridor lined with carpeting, the walls having warm, wooden accents instead of the more sterile metallic silver and whites of the rest of the Rahn'naa. In the middle of the corridor was a single set of doors, also made of highly polished wood. As they approached, the two doors slid to either side, admitting them into a large chamber.

Ardyn stared around the large room. On either side of them were rows of wooden benches, and more carpeting covered the floor. Before them was a raised dais with a long, curved table, behind which sat several familiar faces. Takyra, Mathias, and Taeglyn sat in the three central seats, while Andreesen and Keryth sat on either side. Aerys, Marta, Tomas, and Aron were also there, sitting on a bench facing the dais.

"Jevan and Ardyn, please, come forward," Takyra welcomed them. "I'm sure you both have many questions. Let us answer the one that is probably the foremost in your minds."

"Our people came together in the face of danger, and in the aftermath, we came to recognize that we must continue to work together, for the good of all the people in Vestos," Taeglyn said.

"That is why we've formed this council," Mathias continued. "Currently, we're serving as interim council members until our various peoples can elect permanent ones. I'm representing the Medellans of Vestos, with the blessing of our leadership in Tafaran."

After a pause, Taeglyn spoke next. "I am representing the Athla'naa who have occupied Vestos for the past twelve-hundred cycles of the seasons. Because our people and needs will differ from those aboard the Rahn'naa, it made sense to give our people a unique name. We're going to call ourselves the Athla'bhat."

People of the trees. That's... fitting.

Takyra spoke last. "And I am representing the Athla'naa from the Rahn'naa. As we're technically the oldest among you, we are calling ourselves the Athla'dor."

Ardyn saw Jevan try not to smirk, knowing that could be interpreted as either *The Wise Ones* or simply *The Old Ones*. Looking over those assembled, it amazed Ardyn at how they had come together in this way, especially after the centuries of tension between his people and the Medellans. "What about Andreesen and Keryth?"

"They are serving as advisors to our council, as we work together toward a united Vestos," Takyra replied. "Andreesen brings to us his experience as a past member of the Grand Council of Ateria, while Keryth brings wisdom from the Leadership Conclave on Aria'naa."

"This is amazing," Jevan said. "I never thought I'd see our people work together, but now that you mentioned Aria'naa, the most pressing question I have is regarding the Maara'dahl. Are we still in danger?"

Keryth smiled. "We received news from Commander Aramys last night. Through a coordinated effort, our operatives within the Maara'dahl managed to eliminate their leadership, and the battalion disabled and captured the rest of their fleet. They are no longer a threat."

The relief and joy that flooded through Ardyn left tears stinging his eyes, and he turned to give Jevan a hug. "Finally, we can hope for peace!"

Jevan hugged him back hesitantly, and it reminded Ardyn of how distant he'd been recently, lost within his own existential crisis. He reluctantly backed away from Jevan and turned back toward the council.

Shuffling his feet for a moment, Ardyn finally brought up the one other question he'd been hesitant to ask. "How… how many people did we lose during the battle? I've tried asking, but no one would tell me."

A grave look crossed Takyra's face. "We wanted to wait until Jevan was well and we could tell you both. The good news is that we didn't lose any of the lives we sheltered. The shields on the Rahn'naa did their job. Other than the dozen techs that were working maintenance in the communications section of the observation tower, no one else was hurt."

Mathias cleared his throat and added. "Thankfully, the Maara'dahl concentrated their attack on the Rahn'naa, so none of the unprotected populations were harmed. Everyone on Vestos and Ateria remained safe."

That's a relief.

After Takyra turned to Keryth, he continued. "Besides those techs in the tower, the only other casualties happened during the battle. Every ship in the battalion suffered some damage and at least a handful of casualties, and three ships were destroyed with all hands lost."

Jevan wrapped an arm around Ardyn when he let out an unexpected gasp. *Oh no!* "There were hundreds of people on each of those ships, weren't there?"

Keryth gave a somber nod. "Yes."

Ardyn took a deep breath before stepping away from Jevan, sliding out from under the man's arm. With everything else weighing on him at that moment, he couldn't bear the added weight. *More deaths that wouldn't have happened if I hadn't found that stupid key.*

Takyra had a fleeting look of concern. "You should know, after more deliberation and communication between the Grand Council of Ateria, the Leadership Conclave, and our Council, we have decided that all Athla'naa on Med'nor may choose where they wish to live. They may remain on Med'nor or return to Aria'naa. Since the population of Athla'bhat is so firmly established on Vestos, it makes little sense to relocate them to Maal'dak Five."

"Also," Andreesen spoke up, looking at Jevan. "Any Medellans of Vestos are welcome to visit or relocate to Ateria if they wish. Some of your people may still have distant relations on our continent and we can attempt to reunite those families."

"What about my people? May we also visit Ateria?" Ardyn asked.

At that, Andreesen nervously cleared his throat. "We're still discussing that. Not all Aterians will welcome an alien species. That's not to say some couldn't visit, especially in an official capacity. We just can't ensure the safety of every Athla'naa that visits. *Not yet* anyway."

Cannot ensure our safety? What does that mean?

Before Ardyn could ask for clarification, Takyra changed the subject. "That actually brings us to our final piece of business, and why we asked you both here today."

The three council members rose, and Mathias spoke first. "Jevan of Yanen and Ardyn of Maala'naa, you have both helped set forth a series of events that have had far-reaching consequences."

Suddenly, the feeling of safety and belonging that he had developed since they had discovered the Rahn'naa drained away, as Ardyn felt they were once again being put on trial for their incursion into the Aria'una all those cycles of the moons ago. Looking up at Jevan, he saw the Medellan also had a worried look on his face.

"Ardyn, you were the one who found the key, which led you to delve deeper into the Aria'una," Taeglyn said. "What do you have to say regarding your role in everything that has happened since?"

Oh, great. Here we go again.

CONSEQUENCES

Ardyn's heart hammered in his chest, hearing the doubts that have so often echoed through his mind, spoken aloud. For a moment, he struggled to breathe, let alone speak. It wasn't until Jevan wrapped an arm around his shoulders again that he could take a breath and reply.

"Yes, I know. I set off all the events that have happened. That key made me doubt the history of my people. I had to learn the truth. I don't think I could have lived with myself if I had not."

Jevan squeezed his shoulder and spoke. "You can't lay all the blame on Ardyn. Before I came along, he was determined to leave the Aria'una. If I hadn't been there, we may have never discovered the secrets hidden here."

"No, Jevan," Ardyn said. "Do not take responsibility for my choices. I was the one who wanted to explore further—"

"Enough!" Takyra shouted, bringing Ardyn's attention back to the council, his ears flattening in deference.

It was when all of those on the dais broke into broad smiles that Ardyn thought he may have lost his mind. "Jevan, you also bear part of the *blame* for what happened," Mathias said, looking almost mirthful.

With a warm smile Takyra continued. "It is because of your insightfulness and bravery, despite whatever fate awaited you, that all of us have much to thank you for. The Athla'dor are especially grateful to both of you. We were slowly dying. You found us and saved us."

Wait, what? Did they just praise us? Ardyn felt even more confused.

"Despite the turmoil, you have both ushered in an age of enlightenment for the people of Vestos," Taeglyn said. "You broke our people out of the cycles of lies and secrets we've been perpetuating for centuries, holding both of our people back."

Standing, Keryth smiled down at them. "Because of this, we would like to offer you both the joint positions of ambassadors to Aria'naa."

Ardyn looked at Jevan, and then back to the council, completely confused. "I... thought we were about to face punishment for our crimes."

"You committed no crimes," Takyra reassured them. "You are two of the most selfless people I have ever met."

"But are you sure you want *us* to be ambassadors?" Jevan asked.

"We couldn't think of anyone better," Takyra said. "You would make excellent representatives of the two parts of our world, Medellan and Athla'naa. Despite everything you've been through, you have handled everything remarkably well."

Standing up next to him, Aerys also joined in. "You've both impressed me by how easily you have adapted to living in a more technologically advanced environment. You have both taken everything in stride, always learning and improving yourselves."

"Watching how you helped so many of our people readjust, awakening in such an unexpected situation, you have both shown a lot of empathy. You both put people at ease around you, and that is an excellent skill to have as an ambassador," Takyra added.

Ardyn's mind was whirling at the unexpected change of events. "I am honored you think that highly of me... of us..."

Aerys gave them a knowing smile. "But you need time to consider it?"

"Yes, and to understand what being an ambassador would entail," Ardyn said.

Andreesen nodded. "First, you would need to come to Ateria. If you are to truly represent our planet, you should also learn about our culture and society, and understand the needs of the Aterian people, which will differ from those of the Medellans of Vestos."

"I was hoping to visit and learn more about your culture and our people's history," Jevan said. "But wouldn't it be better to have an Aterian ambassador?"

"I had considered that, and the Grand Council may still insist on one," Andreesen conceded. "However, it would still serve you well to understand the Aterian way of life first."

"Then, once you're ready, you would travel to Aria'naa," Keryth added. "There you would also spend some time learning about our culture before officially taking on your roles as ambassadors."

"What will we be expected to do, as ambassadors?" Ardyn asked.

Takyra replied. "You would be the liaison between our governments, and a central point of communication between our planets. While you would represent our interests on Aria'naa, they would also send ambassadors to Med'nor for the same purpose."

"That's a lot of responsibility," Jevan said.

"It is, but we feel you both would be up for the challenge if you decided to accept the position. However, we expected you would need some time to consider the offer, so we've prepared a little surprise for you both. Aerys, will you escort them, please?"

"It would be my pleasure," Aerys said. "Come on, follow me."

Aerys led them to the elevator. When they exited, they noticed they were on the upper cargo level, with its red-lined corridors. "I don't think I've been on this level since we stumbled on that hatch in the forest," Ardyn remarked. "How long ago was that?"

Aerys spoke to the tablet he held. "Cytra, how many Med'nor days has it been since Ardyn and Jevan reactivated you?"

"One hundred and sixty-seven days."

"That means it's autumn," Jevan said. "You told me you were born in the autumn. I should have realized when you said you recently turned thirty-five. I was born in summer, so that makes me twenty-six now. This is the first time I've missed celebrating."

Ardyn noticed Aerys was leading them down a corridor they hadn't explored the last time they had been here. The floor at the end of the corridor became a ramp that led them upward toward a familiar-looking door. "That door reminds me of the one in that airlock we found all those cycles of the moons ago."

Aerys gave them a knowing look before opening the door, leading them into a small room with another door on the other side of it. This room reminded Ardyn even more of the airlock, and when Aerys opened the other set of doors, he gasped to see the familiar woods beyond them.

A wave of nostalgia came over Ardyn. "This *is* the airlock we found!"

"It is indeed," Aerys confirmed. "I had a team of techs repair the interior door, so you can now safely return to the ship through here instead of hiking through the woods."

"Is that why you've brought us here?" Jevan asked. "So, we can have another way in and out of the Rahn'naa?"

"Yes, and we thought you both may appreciate having some time to yourselves," Aerys said, pointing out some packs and other provisions stashed in a corner. "We've put together enough provisions for you to last at least five days. Take some time away from the ship to reconnect with your world as you consider your futures."

Lowering his ears, Ardyn smiled gratefully at Aerys. "This is a wonderful surprise, thank you. I think this is exactly what we needed."

"If you need anything else," Aerys said. "There is a replicator in a small room around the corner from the airlock. Just let us know when you've returned and made your decisions."

"Thank you, Aerys," Jevan said.

After Aerys left, they looked at each other. "Well, I guess we have a lot to talk about."

Jevan nodded. "Yeah, we definitely do."

RECONCILED

Jevan leaned against the wall, feeling somewhat dumbfounded now that he and Ardyn were finally alone. He couldn't wrap his mind around the idea of being an ambassador when he wasn't even sure where he stood with Ardyn.

"I'm... going to take a little walk and let my family know we're heading away from the ship for a while," Jevan explained as he pushed off the wall and walked toward the outer airlock door. "I won't be gone long."

Ardyn gave him a brief nod. "I'll check the provisions they put together and see if we need to replicate anything."

Stepping outside for the first time in what felt like many cycles of the seasons, Jevan took a deep lungful of fresh air. It was late afternoon, so it wouldn't make sense to head out until the next morning, but it felt good to stretch his legs and feel the natural ground beneath his feet again. Clicking on his communicator, he asked for his sister. "Hey, Jenira!" he greeted.

"Where have you been? Mother is worried sick!"

"Ardyn and I were called into a meeting with this new council they've formed," Jevan explained. "I don't want to go into details right now, but Ardyn and I have a pretty big decision to make. So, we're going away from the ship for a few cycles of the sun. We need to clear our heads and figure out some things."

"What is up with you and Ardyn, anyway? Did he tell you why he stopped coming to the hospital to see you?"

"We haven't had time to talk about that yet, but we will," Jevan reassured her. "Right now, we just need some time alone together."

"Alright, but I'll be checking in with you, so keep that communicator on, okay?"

"I will and tell mother that I love her, and I love you, too."

Ending the conversation, Jevan looked around and saw that he'd wandered farther from the structure than he'd intended and turned to make his way back. He was within sight of the airlock when he heard the snap of a branch, followed by a territorial growl.

Stopped in his tracks, Jevan turned to see a pack of triwolves stalking toward him. *Falx! This must be their autumn hunting grounds.* He slowly backed away, trying not to make any sudden movements.

So far, the pack was only sizing him up, the largest of them giving him a low growl in warning. They looked well-fed, so they weren't eyeing him for dinner, merely letting him know that he'd intruded on their territory.

Jevan tried to back away slowly, heading roughly in the direction of the airlock. His heart was racing as he took a few steps without taking his eyes off the pack. They didn't like that, as they all moved into a crouch, looking ready to rush toward him, when a burst of bright light exploded on the forest floor in front of the pack.

Several more bursts were fired, sending the pack running away, as Ardyn ran toward him with a *rahn'ora.* "Are you okay?"

Taking several deep breaths, Jevan nodded. "Y-yeah, thanks. I thought I was a goner there for a moment. How did you...?"

"I heard the growls," Ardyn pointed to his ears, waggling them back and forth for a moment.

That made Jevan burst out laughing, while Ardyn tried to keep a straight face, but after another waggle of his ears, his lips twitched and finally he couldn't contain his laughter as he doubled over. It took them a moment to regain their composure, but the earlier tension between them was finally gone.

"Thanks for saving me," Jevan said, as they made their way back to the airlock.

"I wasn't about to let you become a feast for that pack of *sar'ora.*"

"Well, after the way you've been acting lately, I wasn't so sure," Jevan admitted.

Back inside, he saw Ardyn had unrolled the two bedrolls next to each other in the middle of the airlock, along with placing out some food and drinks.

"Come and sit with me," Ardyn invited, closing the airlock doors. "It's time we talked."

Nodding in agreement, Jevan sat down. Sitting cross-legged, Jevan waited for Ardyn to speak. At first, Ardyn fiddled with the end of his braid and avoided eye contact with him, so Jevan gave him time to collect his thoughts.

After taking a deep breath, Ardyn raised his eyes to Jevan. "I know I've been distant since we learned about our compatibility for pair-bonding. I... I am sorry for that."

"You seemed willing to pair-bond with me until then," Jevan said. "What changed?"

"Everything."

Jevan's brows knit in confusion. "Have I done something wrong?"

Ardyn shook his head. "No, it's not you."

"Then what is it? Please, talk to me."

Grabbing a cup, Ardyn took a drink before responding. "So much has happened and... I have been feeling lost. I don't know where my future lies anymore. Sometimes I miss the simplicity of my old life."

"That I understand," Jevan replied. "Neither of us will be able to go back to what we were before. You're right, our futures are uncertain. They stopped the Maara'dahl, but what if there are others out there like them?"

Looking straight at him, Ardyn's eyes were full of emotion. "I am *afraid*. Afraid if I get too close to anyone, I'll just lose them," Ardyn confessed. "You... you are the one I want to lose, least of all."

Jevan reached out and took the cup from Ardyn, setting it aside. Then he took Ardyn's hands into his, holding them firm. "I don't want to lose you either. You know, I couldn't sleep that night after Denyra took you. I never want to be separated from you again."

"I have been so unsure of what I want, but I know I feel better when I'm with you, and... *I shouldn't.*"

"Why not?" Jevan asked in confusion.

"I know you really don't want to be locked into a pair-bond. Eventually you must, but... I have been doubting my worthiness to be your bondmate. Especially... considering what may be required to complete the bonding process."

That's when Jevan understood. "You're afraid of being intimate with me."

Nodding, Ardyn ducked his head, his ears flattening. "After we were told it was necessary, I thought I might... be willing to work up to that stage with you, but then everything seemed to happen so fast. Your family seems especially... *eager*... for this ceremony to happen soon. But—"

"But you're not ready yet."

"I'm... I'm not sure I'll ever be ready. I don't know if it's because of my forced mating, but I... I don't enjoy..."

"Oh, I think I understand. You don't enjoy being the penetrating partner, is that it?"

"Yes... *exactly*!" Ardyn sounded relieved that he didn't have to say it.

"Well, there are other ways we can pleasure each other, without having to do that," Jevan said.

Ardyn gave him a quizzical look.

Jevan explained all the ways he and his past partners had pleasured each other. While he enjoyed all ways of giving and receiving, he knew others had their preferences. "I would never expect you to do something with me you're not comfortable with, but would any of the things I just explained be okay with you? I can ask, but I'm sure we can make one of those work to meet the pair-bonding requirements."

There was a lovely blush of lavender on Ardyn's cheeks as he sat silently, thinking through everything Jevan had just told him. Looking back up at Jevan again, he quirked his head to the side. "You find all of that... pleasurable?"

Giving Ardyn a warm smile, he nodded. "Yes, very much so."

"I... might be okay with the one you described, using your mouth," Ardyn said quietly, ducking his head again. "W- would you be... willing to...?"

Jevan's eyebrows rose in surprise when he realized what Ardyn was asking for. "Do you mean right now?"

Another slight nod and Jevan crawled over to Ardyn, looming over the smaller Athla'naa. "Are you sure?"

Ardyn reached up and cupped Jevan's face, meeting his gaze. "Yes."

Waggling his eyebrows, he smirked as he gently pushed Ardyn onto his back and pressed their lips together. Jevan's heart hammered in his chest as Ardyn wrapped his arms around his neck and pulled him closer, deepening the kiss.

This is going to be so much fun.

CLOSEST

Ardyn woke, wrapped in Jevan's arms, like he had many times in the past several cycles of the moons. Yet, this time was different. A smile spread across his face as he remembered last night, and how gentle and patient Jevan was with him. After spending his life fearing intimate touch, Jevan broke through his walls and helped him experience genuine pleasure for the first time.

Now, instead of the usual knot of anxiety, there was a warm, happy feeling in the center of his chest that Ardyn had never experienced before. Turning in Jevan's arms, Ardyn tangled their legs together as he gazed at Jevan's sweet, sleeping face. *I love him so much, it almost hurts.* When Jevan blinked awake and saw Ardyn looking at him, he gave him a big, brilliant smile.

Rubbing the sleep out of his eyes, Jevan stretched his long limbs. "Hey, good morning."

Ardyn responded by snuggling closer to Jevan, ducking his head underneath the larger man's chin. All he wanted right now was to be as close to Jevan as possible. *I never want this feeling to end.*

"Are you alright?" Jevan asked, kissing the top of his head. "Last night wasn't too much, was it?"

Shaking his head, Ardyn curled even closer. "No. It was perfect."

Kissing his head again, Jevan hugged him gently. "Good, I'm glad. It's been so long since I've been intimate with anyone. I almost forgot how good it could be."

A fleeting thought of regret made Ardyn frown. "I'm sorry."

"Hey, it's not your fault. The circumstances weren't right until now, and it was good for me to take a break. It helped me clear my mind and realize what I'd been really wanting in my life. What I was really afraid of, was to pair-bond with the wrong person."

Pulling back and looking at Jevan, Ardyn reached out to trace a thumb over his bottom lip. "And I'm the right person?"

"Absolutely." Jevan leaned down and captured Ardyn's lips in a kiss.

Kissing was something Ardyn learned he really enjoyed, and he eagerly returned it.

●●●

After spending a leisurely morning enjoying each other's bodies once more, they replicated themselves a hearty meal before dressing and packing up their gear. Knowing the pack of *sar'ora* were still in the area, Ardyn replicated another weapon for Jevan, so they were both armed.

Usually, packs of *sar'ora* avoided people. That lone beast that Ardyn had tracked so long ago was an exception. Still, it was better to be safe, especially since they were intruding on their territory.

Shouldering their packs, they closed the airlock behind them and headed out. "Where should we go?" Jevan asked.

Ardyn wasn't sure. "I just want to spend time together. We have a lot more to discuss that we didn't get to last night."

"Hah, good point, but I'm not sorry I distracted you. Hey, do you remember where that cave was? The one where you found the key. Maybe we could head over that way?"

Sorting through his memories of when he'd found that cave and later realized he'd wandered into the Aria'una, Ardyn turned around to orient himself. "The *bhat'laa'arh* perimeter is roughly south of here, and the observation tower is northeast. So... yes, I think I know where it is. It is a journey that would take three cycles of the sun, heading slightly northwest. Are you sure you want to go that far?"

"We can always ask Keryth to bring us back," Jevan pointed out.

"That's true." Ardyn began heading in roughly the direction he thought the cave would be in. "If we can find the clearing where you saved me from that lone *sar'ora*, then I'm sure I can find it again."

"I guess we've both saved each other from those beasts now, haven't we?"

Remembering when he'd heard that distinctive growl the previous afternoon, Ardyn was glad he'd replicated a weapon as he ran out to chase off the pack before they made Jevan their next meal.

"Yes, we have." Ardyn moved closer so he could take Jevan's hand in his.

They hiked for a time, each lost in their own thoughts. Ardyn sorted through all the things he knew they needed to discuss. They'd resolved one hurdle last night, but that didn't quite settle everything between them.

"Oh, I haven't told you yet," Jevan said, breaking the silence. "Tamaryn came to talk to me while I finished my recuperation. He told me he looked at my telomeres more closely, and said they looked stable. I should still have a few cycles of the seasons before I have to pair-bond... so, if you're not ready yet, there's still time."

Ardyn paused, squeezing Jevan's hand. "That's good to know, but that's not the only factor we need to consider. There's also the matter of these ambassadorships they have offered us."

"Good point. Hey, I remembered a suitable spot for us to make camp tonight, but we need to keep moving if we're going to make it before nightfall."

They kept walking, with Jevan taking the lead, while Ardyn mulled over the idea of leaving Med'nor. The thought of visiting his people's homeworld was both exciting and terrifying. It thrilled the adventurous part of him, although recent events with the Maara'dahl made him wary. Ardyn also realized he would miss his infrequent visits with his family.

"We wouldn't have to be ambassadors forever, would we?" Ardyn wondered aloud.

Jevan squeezed his hand. "No, I don't think so, and I'm sure we can come back and visit. Especially if they set up regular trade between our worlds."

"I'm glad they offered it to both of us. If I had to leave you behind, I wouldn't accept the position at all."

"That's probably why they offered it to us both. We've become inseparable!" Jevan laughed.

"Then, I think it depends on when they want us to leave. We should pair-bond before then, shouldn't we? We don't know how long we'll be gone, and we should do it here so our families can attend."

With a snort of laughter, Jevan agreed. "My mother would kill me if I didn't invite her to my pair-bonding."

"Tell me again everything that happens during the ceremony. I know we went through it before, but I'd like to hear it all from you this time. Please?"

For the rest of their hike, Jevan described all the parts of the pair-bonding ceremony, interspersed with funny stories from his friends' pair-bonding celebrations. By the time he finished, they'd reached the clearing Jevan had been heading toward. "I think this was the clearing where we camped the first time after we'd met," he said, as they put down their packs.

Looking around, Ardyn nodded, recalling that first night they'd spent together. "I think you're right. Should I go hunt a couple of *paal'dak* for dinner?"

"I think they packed enough food, but you could help me gather some firewood."

The sun had fully set by the time they had a nice roaring fire going, as they sat beside each other, eating. "At least this stuff tastes better than those ranger rations you used to eat," Jevan teased.

Ardyn laughed. "Those rations weren't *that* bad."

◆◆◆

Ardyn led most of the way, even climbing up a tree to make sure they were still heading in the right direction. They made good time and by early evening, they reached the clearing by the stream where Ardyn had first met Jevan. It was a good place to stop and camp, making love to the sound of the burbling stream.

They took their time the next day, and Ardyn was able to appreciate his surroundings more. "The last time I was in this part of the Aria'una, I was trying to run for the perimeter as fast as my legs could carry me," he said, laughing at himself.

Walking at a leisurely pace, it was late afternoon when they approached the cliffside that Ardyn recognized. They made their way along it, hoping to find the same cave Ardyn had taken shelter in. "It's around here somewhere. I'm still amazed I found it in the downpour I was running through."

The sun was about to set when Jevan spotted it. "Over there, is that it?"

Making their way toward the entrance, Ardyn nodded. "Yes!"

Ardyn pulled out one of the electric lanterns they had in their packs and turned it on before crouching and making his way into the small cave. "Hey, you didn't tell me it was this small!" Jevan grumbled as he crawled through the entrance on his hands and knees.

"Oh, sorry!" Ardyn apologized. "I forgot how much bigger you are than I am. At least the ceiling inside is higher."

Plunking himself down in the middle of the small cave, Jevan could sit upright with a few inches to spare. "Just barely! So, where'd you find that key?"

Crawling over to the far corner of the cave, Ardyn patted the dirt there. "Right around here. A flash of lightning glinted off it, or I would never have seen it."

"How much different all our lives would be if you hadn't spotted it..."

Ardyn turned to look at Jevan, his ears flattening. "You know I've had my regrets over finding it, but... are you regretting it now, too?"

"I'd be lying if I said I don't miss the simplicity of my old life sometimes," Jevan admitted, crawling closer to Ardyn, and reaching out to take his hand. "But I wouldn't change anything that's happened. It's hard losing people, but look at how many we've also saved? All of those aboard the Rahn'naa didn't deserve to die in there."

"You're right. I just wish we could have saved them without losing anyone, but I know I can't put the blame of other's actions on myself. That's something I've been struggling with the most."

Jevan pulled him closer. "We can't change what's happened. All we can do is figure out how to move forward from here. What do you want to do?"

Leaning against Jevan, Ardyn took a moment to collect his thoughts. "I've been thinking a lot about that while we were hiking here today. One fact remains true. I love you... and I don't want to be apart from you. I am no longer afraid of having to be intimate with you after the pair-bonding, and I know your family is eager for the ceremony to proceed. So, I think I'm ready."

Gentle fingers lifted Ardyn's chin until he was staring directly into Jevan's eyes. "Are you sure? I love you, too, but if you're not ready—"

Smiling, Ardyn caressed Jevan's face, and with more confidence, replied. "I am ready."

EXPECTATIONS

After they returned to the Rahn'naa, Jevan felt more relaxed than he had in a long time. The time away, alone with Ardyn, was exactly what he'd needed. Now he had a future to look forward to, with his betrothed by his side. The more he thought about it, the more the opportunity of becoming an ambassador excited and gave him a sense of purpose that he hadn't felt in many cycles of the seasons.

When they were called before the Council of Vestos again, Jevan and Ardyn were better prepared to give a response. As they approached the podium facing the council members, they were holding each other's hand, which made Takyra smile.

"You both seem to be in a much better mood than when we last saw you," Takyra observed. "Have you had enough time to consider our proposal?"

They both nodded and Jevan replied. "Yes, we have. We would be honored to accept the positions as ambassadors of Med'nor."

Ardyn squeezed his hand before asking. "How soon will we have to take these positions?"

"The Grand Council of Ateria are eager to meet you both. I have made arrangements in Donarvon for your accommodations," Andreesen replied. "You could leave at any time."

The council must have noted the look of panic on their faces as they all laughed. "You don't need to hurry. Please, take as much time as you need to prepare."

"Actually, we have an announcement to make," Jevan said, unable to hold back a cheerful grin as he wrapped his arm around Ardyn. "Ardyn has agreed to be my bondmate. Mathias, would you do the honors?"

Springing out of his chair and clapping his hands like an excited schoolboy, Mathias grinned from ear to ear. "It's about time. Young man, I wouldn't think of letting anyone else preside over this joyous occasion."

Mathias ran down from where he sat and embraced them both in a big hug. "Congratulations! They were worried you wouldn't go through with it, but I knew you'd both make up if given enough time alone together."

"How long will it take to plan the ceremony?" Ardyn asked.

Clasping a hand on Ardyn's shoulder, Mathias gave them a knowing look. "If I know Asha, she's already made most of the preparations already. Do you want your family to attend? Then it depends on how long it will take for them to arrive."

"Good point," Ardyn said. "I'll need to talk to them first."

"Since your people are still fearful of the transmat, I can have someone fly you to Maala'naa," Keryth offered, as the rest of them joined them on the council chamber floor. "Anyone you wish to invite can return on the shuttle with you."

"Asha and Jenira have already started planning," Mathias said, still beaming happily. "I think we should be ready in five cycles of the sun. Is that soon enough for you both?"

Jevan's heart lept into his throat. This was all happening so fast, and... *this is why Ardyn freaked out on me, isn't it?* Jevan chuckled to himself. He looked down at Ardyn. "It's a little fast, but I know my mother won't let us drag our feet any longer than necessary."

Mathias clapped his hands together with a grin. "Excellent."

◆◆◆

Later that afternoon found Jevan and Ardyn back in their quarters. Jevan was trying to contain his nervous excitement over everything and was pacing the room while Ardyn watched him with amusement. "You need to relax. I'm sure it will all fall into place."

Taking a deep breath, he sat back down next to Ardyn. "I know, but tell that to the millions of thoughts racing through my head right now. Once we've concluded the ceremony, what next? Do we just leave, or will Andreesen give us some training first? We're supposed to go to Donarvon for a full cycle of the seasons, right? What will that be like?"

Ardyn grabbed one of Jevan's flailing hands and brought it to his lips to kiss it gently. "Breathe, my love. We'll find out in due time."

Taking another deep breath, Jevan smiled at him. "You're right."

"When I'm in Maala'naa tomorrow, do not drive your mother and sister crazy," Ardyn teased him. "Let them fuss over you. It will make them happy."

Jevan was about to respond to that when the chime of their door rang, and Ardyn flung an arm out, preventing him from getting up to answer it. "I will get it."

A moment later, Mathias entered their quarters, holding an ornate wooden box. "We have much to plan before the ceremony," he explained, setting the box on the low table in front of the couch.

"Can I offer you a drink?" Ardyn asked. "Tea, or something stronger?"

"This is a time for celebration! How about some of that *wah'roh* your people are so fond of?"

"I'd wager you're quite fond of it as well," Jevan teased.

Mathias laughed. "You're not wrong about that!"

Once the drinks were served, Mathias sat and opened the box he'd brought, showing off two beautifully wrought daggers laying on a dark red cloth. "These are for you to use during the ceremony," Mathias explained. "I've had them freshly sharpened, so be careful with them."

Jevan carefully lifted one out to look at. The metal was polished to a high sheen and embedded in the elaborate hilt were dark red gems. Ardyn picked up the other, which had purple gems.

"I know there's a less painful way, but I was hoping you both would be willing to go the traditional route, so I had some help from the Athla'dor in replicating those," Mathias explained. "The gems represent the colors of your blood."

Ardyn admired the craftsmanship. "They're beautiful. What a fine gift, thank you," Ardyn said, before looking at Jevan. "What do you think? I would like to follow your traditions if you're willing. The medical techs can always give us something for the pain."

"Yes, I'd like to keep with our traditions," Jevan agreed. "The way Marta explained how they do it in Ateria, it all sounds so... *clinical.*"

After they returned the daggers to the box, Jevan proposed a toast. "To peace and long life, for all of us."

"I'll drink to that!" Mathias said as he raised his glass. "Now, the other thing I wanted to discuss was the ceremony itself. This will be an unprecedented event, and I think we should incorporate elements from both our cultures into the ceremony."

"That's a wonderful idea," Ardyn agreed.

Clearing his throat, Mathias took a long drink before continuing. "So... I know this is a delicate topic, but is there any part of your mating ritual that you would want incorporated into this ceremony? Besides the obvious, of course."

Ardyn went stiff, so Jevan placed a comforting arm around his shoulders. "No, I don't want any reminders of that... but thank you for asking."

Nodding, Mathias sat forward slightly. "I understand. However, is there anything from your culture you think we could incorporate?"

For a long moment, Ardyn was still, completely lost in thought. Jevan was about to change the subject when Ardyn spoke again. "There... there is another ceremony among my people. It's rarely performed, but when two or more feel a deep connection, they may hold a handfasting celebration to profess their commitment to each other."

"Oh, that sounds perfect," Mathias said. "Is there any aspect of that celebration that we could add to your ceremony?"

A small smile came to Ardyn as he remembered something. "Those who took part in the handfasting celebration would weave flowers through their hair."

Picturing it, Jevan smiled. "How lovely! In fact, I know just the blooms that would look perfect with your hair."

"Should we include flowers in any other way?" Mathias asked.

An idea came to Jevan, and he beamed a bright smile. "We could also decorate the traditional archway with flowers," he suggested. "What do you think, Ardyn?"

"What is this archway?" Ardyn asked.

Jevan looked at Mathias to explain. "We take thin branches and weave them into an arch, where the bondmates stand during the ceremony. It's meant as a symbol of their lives and families intertwining."

"That would look beautiful with flowers added," Ardyn agreed.

They discussed several other aspects of the ceremony, including the preparations the two families would make for the betrothed. "Who will you be bringing with you from Maala'naa?" Mathias asked.

"My mother and father, assuming he can set aside his duties as Elder for a while. I may also ask the mother of my oldest child if they would like to attend. Although, she may decline. We've never been very close."

Mathias nodded in understanding. "Under the circumstances, I imagine you wouldn't be. How about your other two children? You have at least three, right?"

"Yes, but they live in other settlements. I haven't seen either of them since our matings."

"Well, I suppose it's for the best. We don't have to invite them. I think smaller ceremonies are better, anyway. That way, the two of you can get to the fun part of the bonding more quickly."

Jevan's face heated at that, and Ardyn was ducking his head as his ears flattened. It took Mathias a moment to realize what he'd said and slapped his hand over his mouth in embarrassment. "I'm so sorry, Ardyn. I shouldn't have implied it was fun... I mean, it usually is for most... but... I'll shut up now."

Looking at each other, Jevan and Ardyn burst out laughing, making Mathias look very confused. "Don't worry about Ardyn," Jevan attempted to explain. "Let's just say we've worked through that issue together."

"Oh?" Mathias asked before coming to another realization. "Oh!"

PREPARATIONS

The next several cycles of the sun sped by as Jevan and Ardyn prepared for both their bonding ceremony and their trip to Donarvon.

"Are you excited to visit Ateria?" Marta asked as they walked together back to their quarters after spending the afternoon together.

"Yes, I am. Life in Donarvon sounds very different from the village I grew up in," Jevan admitted. "Your people have come much farther than ours have, and I'm interested to see how different it is."

"We've also come a long way from who we were, haven't we?" Ardyn mused aloud.

Jevan's mind flooded with memories of his past. The endless cycles of the sun trekking from one village or settlement to the next. Meeting the Athla'naa for the first time and learning their language. All the many happy, intimate encounters he'd had. Life had been simpler back then, but nowhere near as interesting. Wrapping an arm around Ardyn's shoulders, he agreed. "We certainly have."

"How long has it been since either of you have visited your homes?" Marta asked.

"Except for the brief visit on Keryth's shuttle, not since we fled," Jevan replied.

Ardyn nodded. "Other than when we stood in judgement before the Elder Triumvirate, the last time I was in Maala'naa was the morning they sent me to hunt the *sar'ora*. Even then, I had only arrived home the night before."

"Then you both should take some time to visit before leaving," Marta suggested. "So much has happened and you'll be away for a long while. I'm sure your friends will love to see you before you leave."

They paused outside of their quarters and Jevan contemplated it for a moment. "I think that's a great idea. What do you think, Ardyn? We could pack some provisions and make the trek on foot? First to Maala'naa and then to Yanen. I think it would do us both some good."

Ardyn gave him a dismissive shrug. "Didn't we just get back from spending time in the woods? We could ask Keryth to send one of his shuttles."

"I'm sure we'll get used to a lot of advanced conveniences after we visit Donarvon and then move to Aria'naa. This may be our last chance to go on foot like we used to. What do you say? For old time's sake."

Ardyn laughed. "Alright, for old time's sake."

◆◆◆

The ceremony was to take place outside the observation tower. Grateful to Ardyn and Jevan for finding and rescuing them, many of the Athla'dor pitched in and created a beautiful setting for the ceremony. They built several rows of benches hewn from the surrounding forest, which they were planning to clear so they could finally build their city, with help from Aria'naa. Keryth was helping to coordinate all the equipment they would need to dig out the Rahn'naa.

Mathias supervised the construction of the central archway, while Taeglyn advised on which late autumn blossoms to weave into the branches, so it reflected both Medellan and Athla'naa traditions.

A couple of cycles of the sun before the ceremony, Jevan's mother presented him with a package. "I asked Keryth to fly me back to Yanen so I could retrieve these. I've been saving them for you. They are your father's and my bonding garments."

Jevan hesitated to take it. "I... I'm not sure I can accept these. You and father hated each other—"

"Oh, what utter nonsense," Asha exclaimed. "Yes, we fought frequently and passionately, but we didn't hate each other."

Looking up at his mother with astonishment, Jevan couldn't believe it. "You... didn't?"

"Oh, I know everyone assumed we did. We both fought the idea of the pair-bond, as much as you tried to. We thought the old tradition was a foolish way to control us and we hated the idea of being tied down to only a single partner. However, we were secretly in love long before they matched us together. We kept up the charade afterward because we were afraid the Ard would tear us apart if he found out we'd lied."

Shaking his head, Jevan laughed. "Why am I not surprised that even you hid secrets from me? It seems this is the season for uncovering all the hidden truths."

Jevan and his mother spoke for hours, and he gained a new appreciation for his late father that he hadn't had before. That made him sad, knowing his father wouldn't be there to see his bonding ceremony. It also brought him some level of comfort, going into this pair-bond with Ardyn, knowing his mother hadn't suffered in her bond as much as he thought she had.

After the long conversation, Jevan graciously accepted the gift. Then he found someone on the Rahn'naa who could alter the garments, so they would fit both him and Ardyn. He also requested they incorporate both Athla'naa and Medellan designs into them. This ceremony symbolized not only their mutual bond as a couple but the uniting of their two peoples.

The night before the ceremony found Jevan pacing, as he often did.

"If that wasn't a metal floor, I'd admonish you for wearing a hole in it," Ardyn teased. "You're not having second thoughts, are you?"

Settling himself next to Ardyn on the couch, Jevan shook his head. "No, not at all. It's not nerves... it's excitement."

Ardyn rolled his eyes before giving Jevan a cheeky grin. "Well, we don't have to wait for the second part of the bonding tomorrow. We could practice again tonight."

With a playful shove, Jevan laughed. "That's not what I meant, and you know it! It's more like... tomorrow marks the start of our new lives, and after we make our visits back home, we're starting another adventure. For the first time in many cycles of the seasons, I'm excited about what the future brings."

"I know, I am, too," Ardyn said, smiling at him fondly. "So, does that mean you don't want to practice for tomorrow night?"

Jevan stood up and scooped Ardyn into his arms, carrying him towards the bed. "No need to ask me twice!"

THE BONDING

The next morning dawned bright and clear. Keryth had promised them perfect weather for their ceremony, and he'd certainly delivered. Ardyn was thankful for the commander's localized weather control technology making it unseasonably warm for late autumn and perfect for the festivities.

Ardyn was in their quarters, sitting on the couch with Jevan. Earlier that morning, Jevan had gone out to pick the late autumn blooms that he planned to plait into Ardyn's hair. The flowers had petals that went from either a white or pale pink at their center to a deep purple, complementing Ardyn's natural coloring.

Sighing with contentment as Jevan worked on his hair, Ardyn marveled that such a simple thing could make him so happy. "I'm glad we dissuaded your mother from doing my hair. While I have nothing against Asha, I prefer when you do it."

"I still remember the first time I brushed your hair," Jevan said fondly. "I needed something to do that night, and it was frustrating watching you try to untangle it with your fingers."

Laughing, Ardyn shrugged. "My people only use fingers to comb through our hair, so it's what I was used to. Although, now I can't imagine not having you brush it for me."

For the ceremony, Jevan plaited a more elaborate braid, incorporating the flowers and pinning Ardyn's hair up onto the back of his head in a fetching style he'd found in the Athla'naa database. After he was done, Ardyn went to the shower room to view himself in the mirror. The effect of the blooms was magical, and Ardyn loved the effect.

"Thank you, my love," Ardyn said as he came back to the living room and gave Jevan a little kiss on the cheek.

"You look exquisite," Jevan said, pulling his betrothed in for a deeper kiss. "Now, let's get you into those bonding garments."

Ardyn removed the clothes he'd put on after his shower that morning and stood unabashed as he watched Jevan get the garment that Jevan had altered for him. It was a complicated affair, consisting of several layers of textured cloth in various hues of lavender and purple. It had originally been red, the color of bonding among the Medellans, but Jevan asked the Athla'naa techs who had helped him alter the garments if they could change it to match the natural coloring of the Athla'naa people.

While Jevan helped Ardyn into each layer, he peppered Ardyn with little kisses. "Are you ready for tonight?"

Ardyn laughed as his face heated at the thought. "I think we've had enough *practice*. I would be a lot more nervous if we hadn't, so thank you for that."

Jevan stepped back to admire him. "Wow, you look amazing. Are you sure you don't want to practice one more time?"

With an exaggerated roll of his eyes, Ardyn gave Jevan a playful shove. "You're incorrigible. Get dressed. We don't want to be late to our own ceremony."

"Alright, alright, but they can't have the ceremony without us, so technically, we can't be late."

Jevan changed into his bonding garments, which remained dyed in various shades of red. Before putting on the last layer, he stepped up to Ardyn and tucked a stray strand of hair behind his pointed ear. "Okay, all kidding aside, I meant, are you ready for any changes that might happen? They still don't know exactly how the bonding will affect us."

Blushing at his earlier misunderstanding, Ardyn ducked his head and flattened his ears. "Oh... that. Well, I mean, how do you prepare yourself for something like that?"

"Good point," Jevan agreed, as he put the last layer of his garment on and checked the time. "I think we should head up. The ceremony will begin soon. Shall we?"

Jevan offered his hand and Ardyn accepted, realizing that the next time they would be in their quarters together, they would be bonded. A small shiver of excitement ran up his spine at the thought.

When they emerged from the elevator, Ardyn was astonished to see all the Athla'naa lining the way toward the exterior exit of the tower, the path they formed lined with an array of flower petals. Hand-in-hand, they made their way while those gathered cheered and shouted their congratulations. This was the first big celebration they'd had since being awakened, and there was an air of festive excitement. Ardyn was glad to be one reason for the celebration, although it was those aboard the Rahn'naa that really deserved it, after all they'd been through.

Once outside, the path of flowers and well-wishers continued to the benches that had been set up. The path led between the rows of benches and toward the ceremonial arch, where Mathias was waiting, holding the chalice. As they made their way down the aisle, they bowed at each row of guests, as was customary. When they reached the last row of benches, Ardyn smiled to see his parents, Cylaen, and Myria.

After bowing, Ardyn's father pulled him into a hug, followed by his mother.

"Papa Ardyn! You look so pretty!" Myria exclaimed, making Ardyn smile.

Picking her up and giving her a quick kiss on the cheek, he straightened the flower crown she wore. "So do you, little one."

"Thank you for bringing her," Ardyn said to Cylaen, as he set her back down before joining Jevan.

Once together under the arch, they both turned toward the assembled guests and made another bow, before turning and giving a final bow to Mathias. Then, facing each other, they sank to their knees onto the pillows that had been placed at Mathias' feet. Taeglyn had reminded them that kneeling was part of the handfasting celebration, so they added that to this ceremony as well.

Mathias cleared his throat. "We gather here to bear witness to the bonding of Jevan and Ardyn." Raising the chalice before Jevan, he asked. "Jevan, will you spill your life's blood to bond with Ardyn?"

Jevan pulled out the dagger he'd secured within his garment. "I will."

Swiftly sliding the dagger across his palm, Jevan made a fist to squeeze his dark red blood into the chalice. Once the blood stopped dripping, Mathias asked the same of Ardyn, who looked directly into Jevan's eyes as he slid his own dagger across his palm. He tried not to wince at the sharp pain, instead closing his fist tight, letting his dark purple blood drip and mix with Jevan's.

Once Mathias had collected the blood, he turned to the table behind him and began stirring the combined blood with the quickener. Ardyn could hear Mathias count softly to one thousand as he and Jevan cradled their wounded hands and waited. Looking coyly at Jevan, Ardyn kept his ears flat, his heart thumping in anticipation of their impending bond.

Once the mixing was complete, Mathias turned back and held the chalice before them. "Jevan, take Ardyn's hand and wash it in your combined life's blood, so it may renew him in your bond."

Jevan reached out and took Ardyn's injured hand and dipped it into the combined blood in the chalice, massaging the mixed blood as gently as he could into the wound. Mathias then repeated the same words for Ardyn, who took Jevan's hand and, with his four pale fingers, massaged Jevan just as gently.

Next, Mathias turned and placed the chalice behind him and brought forth the herbal poultices that had been prepared. Holding out their injured hands, Mathias first placed a poultice on Jevan's hand, which Ardyn then reached out and held.

"Ardyn, bind Jevan's hand, as you are now bound for eternity."

Unwinding a strip of cloth from his wrist, Ardyn gently wrapped it around Jevan's hand, holding the poultice in place over his wound. Then Jevan repeated the process on Ardyn.

Jevan had just finished tying off the binding, and Mathias was speaking again when Ardyn swayed on his knees. The world was spinning before his eyes and the last thing he heard before his world went black was Jevan's voice crying out. "Ardyn!"

CONNECTING

Jevan lurched forward and caught Ardyn in his arms as his new bondmate passed out. "Someone, help him!"

Amyra and Tamaryn were next to him a moment later, both pulling out their hand scanners. "He's alive, just unconscious," Amyra said with a note of relief.

Tamaryn looked at the readings on his scanner. "It appears the bonding process isn't as harmless as we thought. Can you carry him?"

Jevan nodded and pulled Ardyn into his arms as he stood.

"Let's take him up to your medical bay," Amyra suggested. "It will be faster than carrying him down to the hospital wing."

Cradling Ardyn in his arms, Jevan nodded his consent before Keryth and Takyra ran over to join them, and they were all transported to the Wah'kah'ria together. The medical techs were already waiting for them with an anti-gravity gurney. Jevan laid Ardyn down gently, before following numbly after.

Ardyn's face looked so drawn, and his breathing was too shallow. *No, no, no, no. Don't leave me, Ardyn. Not now,* Jevan pleaded in his mind as his heart raced with worry.

Once in the medical bay, they transferred Ardyn to a stasis bed, and Tamaryn began a full set of scans. Both he and Amyra gasped when they saw the results. "Ardyn is... he's changing. His very genetic structure is transforming."

"Isn't that what you expected to happen?" Jevan asked.

Shaking his head, Tamaryn tried to explain. "Not exactly. We expected that repairing *your* telomeres would modify *your* genetic structure. However, because Ardyn's telomeres aren't damaged, we didn't expect it to affect his genetic structure in any significant way."

"So, what is it doing to him?"

Amyra ran around to the other side of the bed and began tapping on the display there. "I'm not sure. All I can say is that it's affecting his genetic structure in a way our simulations did not anticipate and his physiology is not taking kindly to it."

"How are you feeling?" Tamaryn asked. "Are you feeling any effects at all?"

Jevan took a breath and realized he was slightly lightheaded, but he shrugged it off, wanting them to focus their attention on Ardyn. "I'm fine."

Ardyn began writhing on the bed, moaning in pain, drawing everyone's attention. His body seemed to fight the bonding process, and it broke Jevan's heart to see him in such distress.

Rushing to his bondmate's side, Jevan took Ardyn's hand into his. "Hey, Ardyn? Dear heart, please remain strong. Don't leave me. Not today. Not ever. I came back to you. Please, please come back to me!"

Hot tears streamed down Jevan's face as Ardyn's body arched on the bed and a scream of pain escaped his lips. At the same moment, pain burst throughout Jevan's body and he fell to his knees with an echoed scream.

Tamaryn ran to him and scanned him. "It seems the bonding affected Jevan as well. Everyone, help me get him onto the Medellan-sized bed."

Jevan was still conscious and managed to get his feet under him, and with the support of two medical techs, they guided him toward the larger bed. Collapsing onto it, the techs helped position him properly before they could activate the medical stasis field and begin full scans of him as well.

Writhing in agony, his entire body felt as if it were being burned alive. Still, Jevan tried not to scream so he could hear them speaking. A moment later, he heard Mathias come in and ask. "What's going on? What's wrong with them?"

He heard Tamaryn respond. "It must be the mix of Medellan and Athla'naa genetics. Something has gone terribly wrong. We're not even sure what's happening, so there isn't much we can do except monitor their conditions for now. We can't even risk giving them anything for the pain because we don't fully understand what's going on yet."

Lost in a sea of pain, it burned through Jevan to his very core. It was simultaneously agonizing and oddly cleansing, as if his old self was being stripped bare and being replaced with something new. *Help me!* Jevan screamed to himself.

After what felt like an eternity, Jevan suddenly felt a presence. *"Jevan?! Jevan, where are you?"* Ardyn's voice flooded his mind.

The feeling of Ardyn's presence helped Jevan ignore his own pain. *"Ardyn? I'm here! Are you okay? Where are you?"*

"I don't know. It just hurts so much!"

"I... I'm hurting, too," Jevan admitted. *"What's happening?"*

Pain seared through him again, and all he could hear were Ardyn's screams.

After an eternity of torment, Jevan bolted awake and found himself still on the medical stasis bed. His pain had lessened, but he saw Ardyn was still writhing. "What's happening to us?" he asked as Amyra rushed over to him.

"We don't know. Both of your genetic structures are changing in unexpected ways," Amyra replied. "Your body seems to take it better than Ardyn's. Tamaryn has several techs researching what's going on, to see if there's anything we can do to at least relieve your pain."

Jevan flinched, grunting in pain the next time Ardyn cried out.

"You're feeling pain every time he does, aren't you?" Amyra asked.

Jevan nodded. "Yes, and I think our minds are also connected somehow. Through my mind, I spoke to Ardyn briefly. His pain is much worse than mine."

"Fascinating."

Just then, Andreesen and Marta walked into the medical bay and Amyra filled them in on the situation before bringing them over to Jevan's bed. "I asked them to come because Aterians have somewhat more advanced knowledge of the pair-bond."

"We have some ideas on how the bond links a pair together," Andreesen said. "But I've never seen it on this level before."

Amyra put a comforting hand on Jevan's shoulder. "Try to get some rest. We need to go back to the lab and do more research."

Laying back down, Jevan closed his eyes and did his best to relax, despite the pain he was still feeling. As the pain slowly became more tolerable, his mind drifted in and out of consciousness, and soon he was aware of Ardyn's presence again.

"*Ardyn? How are you?*"

"*I don't know, but the pain has lessened and I can feel everything from you now. It's... a little overwhelming. All your emotions, even your thoughts. I've been struggling to sort them all out. I'm able to focus only when you speak to me,*" Ardyn's voice echoed in Jevan's mind.

Allowing himself to relax, Jevan realized he could feel it, too. A flood of emotions, thoughts, and memories came from Ardyn. Jevan could see pieces of Ardyn's childhood as he ran and laughed, carefree. Then the memories of Ardyn's forced matings came to the surface, and Jevan felt a mix of anger and sadness. The humiliation Ardyn had felt tore at Jevan's very core.

Jevan didn't know what memories Ardyn was seeing, but all he wanted to do was wrap his arms around his bondmate and comfort him. "*I'm so sorry, Ardyn, and I love you so much.*"

"*I know. Yawen asharra'ior,*" Ardyn replied and Jevan felt all the love Ardyn had for him, and it made him weep for joy.

Eventually, both of their pain subsided, and they finally rested. After getting some sleep, Jevan groaned as his eyes fluttered open. Looking over at the bed where Ardyn lay, he saw his bondmate was awake and no longer writhing in pain.

"Hey," Jevan smiled. "How do you feel?"

"Much better now, my love," Ardyn smiled back.

"*I'll* be the judge of that," Tamaryn insisted.

For the next half-hour, Tamaryn and Amyra probed and scanned them, making certain they were okay. "Can we go to the feast?" Jevan asked, beginning to feel hungry after the ordeal.

"Alright, if both of you rest for a little while longer, I'll tell everyone that the bonding feast is back on," Amyra insisted.

Ardyn and Jevan smirked and agreed. "Yes, ma'am."

Once Amyra left them alone, Ardyn glanced towards Jevan. "Do you feel that? Are you feeling what I'm feeling now?"

Jevan concentrated for a moment. "Yes." Then, Jevan thought to Ardyn. *Can you hear my thoughts, too?*

"Yes!" Ardyn thought back.

"Wow," Jevan took a deep breath. "We're bonded more closely than I ever could have imagined."

Ardyn had tears streaming down his face. "The emotions you're feeling, it's almost too much."

"Shh. Come here," Jevan said. "Lie with me."

Ardyn hopped off his bed and joined Jevan in his larger one. Ardyn lay so that his back was to Jevan's chest and Jevan enveloped him in his long arms. Both of their breathing soon calmed, as did their heart rates.

"There, that's better," Jevan soothed. "I never expected such a profound connection, but somehow..."

"... it just feels right," Ardyn agreed.

Jevan pulled Ardyn in a little tighter, and they both allowed themselves to relax and drift into a light slumber.

●●●

As they dozed, the newly forged connection between them and this constant rippling wave of love that flowed from Jevan to him surrounded Ardyn. He never imagined having a connection so deep or so personal. There were also other feelings that drifted through, including *safe* and *home.*

A little while later, Amyra came back and roused them, rechecking one last time before deeming them fit enough to join the bonding feast. "However, I want you both to wear these monitors." She applied the small devices to their necks, just above their collar bones. "I don't need to be physically present, but I want to monitor your vitals when you complete the last phase of your bonding. These will alert me immediately in case anything else goes wrong."

Jevan helped Ardyn redo his hair, that had become mussed in all the commotion. Then they beamed down and headed towards the dining hall where the feast was being held. The hall was all hushed whispers as they approached, but once they appeared in the doorway, cheers erupted upon seeing both alive and well.

Takyra ushered them to their places, a special table raised upon a dais at the one end of the room. Along the way, Jevan saw and hugged his mother and sister, and Ardyn went to his parents and hugged them, reassuring them he and Jevan were fine.

Once seated at their table, they enjoyed the boisterous company and the specially prepared food. Takyra worked with Andreesen, Mathias, and Taeglyn to produce a mix of Aterian and Vestian Medellan delicacies, along with some of Ardyn's favorite Athla'naa dishes. They also had plenty of beverages, including *wah'roh* and whiskey to wash it all down.

The celebrations lasted late into the night, and eventually, Jevan and Ardyn could no longer put off what they needed to solidify their bond.

Jevan smiled at Ardyn. "So, dear heart, are you ready for the last phase of bonding?"

Ardyn looked at Jevan and simply nodded as he conveyed his readiness in other ways. Their newfound connection now made him even more eager for what was to come. The idea of experiencing that level of intimacy with their newfound bond was going to prove interesting.

They both rose from the dais and addressed their guests. "Thank you so much for celebrating our pair-bonding with us. It means so much that you were there to bear witness, regardless of how rocky it was. Ardyn and I must now complete the last part of the ritual in private, so we bid you all good night."

Not everyone was aware of the last requirement of the ritual, and questions arose among the guests. Jevan and Ardyn hoped that Mathias and the Aterians would quell the questions discreetly.

They left the dining hall with their arms wrapped around each other and walked towards their quarters in companionable silence. Everything that needed to be said was being conveyed between them without either having to say a single word.

CONNECTED

The next morning Ardyn awoke in Jevan's arms, much as he'd done for many cycles of the sun. Yet, their new bond made for a deeper connection than he'd ever felt with anyone. While Jevan was still deep asleep, Ardyn could clearly feel his presence in his mind. Ardyn no longer felt alone, and it fulfilled a need he never realized he had.

Whatever it was about his physiology that caused their bond to be much deeper than it ever had been between two Medellans, neither of them was complaining. It had been a painful transition, and they were still navigating the newness of their bond, but the closeness they now shared was worth it.

Before Jevan even opened his eyes, Ardyn was aware of his slow climb into wakefulness. "*Good morning,*" he thought, kissing Jevan's temple as he blinked awake. Ardyn didn't even need to ask how Jevan was feeling. He just *knew*. It was still a little overwhelming.

Jevan pulled him into a tighter embrace. "Good morning yourself," Jevan said with a fond chuckle. "I think you wore me out last night."

Ardyn ducked his head into the crook of Jevan's neck. "Sorry."

Letting out a hearty laugh, Jevan hugged him fondly. "Don't be sorry. It's been a long while since I've had a night like that."

Ardyn blushed at the memories of Jevan's many trysts flooded his thoughts.

"I never imagined having a connection like this with anyone," Ardyn said, snuggling into Jevan's embrace. "It will take time to get used to, but I wouldn't trade it for anything."

"Neither would I, dear heart," Jevan said, conveying all the love he could through their bond.

After spending a lazy morning in bed, they finally rose and showered together before making their way down to the hospital wing. Amyra had made them promise to come by for a full scan after they'd completed the remainder of the bonding ritual and gotten some rest.

Amyra was in a meeting, so the receptionist escorted them to a small lounge that was equipped with a replicator. After replicating some tea, they settled in to wait, having nothing else planned until that evening. Keryth would have already sent one of his techs to fly their families back to their homes in Maala'naa and Yanen, knowing that Jevan and Ardyn were planning to visit soon.

While they waited, they practiced their new telepathic connection. While they appeared to be sitting quietly, they were having a boisterous discussion within their minds. The only outward sign were the occasional laughs they exchanged.

When someone finally escorted them to Amyra's office, she smiled at them both warmly as they entered. "You're both looking a lot better. How are you feeling?"

Pointing to the monitor he still wore, Ardyn asked. "Why don't you tell us?"

Laughing, she shook her head in admonishment. "Your vitals are all good, but that doesn't always tell me how you are."

"Last night was perfect," Jevan replied. "I think this new bond between us made the encounter even more pleasant."

Ardyn agreed, despite feeling bashful talking about it. "It... yes, it did."

"Good, I'm glad," Amyra said, coming over to remove the monitors from each of them. "I've let Tamaryn know you're here and he's going to join us. Follow me, please. We'd like to run some additional scans to make sure everything in your systems has stabilized. I don't want you two to run into any problems during your trek through the forest tomorrow."

As they arrived in the exam room, Tamaryn was just beaming in. "By the looks of things, I take it the consummation was a success?"

Flattening his ears, Ardyn's face heated, even as he nodded shyly.

"Since you were the first one to collapse yesterday, let's get you on the exam bed first, Ardyn," Amyra said, activating the equipment.

After they were both scanned, Tamaryn and Amyra spent a few moments analyzing the data. "The changes in both your genetic structures are remarkable. I've seen nothing like this before," Tamaryn said.

"Thankfully, it doesn't look like the changes are dangerous," Amyra added. "Jevan, your telomeres are longer than we expected and are completely stable. The changes to Ardyn's telomeres are what's most remarkable. They have also lengthened because of your bonding. If our preliminary findings are correct, you could both live very long lives."

"Can you tell how long we'll live?" Ardyn asked.

"We'll need to do a more in-depth analysis," Tamaryn replied. "However, our current estimate is that you both might live close to three hundred years, if the new lengths of telomeres are accurate."

"And you remain healthy and avoid bulkheads from falling on you," Amyra added with a wink.

Jevan whistled. "Three hundred? I'll be old and frail long before that, won't I?"

Tamaryn shook his head. "Your body won't show signs of aging until your telomeres have deteriorated beyond a certain point. We'll need to run additional tests at a few intervals to gauge the rate of deterioration they're showing after your pair-bonding. That will give us a better idea of when you can expect to see significant signs of aging, and give us a more accurate prediction of your potential lifespan."

"You seem really confident, but your analysis before didn't predict this telepathic link that Jevan and I have developed," Ardyn reminded them.

"Good point," Amyra admitted. "We need to analyze all the data more closely. We clearly missed something, so we'll need to go over everything again."

"I'm planning to consult some techs back on Aria'naa, that specialize in other scientific fields," Tamaryn added. "This may take some time, but we'll figure out what we missed. Now that the Medellan and Athla'naa people are no longer holding each other at arm's length, others may eventually wish to pair-bond as you did. So, we'll need to understand how and why this happened."

"Is it safe for us to leave for Maala'naa tomorrow?" Jevan asked.

Amyra looked at Tamaryn with concern but ultimately nodded. "You have both stabilized and we're not seeing the rapid changes in your genetic structure we were seeing yesterday. However, bring your communicators with you, and check in regularly. If anything goes wrong, contact someone immediately so we can beam you to the Wah'kah'ria."

Slipping his hand into Jevan's, Ardyn nodded. "That's easy. It hasn't even been that long, but I don't think I could imagine life without those communicators anymore."

"They are an integral part of our lives," Tamaryn agreed. "If I recall my history correctly, the development of long-range communication systems sped up the technological advancement in our society. Our world transformed from a mostly rural agrarian society to one centered on large urban centers and manufacturing."

Crossing her arms, Amyra frowned. "That's what eventually led to the rise of the Aria'asharra. They were concerned over the environmental effects of everything we were developing."

"They were not entirely wrong," Tamaryn admitted. "We could have caused the ecological collapse of our entire world if we hadn't started paying attention."

Leaning against the medical stasis bed, Amyra sighed. "I know, but their methods were too extreme. Look at what they did! All of us who were left to rot here are now stuck twelve hundred years in the future. Everyone we had ever known on Aria'naa is long gone."

"Why does that matter?" Ardyn wondered. "You left to start a colony that would have taken you over one hundred and thirty cycles of... um... *years*... to travel to. Wouldn't most of the people you knew have been dead by then?"

"Not all of them, especially not those around our age or younger. Plus, with the subspace beacon, we could have still been able to communicate with them."

"Well, you are now part of a new family," Tamaryn said, giving her a coy smile.

Ardyn smirked at their interaction. *"I think they like each other."*

Giving him a look, Jevan agreed.

They headed for the door, and when they turned around, they noticed Tamaryn had stepped closer to Amyra. Ardyn smirked again before clearing his throat. "Thanks again. I'm sure we'll see you both when we get back. We should get our packs and provisions together for tomorrow."

Amyra and Tamaryn realized they'd been caught and stepped apart, their ears flattened and a lavender flush bloomed on their cheeks as they waved goodbye.
"Yeah, they definitely like each other."

HONEYMOON

Shouldering their packs, Jevan and Ardyn set out early the next morning. A small group gathered in the observation tower to wish them farewell, including Takyra, Aerys, Mathias, and Taeglyn.

"Here, take a couple of spare communicators, in case you damage yours," Takyra offered, handing them to Jevan.

Aerys held out a *rahn'ora*. "Did you remember to pack your weapons?"

Pulling a *rahn'ora* from his pocket, Ardyn nodded. "You don't have to worry so much about us. We'll be fine."

"You gave us quite a scare during your bonding ceremony," Takyra reminded him. "What you both have been through is unprecedented, and we want you to return safely."

"Thank you," they both said gratefully.

"Give my best to your father," Taeglyn said, pulling Ardyn aside and handing him a written note.

Everyone followed them outside, and they both turned around and waved at them one last time before they made their way toward Maala'naa. The trek on foot would take them around three cycles of the sun, and they promised to check in with the Rahn'naa regularly and let them know once they had arrived.

Most of the encampment around the Rahn'naa had dispersed, the people returning to their settlements. However, there were some who remained, eager to help clear the land and watch as the ship would be transformed into a settlement.

It took some time for them to pass through the encampment and even then, there were now well-trodden paths through the woods that clearly led to Yanen and Maala'naa.

"*I don't think we'll get lost,*" Jevan joked.

By this point, Ardyn and Jevan were conversing both telepathically and verbally, as they were still working out what felt right. As thoughts of the last time Jevan had been in Maala'naa filtered into his mind, Ardyn spoke up. "This time, I will give you a proper tour of our settlement."

"It will be nice to not have the threat of death hanging over me. Hopefully, that will give me a better appreciation of my surroundings," Jevan joked. Ardyn gave him a gentle punch in his arm as they both laughed.

The weather was turning cooler, and they had asked Keryth not to change the weather just for them, explaining how they'd spent their entire lives living in these forests. However, they appreciated some guidance on warmer clothes to replicate. It wasn't winter yet, but the nights were going to be colder, so they wore pants and jackets that were slightly insulated.

Not needing to blend into their surroundings as they once did, they also chose different colors than the browns and greens they usually wore. Ardyn wore gray pants with black boots, with a dark blue shirt and a jacket that had blocks of both blue and gray. Jevan loved the look and made something similar but went with a combination of tan and red instead, with dark brown boots.

Some of their friends on the Rahn'naa also suggested they bring a tent with them, and they showed them how to replicate one. They liked the design, but it seemed too bulky to take with them when a tech from the Wah'kah'ria showed them the latest in tent designs from Aria'naa.

When collapsed, it was around the size of a tray of food, and after pressing a button, it unfolded itself into a tent easily large enough to sleep two people. It included a small forcefield generator to keep them safe while they slept, so they no longer had to take turns keeping watch.

When they'd reached their planned campsite for the evening, they checked in and let them know they were both doing well, before setting up their camp for the night. Sitting by the fire, Jevan smiled when he realized Ardyn was replaying memories of the consummation of their bond in his mind.

Ardyn's ears went flat when he realized Jevan knew what he was thinking. "This is going to take some getting used to, never having a private thought from you."

"I'm sorry, I wasn't trying to invade your thoughts," Jevan apologized. "I'll try to find a way to not intrude on them, but this is all so new. We need to keep practicing so we can learn how to control it better."

"Agreed. We're bondmates, but we're both entitled to some private thoughts."

"We are, but... since you were having those thoughts, does that mean you would enjoy being intimate with me again?" Jevan asked, giving Ardyn his most charming smile.

Ducking his head, Ardyn nodded, before holding a hand up to keep Jevan from following through with the current thought he was having. "But first, we should eat something."

"Alright, eat first, ravish later," Jevan agreed with a laugh.

◆◆◆

The next cycle of the sun was peaceful as they made their way through the Aria'una and past the *bhat'laa'arh*. "Hey look, the sensors are gone!" Jevan noted as they approached the ancient trees.

"I guess my people took them down," Ardyn thought to him, flooding his mind with memories of the last time they came this way. *"I'm almost disappointed that there's no hunting party to greet us, either."*

Jevan laughed. *"Don't remind me."*

After the incident the night before, they practiced both communicating and blocking each other's thoughts. One thing they both realized was the more emotional the thought was, the harder it was to keep private.

"I guess that's not always a bad thing," Jevan thought. *"At least if one of us is in distress, the other will immediately know, even when we're not together."*

"Good point, but will we still be able to communicate if we're far apart?"

Jevan thought about that for a moment. *"Maybe we can test that? Keryth could beam one of us up to his ship and we could try to communicate."*

"That couldn't possibly work, could it?"

"Why not? These communicators we wear work across vast distances, don't they?"

"I guess we'll have to find out."

MAALA'NAA

They reached Maala'naa by mid-morning. After they let the Rahn'naa know they had arrived, they reached out to Elder Taesys, who was awaiting their arrival along with Saelyn, Cylaen, and little Myria.

"Papa Ardyn!" Myria cried out, running toward them. "I made a gift for you!"

Ardyn dropped his pack and scooped up the young child. "You did? Show me!"

She handed him a small leather pouch.

"Oh, it's beautiful! You made this?" Ardyn asked.

Nodding with a shy smile, she looked up at Jevan. "There's another gift inside, and one is for you, Papa Jevan!"

An unexpected pang of emotion hit Jevan when Myria called him that, and Ardyn smirked as he handed the pouch to him. Opening it, he pulled out a pair of embroidered leather bracelets. "These are beautiful, thank you little one."

Myria buried her head in Ardyn's chest as she mumbled. "You're welcome."

Ardyn set Myria down and let Jevan tie one bracelet on his left wrist and then tied the other on Jevan's right wrist. That way, whenever they held hands, the bracelets would be together. Seeing that thrilled Myria as she ran around the small group while they made their way into the settlement.

"Thank you for coming to visit before leaving," Saelyn said, giving Ardyn a small hug. "It has been too long since you've been home."

"I know, and I'm sorry Mama Saelyn. So much has happened since the day Aelrynd sent me out after that *sar'ora*."

"Oh, don't remind me," Saelyn admonished. "You've both turned our lives upside down. Hopefully for the better, but that's yet to be seen."

Elder Taesys approached Jevan as they walked toward the center of Maala'naa, putting a hand on his upper arm. "You will look after my son and protect him in that distant land you're going to. If you don't, you will have to answer to me. Is that understood?"

Smiling at him, Jevan nodded. "Perfectly clear. I hope you know I will protect Ardyn with my very life."

"Good. That's what I needed to hear," he said, patting Jevan on the back.

Ardyn caught up with them and admonished his father. "Leave my bondmate alone."

"I can't help being protective of you," Taesys said, pulling Ardyn into an embrace. "You're the only child of mine that I'm close to, and I don't want to lose you."

Returning the hug, he pulled something out of his pocket and handed it to Taesys. "I almost forgot. Taeglyn asked me to give this to you."

Taesys looked at it curiously for a moment before slipping it into a pocket in his robes. "I'll read it later. Thank you."

Approaching a rope ladder, Jevan could hear a festive cacophony coming from the largest hut overlooking the center of Maala'naa. The Athla'bhat built the hut in the branches of a large, gnarly old tree. It looked like it served as the central gathering place for celebrations.

Taesys led the way, and a rousing cheer came from those gathered as they entered the large hut. Inside, they saw a feast set up, with at least fifty people gathered. He led them toward a low table in a place for honored guests. This treatment differed from the last time Jevan had been in Maala'naa.

Instead of chairs or benches, there were furs and blankets spread out for the guests to sit on, and the feast before them looked amazing. It must have taken many people to prepare all the food they saw. There was roast *paal'dak*, fish stew, and an array of fresh fruits and root vegetables that the Athla'naa were fond of eating. It had been a long time since they had eaten home-cooked Athla'naa cuisine, and they savored every bite. They may not have seasoned the food with the spices Takyra had introduced them to, but Jevan could feel through Ardyn that it tasted like *home.*

There were many stories to share, and they passed around the *wah'roh* as everyone enjoyed the feast. After everyone finished eating, Taesys stood to address the group gathered. "Today we celebrate one of our own, along with his partner and bondmate. Ardyn opened our eyes to many truths, and we are being led out of the darkness and into a new era of enlightenment."

A hush fell over the crowd and they heard a few disgruntled voices muttering under their breaths.

Holding up his hands, Taesys continued. "I know many of you are still skeptical, but I believe this is the right path for our people. However, tonight is not the time for this debate."

Giving a pointed look to everyone gathered, he waited to see if anyone would challenge him, but none did. "To honor Ardyn for what he has achieved, and for stepping up to represent our people on our ancestral homeworld, I wish to present him with a gift."

Jevan looked at Ardyn, feeling as surprised by this as he could tell Ardyn felt.

"Many cycles of the moons ago, our Triumvirate asked him to track and kill the *sar'ora* that had been preying upon our children. It was that task that led him down the path of discovery that has changed our entire world. We saved the pelt of that beast, and I asked our best craftspeople to make a coat for him to wear on his journey."

A young Athla'naa approached them with a cloth wrapped parcel that must have contained the coat. Accepting it, Ardyn stood and bowed. "I am honored to receive such a fine gift, Elder Taesys. Thank you, Papa."

"Also, for Jevan, whom I believe is the one who killed the beast and saved Ardyn's life," Taesys continued. "I have asked our best bowyer and fletcher to fashion you a new bow and quiver. After all your experiences onboard the Rahn'naa, you probably consider these primitive weapons, but perhaps they may still remind you of home."

Accepting the beautifully crafted bow and quiver filled with arrows, Jevan also tried to stand, but he hit his head on a support beam, making everyone laugh. Opting to bow and then kneel back down, Jevan responded. "Thank you, Elder Taesys. This is a beautiful gift, and no matter how far we travel, it will remind me of our humble beginnings."

After the feast, Ardyn led Jevan to the hut he'd shared with his parents. Taesys and Saelyn had since moved into the huts reserved for the Triumvirate, but they had kept the hut for guests. When they entered, they saw the old packs that had been confiscated next to the pile of furs Ardyn used to sleep on.

"Oh, wow, I can't believe they'd kept these," Jevan said, grabbing his pack, looking through it. It was still filled with all the items he'd traded for all those cycles of the moons ago. "Your people can keep these things. We don't need them, and I'm sure those back in Yanen had given up waiting on them now. I certainly don't want to lug this heavy thing back with me, but I will keep a few of the personal items."

"Yeah, that pack always looked too heavy," Ardyn thought, as he went through his old ranger pack with the same intent, pulling out a few personal items he wanted to keep, putting them into his new pack from the Rahn'naa.

That night, Jevan helped Ardyn replace his terrible memories of Maala'naa by making love to him there in his old home. Using their deep bond, he made it a joyous night, and it deepened the increasing intimacy between them.

YANEN

At dawn the next morning, Ardyn introduced Jevan to his old ritual of taking a brisk bath in the nearby creek. He couldn't help but laugh when Jevan cried out after he jumped into the natural pool, only to shriek a moment later when Jevan splashed him with the icy water.

"Why would you willingly bathe in that freezing water?" Jevan asked through chattering teeth, as he dried himself and dressed quickly, trying to get warm. "I am really missing our hot showers back on the Rahn'naa right now."

"I see now why my ancestors thought technology might spoil us," Ardyn teased.

They broke their fast with Ardyn's parents, and Ardyn took the time to look at some artifacts the Triumvirate had kept hidden from their people all these centuries. Taesys learned of them after the Elders initiated him into the Triumvirate and thought Ardyn and Jevan should see them. "It appears they kept several pieces of technology that they probably used, beyond just the sensors around the Aria'una and life form tracker," Taesys pointed out.

"This is a tissue regenerator," Jevan said, picking up a device. "It's the same kind that Amyra used to heal your arm after the battle, remember?"

Ardyn took it and stared at it for a long moment. "I remember. Well, we've known for a while that our ancestors were hypocrites, so this is unsurprising. Do you plan to return these to the Rahn'naa?"

Taesys looked around at everything gathered there. "I probably should, but I will wait until we've vetted two new elders into the Triumvirate. With all this upheaval, I haven't had the opportunity to do so."

"Two? What about Elder Taeglyn?" Ardyn asked.

"His duties on the Council of Vestos will keep him too busy to attend to the needs of the Athla'bhat," Taesys explained. "The letter he gave you was his resignation from the Triumvirate. Perhaps now that the council exists, we won't need the Triumvirate anymore, but I think it's too soon for us to abandon all our ways."

"You're right," Jevan agreed. "The Medellan leadership isn't disbanding either. The council was created to bring our people together, rather than to replace our governments."

Ardyn put down the scanner he still held and walked to one of the open windows. "I am glad I don't have to worry about any of that. Hopefully, all the changes will continue to move forward peacefully. I noticed some noises of discontent last night."

Taesys came over and put his arm around his son's shoulders. "Not everyone is accepting of the changes, and there will be challenging days ahead. Druyndar stirred up a lot of old prejudices. However, I am determined to maintain the peace we fought so hard for. Therefore, I am relying on Taeglyn to help me vet the next members of the Triumvirate, and we are also holding open discussions with our people from across Vestos. I want to make sure everyone feels they are being heard."

"That's very wise of you, Papa," Ardyn said with a smile. "Our people will be in excellent hands."

After they finished breakfast, it was time for them to set out for the next leg of their journey. They had received so many gifts from old friends and well-wishers that Jevan contacted Keryth and asked if he could send someone to Maala'naa to pick everything up for them. Once they had that arranged, they headed toward Yanen.

Jevan took Ardyn's hand as they made their way, both of their minds filled with the memory of their desperate flight, all those cycles of the moons ago. *"I'm so glad we can take our time."*

"So am I," Ardyn admitted. *"I never want to run that far, for that long, ever again."*

While this time there wasn't a well-defined path through the woods, the hike to Yanen was much shorter, and they arrived by the late evening, where they found Mathias waiting for them in Asha's home, along with Jenira and Micah.

Jevan gave a surprised greeting to his ard. "Mathias! Why didn't you tell me you were going to be here? I thought you were busy with council business back at the Rahn'naa."

"I have been, but Yanen has been without an ard for too long. Keryth transported me here so I could instate Elden as the new ard. After Taeglyn stepped down from the

Triumvirate, I decided to do the same. I know it's unprecedented for an ard to resign, but the work we're doing in the council is more meaningful than anything I've ever done in Yanen."

"You also didn't want to give up those hot showers," Jevan teased.

With a hearty laugh, Mathias patted Jevan on the back. "Hah. You've found me out. Actually, I've put forth a measure before the council to allow Medellans throughout Vestos to have access to their technology. Can you imagine having hot showers and replicated meals right here in Yanen?"

It hadn't occurred to Jevan, and that surprised him. "Wow, that really would change things around here. So, do you think Eldon is ready to take on the role of ard? He hasn't been apprenticed to you that long."

"With all the changes, I think a younger perspective is exactly what Yanen needs right now."

"Speaking of changes," Jevan said, looking around his mother's home. "This place looks different."

Jenira beamed with happiness, placing a hand on her growing belly. "Since Micah has taken on the role of trader for Yanen, we've swapped homes with mother. The trader's cottage was too small for our growing family."

Jevan nodded in agreement. "It is small, but it was perfect for me. I expected you to build an addition to that house, so you'd have room for your child."

Asha patted her son on the back. "That would be silly. This house is much bigger and more suited for raising children, and I was happy to move into your old cottage. It's the right size for an old widow like myself."

"You're not that old yet, Mother," Jevan admonished.

"I turned forty-six this past summer," she reminded him.

Ardyn smiled at the banter and chimed in. "That's not that old at all. I will be thirty-six next autumn."

Asha looked at him in surprise. "You're older than Jevan? You look like you're barely out of your teens!"

"Athla'naa age slower than Medellans," Jevan explained. "His oldest daughter is ten now, but she's more like a Medellan child five cycles of the seasons old."

"That's true," Ardyn said. "We don't even reach sexual maturity before the age of twenty-five."

Instead of responding to that, Asha herded everyone toward the dining table they had set with a late supper. "Well, enough of that talk. We should eat before the food gets cold."

The meal they shared was a less grand affair, with a hearty portion of *paal'dak* and vegetable stew, lightly seasoned with herbs that Medellans favored, and served with a slice of homemade bread. Ardyn smiled as it was Jevan's turn to feel the fondness of *home* when eating his mother's cooking.

"I'm sorry I missed your birthday, mother," Jevan said between bites of his meal. "I usually try to be home for that."

"You mean you're sorry you missed out on some cake?" Jenira teased.

Jevan laughed, as he couldn't deny that. "You're right. You know how much I love mother's fruitcake! Especially when soaked in some whiskey."

Asha smiled at him fondly. "You're in luck. I baked one just for this occasion. We have much to celebrate. I am so proud of you, my son."

A wave of emotions hit Jevan, and he looked over to see tears streaming down Ardyn's face. *"Are you okay, dear heart?"*

Wiping his face, Ardyn nodded. *"Yes, I'm fine. Seeing all the love you and your family have for each other makes me so happy."*

Unprompted, Jevan pulled Ardyn into his arms and planted a quick kiss on his lips, which made Jenira cry out in mock protest. "Ew! Go somewhere else if you're going to do that."

Everyone laughed, and Ardyn ducked his head against Jevan in embarrassment. *"You did that on purpose."*

After dinner, they all enjoyed the special cake Asha made, and Ardyn really loved how some whiskey complemented the flavors of the sweet fruit. "You must give me your recipe so we can replicate this on Aria'naa. I bet this would be just as delicious with some *wah'roh*."

Mathias laughed. "You're not wrong. I tested that out with the replicator in my quarters."

That night, Asha offered them Jevan's former home to sleep in, while she stayed with Jenira and Micah. As they entered the home where Mathias had kept them confined, it didn't evoke as many bad memories as either of them had feared.

"Wow, mother really fixed up this place," Jevan said, noting the new cozy furnishings. Instead of a wooden bench by the fireplace, there was now a comfortable couch. The mattress on the bed was new and much more comfortable. There were herbs hung in the corner by the small table and chairs where he and Jevan had eaten their meals, and they added a lovely aroma to the entire home.

Laying in each other's arms, they couldn't help but reminisce about their time here. "This was the first bed we shared," Jevan recalled. "I tried my best, but I will admit that my thoughts about you weren't always pure."

Jevan flashed some memories of the salacious thoughts he'd had, and Ardyn laughed while snuggling closer. "I suspected as much, but I am glad we spent so much time getting to know each other. It made our first coupling more meaningful."

Hugging him, Jevan lovingly kissed the top of his head. "You are still the most beautiful Athla'naa I've ever met, and I am so grateful you came into my life."

Ardyn leaned his head against Jevan's chest for a moment before tilting his head up to give him a kiss, conveying everything he felt for him. *"Yawen Asharra ior."*

"I love you, too, dear heart. So very much."

NOT THE END

The hike back to the Rahn'naa was uneventful, with thankfully no signs of the *sar'ora* pack they had encountered the last time they had trekked through the forest. They were thankful for the tent on their first night, when it rained not long after they'd set up camp.

Originally, they had planned to hunt some *paal'dak* and roast them over a campfire, but because of the rain, they enjoyed some of the packaged food they had replicated and brought with them instead.

"I'm so glad we did this," Jevan said, as they huddled together under their combined bedrolls for warmth. "It's been good to see everyone and reconnect with our past before moving on."

"It also gave us some time for us to get used to this new bond," Ardyn said. *"Although, I still can't decide if I prefer speaking or thinking to you. What do you prefer?"*

"Thinking feels more intimate," Jevan replied aloud before switching to mere thoughts. *"I enjoy the mix of words and emotions that are conveyed. It tells more than when we just speak, but I also love the sound of your voice. I'd miss it if I didn't hear it occasionally."*

Ardyn conveyed his agreement. "I know what you mean. You have such a wonderfully deep tone to your voice. It vibrates right through me when we're snuggled like this. I'm sure we'll find the right balance, and the telepathic communication will always be useful when we want to speak privately around others."

"That's true. We need to test how far away we can get and still communicate," Jevan remembered. "Let's talk to Keryth about that when we get back."

It was late afternoon when they arrived back at the Rahn'naa, both tired but happy. The first thing they did once they were back in their quarters was to take a hot shower together.

"I used to spend several cycles of the moons ranging the forests around Maala'naa, and only bathed in icy streams," Ardyn laughed as he enjoyed the hot spray on his back while Jevan lathered himself with soap. "Now I can barely stand hiking through them for a few cycles of the sun before I'm longing to return to the comfort of these quarters."

"We *have* been spoiled, but I wonder how different living in Donarvon will be? They aren't as advanced as the Athla'dor, but from what we've seen, they are more advanced than either of our people."

"Marta assured me that the apartment we'll be living in will have hot running water and a shower," Ardyn said as they switched sides, so Jevan could rinse off. "That's all I needed to hear."

◆ ◆ ◆

That evening, they joined Takyra in her favorite restaurant, so everyone could make their farewells and hear about their adventures in Maala'naa and Yanen.

After being teased for lapsing into telepathic communication a few times, Amyra remarked. "That connection you've formed with each other is fascinating. It's far more complex than we originally anticipated, and it may take months to analyze what's really happening. As soon as Tamaryn and I have a better understanding of it, we'll let you know, so please keep those communicators of yours handy."

That reminded Ardyn of something. "Keryth, before you transport us to Donarvon tomorrow, can you help us with something?"

"Of course. What do you need?"

"We'd like to test how far apart our telepathic communication works, so could you transport only one of us to your ship tomorrow?"

"That's an excellent idea!" Tamaryn said. "Could we take some scans of your brains while you're testing this? That data could help us understand what's happening."

Once they agreed on how to conduct the experiment, they returned to the conversation at hand, and stayed up talking late into the night. That meant Jevan and Ardyn got a later start the next morning than they had planned. When they finally woke, they were both reluctant to get out of bed. This time it was Jevan who finally got them moving. "We should get up," he said as he kissed the top of Ardyn's head.

"I know," Ardyn replied reluctantly.

"Come on, sleepyhead," Jevan teased, disentangling himself from Ardyn and pulling the covers off his bondmate.

"Hey!" Ardyn cried out in mock annoyance, even as he threw a pillow at Jevan and laughed.

Since they had already packed and transported all their belongings, there was little else to do. So once they were showered and dressed, they went to meet Marta for a last meal before running through their experiment, and then heading to Donarvon.

They were on their way to the dining hall when they ran into Marta. "There you two are! After how late of a night we had, I had a feeling I'd have to come after you both today."

As they headed toward the dining hall, Jevan asked Marta. "Are you looking forward to going home?"

"Yes, but I will miss this place," Marta admitted. "I know I can always come back, but leaving always makes me a little sad."

"I'm also sad to leave this place behind, but I'm excited for the next adventure," Ardyn admitted. "Hopefully, everyone in Donarvon is as nice as you and Andreesen have been."

"Everyone back in Ateria will love you both, I'm sure," Marta said as they entered the dining hall. "How could they not?"

After they finished a quick meal, Marta beamed up, while Jevan and Ardyn headed to the medical bay where Amyra was waiting for them. She had Ardyn lie on one of the newly installed medical beds so she could monitor his vitals.

Before Jevan beamed aboard the Wah'kah'ria, he leaned down and gave Ardyn a quick kiss. *"I'll see you soon, dear heart."*

When they separated, Jevan tapped the communicator in his ear and let Keryth know he was ready. Once Jevan was gone, Ardyn let go of a breath he hadn't realized he'd been holding. As often as they had used the transmat system, it still left Ardyn with a sense of unease.

While Ardyn waited, he watched Amyra as she activated the scanners on his bed. It felt like it was taking too long when finally he heard from Jevan. *"Are you worried about me already?"*

"It works!" Ardyn said aloud, letting Amyra know. *"Does it feel any different to you from this distance?"*

"No, not at all. I can sense you as if you were standing right next to me."

Ardyn agreed. *"That's exactly what I feel. If I didn't know you were so far away from me right now, I would swear you were right here."*

Ardyn told Amyra what he was experiencing, while also sharing thoughts and emotions with Jevan for another moment before it satisfied them that distances would not be a problem. "Do you have enough data?" Ardyn asked Amyra.

"More than enough, thank you," Amyra replied. "Thank you so much for suggesting this. Hopefully, this will aid in our research."

Getting off the bed, Ardyn was about to tell the Wah'kah'ria he was ready to leave, when Takyra came running in. "Wait, you forgot something!"

Puzzled, it surprised Ardyn when Takyra handed him the old artifact that had started him on all their adventures. He'd left the control access key behind in their quarters because he didn't think it would be of any use in Donarvon.

"I would like you to keep it, as a small memento, to remind you of what led you to where you are. Also, as a thank you for following your instincts and saving us. Those of us from the Rahn'naa will forever be grateful for that."

Stepping closer to her, he gave Takyra a hug. "Thank you for everything. You've opened a whole new world of possibilities for us."

"I'm sure I'll see you again, but until then, take care of yourself," Takyra said.

After he stepped back, Ardyn blinked back tears. He signaled that he was ready and waved to Takyra and Amyra as the transmat beam dematerialized him. A moment later he stood in the transmat room of the Wah'kah'ria and ran into Jevan's arms.

"Are you okay?" Jevan asked.

Nodding, Ardyn took a deep breath and turned to Marta. "Ready to go home?"

The three of them climbed back onto the transmat platform and waved goodbye to Keryth. A mix of excitement and uncertainty filled him as the tingling sensation of the transmat beam engulfed him once again.

GLOSSARY

arh: tall.

aria: world, land, or place. Also, more obscure, *nature.*

aria'asharra: world, land, or place lover (patriot). Also, *nature lover.* The name of the faction that crashed the Rahn'naa.

aria'maal: homeworld.

aria'naa: first world. Also, the name of the Athla'naa homeworld.

aria'nor: our world or our land.

aria'una: forbidden place. Also, the name of the forbidden woods, marked by the border of bhat'laa'arh trees, where the Rahn'naa crashed.

asharra: love.

asharra'dak: make love (have sex).

asharra'ior: I love.

asharra'laa: red love. The name of an Athla'naa delicacy.

athla: people.

athla'bhat: people of the trees. The new name given to Ardyn's people.

athla'dor: wise people. The new name given to Takyra's people aboard the Rahn'naa.

athla'naa: first people. The name of the people who originated on Aria'naa.

athla'maakh: not or less than people (beast). Also, the name the Athla'bhat gave the Medellan people, originally meant as an insult.

baaru: new.

baaru'dak: make new. Also, the name of the Athla'naa class that includes architects, builders, and engineers.

aria'nor: our new world. Also, the name Athla'bhat gave the continent and planet they crashed on.

bhat: tree.

bhat'laa'arh: tall, red tree. A type of tree with bright red leaves that grow very tall, originally native to Aria'naa. Planted around the perimeter of the *aria'una.*

dahl: all.

dak: make.

dor: old or ancient. When used for a person, *wise.*

ior: I or me.

ior'kah: break me. Typically used as an expletive.

ior'uthera: I greet you (hello).

kala: sleep.

kala'dak: make sleep (good night). Also, a type of tea used as a sleep aid.

kah: broken.

kah'dak: make broken (break).

kerros: name.

kerros'nor: my name.

laa: red.

laasa: health or healthy.

laasa'dak: make healthy or heal. Also, the Athla'naa class that includes all medical and science professions.

maala: a dwelling or collection of dwellings (settlement).

maala'dak: make dwelling (building construction).

maala'naa: first settlement. Also, the name the Athla'bhat gave the first settlement they built on Med'nor.

maala'nor: my home (either an individual dwelling or a home settlement).

maakh: not or less than.

maara: death of large or entire populations, either from pandemics or mass murder.

maara'dahl: death of all (genocide). Also, the name of the Baaru'dak faction intent on killing all members and descendants of the Aria'asharra faction, including the Athla'bhat.

med: sphere or ball.

med'nor: our sphere or ball. Also, the new name of the planet shared by the Medellans and Athla'naa.

naa: first, primary, main, or primary.

nor: my, mine, or ours.

ora: death, also to kill, specifically an individual.

ora'dak: make death (premeditated murder).

paahr: grow or raise.

paahr'dak: make grow or raise, pertaining to agriculture, horticulture, and animal domestication.

pah: flying or flight.

pah'maala: flying settlement (colonization ship).

pah'ora: flying death. The name given to an Aria'naa warship that had been decommissioned. The Maara'dahl stole it and used it in the fight over Med'nor.

paal: bounce.
paal'dak: make bounce (jump) A name given to a small species of animal the Medellans call *jumpers*.
roh: fire.
rahn: light.
rahn'naa: first light (dawn). Also, the name of the colonization ship that crashed on Med'nor, the Dawn.
rahn'kala: sleeper light. A non-lethal version of the rahn'ora, that only has a stun setting.
rahn'ora: killer light. The name of the energy weapons used primarily by the Baaru'dak security subclass.
ria: flowing.
sar: silver or gray.
sar'ora: silver death. The name given to a carnivorous species native to the continent of Vestos. Medellans call them *triwolves* for their triple eyes.
toren: follow.
toren'ior: follow me.
una: forbidden.
uthera: greet or acknowledge.
uthera'ior: I greet, or I acknowledge.
vaara: outer space.
wah: water.
wah'dak: make water (urinate).
wah'kah'ria: broken flowing water (delta). Also, the name of Keryth's star cruiser, the Delta.
wah'ria: flowing water (river or stream).
wah'roh: fire water (spirit distilled from fruit).
yat: move forward or travel.
yat'athla: person who travels (traveler).
yawen: you or yours.

ACKNOWLEDGEMENTS

Over the past several years I've had the help of many beta readers who helped me hone this story into what it is today. Thank you so much George Robbert, Susan Wolber, Sandy Bennett, Caroline Ailanthus, and Amy-Alex Campbell.

Also, thank you Dai Ulmo for letting me bounce ideas and my needlessly over-thought Athla'naa vocabulary off you. Your input was invaluable.

Finally, thank you Dave for coming up with the clever title of "Artifact of the Dawn." Cunning in its simplicity but also smart for its deeper meaning.

ABOUT THE AUTHOR

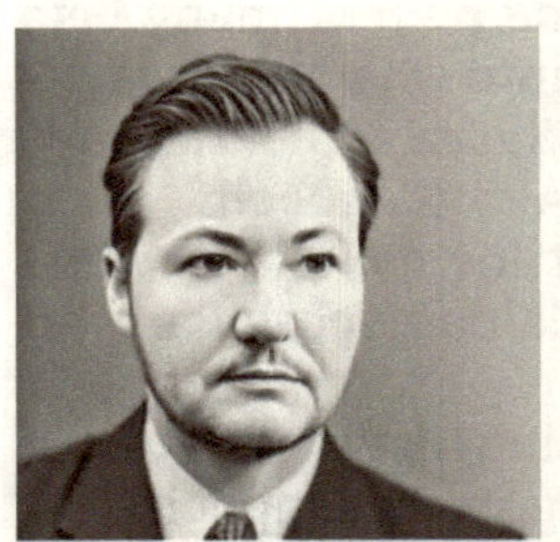 Grayson Bell developed a love affair with the written word before he even attended school. After devouring countless books, he found a love for writing.

Writing has been a part of Grayson's life in one form or another for decades, everything from academic and technical writing to blogging, and writing fanfiction. These days he splits his time between writing articles about LGBTQ issues and writing queer fiction stories.

Sharing his home in Colorado with his dogs, Grayson also enjoys whipping up something creative in the kitchen or escaping into the world of video games. He is an out and proud gay, transgender man.

QUEER FICTION BOOKS BY GRAYSON BELL

Coffee-to-Go

A mutual love of coffee, and an unfortunate accident, brought Leo and Andy together. Will a corrupt immigration system tear them apart?

Mark My Soul

Scott keeps fleeing from his soulmate, Ross. Perhaps a little discipline is in order?

Transcendent

When Cory's new boss makes an indecent proposal, will he risk his heart to advance his career?

Suddenly, Omega

When Pete discovers he's an omega, his entire world is turned upside down. After Dr. Ryan Walsh saves his life, can he also mend Cory's life?